PENGUIN BOOKS

THE FURTHER RIVALS
OF SHERLOCK HOLMES

After a career as a foreign correspondent in several European countries, Hugh Greene joined the BBC in 1940 as head of the German Service, a post he held throughout the war. He went on to become successively Controller of Broadcasting in the British Zone of Germany, head of the BBC East European Service, and head of the Emergency Information Services in Malaya. He was Director-General of the BBC from 1960 to 1969 and is now on the board of The Bodley Head, a major British publisher. Books by him include *The Spy's Bedside Book* (written in collaboration with his brother, Graham Greene) and *The Third Floor Front: A View of Broadcasting in the Sixties.* In addition to *The Further Rivals of Sherlock Holmes*, he has edited *The Rivals of Sherlock Holmes* and *Cosmopolitan Crimes: Foreign Rivals of Sherlock Holmes*, both also published by Penguin.

THE
FURTHER RIVALS
OF
SHERLOCK
HOLMES

Edited by Hugh Greene

Penguin Books Inc
Baltimore • Maryland

FOR GEORGE MARKSTEIN

Penguin Books Inc
7110 Ambassador Road
Baltimore, Maryland 21207, U.S.A.

Originally published in England as *The Crooked Counties*
by The Bodley Head
First published in the United States by Pantheon Books,
a division of Random House, Inc., New York, 1973
Published by Penguin Books Inc, 1974,
by arrangement with Pantheon Books

CONTENTS

Acknowledgments, 7

Introduction, 11

I. The Redhill Sisterhood, *Catherine Louisa Pirkis,* 21

II. The Loss of Sammy Throckett, *Arthur Morrison,* 48

III. The Problem of Dead Wood Hall, *Dick Donovan,* 74

IV. The Case of Janissary, *Arthur Morrison,* 112

V. Murder by Proxy, *M. McD. Bodkin Q.C.,* 138

VI. The Amber Beads, *Fergus Hume,* 162

VII. How He Cut His Stick, *M. McD. Bodkin Q.C.,* 182

VIII. A Race with the Sun, *L. T. Meade and Clifford Halifax,* 194

IX. The Contents of the Coffin, *J. S. Fletcher,* 220

X. The Mystery of Room 666, *Jacques Futrelle,* 238

XI. The Man Who Cut Off My Hair, *Richard Marsh,* 258

XII. The Affair of the German Dispatch-Box, *Victor L. Whitechurch,* 278

XIII. The Tragedy at Brookbend Cottage, *Ernest Bramah,* 292

ACKNOWLEDGMENTS

For permission to publish some of these stories my thanks are due to: the Beneficiaries of the Estate of Arthur Morrison and Ward Lock & Co Ltd for *The Loss of Sammy Throckett* and *The Case of Janissary*; the Estate of Ernest Bramah and Methuen & Co Ltd for *The Tragedy at Brookbend Cottage*; The Hutchinson Publishing Group Ltd for *The Amber Beads*; Mrs Bodkin for *Murder by Proxy* and *How He Cut His Stick*.

Some copyright holders have been very difficult to trace. If in any case I have failed I offer my apologies.

For help on biographical details I am indebted to Father M. Bodkin S.J., Miss J. Houlgate, the B B C Reference Librarian, Reg Courtney-Browne, Thames Television Information Officer, the Deputy Librarian of the British Medical Association, the Press Officer of the National Canine Defence League and the Secretary of the Savage Club.

I am particularly grateful to Mr Jack Kelson of Tunbridge Wells for drawing my attention to Jacques Futrelle's story *The Mystery of Room 666*. I should also like to thank the many people on both sides of the Atlantic who have written to me about my two previous anthologies.

'It is my belief, Watson, founded upon my experience, that the lowest and vilest alleys in London do not present a more dreadful record of sin than does the smiling and beautiful countryside.'

Sherlock Holmes in *The Adventure of the Copper Beeches*

Introduction

This is the third and, I expect, the last of my collections of early detective stories published in the quarter of a century between the arrival on the scene of Sherlock Holmes and the outbreak of war in 1914.

I doubt whether there are many more discoveries to be made. The books—and many, even, of the magazines— in which these stories appeared are more and more difficult to find and, if found, are more and more expensive to buy.

For about ten years from 1950 onwards I kept a list of prices quoted in the catalogues of second-hand booksellers for detective stories of my chosen period. When I look through my notebook today I am struck not only by the cheapness of the books but by the large number listed and by the wide variety of the booksellers represented— many, if not most, of them no longer in existence.

During that decade prices remained fairly steady—apart from a few much-collected authors like Conan Doyle. During the last twelve years prices have multiplied by ten, twenty, even by a hundred times. *The Mystery of the Patrician Club* by a rather obscure writer called Albert Vandam, which seemed over-priced at £2 in a specialist catalogue in 1955, fetched £20 in a Sotheby sale in December 1972. First editions of William Le Queux used to be found in the shilling boxes. Now one may be asked for £5 or more.

But occasionally one can have a piece of luck. The pleasure of the chase has not entirely vanished.

Except in the British Museum Library I have never seen a copy of Victor L. Whitechurch's *Thrilling Stories of the Railway* which was originally published in pictorial wrappers for one shilling: nor have I ever met a second-hand bookseller who has seen one. Should some lucky person find a copy in a dusty pile in a country house library he might well get £100 or more for it from an American collector.

Almost as rare are J. S. Fletcher's *The Adventures of Archer Dawe*, the Paul Beck and Dora Myrl books by M. McD. Bodkin Q.C. (my own copy of *Dora Myrl, the Lady Detective* came, rather appropriately, from the Prison Library at Holloway) and Mrs Pirkis's *Experiences of Loveday Brooke, Lady Detective*. First editions of Arthur Morrison, Fergus Hume and Dick Donovan can sometimes still be found—at a price.

Most of the stories in my earlier collections came from books and magazines on my own shelves. This time I have spent many hours in the British Museum Reading Room, turning over piles of books which, perhaps, have seldom or never been called for in the last sixty or eighty years.

The authors who have been completely forgotten apart from a mention in the Greene/Glover or Ellery Queen bibliographies usually deserve their obscurity. But there is a twilight world of neglected, but not completely forgotten, writers like Dick Donovan, Bodkin, Mrs Pirkis and Mrs L. T. Meade who wrote the occasional story which deserves to be resurrected, if not for its literary quality, then for some ingenuity of plot, some sudden flash of imagination, some light on the late Victorian and Edwardian world.

I put J. S. Fletcher, Victor L. Whitechurch, Richard

Marsh, even Fergus Hume on a higher plane, to say nothing of Arthur Morrison, Ernest Bramah and Jacques Futrelle who figured in one or other of my previous collections.

The idea for the theme of this collection was given to me by Sherlock Holmes. On his way by train to Winchester to investigate the affair of the Copper Beeches he remarked to Watson: 'It is my belief, Watson, founded upon my experience, that the lowest and vilest alleys in London do not present a more dreadful record of sin than does the smiling and beautiful countryside.'

So here we have sin in Yorkshire, Cheshire, Surrey, Sussex, Hampshire, Cornwall, Dorset and other less easily identifiable counties, though on internal evidence the home counties seem to be particularly well represented. It seems to me to be, in general, a more realistic countryside than that of the country house murders so prevalent in the detective stories written between the wars. Nor is murder the invariable subject. The Victorians and Edwardians were just as interested in crimes against property.

The story by Jacques Futrelle, who was the creator of Professor S. F. X. Van Dusen, is set in a seaside hotel and since Sussex is mentioned I allow myself to assume that the hotel was in Brighton. Where else would one expect to find a house detective? This story has been buried since August 1910 in a more or less forgotten magazine called *The Story-Teller*. Original and fascinating though it is, at any rate to my mind, it never seems to have appeared in book form or to have been reprinted anywhere since. Perhaps this is to be explained by the fact that its author was drowned two years later in the Titanic disaster.

I must confess that I have cheated a little in including Fergus Hume's story *The Amber Beads*. Hagar Stanley, the heroine, works in a pawn-shop in Lambeth, but I justify myself by the fact that she is a gypsy girl from the New Forest.

Of the authors represented in this collection I gave some

account of Arthur Morrison, Ernest Bramah and Mrs L. T. Meade in *The Rivals of Sherlock Holmes* and of Jacques Futrelle in *More Rivals of Sherlock Holmes*. Mrs Meade names as her collaborator for the story in this collection a certain Clifford Halifax M.D. Halifax, who makes a personal appearance in other stories as a medical detective, was the pseudonym of Dr Edgar Beaumont, who was born in 1860 and died in 1921. He had a general practice in the neighbourhood of the Crystal Palace and was a keen horseman and sportsman. According to his obituary in the *Lancet* his share in the collaboration was to supply Mrs Meade with the plots.

Mrs Catherine Louisa Pirkis published fourteen novels between 1877 and 1894, *The Experiences of Loveday Brooke, Lady Detective* being the last. After that she became increasingly involved in a variety of good causes, particularly in connection with animals. With her husband, a retired naval officer, she founded the National Canine Defence League, which still flourishes. So far as writing was concerned what was lost to popular literature was gained by the anti-vivisection movement. Her funeral took place at Kensal Green on October 4, 1910.

Dick Donovan's real name was J. E. Muddock (1842–1934), later Preston-Muddock. Under both names he was a remarkably prolific writer. As Dick Donovan he wrote more than fifty detective stories and thrillers between 1889 and 1914, often with himself as the hero. Under his own name he produced an occasional thriller and another fifty or so historical novels and guide books, starting in 1873. His guide book to Switzerland became a standard work for Victorian travellers and went into seven editions. He also wrote an autobiography, *Pages from an Adventurous Life*, which was published by Werner Laurie in 1907. His life really had been adventurous. He had gone through the Indian mutiny as a 12-year-old employee of the East India Company. Like William Le Queux, Dick

Introduction

Donovan took his spy stories very seriously and prided himself on the fact that many people believed he was a real agent in the pay of the Russian Government. His other main interest in life was the Savage Club, some of whose papers he edited. One of the oldest members of the Club today who remembers him well says that, though he was so prolific on paper, he was taciturn in conversation with a somewhat oppressive personality. He had, a picturesque touch, 'downward sprouting hairs which grew not *in* his nose but from the top upper end of his nose'. One can still see a portrait of him by Eyre Macklin on the wall of the Club sitting room, long grey hair, long reddish moustache and a square cut beard. With his loose collar and tie he looks a rather self-conscious Bohemian.

Fergus Hume (1859–1932) was the author of the most successful detective story ever written, *The Mystery of a Hansom Cab*, and I am not forgetting Conan Doyle. The first edition appeared in Melbourne in 1886, a year before the first Sherlock Holmes story, *A Study in Scarlet*. At the time Hume was an impecunious barrister's clerk, and he sold the copyright for £50 to a group of speculators who formed the Hansom Cab Publishing Company. The new company started printing the book in London in July 1887 and by August 1888 it had sold 340,000 copies without its author earning a penny. Hume had been born in England and was taken as a child to Dunedin in New Zealand by his father, a doctor who was proprietor of a mental hospital. He was educated at the Otago Boys High School and the University of Otago and was admitted to the New Zealand Bar in 1885. He immediately left New Zealand for Melbourne where he tried, unsuccessfully, to write plays. After he became famous as the author of *The Mystery of a Hansom Cab* he moved to England where he published nearly 150 detective stories, thrillers and novels, the last of them in the year of his death, without ever attaining a fraction of the success of the book he had sold outright for a song. He was always dogged by bad luck. His great ambition was to see one of his plays produced and finally he had a play accepted by Sir Henry Irving. But Irving died before it could be produced and nothing more was heard of it. Hume remained a poor man and lived for about the last forty years of his life in a cottage at Thundersley in Essex, where he lies buried at the entrance to the churchyard. Thundersley, then a remote village, is now a suburb of Southend-on-Sea. Hume was a Theosophist and accepted his bad luck in life as part of his karma. He believed that he had had a previous existence as a French nobleman in the 18th century and he had vivid memories of being guillotined during the Revolution. His companion for many years at the cottage in Thundersley was a Mr John Joseph Melville, who was, apparently, a reincarnation of Roger Bacon, the 13th century philosopher and scientist.

His Honour Matthias McDonnell Bodkin, Q.C. (he took silk during the reign of Queen Victoria) died in 1933 at the age of 84. He was the author of six books of detective short stories published between 1898 and 1929. He created two detectives: Paul Beck, described as 'the rule of thumb detective', and Dora Myrl, the Lady Detective. Mr Bodkin's son, Father M. Bodkin S.J., has told me that Paul Beck 'was deliberately conceived as the opposite of Sherlock Holmes, unromantic.' He relied more on common sense in solving his cases than on inspiration and in one story it is said that he looked 'more like a respectable retired milkman than a detective'. Dora Myrl was a much more emotional and romantic figure. Mr Bodkin had the brilliant idea of marrying off his two detectives, and in due course they had a son, Young Beck, and a book was devoted to his adventures. Perhaps it is just as well that Mr Bodkin was a busy man or the process might have been continued *ad infinitum*. In fact Mr Bodkin does not seem to have set much store by his detective stories. In his entertaining book of reminiscences, *Recollections of an Irish Judge*, published in 1914, he does not even mention them. He was a member of the Irish Bar and as a young man seems to have earned more money through journalism than through his occasional briefs. In 1892 during Gladstone's last period as Prime Minister he was elected Irish Nationalist M.P. for North Roscommon, and he gives a rather charming account of his short period at Westminster—he did not stand again in the election called by Lord Rosebery. 'A Member of Parliament,' he writes, 'of simple tastes, who makes up his mind, as I did, to dispense with all luxuries, including alcohol and tobacco, and take all his meals except breakfast within the precincts of the House of Commons, can be fairly comfortable on £150 a year.' Although he took silk he evidently continued to devote more of his time to journalism and the theatre in Dublin, and to books on Law and Irish history, than to the Bar until he was appointed County Court Judge of Clare. One could wish that he had made use of his experiences as a Judge for a new series of detective stories. He had the right ideas. During his retirement he used to tell his son that he deplored the fact that the detective story had become a murder story. Murderers, he said, were the most stupid criminals and con-men the best material. During the Irish Rebellion Judge Bodkin courageously denounced acts of violence committed both by the rebels and by the armed forces of the Crown. The Bodkin Report of February 1921, which he read in open court at Ennis, Co Clare, listed 139 cases in which it was proved that criminal injuries were committed by the British regular and auxiliary forces in the County of Clare. Mr Asquith in the House of Commons quoted Judge Bodkin's declaration that 'Law and order could not be upheld by competition in crime' and described the Report as 'one of the gravest indictments ever presented by a judicial officer against the Executive Government in a free country.'

Joseph Smith Fletcher (1863–1935) was one of the most

prolific English writers of all time. Although it is sometimes difficult to disentangle reprints of his books under
new titles from the original publications, he produced, by
my count, close on 200 books between 1879, when he published his juvenile poems, and 1934. What distinguishes
him from other prolific writers of his time, like Fergus
Hume, Dick Donovan, William Le Queux and E. Phillips
Oppenheim is his astounding versatility. Poems, novels,
detective stories, theology, topographical and archaeological
books about Yorkshire, historical works (including a
history of the St Leger and a three-volume Picturesque
History of Yorkshire) biographies (including lives of
Cardinal Newman and Lord Roberts) all poured from his
pen. He found time, too, for a great mass of occasional
journalism and lectures and was a very good cricketer. He
was one of the leading writers of detective stories from 1918
until his death and was given a flying start in the United
States by the praise of President Woodrow Wilson. I find
the earlier stories about Archer Dawe, his tough old Yorkshire private detective, more attractive. 'Archer Dawe was
now a man of sixty—a little squat-figured man, who
dressed, Sunday or week-day, in rusty black; was never
seen, indoors or out, without a very high-crowned, wide-
brimmed silk hat; and who wore old-fashioned stick-up
collars, held tightly to his wizened throat by swathes of
black neck-cloth. He was a notable figure enough, seen in
this wise, and in company with a Gamp-like umbrella
which he always carried with him wherever he went, wet or
fine; but few people noticed his garments when they had
looked at his face. It was at most times more of a mask
than a face: there was a high, bulging forehead; a small
nose; a straight, hard line of a mouth; a square, determined
jaw and chin. And deep-set in the general pallor of the face
were two eyes—dark, inscrutable, steady as steel, with a
curious penetrating light that seemed to burn far back in
mysterious, unreachable recesses.'

Introduction

One would like to know more about Richard Marsh who died of what was described as heart failure at Haywards Heath in Sussex at the age of 57 in 1915. He was the author of some genuinely horrifying horror stories, particularly *The Beetle* and *The Goddess*. The opening chapters of *The Beetle* in which a tramp, taking refuge from the rain in what he believes to be an empty house, is attacked by a monstrous insect can still make the flesh creep. Perhaps this dark and morbid side of his imagination accounts for the aggressive normality of his entry under Recreation in *Who's Who*: 'He loved them all—cricket, football, golf, cycling, billiards, chess, bridge, motoring and a dozen more. A clumsy but enthusiastic student of whatever made for proficiency in the fine art of doing nothing.' He published in all about seventy novels and collections of short stories, most of them mysteries of one sort or another. He had been educated at Eton and Oxford and started writing stories for magazines for boys at the age of twelve. During the last two years of his life he was an invalid and dictated his last books to a secretary. 'Rarely,' says his obituary in the *Mid-Sussex Times*, 'was there occasion to alter a word after he had uttered it.' That, perhaps, had been the trouble all his life. In most of his books there are chapters which make one feel that he had it in him to be a thriller writer of the first rank, but then will come long passages of such slack and careless writing that all tension is lost.

Canon Victor Lorenzo Whitechurch (1868–1933) led a quiet and uneventful life which is reflected in such novels of clerical life as *The Canon in Residence* and *The Bishop out of Residence*, which have been occasionally reprinted. As a country clergyman and later as Honorary Canon of Christ Church, Oxford, he produced in the 1920s a succession of equally quiet and uneventful detective stories set in country places which appealed to the public taste of the time. For some unknown reason the railway crime stories which he had written while still a curate in the early part of the century were never reprinted and some never appeared in book form at all. And yet the young clergyman had invented in Thorpe Hazell, vegetarian, hypochondriac and railway expert, one of the most original detectives of the time, and the stories have a more astringent flavour than his bland later work.

In two of the stories in this book *The Case of Janissary* and *The Amber Beads* I have made some slight changes and omitted a few sentences which would be incomprehensible out of the context of the books in which they originally appeared. In *The Affair of the German Dispatch-Box* I have included at the beginning a description of Thorpe Hazell which is actually taken from another story.

Perhaps I may conclude this introduction by drawing attention to a remark made by Loveday Brooke in *The Redhill Sisterhood*. 'The popular detective stories,' she said, 'for which there seems so large a demand at the present day, must be, at times, uncommonly useful to the criminal classes.'

I

The Redhill Sisterhood

Catherine Louisa Pirkis

'They want you at Redhill, now,' said Mr Dyer, taking a packet of papers from one of his pigeon-holes. 'The idea seems gaining ground in many quarters that in cases of mere suspicion, women detectives are more satisfactory than men, for they are less likely to attract attention. And this Redhill affair, so far as I can make out, is one of suspicion only.'

It was a dreary November morning; every gas jet in the Lynch Court office was alight, and a yellow curtain of outside fog draped its narrow windows.

'Nevertheless, I suppose one can't afford to leave it uninvestigated at this season of the year, with country-house robberies beginning in so many quarters,' said Miss Brooke.

'No; and the circumstances in this case certainly seem to point in the direction of the country-house burglar. Two days ago a somewhat curious application was made privately, by a man giving the name of John Murray, to Inspector Gunning, of the Reigate police—Redhill, I must tell you, is in the Reigate police district. Murray stated that he had been a greengrocer in South London, had sold his business there, and had, with the proceeds of the sale, bought two small houses in Redhill, intending to let the one and live in the other. These houses are situated in a blind alley, known as Paved Court, a narrow turning leading off the London and Brighton coach road. Paved Court has been known to the sanitary authorities for the past ten years as a regular fever nest, and as the houses which Murray bought—numbers 7 and 8—stand at the very end of the blind alley, with no chance of thorough ventilation, I dare say the man got them for next to nothing. He told the Inspector that he had had great difficulty in procuring a tenant for the house he wished to let, number 8, and that consequently when, about three weeks back, a lady, dressed as a nun, made him an offer for it, he immediately closed with her. The lady gave her name simply as "Sister Monica", and stated that she was a member of an undenominational Sisterhood that had recently been founded by a wealthy lady, who wished her name kept a secret. Sister Monica gave no references, but, instead, paid a quarter's rent in advance, saying that she wished to take possession of the house immediately, and open it as a home for crippled orphans.'

'Gave no references—home for cripples,' murmured Loveday, scribbling hard and fast in her note-book.

'Murray made no objection to this,' continued Mr Dyer, 'and, accordingly, the next day, Sister Monica, accompanied by three other Sisters and some sickly children, took possession of the house, which they furnished with the barest possible necessaries from cheap shops in the neighbourhood. For a time, Murray said, he thought he had secured most desirable tenants, but during the last ten days suspicions as to their real character have entered his mind, and these suspicions he thought it his duty to communicate to the police. Among their possessions, it seems, these Sisters number an old donkey and a tiny cart, and this they start daily on a sort of begging tour through the adjoining villages, bringing back every evening a perfect hoard of broken victuals and bundles of old garments. Now comes the extraordinary fact on which Murray bases his suspicions. He says, and Gunning verifies his statement, that in whatever direction those Sisters turn the wheels of their donkey-cart, burglaries, or attempts at burglaries, are sure to follow. A week ago they went along towards Horley, where, at an outlying house, they received much kindness from a wealthy gentleman. That very night an attempt was made to break into that gentleman's house—an attempt, however, that was happily frustrated by the barking of the house-dog. And so on in other instances that I need not go into. Murray suggests that it might be as well to have the daily movements of these Sisters closely watched, and that extra vigilance should be exercised by the police in the districts that have had the honour of a morning call from them. Gunning coincides with this idea, and so has sent to me to secure your services.'

Loveday closed her note-book. 'I suppose Gunning will meet me somewhere and tell me where I'm to take up my quarters?' she said.

'Yes; he will get into your carriage at Merstham—the station before Redhill—if you will put your hand out of the window, with the morning paper in it. By the way, he takes it for granted that you will take the 11.5 train from Victoria. Murray, it seems, has been good enough to place his little house at the disposal of the police, but Gunning does not think espionage could be so well carried on there as from other quarters. The presence of a stranger in an alley of that sort is bound to attract attention. So he has hired a room for you in a draper's shop that immediately faces the head of the court. There is a private door to this shop of which you will have the key, and can let yourself in and out as you please. You are supposed to be a nursery governess on the lookout for a situation, and Gunning will keep you supplied with letters to give colour to the idea. He suggests that you need only occupy the room during the day, at night you will find far more comfortable quarters at Laker's Hotel, just outside the town.'

This was about the sum total of the instructions that Mr Dyer had to give.

The 11.5 train from Victoria, that carried Loveday to her work among the Surrey Hills, did not get clear of the London fog till well away on the other side of Purley. When the train halted at Merstham, in response to her signal, a tall, soldier-like individual made for her carriage, and, jumping in, took the seat facing her. He introduced himself to her as Inspector Gunning, recalled to her memory a former occasion on which they had met, and then, naturally enough, turned the talk upon the present suspicious circumstances they were bent upon investigating.

'It won't do for you and me to be seen together,' he said; 'of course I am known for miles round, and any one seen in my company will be at once set down as my coadjutor, and spied upon accordingly. I walked from Redhill to Merstham on purpose to avoid recognition on the platform at Redhill, and half-way here, to my great annoyance, found that I was being followed by a man in a workman's dress and carrying a basket of tools. I doubled, however, and gave him the slip, taking a short cut down a lane which, if he had been living in the place, he would have known as well as I did. By Jove!' this was added with a sudden start, 'there is the fellow, I declare; he has weathered me after all, and has no doubt taken good stock of us both, with the train going at this snail's pace. It was unfortunate that your face should have been turned towards that window, Miss Brooke.'

'My veil is something of a disguise, and I will put on another cloak before he has a chance of seeing me again,' said Loveday.

All she had seen in the brief glimpse that the train had allowed, was a tall, powerfully-built man walking along the siding of the line. His cap was drawn low over his eyes, and in his hand he carried a workman's basket.

Gunning seemed much annoyed at the circumstance.

'Instead of landing at Redhill,' he said, 'we'll go on to Three Bridges, and wait there for a Brighton train to bring us back, that will enable you to get to your room somewhere between the lights; I don't want to have you spotted before you've so much as started your work.'

Then they went back to their discussion of the Redhill Sisterhood.

'They call themselves "undenominational", whatever that means,' said Gunning, 'they say they are connected with no religious sect whatever, they attend sometimes one place of worship, sometimes another, sometimes none at all. They refuse to give up the name of the founder of their order, and really no one has any right to demand it of them, for, as no doubt you see, up to the present moment the case is one of mere suspicion, and it may be a pure co-incidence that attempts at burglary have followed their footsteps in this neighbourhood. By the way, I have heard of a man's face being enough to hang him, but until I saw Sister Monica's, I never saw a woman's face that could perform the same kind of office for her. Of all the lowest criminal types of faces I have ever seen, I think hers is about the lowest and most repulsive.'

After the Sisters, they passed in review the chief families resident in the neighbourhood.

'This,' said Gunning, unfolding a paper, 'is a map I have specially drawn up for you—it takes in the district for ten miles round Redhill, and every country house of any importance is marked on it in red ink. Here, in addition, is an index of those houses, with special notes of my own to every house.'

Loveday studied the map for a minute or so, then turned her attention to the index.

'Those four houses you've marked, I see, are those that have been already attempted. I don't think I'll run them through, but I'll mark them "doubtful"; you see the gang—for, of course, it is a gang—might follow our reasoning on the matter, and look upon those houses as our weak point. Here's one I'll run through, "house empty during winter months",—that means plate and jewellery sent to the bankers. Oh! and this one may as well be crossed off, "father and four sons all athletes and sportsmen", that means firearms always handy—I don't think burglars will be likely to trouble them. Ah! now we come to something! Here's a house to be marked "tempting" in a burglar's list. "Wootton Hall, lately changed hands and rebuilt, with complicated passages and corridors. Splendid family plate in daily use and left entirely in the care of the butler." I wonder does the master of that house trust to his "complicated passages" to preserve his plate for him? A dismissed dishonest servant would supply a dozen maps of the place for half a sovereign. What do these initials, "E.L." against the next house in the list, North Cape, stand for?'

'Electric lighted. I think you might almost cross that house off also. I consider electric lighting one of the greatest safeguards against burglars that a man can give his house.'

'Yes, if he doesn't rely exclusively upon it; it might be a nasty trap under certain circumstances. I see this gentleman also has magnificent presentation and other plate.'

'Yes . . . Mr Jameson is a wealthy man and very popular in the neighbourhood; his cups and epergnes are worth looking at.'

'Is it the only house in the district that is lighted with electricity?'

'Yes; and, begging your pardon, Miss Brooke, I only wish it were not so. If electric lighting were generally in vogue it would save the police a lot of trouble on these dark winter nights.'

'The burglars would find some way of meeting such a condition of things, depend upon it; they have reached a very high development in these days. They no longer stalk about as they did fifty years ago with blunderbuss and bludgeon; they plot, plan, contrive, and bring imagination and artistic resource to their aid. By the way, it often occurs to me that the popular detective stories, for which there seems so large a demand at the present day, must be, at times, uncommonly useful to the criminal classes.'

At Three Bridges they had to wait so long for a return train that it was nearly dark when Loveday got back to Redhill. Mr Gunning did not accompany her thither, having alighted at a previous station. Loveday had directed her portmanteau to be sent direct to Laker's Hotel, where she had engaged a room by telegram from Victoria Station. So, unburthened by luggage, she slipped quietly out of the Redhill Station and made her way straight for the draper's shop in the London Road. She had no difficulty in finding it, thanks to the minute directions given her by the Inspector.

Street lamps were being lighted in the sleepy little town as she went along, and as she turned into the London Road, shopkeepers were lighting up their windows on both sides of the way. A few yards down this road, a dark patch between the lighted shops showed her where Paved Court led off from the thoroughfare. A side door of one of the shops that stood at the corner of the court seemed to offer a post of observation whence she could see without being seen, and here Loveday, shrinking into the shadows, ensconced herself in order to take stock of the little alley and its inhabitants. She found it much as it had been described to her—a collection of four-roomed houses of which more than half were unlet. Numbers 7 and 8 at the head of the court presented a slightly less neglected appearance than the other tenements. Number 7 stood in total darkness, but in the upper window of number 8 there showed what seemed to be a night-light burning, so Loveday conjectured that this possibly was the room set apart as a dormitory for the little cripples.

While she stood thus surveying the home of the suspected Sisterhood, the Sisters themselves—two, at least, of them—came into view, with their donkey-cart and their cripples, in the main road. It was an odd little cortege. One Sister, habited in a nun's dress of dark blue serge, led the donkey by the bridle; another Sister, similarly attired, walked alongside the low cart, in which were seated two sickly-looking children. They were evidently returning from one of their long country circuits, and, unless they had lost their way and been belated, it certainly seemed a late hour for the sickly little cripples to be abroad.

As they passed under the gas lamp at the corner of the court, Loveday caught a glimpse of the faces of the Sisters. It was easy, with Inspector Gunning's description before her mind, to identify the older and taller woman as Sister Monica, and a more coarse-featured and generally repellent face Loveday admitted to herself she had never before seen. In striking contrast to this forbidding countenance was that of the younger Sister. Loveday could only catch a brief passing view of it, but that one brief view was enough to impress it on her memory as of unusual sadness and beauty. As the donkey stopped at the corner of the court, Loveday heard this sad-looking young woman addressed as 'Sister Anna' by one of the cripples, who asked plaintively when they were going to have something to eat.

'Now, at once,' said Sister Anna, lifting the little one, as it seemed to Loveday, tenderly out of the cart, and carrying him on her shoulder down the court to the door of number 8, which opened to them at their approach. The other Sister did the same with the other child; then both Sisters returned, unloaded the cart of sundry bundles and baskets, and, this done, led off the old donkey and trap down the road, possibly to a neighbouring costermonger's stables.

A man, coming along on a bicycle, exchanged a word of greeting with the Sisters as they passed, then swung himself off his machine at the corner of the court, and walked it along the paved way to the door of number 7. This he opened with a key, and then, pushing the machine before him, entered the house.

Loveday took it for granted that this man must be the John Murray of whom she had heard. She had closely scrutinized him as he had passed her, and had seen that he was a dark, well-featured man of about fifty years of age.

She congratulated herself on her good fortune in having seen so much in such a brief space of time, and, coming forth from her sheltered corner, turned her steps in the direction of the draper's shop on the other side of the road.

It was easy to find. 'Golightly' was the singular name that figured above the shop-front, in which were displayed a variety of goods calculated to meet the wants of servants and the poorer classes generally. A tall, powerfully-built man appeared to be looking in at the window. Loveday's foot was on the doorstep of the draper's private entrance, her hand on the door-knocker, when this individual, suddenly turning, convinced her of his identity with the journeyman workman who had so disturbed Mr Gunning's equanimity. It was true he wore a bowler instead of a journeyman's cap, and he no longer carried a basket of tools, but there was no possibility for any one, with so good an eye for an outline as Loveday possessed, not to recognize the carriage of the head and shoulders as that of the man she had seen walking along the railway siding. He gave her no time to make minute observation of his appearance, but turned quickly away, and disappeared down a by-street.

Loveday's work seemed to bristle with difficulties now. Here was she, as it were, unearthed in her own ambush; for there could be but little doubt that during the whole time she had stood watching those Sisters, that man, from a safe vantage-point, had been watching her.

She found Mrs Golightly a civil and obliging person. She showed Loveday to her room above the shop, brought her the letters which Inspector Gunning had been careful to have posted to her during the day. Then she supplied her with pen and ink and, in response to Loveday's request, with some strong coffee that she said, with a little attempt at a joke, would 'keep a dormouse awake all through the winter without winking.'

While the obliging landlady busied herself about the room, Loveday had a few questions to ask about the Sisterhood who lived down the court opposite. On this head, however, Mrs Golightly could tell her no more than she already knew, beyond the fact that they started every morning on their rounds at eleven o'clock punctually, and that before that hour they were never to be seen outside their door.

Loveday's watch that night was to be a fruitless one. Although she sat, with her lamp turned out and safely screened from observation, until close upon midnight, with eyes fixed upon numbers 7 and 8, Paved Court, not so much as a door opening or shutting at either house rewarded her vigil. The lights flitted from the lower to the upper floors in both houses, and then disappeared, somewhere between nine and ten in the evening; and after that, not a sign of life did either tenement show.

And all through the long hours of that watch, again and again there seemed to flit before her mind's eye, as if in some sort it were fixed upon its retina, the sweet, sad face of Sister Anna.

Why it was this face should so haunt her, she found it hard to say.

'It has a mournful past and a mournful future written upon it as a hopeless whole,' she said to herself. 'It is the face of an Andromeda! "Here am I", it seems to say, "tied to my stake, helpless and hopeless".'

The church clocks were sounding the midnight hour as Loveday made her way through the dark streets to her hotel outside the town. As she passed under the railway arch that ended in the open country road, the echo of not very distant footsteps caught her ear. When she stopped they stopped, when she went on they went on, and she knew that once more she was being followed and watched, although the darkness of the arch prevented her seeing even the shadow of the man who was thus dogging her steps.

The next morning broke keen and frosty. Loveday studied her map and her country-house index over a seven o'clock breakfast, and then set off for a brisk walk along the country road. No doubt in London the streets were walled in and roofed with yellow fog; here, however, bright sunshine playing in and out of the bare tree-boughs and leafless hedges on to a thousand frost spangles, turned the prosaic macadamized road into a gangway fit for Queen Titania herself and her fairy train.

Loveday turned her back on the town and set herself to follow the road as it wound away over the hill in the direction of a village called Northfield. Early as she was, she was not to have that road to herself. A team of strong horses trudged by on their way to their work in the fuller's-earth pits. A young fellow on a bicycle flashed past at a tremendous pace, considering the upward slant of the road. He looked hard at her as he passed, then slackened speed, dismounted, and awaited her coming on the brow of the hill.

'Good-morning, Miss Brooke,' he said, lifting his cap as she came alongside of him. 'May I have five minutes' talk with you?'

The young man who thus accosted her had not the appearance of a gentleman. He was a handsome, bright-faced young fellow of about two-and-twenty, and was dressed in ordinary cyclist's dress; his cap was pushed back from his brow over thick, curly, fair hair, and Loveday, as she looked at him, could not repress the thought how well he would look at the head of a troop of cavalry, giving the order to charge the enemy.

He led his machine to the side of the footpath.

'You have the advantage of me,' said Loveday; 'I haven't the remotest notion who you are.'

'No,' he said; 'although I know you, you cannot possibly know me. I am a north-country man, and I was present, about a month ago, at the trial of old Mr Craven, of Troyte's Hill—in fact, I acted as reporter for one of the local papers. I watched your face so closely as you gave your evidence that I should know it anywhere, among a thousand.'

'And your name is . . .?'

'George White, of Grenfell. My father is part proprietor of one of the Newcastle papers. I am a bit of a literary man myself, and sometimes figure as a reporter, sometimes as leader-writer, to that paper.' Here he gave a glance towards his side pocket, from which protruded a small volume of Tennyson's poems.

The facts he had stated did not seem to invite comment, and Loveday ejaculated merely:

'Indeed!'

The young man went back to the subject that was evidently filling his thoughts. 'I have special reasons for being glad to have met you this morning, Miss Brooke,' he went on, making his footsteps keep pace with hers. 'I am in great trouble, and I believe you are the only person in the whole world who can help me out of that trouble.'

'I am rather doubtful as to my power of helping any one out of trouble,' said Loveday; 'so far as my experience goes, our troubles are as much a part of ourselves as our skins are of our bodies.'

'Ah, but not such trouble as mine,' said White eagerly. He broke off for a moment, then, with a sudden rush of words, told her what that trouble was. For the past year he had been engaged to be married to a young girl, who, until quite recently, had been fulfilling the duties of a nursery governess in a large house in the neighbourhood of Redhill.

'Will you kindly give me the name of that house?' interrupted Loveday.

'Certainly; Wootton Hall, the place is called, and Annie Lee is my sweetheart's name. I don't care who knows it!' He threw his head back as he said this, as if he would be delighted to announce the fact to the whole world. 'Annie's mother,' he went on, 'died when she was a baby, and we both thought her father was dead also, when suddenly, about a fortnight ago, it came to her knowledge that, instead of being dead, he was serving his time at Portland for some offence committed years ago.'

'Do you know how this came to Annie's knowledge?'

'Not the least in the world; I only know that I suddenly got a letter from her announcing the fact, and, at the same time, breaking off her engagement with me. I tore the letter into a thousand pieces, and wrote back saying I would not allow the engagement to be broken off, but would marry her if she would have me. To this letter she did not reply; there came instead a few lines from Mrs Copeland, the lady at Wootton Hall, saying that Annie had thrown up her engagement, and joined some Sisterhood, and that she, Mrs Copeland, had pledged her word to Annie to reveal to no one the name and whereabouts of that Sisterhood.'

'And I suppose you imagine I am able to do what Mrs Copeland is pledged not to do?'

'That's just it, Miss Brooke!' cried the young man enthusiastically. 'You do such wonderful things; everyone knows you do. It seems as if, when anything is wanting to be found out, you just walk into a place, look round you, and, in a moment, everything becomes clear as noonday.'

'I can't quite lay claim to such wonderful powers as that. As it happens, however, in the present instance, no particular skill is needed to find out what you wish to know, for I fancy I have already come upon the traces of Miss Annie Lee.'

'Miss Brooke!'

'Of course, I cannot say for certain, but it is a matter you can easily settle for yourself—settle, too, in a way that will confer a great obligation on me.'

'I shall be only too delighted to be of any, the slightest, service to you!' cried White, enthusiastically as before.

'Thank you. I will explain. I came down here specially to watch the movements of a certain Sisterhood who have somehow aroused the suspicions of the police. Well, I find that instead of being able to do this, I am myself so closely watched—possibly by confederates of these Sisters—that unless I can do my work by deputy I may as well go back to town at once.'

'Ah! I see—you want me to be that deputy.'

'Precisely. I want you to go to the room in Redhill that I have hired, take your place at the window—screened, of course, from observation—at which I ought to be seated—watch as closely as possible the movements of these Sisters, and report them to me at the hotel, where I shall remain shut in from morning till night—it is the only way in which I can throw my persistent spies off the scent. Now, in doing this for me, you will be doing yourself a good turn, for I have little doubt but what under the blue serge hood of one of the Sisters you will discover the pretty face of Miss Annie Lee.'

As they talked they had walked, and now stood on the top of the hill at the head of the one little street that constituted the whole of the village of Northfield.

On their left hand stood the village school and the master's house; nearly facing these, on the opposite side of the road, beneath a clump of elms, stood the village pound. Beyond this pound, on either side of the way, were two rows of small cottages with tiny squares of garden in front, and in the midst of these small cottages a swinging sign beneath a lamp announced a 'Postal and Telegraph Office'.

'Now that we have come into the land of habitations again,' said Loveday, 'it will be best for us to part. It will not do for you and me to be seen together, or my spies will be transferring their attentions from me to you, and I shall have to find another deputy. You had better start on your bicycle for Redhill at once, and I will walk back at leisurely speed. Come to me at my hotel without fail at one o'clock and report proceedings. I do not say anything definite about remuneration, but I assure you, if you carry out my instructions to the letter, your services will be amply rewarded by me and by my employers.'

There were yet a few more details to arrange. White had been, he said, only a day and night in the neighbourhood, and special directions as to the locality had to be given to him. Loveday advised him not to attract attention by going to the draper's private door, but to enter the shop as if he were a customer, and then explain matters to Mrs Golightly, who, no doubt, would be in her place behind the counter; tell her he was the brother of the Miss Smith who had hired her room, and ask permission to go through the shop to that room, as he had been commissioned by his sister to read and answer any letters that might have arrived there for her.

'Show her the key of the side door—here it is,' said Loveday; 'it will be your credentials, and tell her you did not like to make use of it without acquainting her with the fact.'

The young man took the key, endeavouring to put it in his waistcoat pocket, found the space there occupied, and so transferred it to the keeping of a side pocket in his tunic.

All this time Loveday stood watching him.

'You have a capital machine there,' she said, as the young man mounted his bicycle once more, 'and I hope you will turn it to account in following the movements of these Sisters about the neighbourhood. I feel confident you will have something definite to tell me when you bring me your first report at one o'clock.'

White once more broke into a profusion of thanks, and

then, lifting his cap to the lady, started his machine at a fairly good pace.

Loveday watched him out of sight down the slope of the hill, then, instead of following him as she had said she would 'at a leisurely pace,' she turned her steps in the opposite direction along the village street.

It was an altogether ideal country village. Neatly-dressed, chubby-faced children, now on their way to the school, dropped quaint little curtseys, or tugged at curly locks as Loveday passed; every cottage looked the picture of cleanliness and trimness, and, although so late in the year, the gardens were full of late flowering chrysanthemums and early flowering Christmas roses.

At the end of the village, Loveday came suddenly into view of a large, handsome, red-brick mansion. It presented a wide frontage to the road, from which it lay back amid extensive pleasure grounds. On the right hand, and a little in the rear of the house, stood what seemed to be large and commodious stables, and immediately adjoining these stables was a low-built, red-brick shed, that had evidently been recently erected.

That low-built, red-brick shed excited Loveday's curiosity.

'Is this house called North Cape?' she asked of a man, who chanced at that moment to be passing with a pickaxe and shovel.

The man answered in the affirmative, and Loveday then asked another question: Could he tell her what was that small shed so close to the house—it looked like a glorified cowhouse—now what could be its use?

The man's face lighted up as if it were a subject on which he liked to be questioned. He explained that that small shed was the engine-house where the electricity that lighted North Cape was made and stored. Then he dwelt with pride upon the fact, as if he held a personal interest in it, that North Cape was the only house, far or near, that was thus lighted.

'I suppose the wires are carried underground to the house,' said Loveday, looking in vain for signs of them anywhere.

The man was delighted to go into details on the matter. He had helped to lay those wires, he said: they were two in number, one for supply and one for return, and were laid three feet below ground, in boxes filled with pitch. They were switched on to jars in the engine-house, where the electricity was stored, and, after passing underground, entered the family mansion under the flooring at its western end.

Loveday listened attentively to these details, and then took a minute and leisurely survey of the house and its surroundings. This done, she retraced her steps through the village, pausing, however, at the 'Postal and Telegraph Office' to despatch a telegram to Inspector Gunning.

It was one to send the Inspector to his cipher-book. It ran as follows:

Rely solely on chemist and coal-merchant throughout the day. L.B.

After this, she quickened her pace, and in something over three-quarters of an hour was back again at her hotel.

There she found more of life stirring than when she had quitted it in the early morning. There was to be a meeting of the 'Surrey Stags', about a couple of miles off, and a good many hunting men were hanging about the entrance of the house, discussing the chances of sport after last night's frost. Loveday made her way through the throng in leisurely fashion, and not a man but what had keen scrutiny from her sharp eyes. No, there was no cause for suspicion there; they were evidently one and all just what they seemed to be—loud-voiced, hard-riding men, bent on a day's sport; but—and here Loveday's eyes travelled beyond the hotel courtyard to the other side of the road—who was that man with a bill-hook hacking at the hedge there—a thin-featured, round-shouldered old fellow, with a bent-about hat? It might be as well not to take it too rashly for granted that her spies had withdrawn, and had left her free to do her work in her own fashion.

She went upstairs to her room. It was situated on the first floor in the front of the house, and consequently commanded a good view of the high road. She stood well back from the window, and at an angle whence she could see and not be seen, took a long, steady survey of the hedger. And the longer she looked the more convinced she was that the man's real work was something other than the bill-hook seemed to imply. He worked, so to speak, with his head over his shoulder, and when Loveday supplemented her eyesight with a strong field-glass, she could see more than one stealthy glance shot from beneath his bent-about hat in the direction of her window.

There could be little doubt about it: her movements were to be as closely watched to-day as they had been yesterday. Now it was of first importance that she should communicate with Inspector Gunning in the course of the afternoon: the question to solve was how it was to be done?

To all appearance Loveday answered the question in extraordinary fashion. She pulled up her blind, she drew back her curtain, and seated herself, in full view, at a small table in the window recess. Then she took a pocket ink-stand from her pocket, a packet of correspondence cards from her letter-case, and with rapid pen set to work on them.

About an hour and a half afterwards, White, coming in, according to his promise, to report proceedings, found her still seated at the window, not, however, with writing materials before her, but with needle and thread in her hand, with which she was mending her gloves.

'I return to town by the first train tomorrow morning,' she said as he entered, 'and I find these wretched things want no end of stitches. Now for your report.'

White appeared to be in an elated frame of mind. 'I've seen her!' he cried, 'my Annie—they've got her, those confounded Sisters; but they sha'n't keep her—no, not if I have to pull the house down about their ears to get her out!'

'Well, now you know where she is, you can take your time about getting her out,' said Loveday. 'I hope, however, you haven't broken faith with me, and betrayed yourself by trying to speak with her, because, if so, I shall have to look for another deputy.'

'Honour, Miss Brooke!' answered White indignantly. 'I stuck to my duty, though it cost me something to see her hanging over those kids and tucking them into the cart, and never say a word to her, never so much as wave my hand.'

'Did she go out with the donkey-cart to-day?'

'No, she only tucked the kids into the cart with a blanket, and then went back to the house. Two old Sisters, ugly as sin, went out with them. I watched them from the window, jolt, jolt, jolt, round the corner, out of sight, and then I whipped down the stairs, and on to my machine, and was after them in a trice, and managed to keep them well in sight for over an hour and a half.'

'And their destination to-day was?'

'Wootton Hall.'

'Ah, just as I expected.'

'Just as you expected?' echoed White.

'I forgot. You do not know the nature of the suspicions that are attached to this Sisterhood, and the reasons I have for thinking that Wootton Hall, at this season of the year, might have an especial attraction for them.'

White continued staring at her. 'Miss Brooke,' he said presently, in an altered tone, 'whatever suspicions may attach to the Sisterhood, I'll stake my life on it, my Annie has had no share in any wickedness of any sort.'

'Oh, quite so; it is most likely that your Annie has, in some way, been inveigled into joining these Sisters—has been taken possession of by them, in fact, just as they have taken possession of the little cripples.'

'That's it! that's it!' he cried excitedly; 'that was the idea that occurred to me when you spoke to me on the hill about them, otherwise you may be sure . . .'

'Did they get relief of any sort at the Hall?' interrupted Loveday.

'Yes; one of the two ugly old women stopped outside the lodge gates with the donkey-cart, and the other beauty went up to the house alone. She stayed there, I should think, about a quarter of an hour, and when she came back was followed by a servant, carrying a bundle and a basket.'

'Ah! I've no doubt they brought away with them something else beside old garments and broken victuals.'

White stood in front of her, fixing a hard, steady gaze upon her.

'Miss Brooke,' he said presently, in a voice that matched the look on his face, 'what do you suppose was the real object of these women in going to Wootton Hall this morning?'

'Mr White, if I wished to help a gang of thieves break into Wootton Hall to-night, don't you think I should be greatly interested in procuring for them the information that the master of the house was away from home; that two of the men-servants, who slept in the house, had recently been dismissed and their places had not yet been filled; also that the dogs were never unchained at night, and that their kennels were at the side of the house at which the butler's pantry is not situated? These are particulars I have gathered in this house without stirring from my chair, and I am satisfied that they are likely to be true. At the same time, if I were a professional burglar, I should not be content with information that was likely to be true, but would be careful to procure such that was certain to be true, and so would set accomplices to work at the fountain head. Now do you understand?'

White folded his arms and looked down on her.

'What are you going to do?' he asked, in short, brusque tones.

Loveday looked him full in the face. 'Communicate with the police immediately,' she answered; 'and I should feel greatly obliged if you would at once take a note from me to Inspector Gunning at Reigate.'

'And what becomes of Annie?'

'I don't think you need have any anxiety on that head. I have no doubt that when the circumstances of her admission to the Sisterhood are investigated, it will be proved that she has been as much deceived and imposed upon as the man, John Murray, who so foolishly let his house to these women. Remember, Annie has Mrs Copeland's good word to support her integrity.'

White stood silent for awhile.

'What sort of a note do you wish me to take to the Inspector?' he presently asked.

'You shall read it as I write it, if you like,' answered Loveday. She took a correspondence card from her letter-case, and, with an indelible pencil, wrote as follows—

Wootton Hall is threatened to-night—concentrate attention there. L.B.

White read the words as she wrote them with a curious expression passing over his handsome features.

'Yes,' he said, curtly as before; 'I'll deliver that, I give you my word, but I'll bring back no answer to you. I'll do no more spying for you—it's a trade that doesn't suit me. There's a straightforward way of doing straightforward work, and I'll take that way—no other—to get my Annie out of that den.'

He took the note, which she sealed and handed to him, and strode out of the room.

Loveday, from the window, watched him mount his bicycle. Was it her fancy, or did there pass a swift, furtive glance of recognition between him and the hedger on the other side of the way as he rode out of the courtyard?

She seemed determined to make that hedger's work easy for him. The short winter's day was closing in now, and her room must consequently have been growing dim to outside observation. She lighted the gas chandelier which hung from the ceiling, and, still with blinds and curtains undrawn, took her old place at the window, spread writing materials before her, and commenced a long and elaborate report to her chief at Lynch Court.

About half an hour afterwards, she threw a casual glance across the road, and saw that the hedger had disappeared, but that two ill-looking tramps sat munching bread and cheese under the hedge to which his bill-hook had done so little service. Evidently the intention was, one way or another, not to lose sight of her so long as she remained in Redhill.

Meantime, White had delivered Loveday's note to the Inspector at Reigate, and had disappeared on his bicycle once more.

Gunning read it without a change of expression. Then he crossed the room to the fireplace and held the card as close to the bars as he could without scorching it.

'I had a telegram from her this morning,' he explained to his confidential man, 'telling me to rely upon chemicals and coals throughout the day, and that, of course, meant that she would write to me in invisible ink. No doubt this message about Wootton Hall means nothing . . .'

He broke off abruptly, exclaiming: 'Eh! what's this!' as, having withdrawn the card from the fire, Loveday's real message stood out in bold, clear characters between the lines of the false one.

Thus it ran:

North Cape will be attacked to-night—a desperate gang—be prepared for a struggle. Above all, guard the

*electrical engine-house. On no account attempt to com-
municate with me; I am so closely watched that any
endeavour to do so may frustrate your chance of trapping
the scoundrels.* L.B.

That night when the moon went down behind Reigate
Hill an exciting scene was enacted at North Cape. The
Surrey Gazette, in its issue the following day, gave the sub-
joined account of it under the heading, 'Desperate En-
counter with Burglars'.

'Last night, "North Cape", the residence of Mr Jameson,
was the scene of an affray between the police and a desperate gang of burglars. "North Cape" is lighted throughout by electricity, and the burglars, four in number,
divided in half—two being told off to enter and rob the
house, and two to remain at the engine-shed, where the
electricity is stored, so that, at a given signal, should need
arise, the wires might be unswitched, the inmates of the
house thrown into sudden darkness and confusion, and the
escape of the marauders thereby facilitated. Mr Jameson,
however, had received timely warning from the police of
the intended attack, and he, with his two sons, all well-
armed, sat in darkness in the inner hall awaiting the
coming of the thieves. The police were stationed, some in
the stables, some in out-buildings nearer to the house, and
others in more distant parts of the grounds. The burglars
effected their entrance by means of a ladder placed to a
window of the servants' staircase, which leads straight down
to the butler's pantry and to the safe where the silver is
kept. The fellows, however, had no sooner got into the
house than two policemen, issuing from their hiding-place
outside, mounted the ladder after them and thus cut off
their retreat. Mr Jameson and his two sons, at the same
moment, attacked them in front, and thus overwhelmed
by numbers the scoundrels were easily secured. It was at
the engine-house outside that the sharpest struggle took

place. The thieves had forced open the door of this engine-shed with their jemmies immediately on their arrival, under the very eyes of the police, who lay in ambush in the stables, and when one of the men, captured in the house, contrived to sound an alarm on his whistle, these outside watchers made a rush for the electrical jars, in order to unswitch the wires. Upon this the police closed upon them, and a hand-to-hand struggle followed, and if it had not been for the timely assistance of Mr Jameson and his sons, who had fortunately conjectured that their presence here might be useful, it is more than likely that one of the burglars, a powerfully-built man, would have escaped.

'The names of the captured men are John Murray, Arthur and George Lee (father and son), and a man with so many *aliases* that it is difficult to know which is his real name. The whole thing had been most cunningly and carefully planned. The elder Lee, lately released from penal servitude for a similar offence, appears to have been prime mover in the affair. This man had, it seems, a son and a daughter, who, through the kindness of friends, had been fairly well placed in life; the son at an electrical engineer's in London, the daughter as nursery governess at Wootton Hall. Directly this man was released from Portland, he seems to have found out his children and done his best to ruin them both. He was constantly at Wootton Hall endeavouring to induce his daughter to act as an accomplice to a robbery of the house. This so worried the girl that she threw up her situation and joined a Sisterhood that had recently been established in the neighbourhood. Upon this, Lee's thoughts turned in another direction. He induced his son, who had saved a little money, to throw up his work in London, and join him in his disreputable career. The boy is a handsome young fellow, but appears to have in him the makings of a first-class criminal. In his work as an electrical engineer he had made the acquaintance of the man John Murray, who, it is said, has been rapidly going downhill of late. Murray was the owner of the house rented by the Sisterhood that Miss Lee had joined, and the idea evidently struck the brains of these three scoundrels that this Sisterhood, whose antecedents were not generally known, might be utilized to draw off the attention of the police from themselves and from the especial house in the neighbourhood that they had planned to attack. With this end in view, Murray made an application to the police to have the Sisters watched, and still further to give colour to the suspicions he had endeavoured to set afloat concerning them, he and his confederates made feeble attempts at burglary upon the houses at which the Sisters had called, begging for scraps. It is a matter for congratulation that the plot, from beginning to end, has been thus successfully unearthed, and it is felt on all sides that great credit is due to Inspector Gunning and his skilled coadjutors for the vigilance and promptitude they have displayed throughout the affair.'

Loveday read aloud this report, with her feet on the fender of the Lynch Court office.

'Accurate, so far as it goes,' she said, as she laid down the paper.

'But we want to know a little more,' said Mr Dyer. 'In the first place, I would like to know what it was that diverted your suspicions from the unfortunate Sisters?'

'The way in which they handled the children,' answered Loveday promptly. 'I have seen female criminals of all kinds handling children, and I have noticed that although they may occasionally—even this is rare—treat them with a certain rough sort of kindness, of tenderness they are utterly incapable. Now Sister Monica, I must admit, is not pleasant to look at; at the same time, there was something absolutely beautiful in the way in which she lifted the little cripple out of the cart, put his tiny thin hand round her neck, and carried him into the house. By the way, I would like to ask some rabid physiognomist how he would account for Sister Monica's repulsiveness of features as contrasted with young Lee's undoubted good looks—heredity, in this case, throws no light on the matter.'

'Another question,' said Mr Dyer, not paying heed to Loveday's digression; 'how was it you transferred your suspicions to John Murray?'

'I did not do so immediately, although at the very first it had struck me as odd that he should be so anxious to do the work of the police for them. The chief thing I noticed concerning Murray, on the first and only occasion on which I saw him, was that he had had an accident with his bicycle, for in the right-hand corner of his lamp-glass there was a tiny star, and the lamp itself had a dent on the same side, had also lost its hook, and was fastened to the machine by a bit of electric fuse. The next morning, as I was walking up the hill towards Northfield, I was accosted by a young man mounted on that selfsame bicycle—not a doubt of it—star in glass, dent, fuse, all there.'

'Ah, that sounded an important key-note, and led you to connect Murray and the younger Lee immediately.'

'It did, and, of course, also at once gave the lie to his statement that he was a stranger in the place, and confirmed my opinion that there was nothing of the north-countryman in his accent. Other details in his manner and appearance gave rise to other suspicions. For instance, he called himself a press reporter by profession, and his hands were coarse and grimy, as only a mechanic's could be. He said he was a bit of a literary man, but the Tennyson that showed so obtrusively from his pocket was new, and in parts uncut, and totally unlike the well-thumbed volume of the literary student. Finally, when he tried and failed to put my latchkey into his waistcoat pocket, I saw the reason lay in the fact that the pocket was already occupied by a soft coil of electric fuse, the end of which protruded. Now, an electric fuse is what an electrical engineer might almost unconsciously carry about with him, it is so essential a part of his working tools, but it is a thing that a literary man or a press reporter could have no possible use for.'

'Exactly, exactly. And it was, no doubt, that bit of electric fuse that turned your thoughts to the one house in the neighbourhood lighted by electricity, and suggested to your mind the possibility of electrical engineers turning their talents to account in that direction. Now, will you tell me what, at that stage of your day's work, induced you to wire to Gunning that you would bring your invisible ink bottle into use?'

'That was simply a matter of precaution; it did not compel me to the use of invisible ink, if I saw other safe methods of communication. I felt myself being hemmed in on all sides with spies, and I could not tell what emergency might arise. I don't think I have ever had a more difficult game to play. As I walked and talked with the young fellow up the hill, it became clear to me that if I wished to do my work I must lull the suspicions of the gang, and seem to walk into their trap. I saw by the persistent way in which Wootton Hall was forced on my notice that it was wished to fix my suspicions there. I accordingly, to all appearance, did so, and allowed the fellows to think they were making a fool of me.'

'Ha! ha! Capital, that—the biter bit, with a vengeance! Splendid idea to make that young rascal himself deliver the letter that was to land him and his pals in jail. And he all the time laughing in his sleeve and thinking what a fool he was making of you! Ha, ha, ha!' And Mr Dyer made the office ring again with his merriment.

'The only person one is at all sorry for in this affair is poor little Sister Anna,' said Loveday pityingly; 'and yet, perhaps, all things considered, after her sorry experience of life, she may not be so badly placed in a Sisterhood where practical Christianity—not religious hysterics—is the one and only rule of the order.'

II

The Loss of Sammy Throckett

Arthur Morrison

It was, of course, always a part of Martin Hewitt's business to be thoroughly at home among any and every class of people, and to be able to interest himself intelligently, or to appear to do so, in their various pursuits. In one of the most important cases ever placed in his hands, he could have gone but a short way towards success had he not displayed some knowledge of the more sordid aspects of professional sport, and a great interest in the undertakings of a certain dealer therein. The great case itself had nothing to do with sport, and, indeed, from a narrative point of view, was somewhat uninteresting; but the man who alone held the one piece of information wanted was a keeper, backer, or 'gaffer' of professional pedestrians, and it was through the medium of his pecuniary interest in such matters that Hewitt was enabled to strike a bargain with him.

The man was a publican on the outskirts of Padfield, a northern town pretty famous for its sporting tastes, and to Padfield, therefore, Hewitt betook himself, and, arrayed in a way to indicate some inclination of his own toward sport, he began to frequent the bar of the 'Hare and

Hounds'. Kentish, the landlord, was a stout, bullnecked man, of no great communicativeness at first; but after a little acquaintance he opened out wonderfully, became quite a jolly (and rather intelligent) companion, and came out with innumerable anecdotes of his sporting adventures. He could put a very decent dinner on the table, too, at the 'Hare and Hounds', and Hewitt's frequent invitation to him to join therein and divide a bottle of the best in the cellar soon put the two on the very best of terms. Good terms with Mr Kentish was Hewitt's great desire, for the information he wanted was of a sort that could never be extracted by casual questioning, but must be a matter of open communication by the publican, extracted in what way it might be.

'Look here,' said Kentish one day, 'I'll put you on to a good thing, my boy—a real good thing. Of course you know all about the Padfield 135 Yards Handicap being run off now?'

'Well, I haven't looked into it much,' Hewitt replied. 'Ran the first round of heats last Saturday and Monday, didn't they?'

'They did. Well'—Kentish spoke in a stage whisper as he leaned over and rapped the table—'I've got the final winner in this house.' He nodded his head, took a puff at his cigar and added, in his ordinary voice, 'Don't say nothing.'

'No, of course not. Got something on, of course?'

'Rather—what do *you* think? Got any price I like. Been saving him up for this. Why, he's got twenty-o[ ] yards, and he can do even time all the way! Fact! Why, [ ] could win runnin' back'ards. He won his heat on Mond[ ] like—like—like that!' The gaffer snapped his fingers, [ ] default of a better illustration, and went on. 'He might [ ] took it a little easier, *I* think—it's shortened his price [ ] course, him jumpin' in by two yards. But you can [ ] decent odds now, if you go about it right. You take [ ] tip—back him for his heat next Saturday, in the se[ ]

round, and for the final. You'll get a good price for the
final, if you pop it down at once. But don't go makin' a song
of it, will you, now? I'm givin' you a tip I wouldn't give
anybody else.'

'Thanks very much—it's awfully good of you. I'll do what
you advise. But isn't there a dark horse anywhere else?'

'Not dark to me, my boy, not dark to me. I know every
man runnin' like a book. Old Taylor—him over at the
Cop—he's got a very good lad—eighteen yards, and a very
good lad indeed; and he's a tryer this time, I know. But,
bless you, my lad could give him ten, instead o' taking
three, and beat him then! When I'm runnin' a real tryer,
I'm generally runnin' something very near a winner, you
bet; and this time, mind, *this* time, I'm runnin' the cer-
tainest winner I *ever* run—and I don't often make a
mistake. You back him.'

'I shall, if you're as sure as that. But who is he?'

'Oh, Throckett's his name—Sammy Throckett. He's
quite a new lad. I've got young Steggles looking after him—
sticks to him like wax. Takes his little breathers in my bit
o'ground at the back here. I've got a cinder sprint path
there, over behind the trees. I don't let him out o' sight
much, I can tell you. He's a straight lad, and he knows it'll
be worth his while to stick to me; but there's some 'ud
poison him, if they thought he'd spoil their books.'

Soon afterward the two strolled toward the tap-room. 'I
expect Sammy'll be there,' the landlord said, 'with Steggles.
I don't hide him too much—they'd think I'd got something
extra on, if I did.'

In the tap-room sat a lean, wire-drawn-looking youth,
with sloping shoulders and a thin face, and by his side was
a rather short, thick-set man, who had an odd air, no
matter what he did, of proprietorship and surveillance of
the lean youth. Several other men sat about, and there was
loud laughter, under which the lean youth looked sheepishly
angry.

''Tarn't no good, Sammy lad,' some one was saying. 'You a makin' after Nancy Webb—she'll ha' nowt to do with 'ee.'

'Don' like 'em so thread-papery,' added another. 'No, Sammy, you aren't the lad for she. I see her . . .'

'What about Nancy Webb?' asked Kentish, pushing open the door. 'Sammy's all right, anyway. You keep fit, my lad, an' go on improving, and some day you'll have as good a house as me. Never mind the lasses. Had his glass o' beer, has he?' This to Raggy Steggles, who, answering in the affirmative, viewed his charge as though he were a post, and the beer a recent coat of paint.

'Has two glasses of mild a-day,' the landlord said to Hewitt. 'Never puts on flesh, so he can stand it. Come out now.' He nodded to Steggles, who rose, and marched Sammy Throckett away for exercise.

* * *

On the following afternoon (it was Thursday), as Hewitt and Kentish chatted in the landlord's own snuggery, Steggles burst into the room in a great state of agitation and spluttered out: 'He—he's bolted; gone away!'

'What?'

'Sammy—gone. Hooked it. *I* can't find him.'

The landlord stared blankly at the trainer, who stood with a sweater dangling from his hand, and stared blankly back. 'What d'ye mean?' Kentish said at last. 'Don't be a fool. He's in the place somewhere; find him.'

But this Steggles defied anybody to do. He had looked already. He had left Throckett at the cinder-path behind the trees, in his running-gear, with the addition of the long overcoat and cap he used in going between the path and the house, to guard against chill. 'I was goin' to give him a bust or two with the pistol,' the trainer explained, 'but when we got over t'other side, "Raggy," ses he, "it's blawin' a bit chilly. I think I'll ha' a sweater—there's one on my box,

[51]

ain't there?'' So in I coomes for the sweater, and it weren't on his box, and when I found it and got back—he weren't there. They'd seen nowt o' him in t' house, and he weren't nowhere.'

Hewitt and the landlord, now thoroughly startled, searched everywhere, but to no purpose. 'What should he go off the place for?' asked Kentish, in a sweat of apprehension. ''Tain't chilly a bit—it's warm—he didn't want no sweater; never wore one before. It was a piece of kid to be able to clear out. Nice thing, this is. I stand to win two years' takings over him. Here—you'll have to find him.'

'Ah—but how?' exclaimed the disconcerted trainer, dancing about distractedly. 'I've got all I could scrape on him myself: where can I look?'

Here was Hewitt's opportunity. He took Kentish aside and whispered. What he said startled the landlord considerably. 'Yes, I'll tell you all about that,' he said, 'if that's all you want. It's no good or harm to me, whether I tell or no. But can you find him?'

'That I can't promise, of course. But you know who I am now, and what I'm here for. If you like to give me the information I want, I'll go into the case for you, and, of course, I shan't charge any fee. I may have luck, you know, but I can't promise, of course.'

The landlord looked in Hewitt's face for a moment. Then he said, 'Done! It's a deal.'

'Very good,' Hewitt replied; 'get together the one or two papers you have, and we'll go into my business in the evening. As to Throckett, don't say a word to anybody. I'm afraid it must get out, since they all know about it in the house, but there's no use in making any unnecessary noise. Don't make hedging bets or do anything that will attract notice. Now we'll go over to the back and look at this cinder-path of yours.'

Here Steggles, who was still standing near, was struck with an idea. 'How about old Taylor, at the Cop, guv'nor, eh?' he said, meaningly. 'His lad's good enough to win, with Sammy out, and Taylor is backing him plenty. Think he knows anything o' this?'

'That's likely,' Hewitt observed, before Kentish could reply. 'Yes. Look here—suppose Steggles goes and keeps his eye on the Cop for an hour or two, in case there's anything to be heard of? Don't show yourself, of course.'

Kentish agreed, and the trainer went. When Hewitt and Kentish arrived at the path behind the trees, Hewitt at once began examining the ground. One or two rather large holes in the cinders were made, as the publican explained, by Throckett, in practising getting off his mark. Behind these were several fresh tracks of spiked shoes. The tracks led up to within a couple of yards of the high fence bounding the ground, and there stopped abruptly and entirely. In the fence, a little to the right of where the tracks stopped, there was a stout door. This Hewitt tried, and found ajar.

'That's always kept bolted,' Kentish said; 'he's gone out that way—he couldn't have gone any other without comin' through the house.'

'But he isn't in the habit of making a step three yards long, is he?' Hewitt asked, pointing at the last footmark and then at the door, which was quite that distance away from it. 'Besides,' he added, opening the door, 'there's no footprint here nor outside.'

The door opened on a lane, with another fence and a thick plantation of trees at the other side. Kentish looked at the footmarks, then at the door, then down the lane, and finally back towards the house. 'That's a licker,' he said.

'This is a quiet sort of lane,' was Hewitt's next remark. 'No houses in sight. Where does it lead?'

'That way it goes to the Old Kilns—disused. This way down to a turning off the Padfield and Catton Road.'

Hewitt returned to the cinder-path again, and once more examined the footmarks. He traced them back over the grass toward the house. 'Certainly,' he said, 'he hasn't gone back to the house. Here is the double line of tracks, side by side, *from* the house—Steggles's ordinary boots with iron tips and Throckett's running pumps—thus they came out. Here is Steggles's track in the opposite direction alone, made when he went back for the sweater. Throckett remained—you see various prints in those loose cinders at the end of the path where he moved this way and that, and then two or three paces toward the fence—not directly toward the *door*, you notice—and there they stop dead, and there are no more, either back or forward. Now, if he had wings, I should be tempted to the opinion that he flew straight away in the air from that spot—unless the earth swallowed him and closed again without leaving a wrinkle on its face.'

Kentish stared gloomily at the tracks, and said nothing.

'However,' Hewitt resumed, 'I think I'll take a little walk now, and think over it. You go into the house and show yourself at the bar. If anybody wants to know how Throckett is, he's pretty well, thank you. By the bye, can I get to the Cop—this place of Taylor's—by this back lane?'

'Yes, down to the end leading to the Catton Road, turn to the left, and then first on the right. Any one'll show you the Cop,' and Kentish shut the door behind the detective, who straightway walked—toward the Old Kilns.

In little more than an hour he was back. It was now becoming dusk, and the landlord was looking out papers from a box near the side window of his snuggery, for the sake of the extra light. 'I've got these papers together for you,' he said, as Hewitt entered. 'Any news?'

'Nothing very great. Here's a bit of handwriting I want you to recognize, if you can. Get a light.'

Kentish lit a lamp, and Hewitt laid upon the table half a dozen small pieces of torn paper, evidently fragments of a letter which had been torn up.

The landlord turned the scraps over, regarding them dubiously. 'These aren't much to recognize, anyhow. *I* don't know the writing. Where did you find 'em?'

'They were lying in the lane at the back, a little way down. Plainly they are pieces of a note addressed to some one called Sammy or something very like it. See the first piece with its "mmy"? That is clearly from the beginning of the note, because there is no line between it and the smooth, straight edge of the paper above; also, nothing follows on the same line. Some one writes to Throckett— presuming it to be a letter addressed to him, as I do for other reasons—as Sammy. It is a pity that there is no more of the letter to be found than these pieces. I expect the person who tore it up put the rest in his pocket and dropped these by accident.'

Kentish, who had been picking up and examining each piece in turn, now dolorously broke out:—

'Oh, it's plain he's sold us—bolted and done us; me as took him out o'the gutter, too. Look here—"throw them over"; that's plain enough—can't mean anything else. Means throw *me* over, and my friends—me, after what I've done for him. Then "right away"—go right away I s'pose, as he has done. Then,' he was fiddling with the scraps and finally fitted two together, 'why, look here, this one with "lane" on its fits over the one about throwing over, and it says "poor f" where it's torn; that means "poor fool", I s'pose—*me*, or "fathead", or something like that. That's nice. Why, I'd twist his neck if I could get hold of him; and I will!'

Hewitt smiled. 'Perhaps it's not quite so uncomplimentary after all,' he said. 'If you can't recognize the writing, never mind. But if he's gone away to sell you, it isn't much use finding him, is it? He won't win if he doesn't want to.'

'Why, he wouldn't dare to rope under my very eyes. I'd—I'd . . .'

'Well, well; perhaps we'll get him to run after all, and as well as he can. One thing is certain—he left this place of his own will. Further, I think he is in Padfield now—he went toward the town, I believe. And I don't think he means to sell you.'

'Well, he shouldn't. I've made it worth his while to stick to me. I've put a fifty on him out of my own pocket, and told him so; and if he won, that would bring him a lump more than he'd probably get by going crooked, besides the prize money, and anything I might give him over. But it seems to me he's putting me in the cart altogether.'

'That we shall see. Meantime, don't mention anything I've told you to any one—not even to Steggles. He can't help us, and he might blurt things out inadvertently. Don't say anything about these pieces of paper, which I shall keep myself. By the bye, Steggles is indoors, isn't he? Very well, keep him in. Don't let him be seen hunting about this evening. I'll stay here tonight and we'll proceed with Throckett's business in the morning. And now we'll settle *my* business, please.'

* * *

In the morning Hewitt took his breakfast in the snuggery, carefully listening to any conversation that might take place at the bar. Soon after nine o'clock a fast dog-cart stopped outside, and a red-faced, loud-voiced man swaggered in, greeting Kentish with boisterous cordiality. He had a drink with the landlord, and said: 'How's things? Fancy any of 'em for the sprint handicap? Got a lad o' your own in, haven't you?'

'Oh, yes,' Kentish replied. 'Throckett. Only a young 'un—not got to his proper mark yet, I reckon. I think old Taylor's got No. 1 this time.'

'Capital lad,' the other replied, with a confidential nod. 'Shouldn't wonder at all. Want to do anything yourself over it?'

'No—I don't think so. I'm not on at present. Might have a little flutter on the grounds just for fun; nothing else.'

There were a few more casual remarks, and then the red-faced man drove away.

'Who was that?' asked Hewitt, who had watched the visitor through the snuggery window.

'That's Danby—bookmaker. Cute chap; he's been told Throckett's missing, I'll bet anything, and come here to pump me. No good though. As a matter of fact, I've worked Sammy Throckett into his books for about half I'm in for altogether—through third parties, of course.'

Hewitt reached for his hat. 'I'm going out for half an hour now,' he said. 'If Steggles wants to go out before I come back, don't let him. Let him go and smooth over all those tracks on the cinder-path, very carefully. And, by the bye, could you manage to have your son about the place to-day, in case I happen to want a little help out of doors?'

'Certainly; I'll get him to stay in. But what do you want the cinders smoothed for?'

Hewitt smiled and patted his host's shoulder. 'I'll explain all my little tricks when the job's done,' he said, and went out.

*　　*　　*

On the lane from Padfield to Sedby village stood the 'Plough' beerhouse, wherein J. Webb was licensed to sell by retail beer to be consumed on the premises or off, as the thirsty list. Nancy Webb, with a very fine colour, a very curly fringe, and a wide-smiling mouth revealing a fine set of teeth, came to the bar at the summons of a stoutish old gentleman with spectacles, who walked with a stick.

The stoutish old gentleman had a glass of bitter beer and then said, in the peculiarly quiet voice of a very deaf man, 'Can you tell me, if you please, the way into the main Catton Road?'

'Down the lane, turn to the right at the cross roads, then first to the left.'

The old gentleman waited with his hand to his ear for some few seconds after she had finished speaking, and then resumed, in his whispering voice, 'I'm afraid I'm very deaf this morning.' He fumbled in his pocket and produced a notebook and pencil. 'May I trouble you to write it down? I'm so very deaf at times, that I—thank you.'

The girl wrote the direction, and the old gentleman bade her good morning and left. All down the lane he walked slowly with his stick. At the cross roads he turned, put the stick under his arm, thrust the spectacles into his pocket, and strode away in the ordinary guise of Martin Hewitt. He pulled out his note-book, examined Miss Webb's direction very carefully, and then went off another way altogether, towards the 'Hare and Hounds'.

Kentish lounged moodily in his bar. 'Well, my boy,' said Hewitt, 'has Steggles wiped out the tracks?'

'Not yet—I haven't told him. But he's somewhere about—I'll tell him now.'

'No, don't. I don't think we'll have that done, after all. I expect he'll want to go out soon—at any rate, some time during the day. Let him go whenever he likes. I'll sit upstairs a bit in the club-room.'

'Very well. But how do you know Steggles will be going out?'

'Well, he's pretty restless after his lost *protégé*, isn't he. I don't suppose he'll be able to remain idle long.'

'And about Throckett. Do you give him up?'

'Oh, no. Don't you be impatient. I can't say I'm quite confident yet of laying hold of him—the time is so short, you see—but I shall at least have news for you by the evening.'

* * *

Hewitt sat in the club-room until the afternoon, taking his lunch there. At length he saw, through the front window, Raggy Steggles walking down the road. In an instant Hewitt was downstairs and at the door. The road bent eighty yards away, and as soon as Steggles passed the bend the detective hurried after him.

All the way to Padfield town and more than half through it Hewitt dodged the trainer. In the end Steggles stopped at a corner and gave a note to a small boy who was playing near. The boy ran with the note to a bright, well-kept house at the opposite corner. Martin Hewitt was interested to observe the legend 'H. Danby, Contractor', on a board over a gate in the side wall of the garden behind this house. In five minutes a door in the side gate opened, and the head and shoulders of the red-faced man emerged. Steggles immediately hurried across and disappeared through the gate.

This was both interesting and instructive. Hewitt took up a position in a side street and waited. In ten minutes the trainer reappeared and hurried off the way he had come, along the street Hewitt had considerately left clear for him. Then Hewitt strolled toward the smart house and took a good look at it. At one corner of the small piece of forecourt garden, near the railings, a small, baize-covered, glass-fronted notice board stood on two posts. On its top edge appeared the words 'H. Danby. Houses to be Sold or Let'. But the only notice pinned to the green baize within was an old and dusty one, inviting tenants for three shops, which were suitable for any business, and which would be fitted to suit tenants. Apply within.

Hewitt pushed open the front gate and rang the doorbell. 'There are some shops to let, I see,' he said, when a maid appeared. 'I should like to see them, if you will let me have the key.'

'Master's out, sir. You can't see the shops till Monday.'

'Dear me, that's unfortunate. I'm afraid I can't wait till Monday. Didn't Mr Danby leave any instructions, in case anybody should inquire?'

'Yes, sir—as I've told you. He said anybody who called about 'em come again on Monday.'

'Oh, very well, then; I suppose I must try. One of the shops is in High Street, isn't it?'

'No, sir; they're all in the new part—Granville Road.'

'Ah, I'm afraid that will scarcely do. But I'll see. Good day.'

Martin Hewitt walked away a couple of streets' lengths before he inquired the way to Granville Road. When at last he found that thoroughfare, in a new and muddy suburb, crowded with brick-heaps and half-finished streets, he took a slow walk along its entire length. It was a melancholy example of baffled enterprise. A row of a dozen or more shops had been built before any population had arrived to demand goods. Would-be tradesmen had taken many of these shops, and failure and disappointment stared from the windows. Some were half covered by shutters, because the scanty stock scarce sufficed to fill the remaining half. Others were shut almost altogether, the inmates only keeping open the door for their own convenience, and perhaps keeping down a shutter for the sake of a little light. Others again had not yet fallen so low, but struggled bravely still to maintain a show of business and prosperity, with very little success. Opposite the shops there still remained a dusty, ill-treated hedge and a forlorn-looking field, which an old board offered on building leases. Altogether a most depressing spot.

There was little difficulty in identifying the three shops offered for letting by Mr H. Danby. They were all together near the middle of the row, and were the only ones that appeared not yet to have been occupied. A dusty 'To Let' bill hung in each window, with written directions to inquire of Mr H. Danby or at No. 7. Now, No. 7 was a melancholy baker's shop, with a stock of three loaves and a plate of stale buns. The disappointed baker assured Hewitt that he usually kept the keys of the shops, but that the landlord, Mr Danby, had taken them away the day before, to see how the ceilings were standing, and had not returned them. 'But if you was thinking of taking a shop here,' the poor baker added, with some hesitation, 'I—I—if you'll excuse my advising you—I shouldn't recommend it. I've had a sickener of it myself.'

Hewitt thanked the baker for his advice, wished him better luck in future, and left. To the 'Hare and Hounds' his pace was brisk. 'Come,' he said, as he met Kentish's inquiring glance, 'this has been a very good day, on the whole. I know where our man is now, and I think we can get him by a little management.'

'Where is he?'

'Oh, down in Padfield. As a matter of fact, he's being kept there against his will, we shall find. I see that your friend, Mr Danby, is a builder as well as a bookmaker.'

'Not a regular builder. He speculates in a street of new houses now and again, that's all. But is he in it?'

'He's as deep in it as anybody, I think. Now don't fly into a passion. There are a few others in it as well, but you'll do harm if you don't keep quiet.'

'But go and get the police—come and fetch him, if you know where they're keeping him; why . . .'

'So we will, if we can't do it without them. But it's quite possible we can, and without all the disturbance and, perhaps, delay that calling in the police would involve. Consider, now, in reference to your arrangements. Wouldn't it pay you better to get him back quietly, without a soul knowing—perhaps not even Danby knowing—till the heat is run to-morrow?'

'Well, yes, it would, of course.'

'Very good then, so be it. Remember what I have told you about keeping your mouth shut—say nothing to Steggles or anybody. Is there a cab or brougham your son and I can have for the evening?'

'There's an old hiring landau in the stables you can shut up into a cab, if that'll do.'

'Excellent. We'll run·down to the town in it as soon as

it's ready. But, first, a word about Throckett. What sort of a lad is he? Likely to give them trouble, show fight, and make a disturbance?'

'No, I should say not. He's no plucked 'un, certainly—all his manhood's in his legs, I believe. You see, he ain't a big sort o' chap at best, and he'd be pretty easy put upon—at least, I guess so.'

'Very good; so much the better; for then he won't have been damaged, and they will probably only have one man to guard him. Now the carriage, please.'

Young Kentish was a six-foot sergeant of Grenadiers, home on furlough, and luxuriating in plain clothes. He and Hewitt walked a little way towards the town, allowing the landau to catch them up. They travelled in it to within a hundred yards of the empty shops and then alighted, bidding the driver wait.

'I shall show you three empty shops,' Hewitt said, as he and young Kentish walked down Granville Road. 'I am pretty sure that Sammy Throckett is in one of them, and I am pretty sure that this is the middle one. Take a look as we go past.'

When the shops had been slowly passed, Hewitt resumed, 'Now, did you see anything about those shops that told a tale of any sort?'

'No,' Sergeant Kentish replied, 'I can't say I noticed anything beyond the fact that they were empty—and likely to stay so, I should think.'

'We'll stroll back, and look in at the windows, if nobody's watching us,' Hewitt said. 'You see, it's reasonable to suppose they've put him in the middle one, because that would suit their purpose best. The shops at each side of the three are occupied, and if the prisoner struggled, or shouted, or made an uproar, he might be heard if he were in one of the shops next those inhabited. So that the middle shop is the most likely. Now, see there,' he went on, as they stopped before the window of the shop in question, 'over at the back there's a staircase not yet partitioned off. It goes down below and up above; on the stairs and on the floor near them there are muddy footmarks. These must have been made to-day, else they would not be muddy, but dry and dusty, since there hasn't been a shower for a week till to-day. Move on again. Then you notice that there are no other such marks in the shop. Consequently the man with the muddy feet did not come in by the front door, but by the back; otherwise he would have made a trail from the door. So we will go round to the back ourselves.'

It was now growing dusk. The small pieces of ground behind the shops were bounded by a low fence, containing a door for each house.

'This door is bolted inside, of course,' Hewitt said, 'but there is no difficulty in climbing. I think we had better wait in the garden till dark. In the meantime, the gaoler, whoever he is, may come out; in which case we shall pounce on him as soon as he opens the door. You have those few yards of cord in your pocket, I think? And my handkerchief, properly rolled, will make a very good gag. Now over.'

They climbed the fence, and quietly approached the house, placing themselves in the angle of an outhouse out of sight from the windows. There was no sound, and no light appeared. Just above the ground about a foot of window was visible, with a grating over it, apparently lighting a basement. Suddenly Hewitt touched his companion's arm, and pointed towards the window. A faint rustling sound was perceptible, and as nearly as could be discerned in the darkness, some white blind or covering was placed over the glass from the inside. Then came the sound of a striking match, and at the side edge of the window there was a faint streak of light.

'That's the place,' Hewitt whispered. 'Come, we'll make a push for it. You stand against the wall at one side of the door, and I'll stand at the other, and we'll have him as he comes out. Quietly, now, and I'll startle them.'

He took a stone from among the rubbish littering the garden, and flung it crashing through the window. There was a loud exclamation from within, the blind fell, and somebody rushed to the back door and flung it open. Instantly Kentish let fly a heavy right-hander, and the man went over like a skittle. In a moment Hewitt was upon him and the gag was in his mouth.

'Hold him,' Hewitt whispered hurriedly. 'I'll see if there are others.'

He peered down through the low window. Within, Sammy Throckett, his bare legs dangling from beneath his long overcoat, sat on a packing-box, leaning with his head on his hand and his back towards the window. A guttering candle stood on the mantelpiece, and the newspaper which had been stretched across the window lay in scattered sheets on the floor. No other person besides Sammy was visible.

They led their prisoner indoors. Young Kentish recognized him as a public-house loafer and race-course ruffian well known in the neighbourhood.

'So it's you, is it, Browdie?' he said. 'I've caught you one hard clump, and I've half a mind to make it a score more. But you'll get it pretty warm one way or another, before this job's forgotten.'

Sammy Throckett was overjoyed at his rescue. He had not been ill-treated, he explained, but had been thoroughly cowed by Browdie, who had from time to time threatened him savagely with an iron bar, by way of persuading him to quietness and submission. He had been fed, and had taken no worse harm from his adventure than a slight stiffness, due to his light under-attire of jersey and knee-shorts.

Sergeant Kentish tied Browdie's elbows firmly together behind, and carried the line round the ankles, bracing all up tight. Then he ran a knot from one wrist to the other over the back of the neck, and left the prisoner, trussed and helpless, on the heap of straw that had been Sammy's bed.

'You won't be very jolly, I expect,' Kentish said, 'for some time. You can't shout, and you can't walk, and I know you can't untie yourself. You'll get a bit hungry, too, perhaps, but that'll give you an appetite. I don't suppose you'll be disturbed till some time to-morrow, unless our friend Danby turns up in the meantime. But you can come along to gaol instead, if you prefer it.'

They left him where he lay, and took Sammy to the old landau. Sammy walked in slippers, carrying his spiked shoes, hanging by the lace, in his hand.

'Ah,' said Hewitt, 'I think I know the name of the young lady who gave you those slippers.'

Throckett looked ashamed and indignant. 'Yes,' he said, 'they've done me nicely between 'em. But I'll pay her—I'll . . .'

'Hush, hush!' Hewitt said; 'you mustn't talk unkindly of a lady, you know. Get into this carriage, and we'll take you home. We'll see if I can tell you your adventures without making a mistake. First, you had a note from Miss Webb, telling you that you were mistaken in supposing she had slighted you, and that as a matter of fact she had quite done with somebody else—left him—of whom you were jealous. Isn't that so?'

'Well, yes,' Throckett answered, blushing deeply under the carriage-lamp; 'but I don't see how you come to know that.'

'Then she went on to ask you to get rid of Steggles on Thursday afternoon for a few minutes, and speak to her in the back lane. Now, your running pumps, with their thin soles, almost like paper, no heels, and long spikes, hurt your feet horribly if you walk on hard ground, don't they?'

'Ay, that they do—enough to cripple you. I'd never go on much hard ground with 'em.'

'They're not like cricket shoes, I see.'

'Not a bit. Cricket shoes you can walk anywhere in.'

'Well, she knew this—I think I know who told her—and she promised to bring you a new pair of slippers, and to throw them over the fence for you to come out in.'

'I s'pose she's been tellin' you all this?' Throckett said mournfully. 'You couldn't ha' seen the letter—I saw her tear it up and put the bits in her pocket. She asked me for it in the lane, in case Steggles saw it.'

'Well, at any rate, you sent Steggles away, and the slippers did come over, and you went into the lane. You walked with her as far as the road at the end, and then you were seized and gagged, and put into a carriage.'

'That was Browdie did that,' said Throckett, 'and another chap I don't know. But—why, this is Padfield High Street!' He looked through the window and regarded the familiar shops with astonishment.

'Of course it is. Where did you think it was?'

'Why, where was that place you found me in?'

'Granville Road, Padfield. I suppose they told you you were in another town?'

'Told me it was Newstead Hatch. They drove for about three or four hours, and kept me down on the floor between the seats so as I couldn't see where we was going.'

'Done for two reasons,' said Hewitt. 'First, to mystify you, and prevent any discovery of the people directing the conspiracy; and, second, to be able to put you indoors at night and unobserved. Well, I think I have told you all you know yourself now as far as the carriage. But there is the 'Hare and Hounds' just in front. We'll pull up here and I'll get out and see if the coast is clear. I fancy Mr Kentish would rather you came in unnoticed.'

In a few seconds Hewitt was back, and Throckett was conveyed indoors by a side entrance. Hewitt's instructions to the landlord were few, but emphatic. 'Don't tell Steggles about it,' he said; 'make an excuse to get rid of him, and send him out of the house. Take Throckett into some other bedroom, not his own, and let your son look after him. Then come here, and I'll tell you all about it.'

Sammy Throckett was undergoing a heavy grooming with white embrocation at the hands of Sergeant Kentish, when the landlord returned to Hewitt. 'Does Danby know you've got him?' he asked. 'How did you do it?'

'Danby doesn't know yet, and with luck he won't know till he sees Throckett running to-morrow. The man who has sold you is Steggles.'

'Steggles?'

'Steggles it is. At the very first, when Steggles rushed in to report Sammy Throckett missing, I suspected him. You didn't, I suppose?'

'No. He's always been considered a straight man, and he looked as startled as anybody.'

'Yes, I must say he acted it very well. But there was something suspicious in his story. What did he say? Throckett had remarked a chilliness, and asked for a sweater, which Steggles went to fetch. Now just think. You understand these things. Would any trainer who knew his business (as Steggles does) have gone to bring out a sweater for his man to change for his jersey in the open air, at the very time the man was complaining of chilliness? Of course not. He would have taken his man indoors again and let him change there under shelter. Then supposing Steggles had really been surprised at missing Throckett, wouldn't he have looked about, found the gate open, and *told* you it was open, when he first came in? He said nothing of that—we found the gate open for ourselves. So that from the beginning I had a certain opinion of Steggles.'

'What you say seems pretty plain now, although it didn't strike me at the time. But if Steggles was selling us, why couldn't he have drugged the lad? That would have been a deal simpler.'

'Because Steggles is a good trainer, and has a certain reputation to keep up. It would have done him no good to have had a runner drugged while under his care—certainly it would have cooked his goose with *you*. It was much the safer thing to connive at kidnapping. That put all the active work into other hands, and left him safe, even if the trick failed. Now you remember that we traced the prints of Throckett's spiked shoes to within a couple of yards of the fence, and that there they ceased suddenly?'

'Yes. You said it looked as though he had flown up into the air; and so it did.'

'But I was sure that it was by that gate that Throckett had left, and by no other. He couldn't have got through the house without being seen, and there was no other way— let alone the evidence of the unbolted gate. Therefore, as the footprints ceased where they did, and were not repeated anywhere in the lane, I knew that he had taken his spiked shoes off—probably changed them for something else, because a runner anxious as to his chances would never risk walking on bare feet, with a chance of cutting them. Ordinary, broad, smooth-soled slippers would leave no impression on the coarse cinders bordering the track, and nothing short of spiked shoes would leave a mark on the hard path in the lane behind. The spike tracks were leading, not directly toward the door, but in the direction of the fence, when they stopped—somebody had handed, or thrown, the slippers over the fence, and he had changed them on the spot. The enemy had calculated upon the spikes leaving a track in the lane that might lead us in our search, and had arranged accordingly.

'So far, so good. I could see no footprints near the gate in the lane. You will remember that I sent Steggles off to watch at the Cop before I went out to the back—merely, of course, to get him out of the way. I went out into the lane, leaving you behind, and walked its whole length, first towards the Old Kilns, and then back towards the road. I found nothing to help me except these small pieces of paper—which are here in my pocket-book, by the bye. Of course, this "mmy" might have meant "Jimmy" or "Tommy", as possibly as "Sammy", but they were not to be rejected on that account. Certainly Throckett had been decoyed out of your ground, not taken by force, or there would have been marks of a scuffle in the cinders. And as his request for a sweater was probably an excuse—because it was not at all a cold afternoon—he must have previously designed going out—inference, a letter received; and here were pieces of a letter. Now, in the light of what I have said, look at these pieces. First, there is the "mmy"— that I have dealt with. Then, see this "throw them ov"— clearly a part of "throw them over"; exactly what had probably been done with the slippers. Then the "poor f", coming just on the line before, and seen, by joining up with this other piece, might easily be a reference to "poor feet". These coincidences, one on the other, went far to establish the identity of the letter, and to confirm my previous impressions. But then there is something else. Two other pieces evidently mean "left him", and "right away"— send Steggles "right away", perhaps; but there is another, containing almost all of the words "hate his", with the word "hate" underlined. Now, who writes "hate" with the emphasis of underscoring—who but a woman? The writing is large, and not very regular; it might easily be that of a half-educated woman. Here was something more— Sammy had been enticed away by a woman.

'Now I remembered that when we went into the taproom on Wednesday, some of his companions were chaffing Throckett about a certain Nancy Webb, and the chaff went home, as was plain to see. The woman, then, who could most easily entice Sammy Throckett away was Nancy Webb. I resolved to find who Nancy Webb was and learn more of her.

'Meantime I took a look at the road at the end of the lane. It was damper than the lane, being lower, and overhung by trees. There were many wheel tracks, but only one set that turned in the road and went back the way it came—towards the town—and they were narrow wheels, carriage wheels. Throckett tells me now that they drove him about for a long time before shutting him up—probably the inconvenience of taking him straight to the hiding-place didn't strike them when they first drove off.

'A few inquiries soon set me in the direction of the "Plough" and Miss Nancy Webb. I had the curiosity to look round the place as I approached, and there, in the garden behind the house, were Steggles and the young lady in earnest confabulation!

'Every conjecture became a certainty. Steggles was the lover of whom Throckett was jealous, and he had employed the girl to bring Sammy out. I watched Steggles home, and gave you a hint to keep him there.

'But the thing that remained was to find Steggles's employer in this business. I was glad to be in when Danby called—he came, of course, to hear if you would blurt out anything, and to learn, if possible, what steps you were taking. He failed. By way of making assurance doubly sure, I took a short walk this morning in the character of a deaf gentleman, and got Miss Webb to write me a direction that comprised three of the words on these scraps of paper—"left", "right", and "lane"—see, they correspond, the peculiar "f's," "t's," and all.

'Now, I felt perfectly sure that Steggles would go for his pay to-day. In the first place, I knew that people mixed up with shady transactions in professional pedestrianism are not apt to trust one another far—they know better. Therefore, Steggles wouldn't have had his bribe first. But he would take care to get it before the Saturday heats were run, because once they were over the thing was done, and the principal conspirator might have refused to pay up, and Steggles couldn't have helped himself. Again I hinted he should not go out till I could follow him, and this afternoon when he went, follow him I did. I saw him go into

Danby's house by the side way and come away again. Danby it was, then, who had arranged the business; and nobody was more likely, considering his large pecuniary stake against Throckett's winning this race.

'But now, how to find Throckett? I made up my mind he wouldn't be in Danby's own house—that would be a deal too risky, with servants about, and so on. I saw that Danby was a builder, and had three shops to let—it was on a paper before his house. What more likely prison than an empty house? I knocked at Danby's door, and asked for the keys of those shops. I couldn't have them. The servant told me Danby was out (a manifest lie, for I had just seen him), and that nobody could see the shops till Monday. But I got out of her where the shops lay, and that was all I wanted at the time.

'Now, why was nobody to see those shops till Monday? The interval was suspicious—just enough to enable Throckett to be sent away again and cast loose after the Saturday racing, supposing him to be kept in one of the empty buildings. I went off at once and looked at the shops, forming my conclusions as to which would be the most likely for Danby's purpose. Here I had another confirmation of my ideas. A poor, half-bankrupt baker in one of the shops had, by the bills, the custody of a set of keys; but *he*, too, told me I couldn't have them; Danby had taken them away—and on Thursday, the very day—with some trivial excuse, and hadn't brought them back. That was all I wanted, or could expect in the way of guidance; the whole thing was plain. The rest you know all about.'

'Well, you're certainly as smart as they give you credit for, I must say. But suppose Danby had taken down his "to let" notice, what would you have done then?'

'We had our course, even then. We should have gone to Danby, astounded him by telling him all about his little games, terrorized him with threats of the law, and made him throw up his hand and send Throckett back. But as it is, you see, he doesn't know at this moment—probably won't know till to-morrow afternoon—that the lad is safe and sound here. You will probably use the interval to make him pay for posing the game—by some of the ingenious financial devices you are no doubt familiar with.'

'Aye, that I will. He'll give any price against Throckett now, so long as the bet don't come direct from me.'

'But about Throckett, now,' Hewitt went on. 'Won't this confinement be likely to have damaged his speed for a day or two?'

'Ah, perhaps,' the landlord replied; 'but, bless ye, that won't matter. There's four more in his heat to-morrow. Two I know aren't tryers, and the other two I can hold in at a couple of quid apiece any day. The third round and the final won't be till to-morrow week, and he'll be as fit as ever by then. It's as safe as ever it was. How much are you going to have on? I'll lump it on for you safe enough. This is a chance not to be missed—it's picking money up.'

'Thank you; I don't think I'll have anything to do with it. This professional pedestrian business doesn't seem a pretty one at all. I don't call myself a moralist, but, if you'll excuse my saying so, the thing is scarcely the game I care to pick up money at in any way.'

'Oh! very well, if you think so, I won't persuade ye, though I don't think so much of your smartness as I did, after that. Still, we won't quarrel—you've done me a mighty good turn, that I must say, and I only feel I aren't level without doing something to pay the debt. Come, now, you've got your trade as I've got mine. Let me have the bill, and I'll pay it like a lord, and feel a deal more pleased than if you made a favour of it—not that I'm above a favour, of course. But I'd prefer paying, and that's a fact.'

'My dear sir, you have paid,' Hewitt said, with a smile. 'You paid in advance. It was a bargain, wasn't it, that I should do your business if you would help me in mine? Very well, a bargain's a bargain, and we've both performed our parts. And you mustn't be offended at what I said just now.'

'That I won't. But as to that Raggy Steggles, once those heats are over to-morrow, I'll—well . . .!'

*   *   *

It was on the following Sunday week that Martin Hewitt, in his rooms in London, turned over his *Referee* and read, under the head, 'Padfield Annual 135 Yards Handicap', this announcement: 'Final Heat: Throckett, first; Willis, second; Trewby, third; Owen, 0; Howell, 0. A runaway win by nearly three yards.'

III

The Problem of Dead Wood Hall

Dick Donovan

'MYSTERIOUS CASE IN CHESHIRE'. So ran the heading to a paragraph in all the morning papers some years ago, and prominence was given to the following particulars:

A gentleman, bearing the somewhat curious name of Tuscan Trankler, resided in a picturesque old mansion, known as Dead Wood Hall, situated in one of the most beautiful and lonely parts of Cheshire, not very far from the quaint and old-time village of Knutsford. Mr Trankler had given a dinner-party at his house, and amongst the guests was a very well-known county magistrate and landowner, Mr Manville Charnworth. It appeared that, soon after the ladies had retired from the table, Mr Charnworth rose and went into the grounds, saying he wanted a little air. He was smoking a cigar, and in the enjoyment of perfect health. He had drunk wine, however, rather freely, as was his wont, but though on exceedingly good terms with himself and every one else, he was perfectly sober. An hour passed, but Mr Charnworth had not returned to the table. Though this did not arouse any alarm, as it was thought that he had probably joined the ladies, for he was what is called 'a ladies' man,' and preferred the company of females to that of men. A tremendous sensation, however, was caused when, a little later, it was announced that Charnworth had been found insensible, lying on his back in a shrubbery. Medical assistance was at once summoned, and when it arrived the opinion expressed was that the unfortunate gentleman had been stricken with apoplexy. For some reason or other, however, the doctors were led to modify that view, for symptoms were observed which pointed to what was thought to be a peculiar form of poisoning, although the poison could not be determined. After a time, Charnworth recovered consciousness, but was quite unable to give any information. He seemed to be dazed and confused, and was evidently suffering great pain. At last his limbs began to swell, and swelled to an enormous size; his eyes sunk, his cheeks fell in, his lips turned black, and mortification appeared in the extremities. Everything that could be done for the unfortunate man was done, but without avail. After six hours' suffering, he died in a paroxysm of raving madness, during which he had to be held down in the bed by several strong men.

The post-mortem examination, which was necessarily held, revealed the curious fact that the blood in the body had become thin and purplish, with a faint strange odour that could not be identified. All the organs were extremely congested, and the flesh presented every appearance of rapid decomposition. In fact, twelve hours after death putrefaction had taken place. The medical gentlemen who had the case in hand were greatly puzzled, and were at a loss to determine the precise cause of death. The deceased had been a very healthy man, and there was no actual organic disease of any kind. In short, everything pointed to poisoning. It was noted that on the left side of the neck was a tiny scratch, with a slightly livid appearance, such as might have been made by a small sharply pointed instrument. The viscera having been secured for purposes of analysis, the body was hurriedly buried within thirty hours of death.

The result of the analysis was to make clear that the unfortunate gentleman had died through some very powerful and irritant poison being introduced into the blood. That it was a case of blood-poisoning there was hardly room for the shadow of a doubt, but the science of that day was quite unable to say what the poison was, or how it had got into the body. There was no reason—so far as could be ascertained—to suspect foul play, and even less reason to suspect suicide. Altogether, therefore, the case was one of profound mystery, and the coroner's jury were compelled to return an open verdict. Such were the details that were made public at the time of Mr Charnworth's death; and from the social position of all the parties, the affair was something more than a nine days' wonder; while in Cheshire itself, it created a profound sensation. But, as no further information was forthcoming, the matter ceased to interest the outside world, and so, as far as the public were concerned, it was relegated to the limbo of forgotten things.

Two years later, Mr Ferdinand Trankler, eldest son of Tuscan Trankler, accompanied a large party of friends for a day's shooting in Mere Forest. He was a young man, about five and twenty years of age; was in the most perfect health, and had scarcely ever had a day's illness in his life. Deservedly popular and beloved, he had a large circle of warm friends, and was about to be married to a charming young lady, a member of an old Cheshire family who were extensive landed proprietors and property owners. His prospects therefore seemed to be unclouded, and his happiness complete.

The shooting-party was divided into three sections, each agreeing to shoot over a different part of the forest, and to meet in the afternoon for refreshments at an appointed rendezvous.

Young Trankler and his companions kept pretty well together for some little time, but ultimately began to spread about a good deal. At the appointed hour the friends all met, with the exception of Trankler. He was not there. His absence did not cause any alarm, as it was thought he he would soon turn up. He was known to be well acquainted with the forest, and the supposition was he had strayed further afield than the rest. By the time the repast was finished, however, he had not put in an appearance. Then, for the first time, the company began to feel some uneasiness, and vague hints that possibly an accident had happened were thrown out. Hints at last took the form of definite expressions of alarm, and search parties were at once organized to go in search of the absent young man, for only on the hypothesis of some untoward event could his prolonged absence be accounted for, inasmuch as it was not deemed in the least likely that he would show such a lack of courtesy as to go off and leave his friends without a word of explanation. For two hours the search was kept up without any result. Darkness was then closing in, and the now painfully anxious searchers began to feel that they would have to desist until daylight returned. But at last some of the more energetic and active members of the party came upon Trankler lying on his side, and nearly entirely hidden by masses of half withered bracken. He was lying near a little stream that meandered through the forest, and near a keeper's shelter that was constructed with logs and thatched with pine boughs. He was stone dead, and his appearance caused his friends to shrink back with horror, for he was not only black in the face, but his body was bloated, and his limbs seemed swollen to twice their natural size.

Amongst the party were two medical men, who, being hastily summoned, proceeded at once to make an examination. They expressed an opinion that the young man had been dead for some time, but they could not account for his death, as there was no wound to be observed. As a matter of fact, his gun was lying near him with both barrels loaded. Moreover, his appearance was not compatible at all with death from a gun-shot wound. How then had he died? The consternation amongst those who had known him can well be imagined, and with a sense of suppressed horror, it was whispered that the strange condition of the dead man coincided with that of Mr Manville Charnworth, the county magistrate who had died so mysteriously two years previously.

As soon as it was possible to do so, Ferdinand Trankler's body was removed to Dead Wood Hall, and his people were stricken with profound grief when they realized that the hope and joy of their house was dead. Of course an autopsy had to be performed, owing to the ignorance of the medical men as to the cause of death. And this post-mortem examination disclosed the fact that all the extraordinary appearances which had been noticed in Mr Charnworth's case were present in this one. There was the same purplish coloured blood; the same gangrenous condition of the limbs; but as with Charnworth, so with Trankler, all the organs were healthy. There was no organic disease to account for death. As it was pretty certain, therefore, that death was not due to natural causes, a coroner's inquest was held, and while the medical evidence made it unmistakably clear that young Trankler had been cut down in the flower of his youth and while he was in radiant health by some powerful and potent means which had suddenly destroyed his life, no one had the boldness to suggest what those means were, beyond saying that blood poisoning of a most violent character had been set up. Now, it was very obvious that blood-poisoning could not have originated without some specific cause, and the most patient investigation was directed to trying to find out the cause, while exhaustive inquiries were made, but at the end of them, the solution of the mystery was as far off as ever, for these investigations had been in the wrong channel, not one scrap of evidence was brought forward which would have justified a definite statement that this or that had been responsible for the young man's death.

It was remembered that when the post-mortem examination of Mr Charnworth took place, a tiny bluish scratch was observed on the left side of the neck. But it was so small, and apparently so unimportant that it was not taken into consideration when attempts were made to solve the problem of 'How did the man die?' When the doctors examined Mr Trankler's body, they looked to see if there was a similar puncture or scratch, and, to their astonishment, they did find rather a curious mark on the left side of the neck, just under the ear. It was a slight abrasion of the skin, about an inch long as if he had been scratched with a pin, and this abrasion was a faint blue, approximating in colour to the tattoo marks on a sailor's arm. The similarity in this scratch to that which had been observed on Mr Charnworth's body, necessarily gave rise to a good deal of comment amongst the doctors, though they could not arrive at any definite conclusion respecting it. One man went so far as to express an opinion that it was due to an insect or the bite of a snake. But this theory found no supporters, for it was argued that the similar wound on Mr Charnworth could hardly have resulted from an insect or snake bite, for he had died in his friend's garden. Besides, there was no insect or snake in England capable of killing a man as these two men had been killed. That theory, therefore, fell to the ground; and medical science as represented by the local gentlemen had to confess itself baffled; while the coroner's jury were forced to again return an open verdict.

'There was no evidence to prove how the deceased had come by his death.'

This verdict was considered highly unsatisfactory, but what other could have been returned. There was nothing to support the theory of foul play; on the other hand, no evidence was forthcoming to explain away the mystery which surrounded the deaths of Charnworth and Trankler. The two men had apparently died from precisely the same cause, and under circumstances which were as mysterious as they were startling, but what the cause was, no one seemed able to determine.

Universal sympathy was felt with the friends and relatives of young Trankler, who had perished so unaccountably while in pursuit of pleasure. Had he been taken suddenly ill at home and had died in his bed, even though the same symptoms and morbid appearances had manifested themselves, the mystery would not have been so great. But as Charnworth's end came in his host's garden after a dinner-party, so young Trankler died in a forest while he and his friends were engaged in shooting. There was certainly something truly remarkable that two men, exhibiting all the same post-mortem effects, should have died in such a way; their deaths, in point of time, being separated by a period of two years. On the face of it, it seemed impossible that it could be merely a coincidence. It will be gathered from the foregoing, that in this double tragedy were all the elements of a romance well calculated to stimulate public curiosity to the highest pitch; while the friends and relatives of the two deceased gentlemen were of opinion that the matter ought not to be allowed to drop with the return of the verdict of the coroner's jury. An investigation seemed to be urgently called for. Of course, an investigation of a kind had taken place by the local police, but something more than that was required, so thought the friends. And an application was made to me to go down to Dead Wood Hall; and bring such skill as I possessed to bear on the case, in the hope that the veil of mystery might be drawn aside, and light let in where all was then dark.

Dead Wood Hall was a curious place, with a certain gloominess of aspect which seemed to suggest that it was a fitting scene for a tragedy. It was a large, massive house, heavily timbered in front in a way peculiar to many of the old Cheshire mansions. It stood in extensive grounds, and being situated on a rise commanded a very fine panoramic view which embraced the Derbyshire Hills. How it got its name of Dead Wood Hall no one seemed to know exactly. There was a tradition that it had originally been known as Dark Wood Hall; but the word 'Dark' had been corrupted into 'Dead'. The Tranklers came into possession of the property by purchase, and the family had been the owners of it for something like thirty years.

With great circumstantiality I was told the story of the death of each man, together with the results of the post-mortem examination, and the steps that had been taken by the police. On further inquiry I found that the police, in spite of the mystery surrounding the case, were firmly of opinion that the deaths of the two men were, after all, due to natural causes, and that the similarity in the appearance of the bodies after death *was* a mere coincidence. The superintendent of the county constabulary, who had had charge of the matter, waxed rather warm; for he said that all sorts of ridiculous stories had been set afloat, and absurd theories had been suggested, not one of which would have done credit to the intelligence of an average schoolboy.

'People lose their heads so, and make such fools of themselves in matters of this kind,' he said warmly; 'and of course the police are accused of being stupid, ignorant, and all the rest of it. They seem, in fact, to have a notion that we are endowed with superhuman faculties, and that nothing should baffle us. But, as a matter of fact, it is the doctors who are at fault in this instance. They are confronted with a new disease, about which they are ignorant; and, in order to conceal their want of knowledge, they at once raise the cry of "foul play".'

'Then you are clearly of opinion that Mr Charnworth and Mr Trankler died of a disease,' I remarked.

'Undoubtedly I am.'

'Then how do you explain the rapidity of the death in each case, and the similarity in the appearance of the dead bodies?'

'It isn't for me to explain that at all. That is doctors' work not police work. If the doctors can't explain it, how can I be expected to do so? I only know this, I've put some of my best men on to the job, and they've failed to find anything that would suggest foul play.'

'And that convinces you absolutely that there has been no foul play?'

'Absolutely.'

'I suppose you were personally acquainted with both gentlemen? What sort of man was Mr Charnworth?'

'Oh, well, he was right enough, as such men go. He made a good many blunders as a magistrate; but all magistrates do that. You see, fellows get put on the bench who are no more fit to be magistrates than you are, sir. It's a matter of influence more often as not. Mr Charnworth was no worse and no better than a lot of others I could name.'

'What opinion did you form of his private character?'

'Ah, now, there, there's another matter,' answered the superintendent, in a confidential tone, and with a smile playing about his lips. 'You see, Mr Charnworth was a bachelor.'

'So are thousands of other men,' I answered. 'But bachelorhood is not considered dishonourable in this country.'

'No, perhaps not. But they say as how the reason was that Mr Charnworth didn't get married was because he didn't care for having only one wife.'

'You mean he was fond of ladies generally. A sort of general lover.'

'I should think he was,' said the superintendent, with a twinkle in his eye, which was meant to convey a good deal of meaning. 'I've heard some queer stories about him.'

'What is the nature of the stories?' I asked, thinking that I might get something to guide me.

'Oh, well, I don't attach much importance to them myself,' he said, half-apologetically; 'but the fact is, there was some social scandal talked about Mr Charnworth.'

'What was the nature of the scandal?'

'Mind you,' urged the superintendent, evidently anxious to be freed from any responsibility for the scandal whatever it was, 'I only tell you the story as I heard it. Mr Charnworth liked his little flirtations, no doubt, as we all do; but he was a gentleman and a magistrate, and I have no right to say anything against him that I know nothing about myself.'

'While a gentleman may be a magistrate, a magistrate is not always a gentleman,' I remarked.

'True, true; but Mr Charnworth was. He was a fine specimen of a gentleman, and was very liberal. He did me many kindnesses.'

'Therefore, in your sight, at least, sir, he was without blemish.'

'I don't go as far as that,' replied the superintendent, a little warmly; 'I only want to be just.'

'I give you full credit for that,' I answered; 'but please do tell me about the scandal you spoke of. It is just possible it may afford me a clue.'

'I don't think that it will. However, here is the story. A young lady lived in Knutsford by the name of Downie. She is the daughter of the late George Downie, who for many years carried on the business of a miller. Hester Downie was said to be one of the prettiest girls in Cheshire, or, at any rate, in this part of Cheshire, and rumour has it that she flirted with both Charnworth and Trankler.'

'Is that all that rumour says?' I asked.

'No, there was a good deal more said. But, as I have told you, I know nothing for certain, and so must decline to

commit myself to any statement for which there could be
no better foundation than common gossip.'

'Does Miss Downie still live in Knutsford?'

'No; she disappeared mysteriously soon after Charnworth's death.'

'And you don't know where she is?'

'No; I have no idea.'

As I did not see that there was much more to be gained
from the superintendent I left him, and at once sought an
interview with the leading medical man who had made the
autopsy of the two bodies. He was a man who was somewhat puffed up with the belief in his own cleverness, but he
gave me the impression that, if anything, he was a little
below the average country practitioner. He hadn't a single
theory to advance to account for the deaths of Charnworth
and Trankler. He confessed that he was mystified; that all
the appearances were entirely new to him, for neither in his
reading nor his practice had he ever heard of a similar case.

'Are you disposed to think, sir, that these two men came
to their end by foul play?' I asked.

'No, I am not,' he answered definitely, 'and I said so at the
inquest. Foul play means murder, cool and deliberate, and
planned and carried out with fiendish cunning. Besides,
if it was murder how was the murder committed?'

'*If it was murder?*' I asked significantly. 'I shall hope to
answer that question later on.'

'But I am convinced it wasn't murder,' returned the
doctor, with a self-confident air. 'If a man is shot, or
bludgeoned, or poisoned, there is something to go upon. I
scarcely know of a poison that cannot be detected. And not
a trace of poison was found in the organs of either man.
Science has made tremendous strides of late years, and I
doubt if she has much more to teach us in that respect.
Anyway, I assert without fear of contradiction that Charnworth and Trankler did not die of poison.'

'What killed them, then?' I asked, bluntly and sharply.

The doctor did not like the question, and there was a roughness in his tone as he answered—

'I'm not prepared to say. If I could have assigned a precise cause of death the coroner's verdict would have been different.'

'Then you admit that the whole affair is a problem which you are incapable of solving?'

'Frankly, I do,' he answered, after a pause. 'There are certain peculiarities in the case that I should like to see cleared up. In fact, in the interests of my profession, I think it is most desirable that the mystery surrounding the death of the unfortunate men should be solved. And I have been trying experiments recently with a view to attaining that end, though without success.'

My interview with this gentleman had not advanced matters, for it only served to show me that the doctors were quite baffled, and I confess that that did not altogether encourage me. Where they had failed, how could I hope to succeed? They had the advantage of seeing the bodies and examining them, and though they found themselves confronted with signs which were in themselves significant, they could not read them. All that I had to go upon was hearsay, and I was asked to solve a mystery which seemed unsolvable. But, as I have so often stated in the course of my chronicles, the seemingly impossible is frequently the most easy to accomplish, where a mind specially trained to deal with complex problems is brought to bear upon it.

In interviewing Mr Tuscan Trankler, I found that he entertained a very decided opinion that there had been foul play, though he admitted that it was difficult in the extreme to suggest even a vague notion of how the deed had been accomplished. If the two men had died together or within a short period of each other, the idea of murder would have seemed more logical. But two years had elapsed, and yet each man had evidently died from precisely the same cause. Therefore, if it *was* murder, the same hand that had slain Mr Charnworth slew Mr Trankler. There was no getting away from that; and then of course arose the question of *motive*. Granted that the same hand did the deed, did the same motive prompt in each case? Another aspect of the affair that presented itself to me was that the crime, if crime it was, was not the work of any ordinary person. There was an originality of conception in it which pointed to the criminal being, in certain respects, a genius. And, moreover, the motive underlying it must have been a very powerful one; possibly, nay probably, due to a sense of some terrible wrong inflicted, and which could only be wiped out with the death of the wronger. But this presupposed that each man, though unrelated, had perpetrated the same wrong. Now, it was within the grasp of intelligent reasoning that Charnworth, in his capacity of a county justice, might have given mortal offence to some one, who, cherishing the memory of it, until a mania had been set up, resolved that the magistrate should die. That theory was reasonable when taken singly, but it seemed to lose its reasonableness when connected with young Trankler, unless it was that he had been instrumental in getting somebody convicted. To determine this I made very pointed inquiries, but received the most positive assurances that never in the whole course of his life had he directly or indirectly been instrumental in prosecuting any one. Therefore, so far as he was concerned, the theory fell to the ground; and if the same person killed both men, the motive prompting in each case was a different one, assuming that Charnworth's death resulted from revenge for a fancied wrong inflicted in the course of his administration of justice.

Although I fully recognized all the difficulties that lay in the way of a rational deduction that would square in with the theory of murder, and of murder committed by one and the same hand, I saw how necessary it was to keep in view the points I have advanced as factors in the problem that had to be worked out, and I adhered to my first impression, and felt tolerably certain that, granted the men had been murdered, they were murdered by the same hand. It may be said that this deduction required no great mental effort. I admit that that is so; but it is strange that nearly all the people in the district were opposed to the theory. Mr Tuscan Trankler spoke very highly of Charnworth. He believed him to be an upright, conscientious man, liberal to a fault with his means, and in his position of magistrate erring on the side of mercy. In his private character he was a *bon vivant*; fond of a good dinner, good wine, and good company. He was much in request at dinner-parties and other social gatherings, for he was accounted a brilliant *raconteur*, possessed of an endless fund of racy jokes and anecdotes. I have already stated that with ladies he was an especial favourite, for he had a singularly suave, winning way, which with most women was irresistible. In age he was more than double that of young Trankler, who was only five and twenty at the time of his death, whereas Charnworth had turned sixty, though I was given to understand that he was a well-preserved, good-looking man, and apparently younger than he really was.

Coming to young Trankler, there was a consensus of opinion that he was an exemplary young man. He had been partly educated at home and partly at the Manchester Grammar School; and, though he had shown a decided talent for engineering, he had not gone in for it seriously, but had dabbled in it as an amateur, for he had ample means and good prospects, and it was his father's desire that he should lead the life of a country gentleman, devote himself to country pursuits, and to improving and keeping together the family estates. To the lady who was to have become his bride, he had been engaged but six months, and had only known her a year. His premature and mysterious death had caused intense grief in both families; and his intended wife had been so seriously affected that her friends had been compelled to take her abroad.

The Problem of Dead Wood Hall

With these facts and particulars before me, I had to set to work and try to solve the problem which was considered unsolvable by most of the people who knew anything about it. But may I be pardoned for saying very positively that, even at this point, I did not consider it so. Its complexity could not be gainsaid; nevertheless, I felt that there were ways and means of arriving at a solution, and I set to work in my own fashion. Firstly, I started on the assumption that both men had been deliberately murdered by the same person. If that was not so, then they had died of some remarkable and unknown disease which had stricken them down under a set of conditions that were closely allied, and the coincidence in that case would be one of the most astounding the world had ever known. Now, if that was correct, a pathological conundrum was propounded which it was for the medical world to answer, and practically I was placed out of the running, to use a sporting phrase. I found that, with few exceptions—the exceptions· being Mr Trankler and his friends—there was an undisguised opinion that what the united local wisdom and skill had failed to accomplish, could not be accomplished by a stranger. As my experience, however, had inured me against that sort of thing, it did not affect me. Local prejudices and jealousies have always to be reckoned with, and it does not do to be thin-skinned. I worked upon my own lines, thought with my own thoughts, and, as an expert in the art of reading human nature, I reasoned from a different set of premises to that employed by the irresponsible chatterers, who cry out 'Impossible', as soon as the first difficulty presents itself. Marshalling all the facts of the case so far as I had been able to gather them, I arrived at the conclusion that the problem could be solved, and, as a preliminary step to that end, I started off to London, much to the astonishment of those who had secured my services. But my reply to the many queries addressed to me was, 'I hope to find the key-note to the solution in the metropolis.' This reply only increased the astonishment, but later on I will explain why I took the step, which may seem to the reader rather an extraordinary one.

After an absence of five days I returned to Cheshire, and I was then in a position to say, 'Unless a miracle has happened, Charnworth and Trankler were murdered beyond all doubt, and murdered by the same person in such a cunning, novel, and devilish manner, that even the most astute inquirer might have been pardoned for being baffled.' Of course there was a strong desire to know my reasons for the positive statement, but I felt that it was in the interests of justice itself that I should not allow them to be known at that stage of the proceedings.

The next important step was to try and find out what had become of Miss Downie, the Knutsford beauty, with whom Charnworth was said to have carried on a flirtation. Here, again, I considered secrecy of great importance.

Hester Downie was about seven and twenty years of age. She was an orphan, and was believed to have been born in Macclesfield, as her parents came from there. Her father's calling was that of a miller. He had settled in Knutsford about fifteen years previous to the period I am dealing with, and had been dead about five years. Not very much was known about the family, but it was thought there were other children living. No very kindly feeling was shown for Hester Downie, though it was only too obvious that jealousy was at the bottom of it. Half the young men, it seemed, had lost their heads about her, and all the girls in the village were consumed with envy and jealousy. It was said she was 'stuck up', 'above her position', 'a heartless flirt', and so forth. From those competent to speak, however, she was regarded as a nice young woman, and admittedly good-looking. For years she had lived with an old aunt, who bore the reputation of being rather a sullen sort of woman, and somewhat eccentric. The girl had a little over fifty pounds a year to live upon, derived from a small property left to her by her father; and she and her aunt occupied a cottage just on the outskirts of Knutsford. Hester was considered to be very exclusive, and did not associate much with the people in Knutsford. This was sufficient to account for the local bias, and as she often went away from her home for three and four weeks at a time, it was not considered extraordinary when it was known that she had left soon after Trankler's death. Nobody, however, knew where she had gone to; it is right, perhaps, that I should here state that not a soul breathed a syllable of suspicion against her, that either directly or indirectly she could be connected with the deaths of Charnworth or Trankler. The aunt, a widow by the name of Hislop, could not be described as a pleasant or genial woman, either in appearance or manner. I was anxious to ascertain for certain whether there was any truth in the rumour or not that Miss Downie had flirted with Mr Charnworth. If it was true that she did, a clue might be afforded which would lead to the ultimate unravelling of the mystery. I had to approach Mrs Hislop with a good deal of circumspection, for she showed an inclination to resent any inquiries being made into her family matters. She gave me the impression that she was an honest woman, and it was very apparent that she was strongly attached to her niece Hester. Trading on this fact, I managed to draw her out. I said that people in the district were beginning to say unkind things about Hester, and that it would be better for the girl's sake that there should be no mystery associated with her or her movements.

The old lady fired up at this, and declared that she didn't care a jot about what the 'common people' said. Her niece was superior to all of them, and she would 'have the law on any one who spoke ill of Hester.'

'But there is one thing, Mrs Hislop,' I replied, 'that ought to be set at rest. It is rumoured—in fact, something

more than rumoured—that your niece and the late Mr
Charnworth were on terms of intimacy, which, to say the
least, if it is true, was imprudent for a girl in her position.'

'Them what told you that,' exclaimed the old woman,
'is like the adders the woodmen get in Delamere forest:
they're full of poisen. Mr Charnworth courted the girl fair
and square, and led her to believe he would marry her.
But, of course, he had to do the thing in secret. Some folk
will talk so, and if it had been known that a gentleman like
Mr Charnworth was coming after a girl in Hester's position,
all sorts of things would have been said.'

'Did she believe that he was serious in his intentions
towards her?'

'Of course she did.'

'Why was the match broken off?'

'Because he died.'

'Then do you mean to tell me seriously, Mrs Hislop, that
Mr Charnworth, had he lived, would have married your
niece?'

'Yes, I believe he would.'

'Was he the only lover the girl had?'

'Oh dear no. She used to carry on with a man named
Job Panton. But, though they were engaged to be married,
she didn't like him much, and threw him up for Mr Charnworth.'

'Did she ever flirt with young Mr Trankler?'

'I don't know about flirting; but he called here now and
again, and made her some presents. You see, Hester is a
superior sort of girl, and I don't wonder at gentlefolk liking
her.'

'Just so,' I replied; 'beauty attracts peasant and lord
alike. But you will understand that it is to Hester's interest
that there should be no concealment—no mystery; and I
advise that she return here, for her very presence would
tend to silence the tongue of scandal. By the way, where is
she?'

'She's staying in Manchester with a relative, a cousin of hers, named Jessie Turner.'

'Is Jessie Turner a married woman?'

'Oh yes: well, that is, she has been married; but she's a widow now, and has two little children. She is very fond of Hester, who often goes to her.'

Having obtained Jessie Turner's address in Manchester, I left Mrs Hislop, feeling somehow as if I had got the key of the problem, and a day or two later I called on Mrs Jessie Turner, who resided in a small house, situated in Tamworth Street, Hulme, Manchester.

She was a young woman, not more than thirty years of age, somewhat coarse, and vulgar-looking in appearance, and with an unpleasant, self-assertive manner. There was a great contrast between her and her cousin, Hester Downie, who was a remarkably attractive and pretty girl, with quite a classical figure, and a childish, winning way, but a painful want of education which made itself very manifest when she spoke; and a harsh, unmusical voice detracted a good deal from her winsomeness, while in everything she did, and almost everything she said, she revealed that vanity was her besetting sin.

I formed my estimate at once of this young woman—indeed, of both of them. Hester seemed to me to be shallow, vain, thoughtless, giddy; and her companion, artful, cunning, and heartless.

'I want you, Miss Downie,' I began, 'to tell me truthfully the story of your connection, firstly, with Job Panton; secondly, with Mr Charnworth; thirdly, with Mr Trankler.'

This request caused the girl to fall into a condition of amazement and confusion, for I had not stated what the nature of my business was, and, of course, she was unprepared for the question.

'What should I tell you my business for?' she cried snappishly, and growing very red in the face.

'You are aware,' I remarked, 'that both Mr Charnworth and Mr Trankler are dead?'

'Of course I am.'

'Have you any idea how they came by their death?'

'Not the slightest.'

'Will you be surprised to hear that some very hard things are being said about you?'

'About me!' she exclaimed, in amazement.

'Yes.'

'Why about me?'

'Well, your disappearance from your home, for one thing.'

She threw up her hands and uttered a cry of distress and horror, while sudden paleness took the place of the red flush that had dyed her cheeks. Then she burst into almost hysterical weeping, and sobbed out:

'I declare it's awful. To think that I cannot do anything or go away when I like without all the old cats in the place trying to blacken my character! It's a pity that people won't mind their own business, and not go out of the way to talk about that which doesn't concern them.'

'But, you see, Miss Downie, it's the way of the world,' I answered, with a desire to soothe her; 'one mustn't be too thin-skinned. Human nature is essentially spiteful. However, to return to the subject, you will see, perhaps, the importance of answering my questions. The circumstances of Charnworth's and Trankler's deaths are being closely inquired into, and I am sure you wouldn't like it to be thought that you were withholding information which, in the interest of law and justice, might be valuable.'

'Certainly not,' she replied, suppressing a sob. 'But I have nothing to tell you.'

'But you knew the three men I have mentioned.'

'Of course I did, but Job Panton is an ass. I never could bear him.'

'He was your sweetheart, though, was he not?'

'He used to come fooling about, and declared that he couldn't live without me.'

'Did you never give him encouragement?'

'I suppose every girl makes a fool of herself sometimes.'

'Then you did allow him to sweetheart you?'

'If you like to call it sweethearting you can,' she answered, with a toss of her pretty head. 'I did walk out with him sometimes. But I didn't care much for him. You see, he wasn't my sort at all.'

'In what way?'

'Well, surely I couldn't be expected to marry a game-keeper, could I?'

'He is a gamekeeper, then?'

'Yes.'

'In whose employ is he?'

'Lord Belmere's.'

'Was he much disappointed when he found that you would have nothing to do with him?'

'I really don't know. I didn't trouble myself about him,' she answered, with a coquettish heartlessness.

'Did you do any sweethearting with Mr Trankler?'

'No, of course not. He used to be very civil to me, and talk to me when he met me.'

'Did you ever walk out with him?'

The question brought the colour back to her face, and her manner grew confused again.

'Once or twice I met him by accident, and he strolled along the road with me—that's all.'

This answer was not a truthful one. Of that I was con-vinced by her very manner. But I did not betray my mis-trust or doubts. I did not think there was any purpose to be served in so doing. So far the object of my visit was accomplished, and as Miss Downie seemed disposed to resent any further questioning, I thought it was advisable to bring the interview to a close; but before doing so, I said:

'I have one more question to ask you, Miss Downie.

Permit me to preface it, however, by saying I am afraid that, up to this point, you have failed to appreciate the situation, or grasp the seriousness of the position in which you are placed. Let me, therefore, put it before you in a somewhat more graphic way. Two men—gentlemen of good social position—with whom you seem to have been well acquainted, and whose attentions you encouraged— pray do not look at me so angrily as that; I mean what I say. I repeat that you encouraged their attentions, otherwise they would not have gone after you.' Here Miss Downie's nerves gave way again, and she broke into a fit of weeping, and, holding her handkerchief to her eyes, she exclaimed with almost passionate bitterness:

'Well, whatever I did, I was egged on to do it by my cousin, Jessie Turner. She always said I was a fool not to aim at high game.'

'And so you followed her promptings, and really thought that you might have made a match with Mr Charnworth; but, he having died, you turned your thoughts to young Trankler.' She did not reply, but sobbed behind her handkerchief. So I proceeded. 'Now the final question I want to ask you is this: Have you ever had anyone who has made serious love to you but Job Panton?'

'Mr Charnworth made love to me,' she sobbed out.

'He flirted with you,' I suggested.

'No; he made love to me,' she persisted. 'He promised to marry me.'

'And you believed him?'

'Of course I did.'

'Did Trankler promise to marry you?'

'No.'

'Then I must repeat the question, but will add Mr Charnworth's name. Besides him and Panton, is there any one else in existence who has courted you in the hope that you would become his wife?'

'No—no one,' she mumbled in a broken voice.

The Problem of Dead Wood Hall

As I took my departure I felt that I had gathered up a good many threads, though they wanted arranging, and, so to speak, classifying; that done, they would probably give me the clue I was seeking. One thing was clear, Miss Downie was a weak-headed, giddy, flighty girl, incapable, as it seemed to me, of seriously reflecting on anything. Her cousin was crafty and shallow, and a dangerous companion for Downie, who was sure to be influenced and led by a creature like Jessie Turner. But, let it not be inferred from these remarks that I had any suspicion that either of the two women had in any way been accessory to the crime, for crime I was convinced it was. Trankler and Charnworth had been murdered, but by whom I was not prepared to even hint at at that stage of the proceedings. The two unfortunate gentlemen had, beyond all possibility of doubt, both been attracted by the girl's exceptionally good looks, and they had amused themselves with her. This fact suggested at once the question, was Charnworth in the habit of seeing her before Trankler made her acquaintance? Now, if my theory of the crime was correct, it could be asserted with positive certainty that Charnworth was the girl's lover before Trankler. Of course it was almost a foregone conclusion that Trankler must have been aware of her existence for a long time. The place, be it remembered, was small; she, in her way, was a sort of local celebrity, and it was hardly likely that young Trankler was ignorant of some of the village gossip in which she figured. But, assuming that he was, he was well acquainted with Charnworth, who was looked upon in the neighbourhood as 'a gay dog'. The female conquests of such men are often matters of notoriety; though, even if that was not the case, it was likely enough that Charnworth may have discussed Miss Downie in Trankler's presence. Some men—especially those of Charnworth's characteristics—are much given to boasting of their flirtations, and Charnworth may have been rather proud of his ascendency over the simple village beauty. Of course, all this, it will be said, was mere theorizing. So it was; but it will presently be seen how it squared in with the general theory of the whole affair, which I had worked out after much pondering, and a careful weighing and nice adjustment of all the evidence, such as it was, I had been able to gather together, and the various parts which were necessary before the puzzle could be put together.

It was immaterial, however, whether Trankler did or did not know Hester Downie before or at the same time as Charnworth. A point that was not difficult to determine was this—he did not make himself conspicuous as her admirer until after his friend's death, probably not until some time afterwards. Otherwise, how came it about that the slayer of Charnworth waited two years before he took the life of young Trankler? The reader will gather from this remark how my thoughts ran at that time. Firstly, I was clearly of opinion that both men had been murdered. Secondly, the murder in each case was the outcome of jealousy. Thirdly, the murderer must, as a logical sequence, have been a rejected suitor. This would point necessarily to Job Panton as the criminal, assuming my information was right that the girl had not had any other lover. But against that theory this very strong argument could be used: By what extraordinary and secret means—means that had baffled all the science of the district—had Job Panton, who occupied the position of a gamekeeper, been able to do away with his victims, and bring about death so horrible and so sudden as to make one shudder to think of it? Herein was displayed a devilishness of cunning, and a knowledge which it was difficult to conceive that an ignorant and untravelled man was likely to be in possession of. Logic, deduction, and all the circumstances of the case were opposed to the idea of Panton being the murderer at the first blush; and yet, so far as I had gone, I had been irresistibly drawn towards the conclusion that Panton was either directly or indirectly responsible for the death of the two gentlemen. But, in order to know something more of the man whom I suspected, I disguised myself as a travelling showman on the look-out for a good pitch for my show, and I took up my quarters for a day or two at a rustic inn just on the skirts of Knutsford, and known as the Woodman. I had previously ascertained that this inn was a favourite resort of the gamekeepers for miles round about, and Job Panton was to be found there almost nightly.

In a short time I had made his acquaintance. He was a young, big-limbed, powerful man, of a pronounced rustic type. He had the face of a gipsy—swarthy and dark, with keen, small black eyes, and a mass of black curly hair, and in his ears he wore tiny, plain gold rings. Singularly enough his expression was most intelligent; but allied with—as it seemed to me—a certain suggestiveness of latent ferocity. That is to say, I imagined him liable to outbursts of temper and passion, during which he might be capable of anything. As it was, then, he seemed to me subdued, somewhat sullen, and averse to conversation. He smoked heavily, and I soon found that he guzzled beer at a terrible rate. He had received, for a man in his position, a tolerably good education. By that I mean he could write a fair hand, he read well, and had something more than a smattering of arithmetic. I was told also that he was exceedingly skilful with carpenter's tools, although he had had no training that way; he also understood something about plants, while he was considered an authority on the habits, and everything appertaining to game. The same informant thought to still further enlighten me by adding:

'Poor Job beän't the chap he wur a year or more ago. His gal cut un, and that kind a took a hold on un. He doän't say much; but it wur a terrible blow, it wur.'

'How was it his girl cut him?' I asked.

'Well, you see, maäster, it wur this way; she thought hersel' a bit too high for un. Mind you, I bään't a saying as she wur; but when a gel thinks hersel' above a chap, it's no use talking to her.'

'What was the girl's name?'

'They call her Downie. Her father was a miller here in Knutsford, but his gal had too big notions of hersel'; and she chucked poor Job Panton overboard, and they do say as how she took on wi' Meäster Charnworth and also wi' Meäster Trankler. I doän't know nowt for certain myself, but there wur some rum kind o' talk going about. Leastwise, I know that Job took it badly, and he ain't been the same kind o' chap since. But there, what's the use of a braking one's 'art about a gal? Gals is a queer lot, I tell you. My old grandfaither used to say, "Women folk be curious folk. They be necessary evils, they be, and pleasant enough in their way, but a chap mustn't let 'em get the upper hand. They're like harses, they be, and if you want to manage 'em, you must show 'em you're their meäster".'

The garrulous gentleman who entertained me thus with his views on women, was a tough, sinewy, weather-tanned old codger, who had lived the allotted span according to the psalmist, but who seemed destined to tread the earth for a long time still; for his seventy years had neither bowed nor shrunk him. His chatter was interesting to me because it served to prove what I already suspected, which was that Job Panton had taken his jilting very seriously indeed. Job was by no means a communicative fellow. As a matter of fact, it was difficult to draw him out on any subject; and though I should have liked to have heard *his* views about Hester Downie, I did not feel warranted in tapping him straight off. I very speedily discovered, however, that his weakness was beer. His capacity for it seemed immeasurable. He soaked himself with it; but when he reached the muddled stage, there was a tendency on his part to be more loquacious, and, taking advantage at last of one of these opportunities, I asked him one night if he had travelled. The question was an exceedingly pertinent one to my theory, and I felt that to a large extent the theory I had worked out depended upon the answers he gave. He turned his beady eyes upon me, and said, with a sort of sardonic grin—

'Yes, I've travelled a bit in my time, meäster. I've been to Manchester often, and I once tramped all the way to Edinburgh. I had to rough it, I tell thee.'

'Yes, I dare say,' I answered. 'But what I mean is, have you ever been abroad? Have you ever been to sea?'

'No, meäster, not me.'

'You've been in foreign countries?'

'No. I've never been out of this one. England was good enough for me. But I would like to go away now to Australia, or some of those places.'

'Why?'

'Well, meäster, I have my own reasons.'

'Doubtless,' I said, 'and no doubt very sound reasons.'

'Never thee mind whether they are, or whether they beän't,' he retorted warmly. 'All I've got to say is, I wouldn't care where I went to if I could only get far enough away from this place. I'm tired of it.'

In the manner of giving his answer, he betrayed the latent fire which I had surmised, and showed that there was a volcanic force of passion underlying his sullen silence, for he spoke with a suppressed force which clearly indicated the intensity of his feelings, and his bright eyes grew brighter with the emotion he felt. I now ventured upon another remark. I intended it to be a test one.

'I heard one of your mates say that you had been jilted. I suppose that's why you hate the place?'

He turned upon me suddenly. His tanned, ruddy face took on a deeper flush of red; his upper teeth closed almost savagely on his nether lip; his chest heaved, and his great, brawny hands clenched with the working of his passion. Then, with one great bang of his ponderous fist, he struck the table until the pots and glasses on it jumped as if they were sentient and frightened; and in a voice thick with smothered passion, he growled, 'Yes, damn her! She's been my ruin.'

'Nonsense!' I said. 'You are a young man and a young man should not talk about being ruined because a girl has jilted him.'

Once more he turned that angry look upon me, and said fiercely—

'Thou knows nowt about it, governor. Thou're a stranger to me; and I doän't allow no strangers to preach to me. So shut up! I'll have nowt more to say to thee.'

There was a peremptoriness, a force of character, and a display of firmness and self-assurance in his tone and manner, which stamped him with a distinct individualism, and made it evident that in his own particular way he was distinct from the class in which his lot was cast. He, further than that, gave me the idea that he was designing and secretive; and given that he had been educated and well trained, he might have made his mark in the world. My interview with him had been instructive, and my opinion that he might prove a very important factor in working out the problem was strengthened; but at that stage of the inquiry I would not have taken upon myself to say, with anything like definiteness, that he was directly responsible for the death of the two gentlemen, whose mysterious ending had caused such a profound sensation. But the reader of this narrative will now see for himself that of all men, so far as one could determine then, who might have been interested in the death of Mr Charnworth and Mr Trankler, Job Panton stood out most conspicuously. His motive for destroying them was one of the most powerful of human passions—namely, jealousy, which in his case was likely to assume a very violent form, inasmuch as there was no evenly balanced judgment, no capability of philosophical reasoning, calculated to restrain the fierce, crude passion of the determined and self-willed man.

The Problem of Dead Wood Hall

A wounded tiger is fiercer and more dangerous than an unwounded one, and an ignorant and unreasoning man is far more likely to be led to excess by a sense of wrong, than one who is capable of reflecting and moralizing. Of course, if I had been the impossible detective of fiction, endowed with the absurd attributes of being able to tell the story of a man's life from the way the tip of his nose was formed, or the number of hairs on his head, or by the shape and size of his teeth, or by the way he held his pipe when smoking, or from the kind of liquor he consumed, or the hundred and one utterly ridiculous and burlesque signs which are so easily read by the detective prig of modern creation, I might have come to a different conclusion with reference to Job Panton. But my work had to be carried out on very different lines, and I had to be guided by certain deductive inferences, aided by an intimate knowledge of human nature, and of the laws which, more or less in every case of crime, govern the criminal.

I have already set forth my unalterable opinion that Charnworth and Trankler had been murdered; and so far as I had proceeded up to this point, I had heard and seen enough to warrant me, in my own humble judgment, in at least suspecting Job Panton of being guilty of the murder. But there was one thing that puzzled me greatly. When I first commenced my inquiries, and was made acquainted with all the extraordinary medical aspects of the case, I argued with myself that if it *was* murder, it was murder carried out upon very original lines. Some potent, swift and powerful poison must have been suddenly and secretly introduced into the blood of the victim. The bite of a cobra, or of the still more fearful and deadly Fer de lance of the West Indies, might have produced symptoms similar to those observed in the two men; but happily our beautiful and quiet woods and gardens of England are not infested with these deadly reptiles, and one had to search for the causes elsewhere. Now every one knows that the notorious

Lucrezia Borgia, and the Marchioness of Brinvilliers, made use of means for accomplishing the death of those whom they were anxious to get out of the way, which were at once effective and secret. These means consisted, amongst others, of introducing into the blood of the intended victim some subtle poison, by the medium of a scratch or puncture. This little and fatal wound could be given by the scratch of a pin, or the sharpened stone of a ring, and in such a way that the victim would be all unconscious of it until the deadly poison so insidiously introduced began to course through his veins, and to sap the props of his life. With these facts in my mind, I asked myself if in the Dead Wood Hall tragedies some similar means had been used; and in order to have competent and authoritative opinion to guide me, I journeyed back to London to consult the eminent chemist and scientist, Professor Lucraft. This gentleman had made a lifelong study of the toxic effect of ptomaines on the human system, and of the various poisons used by savage tribes for tipping their arrows and spears. Enlightened as he was on the subject, he confessed that there were hundreds of these deadly poisons, of which the modern chemist knew absolutely nothing; but he expressed a decided opinion that there were many that would produce all the effects and symptoms observable in the cases of Charnworth and Trankler. And he particularly instanced some of the herbal extracts used by various tribes of Indians, who wander in the interior of the little known country of Ecuador, and he cited as an authority Mr Hart Thompson, the botanist, who travelled from Quito right through Ecuador to the Amazon. This gentleman reported that he found a vegetable poison in use by the natives for poisoning the tips of their arrows and spears of so deadly and virulent a nature, that a scratch even on a panther would bring about the death of the animal within an hour.

Armed with these facts, I returned to Cheshire, and continued my investigations on the assumption that some such deadly destroyer of life had been used to put Charnworth and Trankler out of the way. But necessarily I was led to question whether or not it was likely that an untravelled and ignorant man like Job Panton could have known anything about such poisons and their uses. This was a stumbling-block; and while I was convinced that Panton had a strong motive for the crime, I was doubtful if he could have been in possession of the means for committing it. At last, in order to try and get evidence on this point, I resolved to search the place in which he lived. He had for a long time occupied lodgings in the house of a widow woman in Knutsford, and I subjected his rooms to a thorough and critical search, but without finding a sign of anything calculated to justify my suspicion.

I freely confess that at this stage I began to feel that the problem was a hopeless one, and that I should fail to work it out. My depression, however, did not last long. It was not my habit to acknowledge defeat so long as there were probabilities to guide me, so I began to make inquiries about Panton's relatives, and these inquiries elicited the fact that he had been in the habit of making frequent journeys to Manchester to see an uncle. I soon found that this uncle had been a sailor, and had been one of a small expedition which had travelled through Peru and Ecuador in search of gold. Now, this was a discovery indeed, and the full value of it will be understood when it is taken in connection with the information given to me by Professor Lucraft. Let us see how it works out logically.

Panton's uncle was a sailor and a traveller. He had travelled through Peru, and had been into the interior of Ecuador.

Panton was in the habit of visiting his uncle.

Could the uncle have wandered through Ecuador without hearing something of the marvellous poisons used by the natives?

Having been connected with an exploring expedition, it

was reasonable to assume that he was a man of good intelligence, and of an inquiring turn of mind.

Equally probable was it that he had brought home some of the deadly poisons or poisoned implements used by the Indians. Granted that, and what more likely than that he talked of his knowledge and possessions to his nephew? The nephew, brooding on his wrongs, and seeing the means within his grasp of secretly avenging himself on those whom he counted his rivals, obtained the means from his uncle's collection of putting his rivals to death, in a way which to him would seem to be impossible to detect. I had seen enough of Panton to feel sure that he had all the intelligence and cunning necessary for planning and carrying out the deed.

A powerful link in the chain of evidence had now been forged, and I proceeded a step further. After a consultation with the chief inspector of police, who, however, by no means shared my views, I applied for a warrant for Panton's arrest, although I saw that to establish legal proof of his guilt would be extraordinarily difficult, for his uncle at that time was at sea, somewhere in the southern hemisphere. Moreover, the whole case rested upon such a hypothetical basis, that it seemed doubtful whether, even supposing a magistrate would commit, a jury would convict. But I was not daunted; and, having succeeded so far in giving a practical shape to my theory, I did not intend to draw back. So I set to work to endeavour to discover the weapon which had been used for wounding Charnworth and Trankler, so that the poison might take effect. This, of course, was the *crux* of the whole affair. The discovery of the medium by which the death-scratch was given would forge almost the last link necessary to ensure a conviction.

Now, in each case there was pretty conclusive evidence that there had been no struggle. This fact justified the belief that the victim was struck silently, and probably unknown to himself. What were the probabilities of that being the case? Assuming that Panton was guilty of the crime, how was it that he, being an inferior, was allowed to come within striking distance of his victims? The most curious thing was that both men had been scratched on the left side of the neck. Charnworth had been killed in his friend's garden on a summer night. Trankler had fallen in mid-day in the depths of a forest. There was an interval of two years between the death of the one man and the death of the other, yet each had a scratch on the left side of the neck. That could not have been a mere coincidence. It was design.

The next point for consideration was, how did Panton— always assuming that he was the criminal—get access to Mr Trankler's grounds? Firstly, the grounds were extensive, and in connection with a plantation of young fir trees. When Charnworth was found, he was lying behind a clump of rhododendron bushes, and near where the grounds were merged into the plantation, a somewhat dilapidated oak fence separating the two. These details before us make it clear that Panton could have had no difficulty in gaining access to the plantation, and thence to the grounds. But how came it that he was there just at the time that Charnworth was strolling about? It seemed stretching a point very much to suppose that he could have been loafing about on the mere chance of seeing Charnworth. And the only hypothesis that squared in with intelligent reasoning, was that the victim had been lured into the grounds. But this necessarily presupposed a confederate. Close inquiry elicited the fact that Panton was in the habit of going to the house. He knew most of the servants, and frequently accompanied young Trankler on his shooting excursions, and periodically he spent half a day or so in the gun room at the house, in order that he might clean up all the guns, for which he was paid a small sum every month. These circumstances cleared the way of difficulties to a very considerable extent. I was unable, however, to go beyond that, for I could not ascertain the means that had been used to lure Mr Charnworth into the garden—if he had been lured; and I felt sure that he had been. But so much had to remain for the time being a mystery.

Having obtained the warrant to arrest Panton, I proceeded to execute it. He seemed thunderstruck when told that he was arrested on a charge of having been instrumental in bringing about the death of Charnworth and Trankler. For a brief space of time he seemed to collapse, and lose his presence of mind. But suddenly, with an apparent effort, he recovered himself, and said, with a strange smile on his face—

'You've got to prove it, and that you can never do.'

His manner and this remark were hardly compatible with innocence, but I clearly recognized the difficulties of proof.

From that moment the fellow assumed a self-assured air, and to those with whom he was brought in contact he would remark:

'I'm as innocent as a lamb, and them as says I done the deed have got to prove it.'

In my endeavour to get further evidence to strengthen my case, I managed to obtain from Job Panton's uncle's brother, who followed the occupation of an engine-minder in a large cotton factory in Oldham, an old chest containing a quantity of lumber. The uncle, on going to sea again, had left this chest in charge of his brother. A careful examination of the contents proved that they consisted of a very miscellaneous collection of odds and ends, including two or three small, carved wooden idols from some savage country; some stone weapons, such as are used by the North American Indians; strings of cowrie shells, a pair of moccasins, feathers of various kinds; a few dried specimens of strange birds; and last, though not least, a small bamboo case containing a dozen tiny sharply pointed darts, feathered at the thick end; while in a stone box, about three inches square, was a viscid thick gummy looking substance of a very dark brown colour, and giving off a sickening and most disagreeable, though faint odour. These things I at once submitted to Professor Lucraft, who expressed an opinion that the gummy substance in the stone box was a vegetable poison, used probably to poison the darts with. He lost no time in experimentalizing with this substance, as well as with the darts. With these darts he scratched guinea-pigs, rabbits, a dog, a cat, a hen, and a young pig, and in each case death ensued in periods of time ranging from a quarter of an hour to two hours. By means of a subcutaneous injection into a rabbit of a minute portion of the gummy substance, about the size of a pea, which had been thinned with alcohol, he produced death in exactly seven minutes. A small monkey was next procured, and slightly scratched on the neck with one of the poisoned darts. In a very short time the poor animal exhibited the most distressing symptoms, and in half an hour it was dead, and a post-mortem examination revealed many of the peculiar effects which had been observed in Charnworth's and Trankler's bodies. Various other exhaustive experiments were carried out, all of which confirmed the deadly nature of these minute poison-darts, which could be puffed through a hollow tube to a great distance, and after some practice, with unerring aim. Analysis of the gummy substance in the box proved it to be a violent vegetable poison; innocuous when swallowed, but singularly active and deadly when introduced direct into the blood.

On the strength of these facts, the magistrate duly committed Job Panton to take his trial at the next assizes, on a charge of murder, although there was not a scrap of evidence forthcoming to prove that he had ever been in possession of any of the darts or the poison; and unless such evidence was forthcoming, it was felt that the case for the prosecution must break down, however clear the mere guilt of the man might seem.

In due course, Panton was put on his trial at Chester, and the principal witness against him was Hester Downie, who was subjected to a very severe cross-examination, which left not a shadow of a doubt that she and Panton had at one time been close sweethearts. But her cousin Jessie Turner proved a tempter of great subtlety. It was made clear that she poisoned the girl's mind against her humble lover. Although it could not be proved, it is highly probable that Jessie Turner was a creature of and in the pay of Mr Charnworth, who seemed to have been very much attracted by him. Hester's connection with Charnworth half maddened Panton, who made frantic appeals to her to be true to him, appeals to which she turned a deaf ear. That Trankler knew her in Charnworth's time was also brought out, and after Charnworth's death she smiled favourably on the young man. On the morning that Trankler's shooting-party went out to Mere Forest, Panton was one of the beaters employed by the party.

So much was proved; so much was made as clear as daylight, and it opened the way for any number of inferences. But the last and most important link was never forthcoming. Panton was defended by an able and unscrupulous counsel, who urged with tremendous force on the notice of the jury, that firstly, not one of the medical witnesses would undertake to swear that the two men had died from the effects of poison similar to that found in the old chest which had belonged to the prisoner's uncle; and secondly, there was not one scrap of evidence tending to prove that Panton had ever been in possession of poisoned darts, or had ever had access to the chest in which they were kept. These two points were also made much of by the learned judge in his summing up. He was at pains to make clear that there was a doubt involved, and that mere inference ought not to be allowed to outweigh the doubt when a human being was on trial for his life. Although circumstantially the evidence very strongly pointed to the probability of the prisoner having killed both men, nevertheless, in the absence of the strong proof which the law demanded, the way was opened for the escape of a suspected man, and it was far better to let the law be cheated of its due, than that an innocent man should suffer. At the same time, the judge went on, two gentlemen had met their deaths in a manner which had baffled medical science, and no one was forthcoming who would undertake to say that they had been killed in the manner suggested by the prosecution, and yet it had been shown that the terrible and powerful poison found in the old chest, and which there was reason to believe had been brought from some part of the little known country near the sources of the mighty Amazon, would produce all the effects which were observed in the bodies of Charnworth and Trankler. The chest, furthermore, in which the poison was discovered, was in the possession of Panton's uncle. Panton had a powerful motive in the shape of consuming jealousy for getting rid of his more favoured rivals; and though he was one of the shooting-party in Mere Forest on the day that Trankler lost his life, no evidence had been produced to prove that he was on the premises of Dead Wood Hall, on the night that Charnworth died. If, in weighing all these points of evidence, the jury were of opinion the circumstantial evidence was inadequate, then it was their duty to give the prisoner—whose life was in their hands—the benefit of the doubt.

The jury retired, and were absent three long hours, and it became known that they could not agree. Ultimately, they returned into court, and pronounced a verdict of 'Not guilty'. In Scotland the verdict must and would have been *non proven*.

And so Job Panton went free, but an evil odour seemed to cling about him; he was shunned by his former companions, and many a suspicious glance was directed to him, and many a bated murmur was uttered as he passed by, until in a while he went forth beyond the seas, to the far wild west, as some said, and his haunts knew him no more.

The mystery is still a mystery; but how near I came to solving the problem of Dead Wood Hall it is for the reader to judge.

IV

The Case of Janissary

Arthur Morrison

I

In the year 1897 a short report of an ordinary sort of inquest
appeared in the London newspapers, and I here transcribe
it.

'Dr McCulloch held an inquest yesterday on the body of
Mr Henry Lawrence, whose body was found on Tuesday
morning last in the river near Vauxhall Bridge. The deceased was well known in certain sporting circles. Sophia
Lawrence, the widow, said that deceased had left home on
Monday afternoon at about five, in his usual health, saying
that he was to dine at a friend's and she saw nothing more
of him till called upon to identify the body. He had no
reason for suicide, and so far as witness knew, was free
from pecuniary embarrassments. He had, indeed, been very
successful in betting recently. He habitually carried a
large pocket-book, with papers in it. Mr Robert Naylor,
commission agent, said that deceased dined with him that
evening at his house in Gold Street, Chelsea, and left for
home at about half-past eleven. He had at the time a sum of
nearly four hundred pounds upon him, chiefly in notes,
which had been paid him by witness in settlement of a bet.

It was a fine night, and deceased walked in the direction of Chelsea Embankment. That was the last witness saw of him. He might not have been perfectly sober, but he was not drunk, and was capable of taking care of himself. The evidence of the Thames police went to show that no money was on the body when found, except a few coppers, and no pocket-book. Dr William Hodgetts said that death was due to drowning. There were some bruises on the arms and head which might have been caused before death. The body was a very healthy one. The coroner said that there seemed to be a strong suspicion of foul play, unless the pocket-book of the deceased had got out of his pocket in the water; but the evidence was very meagre, although the police appeared to have made every possible inquiry. The jury returned a verdict of "Found Drowned, though how the deceased came into the water there was no evidence to show".'

I know no more of the unfortunate man Lawrence than this, and I have only printed the cutting here because it probably induced Dorrington to take certain steps in the case I am dealing with. With that case the fate of the man Lawrence has nothing whatever to do. He passes out of the story entirely.

II

Mr Warren Telfer was a gentleman of means, and the owner of a few—very few—racehorses. But he had a great knack of buying hidden prizes in yearlings, and what his stable lacked in quantity it often more than made up for in quality. Thus he had once bought a St Leger winner for as little as a hundred and fifty pounds. Many will remember his bitter disappointment of ten or a dozen years back, when his horse, Matfelon, starting an odds-on favourite for the Two Thousand, never even got among the crowd, and ambled in streets behind everything. It was freely rumoured (and no doubt with cause) that Matfelon had been 'got at' and in some way 'nobbled'. There were hints of a certain bucket of water administered just before the race—a bucket of water observed in the hands, some said of one, some said of another person connected with Ritter's training establishment. There was no suspicion of pulling, for plainly the jockey was doing his best with the animal all the way along, and never had a tight rein. So a nobbling it must have been, said the knowing ones, and Mr Warren Telfer said so too, with much bitterness. More, he immediately removed his horses from Ritter's stables, and started a small training place of his own for his own horses merely; putting an old steeplechase jockey in charge, who had come out of a bad accident permanently lame, and had fallen on evil days.

The owner was an impulsive and violent-tempered man, who, once a notion was in his head, held to it through everything, and in spite of everything. His misfortune with Matfelon made him the most insanely distrustful man alive. In everything he fancied he saw a trick, and to him every man seemed a scoundrel. He could scarce bear to let the very stable-boys touch his horses, and although for years all went as well as could be expected in his stables, his suspicious distrust lost nothing of its virulence. He was perpetually fussing about the stables, making surprise visits, and laying futile traps that convicted nobody. The sole tangible result of this behaviour was a violent quarrel between Mr Warren Telfer and his nephew Richard, who had been making a lengthened stay with his uncle. Young Telfer, to tell the truth, was neither so discreet nor so exemplary in behaviour as he might have been, but his temper was that characteristic of the family, and when he conceived that his uncle had an idea that he was communicating stable secrets to friends outside, there was an animated row, and the nephew betook himself and his luggage somewhere else. Young Telfer always insisted, however, that his uncle was not a bad fellow on the whole, though he had habits of thought and conduct that made him altogether intolerable at times. But the uncle had no good word for his graceless nephew; and indeed Richard Telfer betted more than he could afford, and was not so particular in his choice of sporting acquaintances as a gentleman should have been.

Mr Warren Telfer's house, Blackhall, and his stables were little more than two miles from Redbury, in Hampshire; and after the quarrel Mr Richard Telfer was not seen near the place for many months—not, indeed, till excitement was high over the forthcoming race for the Redbury Stakes, for which there was an entry from the stable— Janissary, for long ranked second favourite; and then the owner's nephew did not enter the premises, and, in fact, made his visit as secret as possible.

I have said that Janissary was long ranked second favourite for the Redbury Stakes, but a little more than a week before the race he became first favourite, owing to a training mishap to the horse fancied first, which made its chances so poor that it might have been scratched at any moment. And so far was Janissary above the class of the field (though it was a two-year-old race, and there might be a surprise) that it at once went to far shorter odds than the previous favourite, which, indeed, had it run fit and well, would have found Janissary no easy colt to beat.

Mr Telfer's nephew was seen near the stables but two or three days before the race, and that day the owner despatched a telegram to the firm of Dorrington & Hicks. In response to the telegram, Dorrington caught the first available train for Redbury, and was with Mr Warren Telfer in his library by five in the afternoon.

'It is about my horse Janissary that I want to consult you, Mr Dorrington,' said Mr Telfer. 'It's right enough now —or at least was right at exercise this morning—but I feel certain that there's some diabolical plot on hand somewhere to interfere with the horse before the Redbury Stakes day, and I'm sorry to have to say that I suspect my own nephew to be mixed up in it in some way. In the first place I may tell you that there is no doubt whatever that the colt, if let alone, and bar accident, can win in a canter. He could have won even if Herald, the late favourite, had kept well, for I can tell you that Janissary is a far greater horse than anybody is aware of outside my establishment— or at any rate, than anybody ought to be aware of, if the stable secrets are properly kept. His pedigree is nothing very great, and he never showed his quality till quite lately, in private trials. Of course it has leaked out somehow that the colt is exceptionally good—I don't believe I can trust a soul in the place. How should the price have gone up to five to four unless somebody had been telling what he's paid not to tell? But that isn't all, as I have said. I've a conviction that something's on foot—somebody wants to interfere with the horse. Of course we get a tout about now and again, but the downs are pretty big, and we generally manage to dodge them if we want to. On the last three or four mornings, however, wherever Janissary might be taking his gallop, there was a big, hulking fellow, with a red beard and spectacles—not so much watching the horse as trying to get hold of the lad. I am always up at five, for I've found to my cost—you remember about Matfelon—that if a man doesn't want to be ramped he must never take his eye off things. Well, I have scarcely seen the lad ease the colt once on the last three or four mornings without that red-bearded fellow bobbing up from a knoll, or a clump of bushes, or something, close by—especially if Janissary was a bit away from the other horses, and not under my nose, or the head lad's, for a moment. I rode at the fellow, of course, when I saw what he was after, but he was artful as a cartload of monkeys, and vanished somehow before I could get near him. The head lad believes he has seen him about just after dark, too; but I am keeping the stable lads in when they're not riding, and I suppose he finds he has no chance of getting at them except when they're out with the horses. This morning, not only did I see this fellow about, as usual, but, I am ashamed to say, I observed my own nephew acting the part of a common tout. He certainly had the decency to avoid me and clear out, but that was not all, as you shall see. This morning, happening to approach the stables from the back, I suddenly came upon the red-bearded man—giving money to a groom of mine! He ran off at once, as you may guess, and I discharged the groom where he stood, and would not allow him into the stables again. He offered no explanation or excuse, but took himself off, and half an hour afterwards I almost sent away my head boy too. For when I told him of the dismissal, he admitted that he had seen that same groom taking money of my nephew at the back of the stables, an hour before, and had not informed me! He said that he thought that as it was "only Mr Richard" it didn't matter. Fool! Anyway, the groom has gone, and, so far as I can tell as yet, the colt is all right. I examined him at once, of course; and I also turned over a box that Weeks, the groom, used to keep brushes and odd things in. There I found this paper full of powder. I don't yet know what it is, but it's certainly nothing he had any business with in the stable. Will you take it?

'And now,' Mr Telfer went on, 'I'm in such an uneasy state that I want your advice and assistance. Quite apart from the suspicious—more than suspicious—circumstances I have informed you of, I am *certain*—I know it without being able to give precise reasons—I am *certain* that some attempt is being made at disabling Janissary before Thursday's race. I feel it in my bones, so to speak. I had the same suspicion just before that Two Thousand, when Matfelon was got at. The thing was in the air, as it is now. Perhaps it's a sort of instinct; but I rather think it is the result of an unconscious absorption of a number of little indications about me. Be it as it may, I am resolved to leave no opening to the enemy if I can help it, and I want to see if you can suggest any further precautions beyond those I am taking. Come and look at the stables.'

Dorrington could see no opening for any piece of rascality by which he might make more of the case than by serving his client loyally, so he resolved to do the latter. He followed Mr Telfer through the training stables, where eight or nine thoroughbreds stood, and could suggest no improvement upon the exceptional precautions that already existed.

'No,' said Dorrington, 'I don't think you can do any better than this—at least on this, the inner line of defence. But it is best to make the outer lines secure first. By the way, *this* isn't Janissary, is it? We saw him farther up the row, didn't we?'

'Oh no, that's a very different sort of colt, though he does look like, doesn't he? People who've been up and down the stables once or twice often confuse them. They're both bays, much of a build, and about the same height, and both have a bit of stocking on the same leg, though Janissary's is bigger, and this animal has a white star. But you never saw two creatures look so like and run so differently. This is a dead loss—not worth his feed. If I can manage to wind him up to something like a gallop I shall try to work him off in a selling plate somewhere; but as far as I can see he isn't good enough even for that. He's a disappointment. And his stock's far better than Janissary's too, and he cost half as much again! Yearlings are a lottery. Still, I've drawn a prize or two among them, at one time or another.'

'Ah yes, so I've heard. But now as to the outer defences I was speaking of. Let us find out *who* is trying to interfere with your horse. Do you mind letting me into the secrets of the stable commissions?'

'Oh no. We're talking in confidence, of course. I've backed the colt pretty heavily all round, but not too much anywhere. There's a good slice with Barker—you know Barker, of course; Mullins has a thousand down for him, and that was at five to one, before Herald went amiss. Then there's Ford and Lascelles—both good men, and Naylor— he's the smallest man of them all, and there's only a hundred or two with him, though he's been laying the horse pretty freely everywhere, at least until Herald went wrong. And there's Pedder. But there must have been a deal of money laid to outside backers, and there's no telling who may contemplate a ramp.'

'Just so. Now as to your nephew. What of your suspicions in that direction?'

'Perhaps I'm a little hasty as to that,' Mr Telfer answered, a little ashamed of what he had previously said. 'But I'm worried and mystified, as you see, and hardly know what to think. My nephew Richard is a little erratic, and he has a foolish habit of betting more than he can afford. He and I quarrelled some time back, while he was staying here, because I had an idea that he had been talking too freely outside. He had, in fact; and I regarded it as a breach of confidence. So there was a quarrel and he went away.'

'Very well. I wonder if I can get a bed at the "Crown" at Redbury: I'm afraid it'll be crowded, but I'll try.'

'But why trouble? Why not stay with me, and be near the stables?'

'Because then I should be of no more use to you than one of your lads. People who come out here every morning are probably staying at Redbury, and I must go there after them.'

III

The 'Crown' at Redbury was full in anticipation of the races, but Dorrington managed to get a room ordinarily occupied by one of the landlord's family, who undertook to sleep at a friend's for a night or two. This settled, he strolled into the yard, and soon fell into animated talk with the hostler on the subject of the forthcoming races. All the town was backing Janissary for the Stakes, the hostler said, and he advised Dorrington to do the same.

During this conversation two men stopped in the street, just outside the yard gate, talking. One was a big, heavy, vulgar-looking fellow in a box-cloth coat, and with a shaven face and hoarse voice; the other was a slighter, slimmer, younger and more gentlemanlike man, though there was a certain patchy colour about his face that seemed to hint of anything but teetotalism.

'There,' said the hostler, indicating the younger of these two men, 'that's young Mr Telfer, him as whose uncle's owner o' Janissary. He's a young plunger, he is, and he's on Janissary too. He give me the tip, straight, this mornin'. "You put your little bit on my uncle's colt," he said. "It's all right. I an't such pals with the old man as I was, but I've got the tip that *his* money's down on it. So don't neglect your opportunities, Thomas," he says; and I haven't. He's stoppin' in our house, is young Mr Richard.'

'And who is that he is talking to? A bookmaker?'

'Yes, sir, that's Naylor—Bob Naylor. He's got Mr Richard's bets. P'raps he's puttin' on a bit more now.'

The men at the gate separated, and the bookmaker walked off down the street in the fast gathering dusk. Richard Telfer, however, entered the house, and Dorrington followed him. Telfer mounted the stairs and went into his room. Dorrington lingered a moment on the stairs and then went and knocked at Telfer's door.

'Hullo!' cried Telfer, coming to the door and peering out into the gloomy corridor.

'I beg pardon,' Dorrington replied courteously. 'I thought this was Naylor's room.'

'No—it's No. 23, by the end. But I believe he's just gone down the street.'

Dorrington expressed his thanks and went to his own room. He took one or two small instruments from his bag and hurried stealthily to the door of No. 23.

All was quiet, and the door opened at once to Dorrington's picklock, for there was nothing but the common tumbler rimlock to secure it. Dorrington, being altogether an unscrupulous scoundrel, would have thought nothing of entering a man's room thus for purposes of mere robbery. Much less scruple had he in doing so in the present circumstances. He lit the candle in a little pocket lantern, and, having secured the door, looked quickly about the room. There was nothing unusual to attract his attention, and he turned to two bags lying near the dressing-table. One was the usual bookmaker's satchel, and the other was a leather travelling-bag; both were locked. Dorrington unbuckled the straps of the large bag and produced a slender picklock of steel wire, with a sliding joint, which, with a little skilful 'humouring', turned the lock in the course of a minute or two. One glance inside was enough. There on the top lay a large false beard of strong red, and upon the shirts below was a pair of spectacles. But Dorrington went farther, and felt carefully below the linen till his hand met a small, flat, mahogany box. This he withdrew and opened. Within, on a velvet lining, lay a small silver instrument resembling a syringe. He shut and replaced the box, and, having rearranged the contents of the bag, shut, locked and strapped it, and blew out his light. He had found what he came to look for. In another minute Mr Bob Naylor's door was locked behind him, and Dorrington took his picklocks to his own room.

It was a noisy evening in the Commercial Room at the 'Crown'. Chaff and laughter flew thick, and Richard Telfer threatened Naylor with a terrible settling day. More was drunk than thirst strictly justified, and everybody grew friendly with everybody else. Dorrington, sober and keenly alert, affected the reverse, and exhibited especial and extreme affection for Mr Bob Naylor. His advances were unsuccessful at first, but Dorrington's manner and the 'Crown' whisky overcame the bookmaker's reserve, and at about eleven o'clock the two left the house arm in arm for a cooling stroll in the High Street. Dorrington blabbed and chattered with great success, and soon began about Janissary.

'So you've pretty well done all you want with Janissary, eh? Book full? Ah! nothing like keeping a book even all round—it's the safest way—'specially with such a colt as Janissary about. Eh, my boy?' He nudged Naylor genially. 'Ah! no doubt it's a good colt, but old Telfer has rum notions about preparation, hasn't he?'

'I dunno,' replied Naylor. 'How do you mean?'

'Why, what does he have the horse led up and down behind the stable for, half an hour every afternoon?'

'Didn't know he did.'

'Ah! but he does. I came across it only this afternoon. I was coming over the downs, and just as I got round behind Telfer's stables there I saw a fine bay colt, with a white stocking on the off hind leg, well covered up in a suit of clothes, being led up and down by a lad, like a sentry—up and down, up and down—about twenty yards each way, and nobody else about. "Hullo!" says I to the lad, "hullo! what horse is this?" "Janissary," says the boy—pretty free for a stable-lad. "Ah!" says I. "And what are you walking him like that for?" "Dunno," says the boy, "but it's gov'nor's orders. Every afternoon, at two to the minute, I have to bring him out here and walk him like this for half an hour exactly, neither more or less, and then he goes in and has a handful of malt. But I dunno why." "Well," says I, "I never heard of that being done before. But he's a fine colt," and I put my hand under the cloth and felt him—hard as nails and smooth as silk.'

'And the boy let you touch him?'

'Yes; he struck me as a bit easy for a stable-boy. But it's an odd trick, isn't it, that of the half-hour's walk and the handful of malt? Never hear of anybody else doing it, did you?'

'No, I never did.'

They talked and strolled for another quarter of an hour, and then finished up with one more drink.

IV

The next was the day before the race, and in the morning Dorrington, making a circuit, came to Mr Warren Telfer's from the farther side. As soon as they were assured of privacy: 'Have you seen the man with the red beard this morning?' asked Dorrington.

'No; I looked out pretty sharply, too.'

'That's right. If you like to fall in with my suggestions, however, you shall see him at about two o'clock, and take a handsome rise out of him.'

'Very well,' Mr Telfer replied. 'What's your suggestion?'

'I'll tell you. In the first place, what's the value of that other horse that looks so like Janissary?'

'Hamid is his name. He's worth—well, what he will fetch. I'll sell him for fifty and be glad of the chance.'

'Very good. Then you'll no doubt be glad to risk his health temporarily to make sure of the Redbury Stakes, and to get longer prices for anything you may like to put on between now and to-morrow afternoon. Come to the stables and I'll tell you. But first, is there a place where we may command a view of the ground behind the stables without being seen?'

'Yes, there's a ventilation grating at the back of each stall.'

'Good! Then we'll watch from Hamid's stall, which will be empty. Select your most wooden-faced and most careful boy, and send him out behind the stable with Hamid at two o'clock to the moment. Put the horse in a full suit of clothes—it is necessary to cover up that white star—and tell the lad he must *lead* it up and down slowly for twenty yards or so. I rather expect the red-bearded man will be coming along between two o'clock and half-past two. You will understand that Hamid is to be Janissary for the occasion. You must drill your boy to appear a bit of a fool, and to overcome his stable education sufficiently to chatter freely—so long as it is the proper chatter. The man may ask the horse's name, or he may not. Anyway, the boy mustn't forget it is Janissary he is leading. You have an odd fad, you must know (and the boy must know it too) in the matter of training. This ridiculous fad is to have your colt walked up and down for half an hour exactly at two o'clock every afternoon, and then given a handful of malt as he comes in. The boy can talk as freely about this as he pleases, and also about the colt's chances, and anything else he likes; and he is to let the stranger come up, talk to the horse, pat him—in short, to do as he pleases. Is that plain?'

'Perfectly. You have found out something about this red-bearded chap then?'

'Oh, yes—it's Naylor the bookmaker, as a matter of fact, with a false beard.'

'What! Naylor?'

'Yes. You see the idea, of course. Once Naylor thinks he has nobbled the favourite he will lay it to any extent, and the odds will get longer. Then you can make him pay for his little games.'

'Well, yes, of course. Though I wouldn't put too much with Naylor in any case. He's not a big man, and he might break and lose me the lot. But I can get it out of the others.'

'Just so. You'd better see about schooling your boy now, I think. I'll tell you more presently.'

A minute or two before two o'clock Dorrington and Telfer, mounted on a pair of steps, were gazing through the ventilation grating of Hamid's stall, while the colt, clothed completely, was led around. Then Dorrington described his operations of the previous evening.

'No matter what he may think of my tale,' he said,

'Naylor will be pretty sure to come. He has tried to bribe your stablemen, and has been baffled. Every attempt to get hold of the boy in charge of Janissary has failed, and he will be glad to clutch at any shadow of a chance to save his money now. Once he is here, and the favourite apparently at his mercy, the thing is done. By the way, I expect your nephew's little present to the man you sacked was a fairly innocent one. No doubt he merely asked the man whether Janissary was keeping well, and was thought good enough to win, for I find he is backing it pretty heavily. Naylor came afterwards, with much less innocent intentions, but fortunately you were down on him in time. Several considerations induced me to go to Naylor's room. In the first place, I have heard rather shady tales of his doings on one or two occasions, and he did not seem a sufficiently big man to stand to lose a great deal over your horse. Then, when I saw him, I observed that his figure bore a considerable resemblance to that of the man you had described, except as regards the red beard and the spectacles—articles easily enough assumed, and, indeed, often enough used by the scum of the ring whose trade is welshing. And, apart from these considerations, here, at any rate, was one man who had an interest in keeping your colt from winning, and here was his room waiting for me to explore. So I explored it, and the card turned up trumps.'

As he was speaking, the stable-boy, a stolid-looking youngster, was leading Hamid back and forth on the turf before their eyes.

'There's somebody,' said Dorrington suddenly, 'over in that clump of trees. Yes—our man, sure enough. I felt pretty sure of him after you had told me that he hadn't thought it worth while to turn up this morning. Here he comes.'

Naylor, with his red beard sticking out over the collar of his big coat, came slouching along with an awkwardly assumed air of carelessness and absence of mind.

'Hullo!' he said suddenly, as he came abreast of the

horse, turning as though but now aware of its presence, 'that's a valuable sort of horse, ain't it, my lad?'

'Yes,' said the boy, 'it is. He's goin' to win the Redbury Stakes to-morrow. It's Janissary.'

'Oh! Janey Sairey, is it?' Naylor answered, with a quaint affectation of gaping ignorance. 'Janey Sairey, eh? Well, she do look a fine 'orse, what I can see of 'er. What a suit o' clo'es! An' so she's one o' the 'orses that runs in races, is she? Well, I never! Pretty much like other 'orses, too, to look at, ain't she? Only a bit thin in the legs.'

The boy stood carelessly by the colt's side, and the man approached. His hand came quickly from an inner pocket, and then he passed it under Hamid's cloths, near the shoulder. 'Ah, it do feel a lovely skin, to be sure!' he said. 'An' so there's goin' to be races at Redbury to-morrow, is there? I dunno anythin' about races myself, an'— Oo my!'

Naylor sprang back as the horse, flinging back its ears, started suddenly, swung round, and reared. 'Lor,' he said, 'what a vicious brute! Jist because I stroked her! I'll be careful about touching racehorses again.' His hand passed stealthily to the pocket again, and he hurried on his way, while the stable-boy steadied and soothed Hamid.

Telfer and Dorrington sniggered quietly in their concealment. 'He's taken a deal of trouble, hasn't he?' Dorrington remarked. 'It's a sad case of the biter bit for Mr Naylor, I'm afraid. That was a prick the colt felt— hypodermic injection with the syringe I saw in the bag, no doubt. The boy won't be such a fool as to come in again at once, will he? If Naylor's taking a look back from anywhere, that may make him suspicious.'

'No fear. I've told him to keep out for the half-hour, and he'll do it. Dear, dear, what an innocent person Mr Bob Naylor is! "Well, I never! Pretty much like other horses!" He didn't know there were to be races at Redbury! "Janey Sairey," too—it's really very funny!'

Ere the half-hour was quite over, Hamid came stumbling and dragging into the stable yard, plainly all amiss, and collapsed on his litter as soon as he gained his stall. There he lay, shivering and drowsy.

'I expect he'll get over it in a day or two,' Dorrington remarked. 'I don't suppose a vet could do much for him just now, except, perhaps, give him a drench and let him take a rest. Certainly, the effect will last over tomorrow. That's what it is calculated for.'

V

The Redbury Stakes were run at three in the afternoon, after two or three minor events had been disposed of. The betting had undergone considerable fluctuations during the morning, but in general it ruled heavily against Janissary. The story had got about, too, that Mr Warren Telfer's colt would not start. So that when the numbers went up, and it was seen that Janissary was starting after all, there was much astonishment, and a good deal of uneasiness in the ring.

'It's a pity we can't see our friend Naylor's face just now, isn't it?' Dorrington remarked to his client, as they looked on from Mr Telfer's drag.

'Yes; it would be interesting,' Telfer replied. 'He was quite confident last night, you say.'

'Quite. I tested him by an offer of a small bet on your colt, asking some points over the odds, and he took it at once. Indeed, I believe he has been going about gathering up all the wagers he could about Janissary, and the market has felt it. Your nephew has risked some more with him, I believe, and altogether it looks as though the town would spoil the "bookies" badly.'

As the horses came from the weighing enclosure, Janissary was seen conspicuous among them, bright, clean, and firm, and a good many faces lengthened at the sight. The start was not so good as it might have been, but the favourite (the starting-price had gone to evens) was not left, and got away well in the crowd of ten starters. There he lay till rounding the bend, when the Telfer blue and chocolate was seen among the foremost, and near the rails. Mr Telfer almost trembled as he watched through his glasses.

'Hang that Willett!' he said, almost to himself. 'He's *too* clever against those rails before getting clear. All right, though, all right! He's coming!'

Janissary, indeed, was showing in front, and as the horses came along the straight it was plain that Mr Telfer's colt was holding the field comfortably. There were changes in the crowd; some dropped away, some came out and attempted to challenge for the lead, but the favourite, striding easily, was never seriously threatened, and in the end, being a little let out, came in a three-lengths winner, never once having been made to show his best.

'I congratulate you, Mr Telfer,' said Dorrington, 'and you may congratulate me.'

'Certainly, certainly,' said Mr Telfer hastily, hurrying off to lead in the winner.

It was a bad race for the ring, and in the open parts of the course many a humble fielder grabbed his satchel ere the shouting was over, and made his best pace for the horizon; and more than one pair of false whiskers, as red as Naylor's, came off suddenly while the owner betook himself to a fresh stand. Unless a good many outsiders sailed home before the end of the week there would be a bad Monday for layers. But all sporting Redbury was jubilant. They had all been 'on' the local favourite for the local race, and it had won.

VI

Mr Bob Naylor 'got a bit back', in his own phrase, on other races by the end of the week, but all the same he saw a black settling day ahead. He had been done—done for a certainty. He had realized this as soon as he saw the numbers go up for the Redbury Stakes. Janissary had not been drugged after all. That meant that another horse had been substituted for him, and that the whole thing was an elaborate plant. He thought he knew Janissary pretty well by sight, too, and rather prided himself on having an eye for a horse. But clearly it was a plant—a complete do. Telfer was in it, and so of course was that gentlemanly stranger who had strolled along Redbury High Street with him that night, telling that cock-and-bull story about the afternoon walks and the handful of malt. There was a nice schoolboy tale to take in a man who thought himself broad as Cheapside! He cursed himself high and low. To be done, and to know it, was a galling thing, but this would be worse. The tale would get about. They would boast of a clever stroke like that, and that would injure him with everybody; with honest men, because his reputation, as it was, would bear no worsening, and with knaves like himself, because they would laugh at him, and leave him out when any little co-operative swindle was in contemplation. But though the chagrin of the defeat was bitter bad enough, his losses were worse. He had taken everything offered on Janissary after he had nobbled the wrong horse, and had given almost any odds demanded. Do as he might, he could see nothing but a balance against him on Monday, which, though he might pay out his last cent, he could not cover by several hundred pounds.

But on the day he met his customers at his club, as usual, and paid out freely. Young Richard Telfer, however, with whom he was heavily 'in', he put off till the evening. 'I've been a bit disappointed this morning over some ready that was to be paid over,' he said, 'and I've used the last cheque-form in my book. You might come and have a bit of dinner with me to-night, Mr Telfer, and take it then.'

Telfer assented without difficulty.

'All right, then, that's settled. You know the place—
Gold Street. Seven sharp. The missis 'll be pleased to see
you, I'm sure, Mr Telfer. Let's see—it's fifteen hundred and
thirty altogether, isn't it?'

'Yes, that's it. I'll come.'

Young Telfer left the club, and at the corner of the street
ran against Dorrington. Telfer, of course, knew him as his
late fellow-guest at the 'Crown' at Redbury, and this was
their first meeting in London after their return from the
races.

'Ah!' said Telfer. 'Going to draw a bit of Janissary
money, eh?'

'Oh, I haven't much to draw,' Dorrington answered.
'But I expect your pockets are pretty heavy, if you've just
come from Naylor.'

'Yes, I've just come from Naylor, but I haven't touched
the merry sovs just yet,' replied Telfer cheerfully. 'There's
been a run on Naylor, and I'm going to dine with him and
his respectable missis this evening, and draw the plunder
then. I feel rather curious to see what sort of establishment
a man like Naylor keeps going. His place is in Gold Street,
Chelsea.'

'Yes, I believe so. Anyhow, I congratulate you on your
haul, and wish you a merry evening.' And the two men
parted.

Dorrington had, indeed, a few pounds to draw as a result
of his 'fishing' bet with Naylor, but now he resolved to ask
for the money at his own time. This invitation to Telfer took
his attention, and it reminded him oddly of the circumstances detailed in the report of the inquest on Lawrence,
transcribed at the beginning of this paper. He had cut out
this report at the time it appeared, because he saw certain
singularities about the case, and he had filed it, as he had
done hundred of other such cuttings. And now certain
things led him to fancy that he might be much interested to
observe the proceedings at Naylor's house on the evening

after a bad settling-day. He resolved to gratify himself with a strict professional watch in Gold Street that evening, on chance of something coming of it. For it was an important thing in Dorrington's rascally trade to get hold of as much of other people's private business as possible, and to know exactly in what cupboard to find every man's skeleton. For there was no knowing but it might be turned into money sooner or later. So he found the number of Naylor's house from the handiest directory, and at six o'clock, a little disguised by a humbler style of dress than usual, he began his watch.

Naylor's house was at the corner of a turning, with the flank wall blank of windows, except for one at the top; and a public-house stood at the opposite corner. Dorrington, skilled in watching without attracting attention to himself, now lounged in the public-house bar, now stood at the street corner, and now sauntered along the street, a picture of vacancy of mind, and looking, apparently, at everything in turn, except the house at the corner. The first thing he noted was the issuing forth from the area steps of a healthy-looking girl in much gaily beribboned finery. Plainly a servant taking an evening out. This was an odd thing, that a servant should be allowed out on an evening when a guest was expected to dinner; and the house looked like one where it was more likely that one servant would be kept than two. Dorrington hurried after the girl, and, changing his manner of address, to that of a civil labourer, said—

'Beg pardon, Miss, but is Mary Walker still in service at your 'ouse?'

'Mary Walker?' said the girl. 'Why, no. I never 'eard the name. And there ain't nobody in service there but me.'

'Beg pardon—it must be the wrong 'ouse. It's my cousin, Miss, that's all.'

Dorrington left the girl and returned to the public-house. As he reached it he perceived a second noticeable thing. Although it was broad daylight, there was now a light behind the solitary window at the top of the side-wall of Naylor's house. Dorrington slipped through the swing-doors of the public-house and watched through the glass.

It was a bare room behind the high window—it might have been a bathroom—and its interior was made but dimly visible from outside by the light. A tall, thin woman was setting up an ordinary pair of house-steps in the middle of the room. This done, she turned to the window and pulled down the blind, and as she did so Dorrington noted her very extreme thinness, both of face and body. When the blind was down the light still remained within. Again there seemed some significance in this. It appeared that the thin woman had waited until her servant had gone before doing whatever she had to do in that room. Presently the watcher came again into Gold Street, and from there caught a passing glimpse of the thin woman as she moved busily about the front room over the breakfast parlour.

Clearly, then, the light above had been left for future use. Dorrington thought for a minute, and then suddenly stopped, with a snap of the fingers. He saw it all now. Here was something altogether in his way. He would take a daring course.

He withdrew once more to the public-house, and ordering another drink, took up a position in a compartment from which he could command a view both of Gold Street and the side turning. The time now, he saw by his watch, was ten minutes to seven. He had to wait rather more than a quarter of an hour before seeing Richard Telfer come walking jauntily down Gold Street, mount the steps, and knock at Naylor's door. There was a momentary glimpse of the thin woman's face at the door, and then Telfer entered.

It now began to grow dusk, and in about twenty minutes more Dorrington took to the street again. The room over the breakfast-parlour was clearly the dining-room. It was lighted brightly, and by intent listening the watcher could distinguish, now and again, a sudden burst of laughter from Telfer, followed by the deeper grunts of Naylor's voice, and once by sharp tones that it seemed natural to suppose were the thin woman's.

Dorrington waited no longer, but slipped a pair of thick sock-feet over his shoes, and, after a quick look along the two streets, to make sure nobody was near, he descended the area steps. There was no light in the breakfast-parlour. With his knife he opened the window-catch, raised the sash quietly and stepped over the sill, and stood in the dark room within.

All was quiet, except for the talking in the room above. He had done but what many thieves—'parlour-jumpers'—do every day; but there was more ahead. He made his way silently to the basement passage, and passed into the kitchen. The room was lighted, and cookery utensils were scattered about, but nobody was there. He waited till he heard a request in Naylor's gruff voice for 'another slice' of something, and noiselessly mounted the stairs. He noticed that the dining-room door was ajar, but passed quickly on to the second flight, and rested on the landing above. Mrs Naylor would probably have to go downstairs once or twice again, but he did not expect anybody in the upper part of the house just yet. There was a small flight of stairs above the landing whereon he stood, leading to the servant's bedroom and the bathroom. He took a glance at the bathroom with its feeble lamp, its steps, and its open ceiling-trap, and returned again to the bedroom landing. There he stood, waiting watchfully.

Twice the thin woman emerged from the dining-room, went downstairs and came up again, each time with food and plates. Then she went down once more, and was longer gone. Meantime Naylor and Telfer were talking and joking loudly at the table.

When once again Dorrington saw the crown of the thin woman's head rising over the bottom stair, he perceived that she bore a tray set with cups already filled with coffee. These she carried into the dining-room, whence presently came the sound of striking matches. After this the conversation seemed to flag, and Telfer's part in it grew less and less, till it ceased altogether, and the house was silent, except for a sound of heavy breathing. Soon this became almost a snore, and then there was a sudden noisy tumble, as of a drunken man; but still the snoring went on, and the Naylors were talking in whispers.

There was a shuffling and heaving sound, and a chair was knocked over. Then at the dining-room door appeared Naylor, walking backward, and carrying the inert form of Telfer by the shoulders, while the thin woman followed, supporting the feet. Dorrington retreated up the small stair-flight, cocking a pocket revolver as he went.

Up the stairs they came, Naylor puffing and grunting with exertion, and Telfer still snoring soundly on, till at last, having mounted the top flight, they came in at the bathroom door, where Dorrington stood to receive them, smiling and bowing pleasantly, with his hat in one hand and his revolver in the other.

The woman, from her position, saw him first, and dropped Telfer's legs with a scream. Naylor turned his head and then also dropped his end. The drugged man fell in a heap, snoring still.

Naylor, astounded and choking, made as if to rush at the interloper, but Dorrington thrust the revolver into his face, and exclaimed, still smiling courteously, 'Mind, mind! It's a dangerous thing, is a revolver, and apt to go off if you run against it!'

He stood thus for a second, and then stepped forward and took the woman—who seemed like to swoon—by the arm, and pulled her into the room. 'Come, Mrs Naylor,' he said, 'you're not one of the fainting sort, and I think I'd better keep two such clever people as you under my eye, or one of you may get into mischief. Come now, Naylor, we'll talk business.'

Naylor, now white as a ghost, sat on the edge of the bath, and stared at Dorrington as though in a fascination of terror. His hands rested on the bath at each side, and an odd sound of gurgling came from his thick throat.

'We will talk business,' Dorrington resumed. 'Come, you've met me before now you know—at Redbury. You can't have forgotten Janissary, and the walking exercise and the handful of malt. I'm afraid you're a clumsy sort of rascal, Naylor, though you do your best. I'm a rascal myself (though I don't often confess it), and I assure you that your conceptions are crude as yet. Still, that isn't a bad notion in its way, that of drugging a man and drowning him in your cistern up there in the roof, when you prefer not to pay him his winnings. It has the very considerable merit that, after the body has been fished out of any river you may choose to fling it into, the stupid coroner's jury will never suspect that it was drowned in any other water but that. Just as happened in the Lawrence case, for instance. You remember that, eh? So do I, very well, and it was because I remembered that that I paid you this visit to-night. But you do the thing much too clumsily, really. When I saw a light up here in broad daylight I knew at once it must be left for some purpose to be executed later in the evening; and when I saw the steps carefully placed at the same time, after the servant had been sent out, why the thing was plain, remembering, as I did, the curious coincidence that Mr Lawrence was drowned the very evening he had been here to take away his winnings. The steps *must* be intended to give access to the roof, where there was probably a tank to feed the bath, and what more secret place to drown a man than there? And what easier place, so long as the man was well drugged, and there was a strong lid to the tank? As I say, Naylor, your notion was meritorious, but your execution was wretched—perhaps because you had no notion that I was watching you.'

He paused, and then went on. 'Come,' he said, 'collect

your scattered faculties, both of you. I shan't hand you over to the police for this little invention of yours; it's too useful an invention to give away to the police. I shan't hand you over, that is to say, as long as you do as I tell you. If you get mutinous, you shall hang, both of you, for the Lawrence business. I may as well tell you that I'm a bit of a scoundrel myself, by way of profession. I don't boast about it, but it's well to be frank in making arrangements of this sort. I'm going to take you into my service. I employ a few agents, and you and your tank may come in very handy from time to time. But we must set it up, with a few improvements, in another house—a house which hasn't quite such an awkward window. And we mustn't execute our little suppressions so regularly on settling-day; it looks suspicious. So as soon as you can get your faculties together we'll talk over this thing.'

The man and the woman had exchanged glances during this speech, and now Naylor asked, huskily, jerking his thumb toward the man on the floor, 'An'—an' what about 'im?'

'What about him? Why, get rid of him as soon as you like. Not that way, though.' (He pointed toward the ceiling trap.) 'It doesn't pay *me*, and I'm master now. Besides, what will people say when you tell the same tale at his inquest that you told at Lawrence's? No, my friend, bookmaking and murder don't assort together, profitable as the combination may seem. Settling-days are too regular. And I'm not going to be your accomplice, mind. You are going to be mine. Do what you please with Telfer. Leave him on somebody's doorstep if you like.'

'But I owe him fifteen hundred, and I ain't got more than half of it! I'll be ruined!'

'Very likely,' Dorrington returned placidly. 'Be ruined as soon as possible, then, and devote all your time to my business. You're not to ornament the ring any longer, remember—you're to assist a private inquiry agent, you and your wife and your charming tank. Repudiate the debt if you like—it's a mere gaming transaction, and there is no legal claim—or leave him in the street and tell him he's been robbed. Please yourself as to this little roguery— you may as well, for it's the last you will do on your own account. For the future your respectable talents will be devoted to the service of Dorrington & Hicks, private inquiry agents; and if you don't give satisfaction, that eminent firm will hang you, with the assistance of the judge at the Old Bailey. So settle your business yourselves, and quickly, for I've a good many things to arrange with you.'

And, Dorrington watching them continually, they took Telfer out by the side gate in the garden wall and left him in a dark corner.

V

Murder by Proxy

M. McD. Bodkin Q.C.

At two o'clock precisely on that sweltering 12th of August, Eric Neville, young, handsome, *debonair*, sauntered through the glass door down the wrought-iron staircase into the beautiful, old-fashioned garden of Berkly Manor, radiant in white flannel, with a broad-brimmed Panama hat perched lightly on his glossy black curls, for he had just come from lazing in his canoe along the shadiest stretches of the river, with a book for company.

The back of the Manor House was the south wall of the garden, which stretched away for nearly a mile, gay with blooming flowers and ripening fruit. The air, heavy with perfume, stole softly through all the windows, now standing wide open in the sunshine, as though the great house gasped for breath.

When Eric's trim, tan boot left the last step of the iron staircase it reached the broad gravelled walk of the garden. Fifty yards off the head gardener was tending his peaches, the smoke from his pipe hanging like a faint blue haze in the still air that seemed to quiver with the heat. Eric, as he reached him, held out a petitionary hand, too lazy to speak.

Without a word the gardener stretched for a huge peach that was striving to hide its red face from the sun under narrow ribbed leaves, plucked it as though he loved it, and put it softly in the young man's hand.

Eric stripped off the velvet coat, rose-coloured, green, and amber, till it hung round the fruit in tatters, and made his sharp, white teeth meet in the juicy flesh of the ripe peach.

BANG!

The sudden shock of sound close to their ears wrenched the nerves of the two men; one dropped his peach, and the other his pipe. Both stared about them in utter amazement.

'Look there, sir,' whispered the gardener, pointing to a little cloud of smoke oozing lazily through a window almost directly over their head, while the pungent spice of gunpowder made itself felt in the hot air.

'My uncle's room,' gasped Eric. 'I left him only a moment ago fast asleep on the sofa.'

He turned as he spoke, and ran like a deer along the garden walk, up the iron steps, and back through the glass door into the house, the old gardener following as swiftly as his rheumatism would allow.

Eric crossed the sitting-room on which the glass door opened, went up the broad, carpeted staircase four steps at a time, turned sharply to the right down a broad corridor, and burst straight through the open door of his uncle's study.

Fast as he had come, there was another before him. A tall, strong figure, dressed in light tweed, was bending over the sofa where, a few minutes before, Eric had seen his uncle asleep.

Eric recognized the broad back and brown hair at once.

'John,' he cried, 'John, what is it?'

His cousin turned to him a handsome, manly face, ghastly pale now even to the lips.

'Eric, my boy,' he answered falteringly, 'this is too awful. Uncle has been murdered—shot stone dead.'

'No, no; it cannot be. It's not five minutes since I saw

him quietly sleeping,' Eric began. Then his eyes fell on the still figure on the sofa, and he broke off abruptly.

Squire Neville lay with his face to the wall, only the outline of his strong, hard features visible. The charge of shot had entered at the base of the skull, the grey hair was all dabbled with blood, and the heavy, warm drops still fell slowly on to the carpet.

'But who can have . . .' Eric gasped out, almost speechless with horror.

'It must have been his own gun,' his cousin answered. 'It was lying there on the table, to the right, barrel still smoking, when I came in.'

'It wasn't suicide—was it?' asked Eric, in a frightened whisper.

'Quite impossible, I should say. You see where he is hit.'

'But it was so sudden. I ran the moment I heard the shot, and you were before me. Did you see anyone?'

'Not a soul. The room was empty.'

'But how could the murderer escape?'

'Perhaps he leapt through the window. It was open when I came in.'

'He couldn't do that, Master John.' It was the voice of the gardener at the door. 'Me and Master Eric was right under the window when the shot came.'

'Then how in the devil's name did he disappear, Simpson?'

'It's not for me to say, sir.'

John Neville searched the room with eager eyes. There was no cover in it for a cat. A bare, plain room, panelled with brown oak, on which hung some guns and fishing-rods—old fashioned for the most part, but of the finest workmanship and material. A small bookcase in the corner was the room's sole claim to be called 'a study'. The huge leather-covered sofa on which the corpse lay, a massive round table in the centre of the room, and a few heavy chairs completed the furniture. The dust lay thick on everything, the fierce sunshine streamed in a broad band across the room. The air was stifling with the heat and the acrid smoke of gunpowder.

John Neville noticed how pale his young cousin was. He laid his hand on his shoulder with the protecting kindness of an elder brother.

'Come, Eric,' he said softly, 'we can do no good here.'

'We had best look round first, hadn't we, for some clue?' asked Eric, and he stretched his hand towards the gun; but John stopped him.

'No, no,' he cried hastily, 'we must leave things just as we find them. I'll send a man to the village for Wardle and telegraph to London for a detective.'

He drew his young cousin gently from the room, locked the door on the outside and put the key in his pocket.

'Who shall I wire to?' John Neville called from his desk with pencil poised over the paper, to his cousin, who sat at the library table with his head buried in his hands. 'It will need be a sharp man—one who can give his whole time to it.'

'I don't know any one. Yes, I do. That fellow with the queer name that found the Duke of Southern's opal— Beck. That's it. Thornton Crescent, W.C., will find him.'

John Neville filled in the name and address to the telegram he had already written—

'Come at once. Case of murder. Expense no object. John Neville, Berkly Manor, Dorset.'

Little did Eric guess that the filling in of that name was to him a matter of life or death.

John Neville had picked up a time-table and rustled through the leaves. 'Hard lines, Eric,' he said, 'do his best, he cannot get here before midnight. But here's Wardle already, anyhow; that's quick work.'

A shrewd, silent man was Wardle, the local constable, who now came briskly up the broad avenue; strong and active too, though well over fifty years of age.

John Neville met him at the door with the news. But the groom had already told of the murder.

'You did the right thing to lock the door, sir,' said Wardle, as they passed into the library where Eric still sat apparently unconscious of their presence, 'and you wired for a right good man. I've worked with this here Mr Beck before now. A pleasant man and a lucky one. "No hurry, Mr Wardle," he says to me, "and no fuss. Stir nothing. The things about the corpse have always a story of their own if they are let tell it, and I always like to have the first quiet little chat with them myself".'

So the constable held his tongue and kept his hands quiet and used his eyes and ears, while the great house buzzed with gossip. There was a whisper here and a whisper there, and the whispers patched themselves into a story. By slow degrees dark suspicion settled down and closed like a cloud round John Neville.

Its influence seemed to pass in some strange fashion through the closed doors of the library. John began pacing the room restlessly from end to end.

After a little while the big room was not big enough to hold his impatience. He wandered out aimlessly, as it seemed, from one room to another; now down the iron steps to gaze vacantly at the window of his uncle's room, now past the locked door in the broad corridor.

With an elaborate pretence of carelessness Wardle kept him in sight through all his wanderings, but John Neville seemed too self-absorbed to notice it.

Presently he returned to the library. Eric was there, still sitting with his back to the door, only the top of his head showing over the high chair. He seemed absorbed in thought or sleep, he sat so still.

But he started up with a quick cry, showing a white, frightened face, when John touched him lightly on the arm.

'Come for a walk in the grounds, Eric?' he said. 'This

waiting and watching and doing nothing is killing work; I cannot stand it much longer.'

'I'd rather not, if you don't mind,' Eric answered wearily, 'I feel completely knocked over.'

'A mouthful of fresh air would do you good, my poor boy; you do look done up.'

Eric shook his head.

'Well, I'm off,' John said.

'If you leave me the key, I will give it to the detective, if he comes.'

'Oh, he cannot be here before midnight, and I'll be back in an hour.'

As John Neville walked rapidly down the avenue without looking back, Wardle stepped quietly after, keeping him well in view.

Presently Neville turned abruptly in amongst the woods, the constable still following cautiously. The trees stood tall and well apart, and the slanting sunshine made lanes of vivid green through the shade. As Wardle crossed between Neville and the sun his shadow fell long and black on the bright green.

John Neville saw the shadow move in front of him and turned sharp round and faced his pursuer.

The constable stood stock still and stared.

'Well, Wardle, what is it? Don't stand there like a fool fingering your baton! Speak out, man—what do you want of me?'

'You see how it is, Master John,' the constable stammered out, 'I don't believe it myself. I've known you twenty-one years—since you were born, I may say—and I don't believe it, not a blessed word of it. But duty is duty, and I must go through with it; and facts is facts, and you and he had words last night, and Master Eric found you first in the room when . . .'

John Neville listened, bewildered at first. Then suddenly, as it seemed to dawn on him for the first time that he *could* be suspected of this murder, he kindled a sudden hot blaze of anger.

He turned fiercely on the constable. Broad-chested, strong limbed, he towered over him, terrible in his wrath; his hands clenched, his muscles quivered, his strong white teeth shut tight as a rat-trap, and a reddish light shining at the back of his brown eyes.

'How dare you! how dare you!' he hissed out between his teeth, his passion choking him.

He looked dangerous, that roused young giant, but Wardle met his angry eyes without flinching.

'Where's the use, Master John?' he said soothingly. 'It's main hard on you, I know. But the fault isn't mine, and you won't help yourself by taking it that way.'

The gust of passion appeared to sweep by as suddenly as it arose. The handsome face cleared and there was no trace of anger in the frank voice that answered. 'You are right, Wardle, quite right. What is to be done next? Am I to consider myself under arrest?'

'Better not, sir. You've got things to do a prisoner couldn't do handy, and I don't want to stand in the way of your doing them. If you give me your word it will be enough.'

'My word for what?'

'That you'll be here when wanted.'

'Why, man, you don't think I'd be fool enough—innocent or guilty—to run away. My God! run away from a charge of murder!'

'Don't take on like that, sir. There's a man coming from London that will set things straight, you'll see. Have I your word?'

'You have my word.'

'Perhaps you'd better be getting back to the house, sir. There's a deal of talking going on amongst the servants. I'll keep out of the way, and no one will be the wiser for anything that has passed between us.'

Half-way up the avenue a fast-driven dog-cart overtook John Neville, and pulled up so sharply that the horse's hoofs sent the coarse gravel flying. A stout, thick-set man, who up to that had been in close chat with the driver, leapt out more lightly than could have been expected from his figure.

'Mr John Neville, I presume? My name is Beck—Mr Paul Beck.'

'Mr Beck! Why, I thought you couldn't have got here before midnight.'

'Special train,' Mr Beck answered pleasantly. 'Your wire said "Expense no object". Well, time is an object, and comfort is an object too, more or less, in all these cases; so I took a special train, and here I am. With your permission, we will send the trap on and walk to the house together. This seems a bad business, Mr Neville. Shot dead, the driver tells me. Any one suspected?'

'I'm suspected.' The answer broke from John Neville's lips almost fiercely.

Mr Beck looked at him for a minute with placid curiosity, without a touch of surprise in it.

'How do you know that?'

'Wardle, the local constable, has just told me so to my face. It was only by way of a special favour he refrained from arresting me then and there.'

Mr Beck walked on beside John Neville ten or fifteen paces before he spoke again.

'Do you mind,' he said, in a very insinuating voice, 'telling me exactly why you are suspected?'

'Not in the very least.'

'Mind this,' the detective went on quickly, 'I give you no caution and make you no pledge. It's my business to find out the truth. If you think the truth will help you, then you ought to help me. This is very irregular, of course, but I don't mind that. When a man is charged with a crime there is, you see, Mr Neville, always one witness who knows whether he is guilty or not. There is very often only that one. The first thing the British law does by way of discovering the truth is to close the mouth of the only witness that knows it. Well, that's not my way. I like to give an innocent man a chance to tell his own story, and I've no scruple in trapping a guilty man if I can.'

He looked John Neville straight in the eyes as he spoke.

The look was steadily returned. 'I think I understand. What do you want to know? Where shall I begin?'

'At the beginning. What did you quarrel with your uncle about yesterday?'

John Neville hesitated for a moment, and Mr Beck took a mental note of his hesitation.

'I didn't quarrel with him. He quarrelled with me. It was this way: There was a bitter feud between my uncle and his neighbour, Colonel Peyton. The estates adjoin, and the quarrel was about some shooting. My uncle was very violent—he used to call Colonel Peyton "a common poacher". Well, I took no hand in the row. I was rather shy when I met the Colonel for the first time after it, for I knew my uncle had the wrong end of the stick. But the Colonel spoke to me in the kindest way. "No reason why you and I should cease to be friends, John," he said. "This is a foolish business. I would give the best covert on my estate to be out of it. Men cannot fight duels in these days, and gentlemen cannot scold like fishwives. But I don't expect people will call me a coward because I hate a row."

'"Not likely," I said.

'The Colonel, you must know, had distinguished himself in a dozen engagements, and has the Victoria Cross locked up in a drawer of his desk. Lucy once showed it to me. Lucy is his only daughter, and he is devoted to her. Well, after that, of course, the Colonel and I kept on good terms, for I liked him, and I like going there and all that. But our friendship angered my uncle. I had been going to the Grange pretty often of late, and my uncle heard of it. He spoke to me in a very rough fashion of Colonel Peyton and his daughter at dinner last night, and I stood up for them.

'"By what right, you insolent puppy," he shouted, "do you take this upstart's part against me?"

'"The Peytons are as good a family as our own, sir," I said—that was true—"and as for right, Miss Lucy Peyton has done me the honour of promising to be my wife."

'At that he exploded in a very tempest of rage. I cannot repeat his words about the Colonel and his daughter. Even now, though he lies dead yonder, I can hardly forgive them. He swore he would never see or speak to me again if I disgraced myself by such a marriage. "I cannot break the entail," he growled, "worse luck. But I can make you a beggar while I live, and I shall live forty years to spite you. The poacher can have you a bargain for all I care. Go, sell yourself as dearly as you can, and live on your wife's fortune as soon as you please."

'Then I lost my temper, and gave him a bit of my mind.'

'Try and remember what you said; it's important.'

'I told him that I cast his contempt back in his face; that I loved Lucy Peyton, and that I would live for her, and die for her, if need be.'

'Did you say "it was a comfort he could not live for ever"? You see the story of your quarrel has travelled far and near. The driver told me of it. Try and remember—did you say that?'

'I think I did. I'm sure I did now, but I was so furious I hardly knew what I said. I certainly never meant . . .'

'Who was in the room when you quarrelled?'

'Only Cousin Eric and the butler.'

'The butler, I suppose, spread the story?'

'I suppose so. I'm sure Cousin Eric never did. He was as much pained at the scene as myself. He tried to interfere at the time, but his interference only made my uncle more furious.'

'What was your allowance from your uncle?'

'A thousand a year.'

'He had power to cut it off, I suppose?'

'Certainly.'

'But he had no power over the estate. You were heir-apparent under the entail, and at the present moment you are owner of Berkly Manor?'

'That is so; but up to the moment you spoke I assure you I never even remembered . . .'

'Who comes next to you in the entail?'

'My first cousin, Eric. He is four years younger than I am.'

'After him?'

'A distant cousin. I scarcely know him at all; but he has a bad reputation, and I know my uncle and he hated each other cordially.'

'How did your uncle and your cousin hit it off?'

'Not too well. He hated Eric's father—his own youngest brother—and he was sometimes rough on Eric. He used to abuse the dead father in the son's presence, calling him cruel and treacherous, and all that. Poor Eric had often had a hard time of it. Uncle was liberal to him so far as money went—as liberal as he was to me—had him to live at the Manor and denied him nothing. But now and again he would sting the poor lad by a passionate curse or a bitter sneer. It spite of all, Eric seemed fond of him.'

'To come now to the murder; you saw your uncle no more that night, I suppose?'

'I never saw him alive again.'

'Do you know what he did next day?'

'Only by hearsay.'

'Hearsay evidence is often first-class evidence, though the law doesn't think so. What did you hear?'

'My uncle was mad about shooting. Did I tell you his quarrel with Colonel Peyton was about the shooting? He had a grouse moor rented about twelve miles from here, and he never missed the first day. He was off at cock-shout with the head gamekeeper, Lennox. I was to have gone with him, but I didn't of course. Contrary to his custom he came back about noon and went straight to his study. I was writing in my own room and heard his heavy step go past the door. Later on Eric found him asleep on the great leather couch in his study. Five minutes after Eric left I heard the shot and rushed into his room.'

'Did you examine the room after you found the body?'

'No. Eric wanted to, but I thought it better not. I simply locked the door and put the key in my pocket till you came.'

'Could it have been suicide?'

'Impossible, I should say. He was shot through the back of the head.'

'Had your uncle any enemies that you know of?'

'The poachers hated him. He was relentless with them. A fellow once shot at him, and my uncle shot back and shattered the man's leg. He had him sent to hospital first and cured, and then prosecuted him straight away, and got him two years.'

'Then you think a poacher murdered him?' Mr Beck said blandly.

'I don't well see how he could. I was in my own room on the same corridor. The only way to or from my uncle's room was past my door. I rushed out the instant I heard the shot, and saw no one.'

'Perhaps the murderer leapt through the window?'

'Eric tells me that he and the gardener were in the garden almost under the window at the time.'

'What's your theory, then, Mr Neville?'

'I haven't got a theory.'

'You parted with your uncle in anger last night?'

'That's so.'

'Next day your uncle is shot, and you are found—I won't say caught—in his room the instant afterwards.'

John Neville flushed crimson; but he held himself in and nodded without speaking.

The two walked on together in silence.

They were not a hundred yards from the great mansion—John Neville's house—standing high above the embowering trees in the glow of the twilight, when the detective spoke again.

'I'm bound to say, Mr Neville, that things look very black against you, as they stand. I think that constable Wardle ought to have arrested you.'

'It's not too late yet,' John Neville answered shortly, 'I see him there at the corner of the house and I'll tell him you said so.'

He turned on his heel, when Mr Beck called quickly after him: 'What about that key?'

John Neville handed it to him without a word. The detective took it as silently and walked on to the entrance and up the great stone steps alone, whistling softly.

Eric welcomed him at the door, for the driver had told of his coming.

'You have had no dinner, Mr Beck?' he asked courteously.

'Business first; pleasure afterwards. I had a snack in the train. Can I see the gamekeeper, Lennox, for five minutes alone?'

'Certainly. I'll send him to you in a moment here in the library.'

Lennox, the gamekeeper, a long-limbed, high-shouldered, elderly man, shambled shyly into the room, consumed by nervousness in the presence of a London detective.

'Sit down, Lennox, sit down,' said Mr Beck kindly. The very sound of his voice, homely and good-natured, put the man at ease. 'Now, tell me, why did you come home so soon from the grouse this morning?'

'Well, you see, sir, it was this ways. We were two hours hout when the Squire, 'e says to me, "Lennox," 'e says, "I'm sick of this fooling. I'm going 'ome."'

'No sport?'

'Birds wor as thick as blackberries, sir, and lay like larks.'

'No sportsman, then?'

'Is it the Squire, sir?' cried Lennox, quite forgetting his shyness in his excitement at this slur on the Squire. 'There wasn't a better sportsman in the county—no, nor as good. Real, old-fashioned style, 'e was. "Hang your barnyard shooting," 'e'd say when they'd ask him to go kill tame pheasants. 'E put up 'is own birds with 'is own dogs, 'e did. 'E'd as soon go shooting without a gun very near as without a dog any day. Aye and 'e stuck to 'is old "Manton" muzzle-loader to the last. "'Old it steady, Lennox," 'ed say to me oftentimes, "and point it straight. It will hit harder and further than any of their telescopes, and it won't get marked with rust if you don't clean it every second shot."

'"Easy to load, Squire," the young men would say, cracking up their hammerless breech-loaders.

'"Aye," he'd answer them back, "and spoil your dog's work. What's the good of a dog learning to 'down shot,' if you can drop in your cartridges as quick as a cock can pick corn."

'A dead shot the Squire was, too, and no mistake, sir, if he wasn't flurried. Many a time I've seen him wipe the eyes of gents who thought no end of themselves with that same old muzzle-loader that shot hisself in the long run. Many a time I seen . . .'

'Why did he turn his back on good sport yesterday?' asked Mr Beck, cutting short his reminiscences.

'Well, you see, it was scorching hot for one thing, but that wasn't it, for the infernal fire would not stop the Squire if he was on for sport. But he was in a blazing temper all the morning, and temper tells more than most anything on a man's shooting. When Flora sprung a pack—she's a young dog, and the fault wasn't hers either—for she came down the wind on them—but the Squire had the gun to his shoulder to shoot her. Five minutes after she found another pack and set like a stone. They got up as big as haycocks and as lazy as crows, and he missed right and left—never touched a feather—a thing I haven't seen him do since I was a boy.

'"It's myself I should shoot, not the dog" he growled and he flung me the gun to load. When I'd got the caps on and had shaken the powder into the nipples, he ripped out an oath that 'e'd have no more of it. 'E walked right across country to where the trap was. The birds got up under his feet, but divil a shot he'd fire, but drove straight 'ome.

'When we got to the 'ouse I wanted to take the gun and fire it off, or draw the charges. But 'e told me to go to . . ., and carried it up loaded as it was to his study, where no one goes unless they're sent for special. It was better than an hour afterwards I heard the report of the "Manton"; I'd know it in a thousand. I ran for the study as fast as . . .'

Eric Neville broke suddenly into the room, flushed and excited.

'Mr Beck,' he cried, 'a monstrous thing has happened. Wardle, the local constable, you know, has arrested my cousin on a charge of wilful murder of my uncle.'

Mr Beck, with his eyes intent on the excited face, waved a big hand soothingly.

'Easy,' he said, 'take it easy, Mr Neville. It's hurtful to your feelings, no doubt; but it cannot be helped. The constable has done no more than his duty. The evidence is very strong, as you know, and in such cases it's best for all parties to proceed regularly.'

'You can go,' he went on, speaking to Lennox, who stood dumbfounded at the news of John Neville's arrest, staring with eyes and mouth wide open.

Then turning again very quietly to Eric: 'Now, Mr Neville, I would like to see the room where the corpse is.'

The perfect flaccidity of his manner had its effect upon the boy, for he was little more than a boy, calming his excitement as oil smooths troubled water.

'My cousin has the key,' he said, 'I will get it.'

'There is no need,' Mr Beck called after him, for he was

half-way out of the room on his errand: 'I've got the key if you will be good enough to show me the room.'

Mastering his surprise, Eric showed him upstairs, and along the corridor to the locked door. Half unconsciously, as it seemed, he was following the detective into the room, when Mr Beck stopped him.

'I know you will kindly humour me, Mr Neville,' he said, 'but I find that I can look closer and think clearer when I'm by myself. I'm not exactly shy you know, but it's a habit I've got.'

He closed the door softly as he spoke, and locked it on the inside, leaving the key in the lock.

The mask of placidity fell from him the moment he found himself alone. His lips tightened, and his eyes sparkled, and his muscles seemed to grow rigid with excitement, like a sporting dog's when he is close upon the game.

One glance at the corpse showed him that it was not suicide. In this, at least, John Neville had spoken the truth.

The back of the head had literally been blown in by the charge of heavy shot at close quarters. The grey hair was clammy and matted, with little white angles of bone protruding. The dropping of the blood had made a black pool on the carpet, and the close air of the room was foetid with the smell of it.

The detective walked to the table where the gun, a handsome, old-fashioned muzzle loader, lay, the muzzle still pointed at the corpse. But his attention was diverted by a water-bottle, a great globe of clear glass quite full, and perched on a book a little distance from the gun, and between it and the window. He took it from the table and tested the water with the tip of his tongue. It had a curious insipid, parboiled taste, but he detected no foreign flavour in it. Though the room was full of dust there was almost none on the cover of the book where the water-bottle stood, and Mr Beck noticed a gap in the third row of the bookcase where the book had been taken.

After a quick glance round the room Mr Beck walked to the window. On a small table there he found a clear circle in the thick dust. He fitted the round bottom of the water-bottle to this circle and it covered it exactly. While he stood by the window he caught sight of some small scraps of paper crumbled up and thrown into a corner. Picking them up and smoothing them out he found they were curiously drilled with little burnt holes. Having examined the holes minutely with his magnifying glass, he slipped these scraps folded on each other into his waistcoat pocket.

From the window he went back to the gun. This time he examined it with the minutest care. The right barrel he found had been recently discharged, the left was still loaded. Then he made a startling discovery. *Both barrels were on half cock*. The little bright copper cap twinkled on the nipple of the left barrel, from the right nipple the cap was gone.

How had the murderer fired the right barrel without a cap? How and why did he find time in the midst of his deadly work to put the cock back to safety?

Had Mr Beck solved this problem? The grim smile deepened on his lips as he looked, and there was an ugly light in his eyes that boded ill for the unknown assassin. Finally he carried the gun to the window and examined it carefully through a magnifying glass. There was a thin dark line, as if traced with the point of a red-hot needle, running a little way along the wood of the stock and ending in the right nipple.

Mr Beck put the gun back quietly on the table. The whole investigation had not taken ten minutes. He gave one look at the still figure on the couch, unlocked the door, locking it after him, and walked out through the corridor, the same cheerful imperturbable Mr Beck that had walked into it ten minutes before.

He found Eric waiting for him at the head of the stairs. 'Well?' he said when he saw the detective.

'Well,' replied Mr Beck, ignoring the interrogation in his voice, 'when is the inquest to be? That's the next thing to be thought of; the sooner the better.'

'To-morrow, if you wish. My cousin John sent a messenger to Mr Morgan, the coroner. He lives only five miles off, and he has promised to be here at twelve o'clock to-morrow. There will be no difficulty in getting a jury in the village.'

'That's right, that's all right,' said Mr Beck, rubbing his hands, 'the sooner and the quieter we get those preliminaries over the better.'

'I have just sent to engage the local solicitor on behalf of my cousin. He's not particularly bright, I'm afraid, but he's the best to be had on a short notice.'

'Very proper and thoughtful on your part—very thoughtful indeed. But solicitors cannot do much in such cases. It's the evidence we have to go by, and the evidence is only too plain, I'm afraid. Now, if you please,' he went on more briskly, dismissing the disagreeable subject, as it were, with a wave of his hand, 'I'd be very glad of that supper you spoke about.'

Mr Beck supped very heartily on a brace of grouse—the last of the dead man's shooting—and a bottle of ripe Burgundy. He was in high good-humour, and across 'the walnuts and the wine' he told Eric some startling episodes in his career, which seemed to divert the young fellow a little from his manifest grief for his uncle and anxiety for his cousin.

Meanwhile John Neville remained shut close in his own room, with the constable at the door.

The inquest was held at half-past twelve next day in the library.

The Coroner, a large, red-faced man, with a very affable manner, had got to his work promptly.

The jury 'viewed the body' steadily, stolidly, with a kind of morose delectation in the grim spectacle.

In some unaccountable way Mr Beck constituted himself a master of the ceremonies, a kind of assessor to the court.

'You had best take the gun down,' he said to the Coroner as they were leaving the room.

'Certainly, certainly,' replied the Coroner.

'And the water-bottle,' added Mr Beck.

'There is no suspicion of poison, is there?'

'It's best not to take anything for granted,' replied Mr Beck sententiously.

'By all means if you think so,' replied the obsequious Coroner. 'Constable, take the water-bottle down with you.'

The large room was filled with the people of the neighbourhood, mostly farmers from the Berkly estate and small shopkeepers from the neighbouring village.

A table had been wheeled to the top of the room for the Coroner, with a seat at it for the ubiquitous local newspaper correspondent. A double row of chairs were set at the right hand of the table for the jury.

The jury had just returned from viewing the body when the crunch of wheels and hoofs was heard on the gravel of the drive, and a two-horse phaeton pulled up sharp at the entrance.

A moment later there came into the room a handsome, soldier-like man, with a girl clinging to his arm, whom he supported with tender, protecting fondness that was very touching. The girl's face was pale, but wonderfully sweet and winsome; cheeks with the faint, pure flush of the wild rose, and eyes like a wild fawn's.

No need to tell Mr Beck that here were Colonel Peyton and his daughter. He saw the look—shy, piteous, loving—that the girl gave John Neville as she passed close to the table where he sat with his head buried in his hands; and the detective's face darkened for a moment with a stern purpose, but the next moment it resumed its customary look of good-nature and good-humour.

The gardener, the gamekeeper, and the butler were

briefly examined by the Coroner, and rather clumsily cross-examined by Mr Waggles, the solicitor whom Eric had thoughtfully secured for his cousin's defence.

As the case against John Neville gradually darkened into grim certainty, the girl in the far corner of the room grew white as a lily, and would have fallen but for her father's support.

'Does Mr John Neville offer himself for examination?' said the Coroner, as he finished writing the last word of the butler's deposition describing the quarrel of the night before.

'No, sir,' said Mr Waggles. 'I appear for Mr John Neville, the accused, and we reserve our defence.'

'I really have nothing to say that hasn't been already said,' added John Neville quietly.

'Mr Neville,' said Mr Waggles pompously, 'I must ask you to leave yourself entirely in my hands.'

'Eric Neville!' called out the Coroner. 'This is the last witness, I think.'

Eric stepped in front of the table and took the Bible in his hand. He was pale, but quiet and composed, and there was an unaffected grief in the look of his dark eyes and in the tone of his soft voice that touched every heart—except one.

He told his story shortly and clearly. It was quite plain that he was most anxious to shield his cousin. But in spite of this, perhaps because of this, the evidence went horribly against John Neville.

The answers to questions criminating his cousin had to be literally dragged from him by the Coroner.

With manifest reluctance he described the quarrel at dinner the night before.

'Was your cousin very angry?' the Coroner asked.

'He would not be human if he were not angry at the language used.'

'What did he say?'

'I cannot remember all he said.'

'Did he say to your uncle: "Well, you will not live for ever"?'

No answer.

'Come, Mr Neville, remember you are sworn to tell the truth.'

In an almost inaudible whisper came the words: 'He did.'

'I'm sorry to pain you, but I must do my duty. When you heard the shot you ran straight to your uncle's room, about fifty yards, I believe?'

'About that.'

'Whom did you find there bending over the dead man?'

'My cousin. I am bound to say he appeared in the deepest grief.'

'But you saw no one else?'

'No.'

'Your cousin is, I believe, the heir to Squire Neville's property; the owner I should say now?'

'I believe so.'

'That will do; you can stand down.'

This interchange of question and answer, each one of which seemed to fit the rope tighter and tighter round John Neville's neck, was listened to with hushed eagerness by the room full of people.

There was a long, deep drawing-in of breath when it ended. The suspense seemed over, but not the excitement.

Mr Beck rose as Eric turned from the table, quite as a matter of course, to question him.

'You say you *believe* your cousin was your uncle's heir—don't you *know* it?'

Then Mr Waggles found his voice.

'Really, sir,' he broke out, addressing the Coroner, 'I must protest. This is grossly irregular. This person is not a professional gentleman. He represents no one. He has no *locus standi* in court at all.'

No one knew better than Mr Beck that technically he had no title to open his lips; but his look of quiet assurance, his calm assumption of unmistakable right, carried the day with the Coroner.

'Mr Beck,' he said, 'has, I understand, been brought down specially from London to take charge of this case, and I shall certainly not stop him in any question he may desire to ask.'

'Thank you, sir,' said Mr Beck, in the tone of a man whose clear right has been allowed. Then again to the witness: 'Didn't you know John Neville was next heir to Berkly Manor?'

'I know it, of course.'

'And if John Neville is hanged you will be the owner?'

Every one was startled at the frank brutality of the question so blandly asked. Mr Waggles bobbed up and down excitedly; but Eric answered, calmly as ever:

'That's very coarsely and cruelly put.'

'But it's true?'

'Yes, it's true.'

'We will pass from that. When you came into the room after the murder, did you examine the gun?'

'I stretched out my hand to take it, but my cousin stopped me. I must be allowed to add that I believe he was actuated, as he said, by a desire to keep everything in the room untouched. He locked the door and carried off the key. I was not in the room afterwards.'

'Did you look closely at the gun?'

'Not particularly.'

'Did you notice that both barrels were at half cock?'

'No.'

'Did you notice that there was no cap on the nipple of the right barrel that had just been fired?'

'Certainly not.'

'That is to say you did not notice it?'

'Yes.'

'Did you notice a little burnt line traced a short distance on the wood of the stock towards the right nipple?'

'No.'

Mr Beck put the gun into his hand.

'Look close. Do you notice it now?'

'I can see it now for the first time.'

'You cannot account for it, I suppose?'

'No.'

'Sure?'

'Quite sure.'

All present followed this strange, and apparently purposeless cross-examination with breathless interest, groping vainly for its meaning.

The answers were given calmly and clearly, but those that looked closely saw that Eric's nether lip quivered, and it was only by a strong effort of will that he held his calmness.

Through the blandness of Mr Beck's voice and manner a subtle suggestion of hostility made itself felt, very trying to the nerves of the witness.

'We will pass from that,' said Mr Beck again. 'When you went into your uncle's room before the shot why did you take a book from the shelf and put it on the table?'

'I really cannot remember anything about it.'

'Why did you take the water-bottle from the window and stand it on the book?'

'I wanted a drink.'

'But there was none of the water drunk.'

'Then I suppose it was to take it out of the strong sun.'

'But you set it in the strong sun on the table?'

'Really I cannot remember those trivialities.' His self-control was breaking down at last.

'Then we will pass from that,' said Mr Beck a third time.

He took the little scraps of paper with the burnt holes through them from his waistcoat pocket, and handed them to the witness.

'Do you know anything about these?'

There was a pause of a second. Eric's lips tightened as if

with a sudden spasm of pain. But the answer came clearly enough:

'Nothing whatever.'

'Do you ever amuse yourself with a burning glass?'

This seeming simple question was snapped suddenly at the witness like a pistol-shot.

'Really, really,' Mr Waggles broke out, 'this is mere trifling with the Court.'

'That question does certainly seem a little irrelevant, Mr Beck" mildly remonstrated the Coroner.

'Look at the witness, sir,' retorted Mr Beck sternly. 'He does not think it irrelevant.'

Every eye in court was turned on Eric's face and fixed there.

All colour had fled from his cheeks and lips; his mouth had fallen open, and he stared at Mr Beck with eyes of abject terror.

Mr Beck went on remorselessly: 'Did you ever amuse yourself with a burning glass?'

No answer.

'Do you know that a water-bottle like this makes a capital burning glass?'

Still no answer.

'Do you know that a burning glass has been used before now to touch off a cannon or fire a gun?'

Then a voice broke from Eric at last, as it seemed in defiance of his will; a voice unlike his own—loud, harsh, hardly articulate; such a voice might have been heard in the torture chamber in the old days when the strain on the rack grew unbearable.

'You devilish bloodhound!' he shouted. 'Curse you, curse you, you've caught me! I confess it—I was the murderer!' He fell on the ground in a fit.

'And you made the sun your accomplice!' remarked Mr Beck, placid as ever.

VI

The Amber Beads

Fergus Hume

It was drawing to night one August evening when the woman made her appearance, and the atmosphere of the pawnshop was darker than usual. Still, it was sufficiently light for Hagar to see that her customer was a tall and bulky negress, arrayed in a gaudy yellow dress, neutralized by trimmings of black jet beading. As the evening was hot and close, she wore neither cloak nor jacket, but displayed her somewhat shapeless figure to the full in this decidedly startling costume. Her hat was a garden of roses—red, white and yellow; she wore a large silver brooch like a shield, an extensive necklace of silver coins, and many bangles of the same metal on her black wrists. As a contrast to these splendours she wore no gloves, nor did she hide her coal-black face with a veil. Altogether, this odd customer was the blackest and most fantastically-dressed negress that Hagar had ever seen, and in the dim light she looked a striking but rather alarming figure.

On Hagar coming to the counter this black woman produced out of a silver-clasped sealskin satchel a necklace, which she handed silently to Hagar for inspection. As the light was too imperfect to admit of a close examination, Hagar lighted the gas, but when it flamed up the negress, as though unwilling to be seen too clearly in the searching glare, stepped back hastily into the darkness. Hagar put this retrograde movement down to the natural timidity of a person unaccustomed to pawning, and took but little notice of it at the time. Afterwards she had cause to remember it.

The necklace was a string of magnificent amber beads threaded on a slender chain of gold. Each bead was as large as the egg of a sparrow, and round the middle of every single one there was a narrow belt of tiny diamonds. The clasp at the back was of fine gold, square in shape, and curiously wrought to the representation of a hideous Ethiopian face, with diamonds for eyes. This queer piece of jewellery was unique of its kind, and, as Hagar rapidly calculated, of considerable value. Nevertheless, she offered, according to custom, as low a sum as she well could.

'I'll give five pounds on it,' said she, returning to the counter.

Rather to her surprise, the negress accepted with a sharp nod, and then took out of her bag a scrap of paper. On this was written laboriously: 'Rosa, Marylebone Road'. The name and address were so imperfect that Hagar hesitated before making out the pawn-ticket.

'Have you no other name but Rosa?' she asked, sharply.

The negress shook her head, and kept well in the shadow.

'And no more particular address than Marylebone Road?'

Again the black woman made a negative sign, whereat, annoyed by these gestures, Hagar grew angered.

'Can't you speak?' she demanded, tartly. 'Are you dumb?'

At once the negress nodded, and laid a finger on her lips. Hagar drew back. This woman was black, she was dumb, she gave half a name, half an address, and she wished to pawn a valuable and unique piece of jewellery. The whole affair was queer, and, as Hagar considered, might be rather dangerous. Perhaps this silent negress was disposing of stolen goods, as the necklace seemed too fine for her to possess. For the moment Hagar was inclined to refuse to do business; but a glance at the amber beads decided her to make the bargain. She could get it cheap; she was acting well within the legal limits of business; and if the police did appear in the matter, no blame could be attached to her for the transaction. Biased by these considerations, Hagar made out the ticket in the name Rosa, and took a clean new five-pound note out of the cash-box. As she was about to give ticket and money across the counter she paused. 'I'll take the number of this note,' she thought, going to the desk; 'if this negress can't be traced by name or address, the bank-note number will find her if it is necessary.'

Deeming this precaution judicious, Hagar hastily scribbled down the number of the five-pound note, and returning to the counter, gave it and the ticket to her queer customer. The negress stretched out her right hand for them; and then Hagar made a discovery which she noted mentally as a mark of identification if necessary. However, she said nothing, but tried to get a good look at the woman's face. The customer, however, kept well in the shadow, and swept note and ticket into her bag hurriedly. Then she bowed and left the shop.

Six days later Hagar received a printed notice from New Scotland Yard, notifying to all pawn-brokers that the police were in search of a necklace of amber beads set with diamonds, and clasped with a negro's face wrought in gold. Notice of its whereabouts was to be sent to the Detective Department without delay. Remembering her suspicions, and recalling the persistent way in which the negress had averted her face, Hagar was not much surprised by this communication. Curious to know the truth, and to learn what crime might be attached to the necklace, she wrote at once about the matter. Within four hours a stranger presented himself to see the amber beads, and to question her concerning the woman who had pawned the same. He was a fat little man, with a healthy red face and shrewd twinkling eyes. Introducing himself as Luke Horval, of the detective service, he asked Hagar to relate the circumstances of the pawning. This the girl did frankly enough, but without communicating her own suspicions. At the conclusion of her narrative she displayed the amber beads, which were carefully examined by Mr Horval. Then he slapped his knee, and whistled in a thoughtful sort of way.

'I guessed as much,' said he, staring hard at Hagar. 'The negress did it.'

'Did what?' asked the girl, curiously.

'Why,' said Horval, 'murdered the old woman.'

Murder! The word had a gruesome and cruel sound, which caused Hagar's cheek to pale when it rang in her ears. She had connected the amber beads with robbery, but scarcely with the taking of life. The idea that she had been in the company of a murderess gave Hagar a qualm; but, suppressing this as a weakness, she asked Horval to tell her the details of the crime and how it bore on the pawning of the amber beads.

'It's just this way, miss,' explained the detective, easily. 'This Rosa is the nigger girl of Mrs Arryford . . .'

'Is Rosa her real name?'

'Oh, yes; I s'pose she thought she might lose the beads if she gave a wrong one; but the address ain't right. It's the other end of London as Mrs Arryford lives—or rather lived,' added Horval, correcting himself, 'seeing she now occupies a Kensal Green grave—Campden Hill, miss; a sweet little house in Bedford Gardens, where she lived with Rosa and Miss Lyle.'

'And who is Miss Lyle?'

'The companion of Mrs Arryford. A dry stick of a spinster, miss; not to be compared with a fine girl like you.'

Hagar did not deign to notice the compliment, but sharply requested Mr Horval to continue his story, which he did, in no wise abashed by her cold demeanour.

'It's just this way, miss,' said he again; 'the old lady, the old maid and the nigger wench lived together in Bedford Gardens, a kind of happy family, as one might say. Mrs Arryford was the widder of a West Indian gent, and as rich as Solomon. She brought those amber beads from Jamaica, and Rosa was always wanting them.'

'Why? The necklace was very unsuitable to one of her condition.'

''Twasn't exactly the cost of it as she thought about,' said Horval, nursing his chin, 'but it seems that the necklace is a fetish, or charm, or lucky-penny, as you might say, to bring good fortune to the wearer. Mrs Arryford was past wanting good luck, so hadn't no need for the beads. Rosa asked her for them, just for the good luck of them, as you might say. The old girl wouldn't part, as she was as superstitious as Rosa herself over that necklace; so in the end Rosa murdered her to get it.'

'How do you know she did?' asked Hagar, doubtfully.

'How do I know?' echoed the detective in surprise. ''Cause I ain't a fool, miss. Last week Mrs Arryford was found in her bed with a carving knife in her heart, as dead as a door-nail, and the beads were missing. Miss Lyle, she didn't know anything about it, and Rosa swore she hadn't left her room, so, you see, we couldn't quite hit on who finished off Mrs Arryford. But now as I know Rosa pawned these beads, I'm sure she did the job.'

'What made you think that the beads might have been pawned?'

'Oh, that was Miss Lyle's idea; a sharp old girl she is, miss. She was very fond of Mrs Arryford, as she well might be, seeing as the old lady was rich and kept her like a princess. Often she heard Rosa ask for those beads, so when Mrs Arryford was killed and the beads missing she told me as she was sure Rosa had done the trick.'

'But the pawning?'

'Well, miss,' said Horval, scratching his chin, 'it was

just this way. Miss Lyle said as how Rosa, to get rid of the necklace until the affair of the murder was blown over, might pawn it. I thought so too, so I sent a printed slip to all the pop-shops in London. You wrote that the beads were here, so it seems as Miss Lyle was right.'

'Evidently. By the way, who gets the money of Mrs Arryford?'

'A Mr Frederick Jevons; he's a nephew of Miss Lyle's.'

'A nephew of Miss Lyle's!' echoed Hagar, in surprise. 'And why did Mrs Arryford leave her money to him instead of to her relatives?'

'Well, it's just this way, miss,' said Horval, rising. 'She hadn't got no relatives; and as Mr Jevons was a good-looking young chap, always at the house to see his aunt, she took a fancy to him and left the money his way.'

'You are sure that Miss Lyle is no relation to Mrs Arryford?'

'Quite sure. She was only the old girl's companion.'

'Was Mrs Arryford weak in the head?'

'Not as I ever heard of,' said Mr Horval, with a stare, 'but you can find out, if you like, from Miss Lyle.'

'Miss Lyle? How am I to see her?'

'Why,' said the detective, clapping on his hat, 'when you come to see if Rosa is the same nigger as pawned the amber beads. Just leave someone to look after the shop, miss, and come with me right away.'

With true feminine curiosity, Hagar agreed at once to accompany the detective to Campden Hill. The shop was delivered into the charge of Bolker, a misshapen imp of sixteen, who for some months had been the plague of Hagar's life. He had a long body and long arms, short legs and a short temper, and also a most malignant eye, which indicated only too truly his spiteful nature. Having given a few instructions to this charming lad, Hagar departed with Horval in the omnibus, and arrived at Bedford Gardens early in the afternoon.

The Amber Beads

The house was a quaint, pretty cottage, which stood in a delightful garden—once the solace of poor dead Mrs Arryford's soul—and was divided from the road by a tall fence of iron railings closed in with wooden planks painted a dark green. The room into which the detective and gipsy were shown was a prim and rather cosy apartment, which bore the impress of Miss Lyle's old-maidism in the deposition of the furniture. When they were seated here, and were waiting for Miss Lyle, who had been advised of their arrival, Hagar suddenly asked Horval a leading question.

'Is Rosa dumb?' she demanded.

'Bless you, no!' answered Horval. 'It's true as she don't talk much, but she can use her tongue in nigger fashion. Why do you ask?'

'She said she was dumb when she pawned the beads.'

'Oh, that was 'cause she was too 'cute to let her voice betray her,' replied Horval, smiling. He had humour enough to note Hagar's unconscious bull; but as she was likely to be useful to him in the conduct of the case, he did not wish to anger her by remarking on it.

When Miss Lyle made her appearance, Hagar, after the manner of women, took immediate note of her looks and manner. The old maid was tall and lean and yellow, with grey eyes, and a thin-lipped, hard-tempered mouth, turned down at the curves. Her iron-grey hair was drawn tightly off her narrow forehead and screwed into a hard-looking knob behind. She wore a black stuff gown, sombre and lustreless; collar and cuffs of white linen, and cloth slippers, in which she glided noiselessly. Altogether an unpromising, hard woman, acidulated and narrow-minded, who looked disapprovingly on the rich beauty of Hagar, and remarked her graces with a jaundiced eye and a vinegary look. The cough with which she ended her inspection shewed that she condemned the girl at first sight.

'Is this young person necessary to your conduct of the

[168]

case?' said Miss Lyle, addressing herself to Horval, and ignoring Hagar altogether.

'Why, yes, miss,' replied Horval, on whom the antagonistic attitude of the two women was not lost. 'She keeps the pawn-shop at which Rosa pawned the beads!'

Miss Lyle gave a start of virtuous horror, and her thin lips wreathed in a viperous smile. 'The wretch did kill my poor friend, then,' she said in a soft and fluty voice. 'I knew it!'

'She pawned the amber beads, Miss Lyle, but . . .'

'Now, don't say the wretch didn't kill my martyred friend,' snapped Miss Lyle, going to the bell-rope, 'but we'll have her in, and perhaps this young person will recognise her as the viper who pawned the beads.'

'It is to be hoped so,' said Hagar, very drily, not approving of being spoken at in the third person, 'but the negress kept her face turned away, and I might not . . .'

'It is your duty to recognize her,' exclaimed Miss Lyle, addressing herself to the girl for once. 'I am convinced that Rosa is a dangerous criminal. Here she is—the black Jezebel!'

As the last word fell from her mouth the door opened, and Rosa entered the room, whereat Hagar uttered an exclamation of surprise. This negress was rather short, and more than a trifle stout. It is true that she wore a yellow dress trimmed with black jet beading; that silver ornaments were on her neck and wrists; also that she was without the wonderful hat. Still, Hagar was surprised, and explained her ejaculation forthwith.

'That is not the woman who pawned the beads!' she declared, rising.

'Not the woman?' echoed Miss Lyle, virulently. 'She must be! This is Rosa!'

'Yis, yis! I Rosa,' said the negress, beginning to weep, 'but I no kill my poo' dear missy. Dat one big lie.'

'Are you sure, miss, that this is not the woman?' asked Horval, rather dismayed.

Hagar stepped forward, and looked sharply at the sobbing negress up and down. Then she glanced at the woman's hands and shook her head.

'I am prepared to swear in a court of law that this is not the woman,' she said, quietly.

'Rubbish, rubbish!' cried Miss Lyle, flushing. 'Rosa coveted the necklace, as it was connected with some debased African superstition, and . . .'

'It one ole fetish!' interrupted Rosa, her eyes sparkling fire at the old maid, 'and ole missy she did wish to gib it me, but you no let her.'

'Certainly not!' said Miss Lyle, with dignity. 'The necklace was not fit for you to wear. And because I persuaded Mrs Arryford not to give it to you, you murdered her, you wretch! Down on your knees, woman, and confess!'

'I no 'fess!' exclaimed the terrified negress. 'I no kill my missy! I no gib dose amber beads for money. If dose beads mine, I keep dem; dey a mighty big fetish, for sure!'

'One moment,' said Horval, as Miss Lyle was about to speak again, 'let us conduct this inquiry calmly, and give the accused every chance. Miss,' he said, turning to Hagar, 'on what day, at what time, was it that the beads were pawned?'

Hagar calculated rapidly, and answered promptly: 'On the evening of the 23rd of August, between six and seven o'clock.'

'Ah!' exclaimed Miss Lyle, joyfully—'and on that very evening Rosa was out, and did not return till nine!'

'Me went to see Massa Jevons for you!' said Rosa vehemently, 'you send me.'

'I send you! Just listen to the creature's lies! Besides, Mr Jevons's rooms are in Duke Street, St James's, whereas it was at Lambeth you were.'

'I no go to dat gem'man's house. You send me to de train Waterloo!'

'Waterloo!' said Horval, looking sharply at Rosa. 'You were there?'

'Yis, massa; me dere at seven and eight.'

'In the neighbourhood of Lambeth,' murmured Horval. 'She might have gone to the pawn-shop after all.'

'Of course she did!' cried Miss Lyle, vindictively—'and pawned the amber beads of my poor dead friend!'

'She did nothing of the sort!' interposed Hagar, with spirit. 'Whosoever pawned the beads, it was not this woman. Besides, how do you know that Rosa killed Mrs Arryford?'

'She wanted the beads, young woman, and she killed my friend to obtain them.'

'No, no! dat one big lie!'

'I am sure it is!' said Hagar, her face aflame. 'I believe in your innocence, Rosa. Mr Horval,' she added, turning to the detective, 'you can't arrest this woman, as you have no grounds to do so.'

'Well, if she didn't pawn those beads . . .'

'She did not, I tell you.'

'She did!' cried Miss Lyle angrily. 'I believe you are an accomplice of the creature's!'

What reply Hagar would have made to this accusation it is impossible to say, for at this moment a young man walked into the room. He was good-looking in appearance, and smart in dress, but there was a haggard look about his face which betokened dissipation.

'This,' said Miss Lyle, introducing him, 'is my nephew, the heir to the property of my late dear friend. He is resolved, as such heir, to find out and punish the assassin of his benefactress. For my part, I believe Rosa to be guilty.'

'And I,' cried Hagar, with energy, 'believe her to be innocent!'

'Let us hope she is,' said Jevons, in a weary voice, as he removed his gloves. 'I am tired of the whole affair.'

'You are bound to punish the guilty!' said Miss Lyle, in hard tones.

'But not the innocent,' retorted Hagar, rising.

'Young woman, you are insolent!'

Hagar looked Miss Lyle up and down in the coolest manner; then her eyes wandered to the well-dressed figure of Jevons, the heir. What she saw in him to startle her it is difficult to say; but after a moment's inspection she turned pale with suppressed emotion. Stepping forward, she was about to speak, when, checking herself suddenly, she beckoned to Horval, and advanced towards the door.

'My errand here is fulfilled,' she said, quietly. 'Mr Horval, perhaps you will come with me.'

'Yes, and you can go also, Rosa,' cried Miss Lyle, angered by the insulting gaze of the girl. 'I am mistress here in my nephew's house, and I refuse to let a murderess remain under its roof!'

'Be content,' said Hagar, pausing at the door. 'Rosa shall come with me; and when you see us again with Mr Horval, you will then learn who killed Mrs Arryford, and why.'

'Insolent hussy!' muttered Miss Lyle, and closed the door on Hagar, Horval and the black woman.

The trio walked away, and shortly afterwards picked up an omnibus, in which they returned to the Lambeth pawnshop. Hagar talked earnestly to Horval the whole way; and from the close attention which the detective paid to her it would seem that the conversation was of the deepest interest. Rosa, a dejected heap of misery, sat with downcast eyes, and at intervals wiped away the tears which ran down her black cheeks. The poor negress, under suspicion as a thief and a murderess, turned out of house and home, desolate and forsaken, was crushed to the earth under the burden of her woes. On her the fetish necklace of amber beads had brought a curse.

On arriving at the shop Hagar conducted Rosa into the

back parlour; and after a further conference she dismissed the detective.

'You can stay with me for a week,' she said to Rosa.

'And den what you do?'

'Oh,' said Hagar, with an agreeable smile, 'I shall take you with me to denounce the assassin of your late mistress.'

All that week Rosa stayed in the domestic portion of the pawn-shop, and made herself useful in cooking and cleaning. Hagar questioned her closely concerning the events which had taken place on the night of the murder in the house at Bedford Gardens, and elicited certain information which gave her great satisfaction. This she communicated to Horval when he one day paid her a hurried visit. When in possession of the facts, Horval looked at her with admiration, and on taking his leave he paid her a compliment.

'You ought to be a man, with that head of yours,' he said; 'you're too good to be a woman!'

'And not bad enough to be a man,' retorted Hagar, laughing. 'Be off with you, Mr Horval, and let me know when you want me up West.'

In four more days Horval again made his appearance, this time in a state of the greatest excitement. He was closeted with Hagar for over an hour, and at its conclusion he departed in a great hurry. Shortly after noon Hagar resigned the shop into Bolker's charge, put on hat and cloak, and ordered Rosa to come with her. What the reason of this unexpected departure might be she did not inform the negress immediately; but before they reached their destination Rosa knew all, and was much rejoiced thereat.

Hagar took Rosa as far as Duke Street, St James's, and here, at the door of a certain house, they found the detective impatiently waiting for them.

'Well, Mr Horval,' said Hagar, coming to a stop, 'is he indoors?'

'Safe and sound!' replied Horval, tapping his breast-coat pocket—'and I have got you know what here. Shall we come up?'

'Not immediately. I wish to see him by myself first. You remain outside his door, and enter with Rosa when I call you.'

Mr Horval nodded, with a full comprehension of what was required of him, and the trio ascended the dark stair-case. They paused at a door on the second landing. Then Hagar, motioning to her companions that they should withdraw themselves into the gloom, rapped lightly on the portal. Shortly afterwards it was opened by Mr Frederick Jevons, who looked inquiringly at Hagar. She turned her face towards the light which fell through the murky stair-case window, whereat, recognizing her, he stepped back in dismay.

'The pawn-shop girl!' said he in astonishment. 'What do you want?'

'I wish to see you,' replied Hagar, composedly, 'but it is just as well that our conversation should be in private.'

'Why, you can have nothing to say to me but what the whole world might hear!'

'After I have mentioned the object of my visit you may think differently,' said Hagar, with some dryness. 'However, we'll talk here if you wish.'

'No, no; come in,' said Jevons, standing on one side. 'Since you insist upon privacy, you shall have it. This way.'

He shewed her into a large and rather badly-furnished room. Evidently Mr Fred Jevons had not been rich until he inherited the fortune of Mrs Arryford.

'I suppose you will be moving to the Bedford Gardens house soon?' said Hagar, sitting composedly in a large armchair.

'Is that what you came to speak to me about?' retorted Jevons, rudely.

'Not exactly. Perhaps, as you are impatient, we had better get to business.'

'Business! What business can I have to do with you?'

'Why,' said Hagar, quietly, and looking directly at him, 'the business of those amber beads which you—pawned.'

'I,' stammered Jevons, drawing back with a pale face.

'Also,' added Hagar, solemnly, 'the business which concerns the commission of a crime.'

'A—a—a crime!' gasped the wretched creature.

'Yes—the most terrible of all crimes—murder!'

'What—what—what do you—you mean?'

Hagar rose from her chair, and, drawn to her full height, stretched out an accusing arm towards the young man. 'What I mean you know well enough!' she said, sternly. 'I mean that you murdered Mrs Arryford!'

'It's a lie!' cried Jevons, sinking into a chair, for his legs refused to support him longer.

'It is not a lie—it is the truth! I have evidence!'

'Evidence!' He started up with dry and trembling lips.

'Yes. Through her influence over Mrs Arryford, your aunt induced her to make you her heir. You are fond of money; you are in debt, and you could not wait until the old lady died in the course of nature. On the night of the murder you were in the house.'

'No, no! I swear . . .'

'You need not; you were seen leaving the house. To throw suspicion on Rosa you disguised yourself as a negress, and came to pawn the amber bead necklace at my shop. I recognized that the supposed black woman was minus the little finger of the right hand. You, Mr Jevons, are mutilated in the same way. Again, I paid you with a five-pound note. Of that note I took the number. It has been traced by the number, and you are the man who paid it away. I saw . . .'

Jevons jumped up, still white and shaking. 'It's a lie!

a lie!' he said, hoarsely. 'I did not kill Mrs Arryford; I did not pawn the beads. I did . . .'

'You did both those things!' said Hagar, brushing past him. 'I have two witnesses who can prove what I say is true. Rosa! Mr Horval!'

She flung the outside door wide open, while Jevons again sank into the arm-chair, with an expression of horror on his white face. 'Rosa! Horval!' he muttered. 'I am lost!'

Rosa and the detective entered quickly in response to Hagar's call, and with her looked down on the shrinking figure of the accused man.

'These are my witnesses,' said Hagar, slowly. 'Rosa!'

'I saw dat man in de house when my missy died,' said the negress. 'I hear noise in de night; I come down, and I see Massa Jevons run away from de room of my missy, and Missus Lyle let him out by de side door. He kill my poo' missy—yes, I tink dat.'

'You hear,' said Hagar to the terrified man. 'Now, Mr Horval.'

'I traced the five-pound note you gave him by its number,' said the detective. 'Yes, he paid it away at his club; I can bring a waiter to prove it.'

'You hear,' said Hagar again; 'and I know by the evidence of your lost finger that you are the man, disguised as a negress, who pawned the necklace which was stolen from the person of Mrs Arryford, after you murdered her. The dead woman, as Rosa tells us, wore that necklace night and day. Only with her death could it have been removed. You murdered her; you stole the necklace of amber beads.'

Jevons leaped up. 'No, no, no!' he cried, loudly, striking his hands together in despair. 'I am innocent!'

'That,' said Horval, slipping the handcuffs on his wrists, 'you shall prove before a judge and jury.'

When Jevons, still protesting his innocence, was removed to prison, Hagar and the negress returned to Carby's

Crescent. It can easily be guessed how she had traced the crime home to Jevons. She had noticed that the negress who pawned the beads had no little finger. On being brought face to face with Rosa, she had seen that the woman had not lost the finger; and when Jevons had removed his gloves she had seen in his right hand the evidence that he was one with the mysterious black woman of the pawn-shop. Still, she was not certain; and it was only when Rosa had deposed to the presence of the man at midnight in the Bedford Gardens house, and when Horval had traced the five-pound note of which she had taken the number, that she was certain that Jevons was the murderer. Hence the accusation; hence the arrest. But now the fact of his guilt was clearly established. To obtain the wealth of Mrs Arryford the wretched man had committed a crime; to hide that crime and throw the blame on Rosa he had pawned the amber beads; and now the amber beads were about to hang him. In the moment of his triumph, when preparing to enjoy the fruits of his crime, Nemesis had struck him down.

The news of the arrest, the story of the amber beads, was in all the papers next day; and next day, also, Miss Lyle came to see Hagar. Pale and stern, she swept into the shop, and looked at Hagar with a bitter smile.

'Girl!' she said, harshly, 'you have been our evil genius!'

'I have been the means of denouncing your accomplice, you mean,' returned Hagar, composedly.

'My accomplice—no, my son!'

'Your son!' Hagar recoiled, with a startled expression. 'Your son, Miss Lyle?'

'Not Miss, but Mrs Lyle,' returned the gaunt, pale woman; 'and Frederick Jevons is my son by my first husband. You think he is guilty; you are wrong, for he is innocent. You believe that you will hang him; but I tell you, girl, he will go free. Read this paper,' she said, thrusting an envelope into the hand of Hagar, 'and you will see how you have been mistaken. I shall never see you again in this life; but I leave my curse on you!'

Before Hagar could collect her wits, Miss—or rather Mrs—Lyle, as she called herself, went hurriedly out of the shop. Her manner was so wild, her words so ominous of evil, that Hagar had it on her mind to follow her, and, if possible, prevent the consequences of her despair. She hurried to the door, but Mrs Lyle had disappeared, and as there was no one to mind the shop, Hagar could not go after her. Luckily, at this moment Horval turned the corner, and at once the girl beckoned to him.

'Miss Lyle—did you see her?'

'Yes,' said Horval, with a nod 'she's on her way across Westminster Bridge.'

'Oh, follow her—follow her quickly!' cried Hagar, wildly, 'she is not herself; she is bent on some rash deed!'

Horval paused a moment in bewilderment; then, grasping the situation, he turned, without a word, and raced down the street in the trail of Miss Lyle. Hagar watched his hurrying figure until it turned the corner; then she retreated to the back parlour, and hurriedly opened the envelope. On the sheet of paper she found within the following confession was written:

'I am not a spinster, but a widow,' began the document abruptly—'a twice-married woman. By my first husband I had Frederick Jevons, who passes as my nephew, and whom I love better than my own soul. When my second husband, Mr Lyle, died, I cast about for some means of employment, as I was poor. Mrs Arryford advertised for an unmarried woman as a companion; she absolutely refused to have any companion but a spinster. To get the situation, which was a good one, as Mrs Arryford was rich, I called myself Miss Lyle, and obtained the place. Mrs Arryford had no relatives and much money, so I schemed to

obtain her wealth for my son, whom I introduced as
my nephew. Rosa, the black maid, had a great deal
of influence over her weak-minded mistress, and in
some way—I don't know how—she fathomed my
purpose. It was a battle between us, as Rosa was
determined that I should not get the money of Mrs
Arryford for my son. Finally I triumphed, and Frederick was left sole heir of all the old lady's wealth.
Then Rosa learnt, by eavesdropping, the true relation-
ship between myself and Frederick. She told her
mistress, and with Mrs Arryford I had a stormy scene,
in which she declared her intention of revoking her will
and turning me and my son out on the world as paupers.
I begged, I implored, I threatened; but Mrs Arryford,
backed up by that wicked Rosa, was firm. I sent for my
son to try and soften the old lady, but he was not in
town, and did not come to see me till late at night.
When he arrived I told him that I had killed Mrs
Arryford. I did so to prevent her altering her will, and
out of love for my dear son, lest he should lose the
money. Frederick was horrified, and rushed from the
house. I believe Rosa saw me let him out by the side
door. I was determined to throw the blame on Rosa, as
I hated her so. Knowing that she coveted the necklace of amber beads, I stole it from the neck of the
dead woman and gave it to my son next day. I
suggested that he should dress up as Rosa, and pawn
the necklace, so that she might be suspected. To save
me, he did so. I obtained a dress that Rosa was fond of
wearing—yellow silk trimmed with black beads; also
the jewellery of the creature. Frederick blackened his
face, and pawned the beads in a pawn-shop at Lambeth.
I sent Rosa on a pretended errand to Waterloo
Station, at the time Frederick was pawning the beads,
so as to get evidence against her that she was in the
neighbourhood. Then I suggested to Horval, the

detective, that the beads might have been pawned. He found the shop, and I thought my plot had succeeded; that Rosa would be condemned and hanged. Unfortunately, the woman who kept the pawn-shop was clever, and traced Frederick by means of his mutilated right hand. I hate her! Frederick is now in prison on a charge of murder, which he did not commit. I am guilty. I killed Mrs Arryford. Frederick knows nothing. He helped me to save myself by trying to throw the blame on Rosa. All useless. I am guilty, and I am determined that he shall not suffer for my sin. Officers of the law, I command you to release my son and arrest me. I am the murderess of Mrs Arryford. I swear it.

Julia Lyle.

'Witnesses:
   'Amelia Tyke (housemaid).
   'Mark Drew (butler).'

Hagar let the document fall from her hands with a sensation of pity for the wretched woman.

'How she must love her son,' thought the girl, 'to have murdered a kind and good woman for his sake! It is terrible! Well, I suppose he will now be released and will enter into possession of the wealth his mother schemed to obtain for him. But he must do justice to Rosa for all the trouble he has caused her. He must give her an annuity, and also the necklace of amber beads, which has been the cause of tracing the crime home to its door. As for Mrs Lyle . . .'

At this moment, white and breathless, Horval rushed into the parlour. Hagar sprang to her feet, and looked anxiously at him, expectant of bad news. She was right.

'My girl,' cried Horval, hoarscly, 'Miss Lyle is dead!'

'Dead? Ah!' said Hagar to herself. 'I thought as much.'

'She threw herself over Westminster Bridge, and has just been picked out of the water—dead!'

'Dead!' said Hagar again. 'Dead!'

'As a door-nail!' replied the detective in a perplexed tone. 'But why—why did she commit suicide?'

Hagar sighed, and in silence handed to the detective the confession of the dead woman.

VII

How He Cut His Stick

M. McD. Bodkin Q.C.

He breathed freely at last as he lifted the small black Gladstone bag of stout calfskin, and set it carefully on the seat of the empty railway carriage close beside him.

He lifted the bag with a manifest effort. Yet he was a big powerfully built young fellow; handsome too in a way; with straw-coloured hair and moustache and a round face, placid, honest-looking but not too clever. His light blue eyes had an anxious, worried look. No wonder, poor chap! he was weighted with a heavy responsibility. That unobtrusive black bag held £5,000 in gold and notes which he—a junior clerk in the famous banking house of Gower and Grant— was taking from the head office in London to a branch two hundred miles down the line.

The older and more experienced clerk whose ordinary duty it was to convey the gold had been taken strangely and suddenly ill at the last moment.

'There's Jim Pollock,' said the bank manager, looking round for a substitute, 'he'll do. He is big enough to knock the head off anyone that interferes with him.'

So Jim Pollock had the heavy responsibility thrust upon him. The big fellow who would tackle any man in England in a football rush without a thought of fear was as nervous as a two-year-old child. All the way down to this point his watchful eyes and strong right hand had never left the bag for a moment. But here at the Eddiscombe Junction he had got locked in alone to a single first-class carriage, and there was a clear run of forty-seven miles to the next stoppage.

So with a sigh and shrug of relief, he threw away his anxiety, lay back on the soft seat, lit a pipe, drew a sporting paper from his pocket, and was speedily absorbed in the account of the Rugby International Championship match, for Jim himself was not without hopes of his 'cap' in the near future.

The train rattled out of the station and settled down to its smooth easy stride—a good fifty miles an hour through the open country.

Still absorbed in his paper he did not notice the gleam of two stealthy keen eyes that watched him from the dark shadow under the opposite seat. He did not see that long lithe wiry figure uncoil and creep out, silently as a snake, across the floor of the carriage.

He saw nothing, and felt nothing till he felt two murderous hands clutching at his throat and a knee crushing his chest in.

Jim was strong, but before his sleeping strength had time to waken, he was down on his back on the carriage floor with a handkerchief soaked in chloroform jammed close to his mouth and nostrils.

He struggled desperately for a moment or so, half rose and almost flung off his clinging assailant. But even as he struggled the dreamy drug stole strength and sense away; he fell back heavily and lay like a log on the carriage floor.

The faithful fellow's last thought as his senses left him was 'The gold is gone.' It was his first thought as he awoke with dizzy pain and racked brain from the deathlike swoon. The train was still at full speed; the carriage doors were still locked; but the carriage empty and the bag was gone.

He searched despairingly in the racks, under the seats—all empty. Jim let the window down with a clash and bellowed.

The train began to slacken speed and rumble into the station. Half a dozen porters ran together—the station-master following more leisurely as beseemed his dignity. Speedily a crowd gathered round the door.

'I have been robbed,' Jim shouted, 'of a black bag with £5,000 in it!'

Then the superintendent pushed his way through the crowd.

'Where were you robbed, sir?' he said with a suspicious look at the dishevelled and excited Jim.

'Between this and Eddiscombe Junction.'

'Impossible, sir, there is no stoppage between this and Eddiscombe, and the carriage is empty.'

'I thought it was empty at Eddiscombe, but there must have been a man under the seat.'

'There is no man under the seat now,' retorted the superintendent curtly, 'you had better tell your story to the police. There is a detective on the platform.'

Jim told his story to the detective, who listened gravely and told him that he must consider himself in custody pending inquiries.

A telegram was sent to Eddiscombe and it was found that communication had been stopped. This must have happened quite recently, for a telegram had gone through less than an hour before. The breakage was quickly located about nine miles outside Eddiscombe. Some of the wires had been pulled down half way to the ground, and the insulators smashed to pieces on one of the poles. All round the place the ground was trampled with heavy footprints which passed through a couple of fields out on the high road and were lost. No other clue of any kind was forthcoming.

The next day but one, a card, with the name 'Sir Gregory Grant', was handed to Dora Myrl as she sat hard at work in the little drawing-room which she called her study. A portly, middle-aged, benevolent gentleman followed the card into the room.

'Miss Myrl?' he said, extending his hand, 'I have heard of you from my friend, Lord Millicent. I have come to entreat your assistance. I am the senior partner of the banking firm of Gower and Grant. You have heard of the railway robbery, I suppose?'

'I have heard all the paper had to tell me.'

'There is little more to tell. I have called on you personally, Miss Myrl, because, personally, I am deeply interested in the case. It is not so much the money—though the amount is, of course, serious. But the honour of the bank is at stake. We have always prided ourselves on treating our clerks well, and heretofore we have reaped the reward. For nearly a century there has not been a single case of fraud or dishonesty amongst them. It is a proud record for our bank, and we should like to keep it unbroken if possible. Suspicion is heavy on young James Pollock. I want him punished, of course, if he is guilty, but I want him cleared if he is innocent. That's why I came to you.'

'The police think?'

'Oh, they think there can be no doubt about his guilt. They have their theory pat. No one was in the carriage— no one could leave it. Pollock threw out the bag to an accomplice along the line. They even pretend to find the mark in the ground where the heavy bag fell—a few hundred yards nearer to Eddiscombe than where the wires were pulled down.'

'What has been done?'

'They have arrested the lad and sent out the "Hue and Cry" for a man with a very heavy calfskin bag—that's all. They are quite sure they have caught the principal thief anyway.'

'And you?'

'I will be frank with you, Miss Myrl. I have my doubts. The case *seems* conclusive. It is impossible that anybody could have got out of the train at full speed. But I have seen the lad, and I have my doubts.'

'Can I see him?'

'I would be very glad if you did.'

After five minutes' conversation with Jim Pollock, Dora drew Sir Gregory aside.

'I think I see my way,' she said, 'I will undertake the case on one condition.'

'Any fee that . . .'

'It's not the fee. I never talk of the fee till the case is over. I will undertake the case if you give me Mr Pollock to help me. Your instinct was right, Sir Gregory: the boy is innocent.'

There was much grumbling amongst the police when a *nolle prosequi* was entered on behalf of the bank, and James Pollock was discharged from custody, and it was plainly hinted the Crown would interpose.

Meanwhile Pollock was off by a morning train with Miss Dora Myrl, from London to Eddiscombe. He was brimming over with gratitude and devotion. Of course they talked of the robbery on the way down.

'The bag was very heavy, Mr Pollock?' Dora asked.

'I'd sooner carry it one mile than ten, Miss Myrl.'

'Yet you are pretty strong, I should think.'

She touched his protruding biceps professionally with her finger tips, and he coloured to the roots of his hair.

'Would you know the man that robbed you if you saw him again?' Dora asked.

'Not from Adam. He had his hands on my throat, the chloroform crammed into my mouth before I knew where I was. It was about nine or ten miles outside Eddiscombe. You believe there *was* a man—don't you, Miss Myrl? You are about the only person that does. I don't blame them, for how did the chap get out of the train going at the rate of sixty miles an hour—that's what fetches me, 'pon my word,' he concluded incoherently; 'if I was any other chap I'd believe myself guilty on the evidence. Can you tell me how the trick was done, Miss Myrl?'

'That's my secret for the present, Mr Pollock, but I may tell you this much, when we get to the pretty little town of Eddiscombe I will look out for a stranger with a crooked stick instead of a black bag.'

There were three hotels in Eddiscombe, but Mr Mark Brown and his sister were hard to please. They tried the three in succession, keeping their eyes about them for a stranger with a crooked stick, and spending their leisure time in exploring the town and country on a pair of capital bicycles, which they hired by the week.

As Miss Brown (alias Dora Myrl) was going down the stairs of the third hotel one sunshiny afternoon a week after their arrival, she met midway, face to face, a tall middle-aged man limping a little, a very little, and leaning on a stout oak stick, with a dark shiny varnish, and a crooked handle. She passed him without a second glance. But that evening she gossiped with the chambermaid, and learned that the stranger was a commercial traveller—Mr McCrowder—who had been staying some weeks at the hotel, with an occasional run up to London in the train, and run round the country on his bicycle, 'a nice, easily-pleased, pleasant-spoken gentleman,' the chambermaid added on her own account.

Next day Dora Myrl met the stranger again in the same place on the stairs. Was it her awkwardness or his? As she moved aside to let him pass, her little foot caught in the stick, jerked it from his hand, and sent it clattering down the stairs into the hall.

She ran swiftly down the stairs in pursuit, and carried it back with a pretty apology to the owner. But not before she had seen on the inside of the crook a deep notch, cutting through the varnish into the wood.

At dinner that day their table adjoined Mr McCrowder's. Half way through the meal she asked Jim to tell her what the hour was, as her watch had stopped. It was a curious request, for she sat facing the clock, and he had to turn round to see it. But Jim turned obediently, and came face to face with Mr McCrowder, who started and stared at the sight of him as though he had seen a ghost. Jim stared back stolidly without a trace of recognition in his face, and Mr McCrowder, after a moment, resumed his dinner. Then Dora set, or seemed to set and wind, her watch, and so the curious little incident closed.

That evening Dora played a musical little jingle on the piano in their private sitting-room, touching the notes abstractedly and apparently deep in thought. Suddenly she closed the piano with a bang.

'Mr Pollock?'

'Well, Miss Myrl,' said Jim, who had been watching her with the patient, honest, stupid admiration of a big New-foundland dog.

'We will take a ride together on our bicycles to-morrow. I cannot say what hour, but have them ready when I call for them.'

'Yes, Miss Myrl.'

'And bring a ball of stout twine in your pocket.'

'Yes, Miss Myrl.'

'By the way, have you a revolver?'

'Never had such a thing in my life.'

'Could you use it if you got it?'

'I hardly know the butt from the muzzle, but'—modestly —'I can fight a little bit with my fists if that's any use.'

'Not the least in this case. An ounce of lead can stop a fourteen-stone champion. Besides one six-shooter is enough and I'm not too bad a shot.'

'You don't mean to say, Miss Myrl, that you . . .'

'I don't mean to say one word more at present, Mr Pollock, only have the bicycles ready when I want them and the twine.'

Next morning, after an exceptionally early breakfast, Dora took her place with a book in her hand coiled up on a sofa in a bow-window of the empty drawing-room that looked out on the street. She kept one eye on her book and the other on the window from which the steps of the hotel were visible.

About half-past nine o'clock she saw Mr McCrowder go down the steps, not limping at all, but carrying his bicycle with a big canvas bicycle-bag strapped to the handle bar.

In a moment she was down in the hall where the bicycles stood ready; in another she and Pollock were in the saddle sailing swiftly and smoothly along the street just as the tall figure of Mr McCrowder was vanishing round a distant corner.

'We have got to keep him in sight,' Dora whispered to her companion as they sped along, 'or rather I have got to keep him and you to keep me in sight. Now let me go to the front; hold as far back as you can without losing me, and the moment I wave a white handkerchief—scorch!'

Pollock nodded and fell back, and in this order—each about half a mile apart—the three riders swept out of the town into the open country.

The man in front was doing a strong steady twelve miles an hour, but the roads were good and Dora kept her distance without an effort, while Pollock held himself back. For a full hour this game of follow-my-leader was played without a change. Mr McCrowder had left the town at the opposite direction to the railway, but now he began to wheel round towards the line. Once he glanced behind and saw only a single girl cycling in the distance on the deserted road. The next time he saw no one, for Dora rode close to the inner curve.

They were now a mile or so from the place where the telegraph wires had been broken down, and Dora, who knew the lie of the land, felt sure their little bicycle trip was drawing to a close.

The road climbed a long easy winding slope thickly wooded on either side. The man in front put on a spurt; Dora answered it with another, and Pollock behind sprinted fiercely, lessening his distance from Dora. The leader crossed the top bend of the slope, turned a sharp curve, and went swiftly down a smooth decline, shaded by the interlacing branches of great trees.

Half a mile down at the bottom of the slope, he leaped suddenly from his bicycle with one quick glance back the way he had come. There was no one in view, for Dora held back at the turn. He ran his bicycle close into the wall on the left hand side where a deep trench hid it from the casual passers by; unstrapped the bag from the handle bar, and clambered over the wall with an agility that was surprising in one of his (apparent) age.

Dora was just round the corner in time to see him leap from the top of the wall into the thick wood. At once she drew out and waved her white handkerchief, then settled herself in the saddle and made her bicycle fly through the rush of a sudden wind, down the slope.

Pollock saw the signal; bent down over his handle bar and pedalled uphill like the piston rods of a steam engine.

The man's bicycle by the roadside was a finger post for Dora. She, in her turn, over-perched the wall as lightly as a bird. Gathering her tailor-made skirt tightly around her, she peered and listened intently. She could see nothing, but a little way in front a slight rustling of the branches caught her quick ears. Moving in the underwood, stealthily and silently as a rabbit, she caught a glimpse through the leaves of a dark grey tweed suit fifteen or twenty yards off. A few steps more and she had a clear view. The man was on his knees; he had drawn a black leather bag from a thick tangle of ferns at the foot of a great old beech tree, and was busy cramming a number of small canvas sacks into his bicycle bag.

Dora moved cautiously forward till she stood in a little opening, clear of the undergrowth, free to use her right arm.

'Good morning, Mr McCrowder!' she cried sharply.

The man started, and turned and saw a girl half a dozen yards off standing clear in the sunlight, with a mocking smile on her face.

His lips growled out a curse; his right hand left the bags and stole to his side pocket.

'Stop that!' The command came clear and sharp. 'Throw up your hands!'

He looked again. The sunlight glinted on the barrel of a revolver, pointed straight at his head, with a steady hand.

'Up with your hands, or I fire!' and his hands went up over his head. The next instant Jim Pollock came crashing through the underwood, like an elephant through the jungle.

He stopped short with a cry of amazement.

'Steady!' came Dora's quiet voice; 'don't get in my line of fire. Round there to the left—that's the way. Take away his revolver. It is in his right-hand coat pocket. Now tie his hands!'

Jim Pollock did his work stolidly as directed. But while he wound the strong cord round the wrists and arms of Mr McCrowder, he remembered the railway carriage and the strangling grip at his throat, and the chloroform, and the disgrace that followed, and if he strained the knots extra tight it's hard to blame him.

'Now,' said Dora, 'finish his packing,' and Jim crammed the remainder of the canvas sacks into the big bicycle bag.

'You don't mind the weight?'

He gave a delighted grin for answer, as he swung both bags in his hands.

'Get up!' said Dora to the thief, and he stumbled to his

feet sulkily. 'Walk in front. I mean to take you back to Eddiscombe with me.'

When they got on the road-side Pollock strapped the bicycle bag to his own handle-bar.

'May I trouble you, Mr Pollock, to unscrew one of the pedals of this gentleman's bicycle?' said Dora.

It was done in a twinkling. 'Now give him a lift up,' she said to Jim, 'he is going to ride back with one pedal.'

The abject thief held up his bound wrists imploringly.

'Oh, that's all right. I noticed you held the middle of your handle-bar from choice coming out. You'll do it from necessity going back. We'll look after you. Don't whine; you've played a bold game and lost the odd trick, and you've got to pay up, that's all.'

There was a wild sensation in Eddiscombe when, in broad noon, the bank thief was brought in riding on a one-pedalled machine to the police barrack and handed into custody. Dora rode on through the cheering crowd to the hotel.

A wire brought Sir Gregory Grant down by the afternoon train, and the three dined together that night at his cost; the best dinner and wine the hotel could supply. Sir Gregory was brimming over with delight, like the bubbling champagne in his wine glass.

'Your health, Mr Pollock,' said the banker to the junior clerk. 'We will make up in the bank to you for the annoyance you have had. You shall fix your own fee, Miss Myrl— or, rather, I'll fix it for you if you allow me. Shall we say half the salvage? But I'm dying with curiosity to know how you managed to find the money and thief.'

'It was easy enough when you come to think of it, Sir Gregory. The man would have been a fool to tramp across the country with a black bag full of gold while the "Hue and Cry" was hot on him. His game was to hide it and lie low, and he did so. The sight of Mr Pollock at the hotel hurried him up as I hoped it would; that's the whole story.'

'Oh, that's not all. How did you find the man? How did the man get out of the train going at the rate of sixty miles an hour? But I suppose I'd best ask that question of Mr Pollock, who was there?'

'Don't ask me any questions, sir,' said Jim, with a look of profound admiration in Dora's direction. 'She played the game off her own bat. All I know is that the chap cut his stick after he had done for me. I cannot in the least tell how.'

'Will you have pity on my curiosity, Miss Myrl.'

'With pleasure, Sir Gregory. You must have noticed, as I did, that where the telegraph was broken down the line was embanked and the wires ran quite close to the railway carriage. It is easy for an active man to slip a crooked stick like this' (she held up Mr McCrowder's stick as she spoke) 'over the two or three of the wires and so swing himself into the air clear of the train. The acquired motion would carry him along the wires to the post and give him a chance of breaking down the insulators.'

'By Jove! you're right, Miss Myrl. It's quite simple when one comes to think of it. But, still, I don't understand how . . .'

'The friction of the wire,' Dora went on in the even tone of a lecturer, 'with a man's weight on it, would bite deep into the wood of the stick, like that!' Again she held out the crook of a dark thick oak stick for Sir Gregory to examine, and he peered at it through his gold spectacles.

'The moment I saw that notch,' Dora added quietly, 'I knew how Mr McCrowder had "*Cut his stick*".'

VIII

A Race with the Sun

L. T. Meade
and Clifford Halifax

It was in the spring of 1895 that the following apparently unimportant occurrence took place. I returned home somewhat late one evening, and was met by my servant, Silva, with the words:

'A lady, sir—a nun, I think, from her dress—is waiting for you in your study.'

'What can she want with me?' I asked. I felt annoyed, as I was anxious to get to work on some important experiments.

'She is very anxious to have an interview with you, sir; she called almost immediately after you had gone out, and said if I would allow her she would wait to speak to you, as her mission was of some importance. I showed her into the study, and after a quarter of an hour she rang the bell, and desired me to tell you that she would not wait now, but would call again later. She left the house, but came back about ten minutes ago. I did not like to refuse her, and . . .'

'Quite right, Silva; I will see to the matter,' I answered.

I went straight to the study, where a bright, young-looking woman, in the full costume of a nun of the Church of Rome, started up and came forward to meet me. She made a brief apology for intruding upon me, and almost before I could reply to her, plunged into the object of her visit. It so happened that she knew a young man in whom I was interested, having come across him when in hospital—she confirmed my views with regard to him—told me a subscription was being got up for his benefit, and asked if I would contribute towards it. I gave her two sovereigns—she expressed much gratitude, and speedily left the house.

At this time I was lecturing in several quarters, and did not give another thought to such an apparently uninteresting event. In the autumn of the same year, however, I was destined to recall it with vivid and startling distinctness.

During this special autumn I was, as I fondly hoped, approaching the *magnum opus* of my life—I was in a fair way to the discovery of a new explosive which would put gunpowder, dynamite, and all other explosives completely in the shade. It was to be smokeless, devoid of smell, and also of such a nature that it would be impossible for it to ignite except when placed in certain combinations. Its propelling power would be greater than anything in existence; in short, if it turned out what I dreamed, it would be a most important factor in case of war, and of immense use to England as a nation. Giddy hopes often throbbed in my head as I worked over it.

My experiments were progressing favourably, but I still wanted one link. Try as I would I could not obtain it. No combinations that I attempted would produce the desired result, and in much vexation of spirit I was wondering if, after all, the secret of my life would never reveal itself, when on a certain afternoon Silva opened the door of my laboratory and announced two visitors. This was an unusual thing for him to do, and I started up in surprise and some involuntary annoyance. A tall man had entered the room—he was dark, with the swarthy complexion of a gipsy; his eyes were small, closely-set, and piercing; he had a long beard and a quantity of thick hair falling in profusion round his neck. Immediately following him was a little man, in every sense of the word his antitype. He was thin and small, clean-shaven, and with a bald head. The two men were total strangers to me, and I stood still for a moment unable to account for this intrusion. The elder of the two came forward with outstretched hands.

'Pardon me,' he said, 'I know I am intruding. My name is Paul Lewin—this is my friend, Carl Kruse. We have had the pleasure of listening to your lecture at the Royal Society, and have taken these unceremonious means of forcing ourselves upon you, for you are the only man in England who can do what we want.'

'Pray sit down,' I said to them both. I hastily cleared two chairs, and my uninvited guests seated themselves. Lewin's face seemed fairly to twitch with eagerness, but Kruse, on the contrary, was very quiet and calm. He was as immovable in expression as his companion was the reverse. The elder man's deep-set eyes flashed; he looked me all over from head to foot.

'You are the only person who can help us,' he repeated, breathing quickly as he spoke.

'Pray explain yourself,' I said to him.

'I will do so, and in a few words. Mr Kruse and I heard you lecture in the early part of last summer. From hints you let drop it became abundantly clear to us both that you were in the pursuit of a discovery which has occupied the best part of both our lives. We are in a difficulty which we believe that you can explain away. We had hoped not to ask you for any assistance, but time is precious—any moment you may perfect your most interesting experiments. In that case the patent and the honour would be yours, and we should be out of it. Now, we don't want to be out of it, and we have come here to ask you frankly if you will co-operate with us.'

I felt a warm blood rushing into my face.

'I don't understand you,' I said; 'to what discovery do you allude?'

'To that of the great new explosive,' said Kruse.

I sprang to my feet in ill-suppressed excitement.

'You must be making a mistake,' I said. 'I have not breathed a word of the matter over which I am engaged to a living soul.'

'You dropped hints at your lecture, which made it plain to us that you and we were on the same track,' said Kruse. 'But here, I can prove the matter.' He took a note-book hurriedly out of his pocket and began to read from it.

I listened to him in dismay and astonishment. There was not the least doubt that these men were working on my own lines—nay, more, that their intelligence was equal to my own, and it was highly probable that they would be first in the field.

'The fact is this,' said Lewin. 'My friend and I have been really working with you step by step. While you have been perfecting your great explosive in your London laboratory, we have been conducting matters on a larger and freer scale in our more extensive laboratories off the Cornish coast. The solitude of our place, too, enables us to test our explosive in the open air. Now, we know exactly the point to which you have come, and your present difficulty is'—he dropped his voice to a semi-whisper—'you are trying to combine certain gases to produce a certain result. Now we have discovered what you want, but our explosive is still far from perfect, owing to the instability of nitrogen chloride'—he dropped his voice again.

'You can help us,' he said abruptly. 'I see by your face that you have certain information which will be valuable to us. Now we, on our side, have information which will be of immense benefit to you. Will you join us in the matter? You have but to name your own price.'

I could not help staring at Lewin in astonishment—he started impatiently from his seat.

'This is the state of the case, sir,' he continued. 'Our lives have been spent over this matter—it is a great work— a magnificent discovery, it is nearly complete. When absolutely completed we intend to offer it to the German Government for something like a million sterling—but there is a probability that you may be first in the field. If you patent your discovery before ours, we are done men. Will you be content to work with us, or . . .' He stopped, his face was crimson, his eyes seemed to start from his head.

'My friend is right,' said Kruse, 'but he is far too excitable; I have told him so over and over. We know of your discovery, Mr Gilchrist; we believe that you can help us, and we know that we can help you. We are working on the same lines. The discovery of this new explosive means money, a very large fortune, and fame. Now, we don't mean to resign our own share in this without a struggle, but we are satisfied to go hand in glove with you. Will you visit us in Cornwall and help us with our experiment? We will impart to you gladly what we know, on condition that you in your turn give us information. You thus see that between us the discovery is complete; without our united efforts it may be a very long time before it is ready for use. Let us go shares in the matter.'

'I am not working at this thing for money,' I said. 'I am an unmarried man, and have as much money as I need. When my discovery is complete I shall offer it to the English Government—they can do what they please with it—my reward will be the gain which it will give to my country. This is a time of peace, but on all hands men are armed to the teeth. The discovery of this explosive, if it means all that I hope it may mean, will be a most important factor in case of war.'

Kruse laughed somewhat nervously.

'We are not so quixotic as you are,' he said; 'I have a

wife, and my friend Lewin has large claims upon him which made it essential that he should make money where he can. Now, will you come to terms or not? The fact is this, our knowledge is indispensable to you, your knowledge is indispensable to us—shall we go shares or not?'

I thought for a little. I had begun by being much annoyed with my strange visitors, but now, in spite of myself, I was interested. They not only knew what they were talking about, but they had something to sell, which I was only too willing to buy.

'Can I look at your notes for a moment?' I said to Kruse.

He immediately handed me his note-book. I glanced over what he had written down—his statements were clear and to the point. There was no doubt that he and his companion were working on identical lines with myself.

'I cannot give you an answer immediately,' I said. 'Your visit has astonished me; the knowledge that you and I are working at a similar discovery has amazed me still more. Will you call upon me again tomorrow? I may then be in a position to speak to you.'

They rose at once, Lewin with ill-suppressed irritation, but Kruse quietly.

The moment I was alone I gave myself up to anxious thought. It was impossible to pursue any further investigations that day, and leaving the laboratory, I spent the rest of the evening in my study. At night I slept little, and on the following morning had resolved to make terms with the Cornish men. They both arrived at ten o'clock, accompanied now by a pretty young woman, whom Kruse introduced as his wife. The moment I saw her face I was puzzled by an intangible likeness to somebody else—she was fair-haired, and, I had little doubt, had German blood in her veins—her eyes were large and blue, and particularly innocent in expression—her mouth was softly curved; she had pretty teeth and a bright smile—she was like thousands of other women, and yet there was a difference. I felt certain that she was not a stranger to me, but where and under what possible circumstances I had met her before was a mystery which I could not fathom. She apologized in a pretty way for forcing herself into my presence, but told me she was really as much interested in the discovery as her husband and friend, and as the matter was of the utmost importance, had insisted on coming with them to visit me today.

Having asked my guests to be seated, I immediately proceeded to the subject of their visit.

'I have thought very carefully over this matter,' I said, 'and perceive that it may be the best in the end for us to come to a mutual arrangement, but I can only do so on the distinct understanding that if this explosive is completed it is not to be offered to a foreign nation, except in the event of the English Government refusing it. That is extremely unlikely, as, if it is perfected on the lines which I have sketched out in my mind, it will be too valuable for us as a nation to lose. I am willing, gentlemen,' I continued, 'to help you with my knowledge, provided you allow a proper legal document to be drawn up, in which each of us pledges the other that we will take no steps with regard to the use of the explosive or the surrendering our rights in it, but with the concurrence of all three. My lawyer can easily prepare such a document, and we will all sign it. On those terms and those alone I am willing to go with you.'

Lewin looked by no means satisfied, but Kruse and his wife eagerly agreed to everything that I suggested.

'It is perfectly fair,' said Mrs Kruse, speaking in a bright, crisp voice, 'we give you something, you give us something. When the explosive is complete we go shares in the matter. We are willing to sign the document you speak of. Is it not so, Carl?'

'Certainly,' said her husband. 'Mr Gilchrist's terms are quite reasonable.'

Lewin still remained silent.

'I have nothing else to suggest,' I said, looking at him.

'Oh, I am in your hands,' he said then. 'The fact is, the thing that worries me is having to offer this to England. I am not a patriot in any sense of the word, and I believe Germany would give us more for it.'

'My terms are absolute,' I repeated. 'I am rather nearer to perfect discovery than you are, and the matter must drop, and we must both take our chances of being first in the field, if you do not agree to what I suggest.'

'I am in your hands,' repeated the man. 'When the legal document is drawn up I am willing to sign it.'

'And now,' said Mrs Kruse, coming forward and pushing back the fluffy hair from her forehead, 'you will immediately arrange to come to us in Cornwall, will you not Mr Gilchrist?'

'Certainly,' I replied, 'and the sooner the better, for if this thing is to be completed, we have really no time to lose. I can go to Cornwall the day after tomorrow, and bring my lawyer's document with me.'

'That will do capitally,' said Mrs Kruse. 'We ourselves go home tonight. We are greatly obliged to you. This is our address.' She took out her card-case as she spoke, extracted a card, and hastily scribbled some directions on the back.

'Our place is called Castle Lewin,' she said. 'It is situated on the coast not far from Chrome Ash—the country around is very wild, but there is a magnificent view and some splendid cliffs. Your nearest station is Chrome Ash. Our carriage shall meet you there and bring you straight to Castle Lewin.'

'You had best take an early train,' said Lewin, 'that is, if you want to arrive in time for dinner. A good train leaves Paddington at 5.50 in the morning. I am sorry we are asking you to undertake so long a journey.'

'Pray do not mention it,' I answered. 'I am quite accustomed to going about the country, and think nothing of a few hours on the railway.'

'We will expect you the day after tomorrow,' said Mrs

Kruse. 'We are greatly obliged to you. I am quite sure you will never repent of the kindness you are about to show us.' She held out her hand frankly, her blue eyes looked full into mine. Again I was puzzled by an intangible likeness. Where, when, how had I met the gaze of those eyes before? My memory would not supply the necessary link. I took the hand she offered, and a few moments later my guests had left me alone.

I went out at once to consult my lawyer, and to tell him of the curious occurrence which had taken place. He promised to draw up the necessary document, and begged of me to be careful how far I gave myself away.

'There is no doubt that the men are enthusiastic scientists,' I said. 'It is plainly a case of give-and-take, and I believe I cannot do better than go shares with them in the matter.'

Mr Scrivener promised that I should have the terms of agreement in my possession that evening, and I returned home.

The next day I made further preparations for my Cornish visit, and on the following morning, at an early hour, took train from Paddington to Chrome Ash. The season of year was late October, and as I approached the coast I noticed that a great gale was blowing seawards. I am fond of Nature in her stormy moods, and as I had the compartment to myself, I opened the window and put out my head to inhale the breeze.

I arrived at Chrome Ash between five and six in the evening. Twilight was already falling and rain was pouring in torrents. It was a desolate little wayside station, and I happened to be the only passenger who left the train. A nicely-appointed brougham and a pair of horses were waiting outside, and with her head poked out of the window, looking eagerly around, I saw the pretty face of Mrs Kruse.

'Ah, you have come; that is good,' she said. 'I determined to meet you myself. Now, step in, won't you? I have brought the brougham, for the night is so wild. We have a long drive before us, over ten miles—I hope you won't object to my company.'

I assured her to the contrary, and seated myself by her side. As I intended to return to town on the following day, I had only brought my suit-case with me. This was placed beside the driver, and we started off at a round pace in the direction of Castle Lewin.

To get to this out-of-the-way part of the country we had to skirt the coast, and the wind was now so high that the horses had to battle against it. The roads were in many places unprotected, and less sure-footed beasts might have been in danger of coming to grief as they rounded promontories and skirted suspicious-looking landslips.

The drive took over an hour, and long before we reached Castle Lewin darkness enveloped us. But at last we entered a long avenue, the horses dashed forward, the carriage made an abrupt turn, and I saw before me an old-fashioned, low house with a castellated roof and a tower at one end. We drew up before a deep porch, a manservant ran down some steps, flung open the door of the brougham, and helped Mrs Kruse to alight.

'See that Mr Gilchrist's luggage is taken to his room,' she said, 'and please tell your master and Mr Lewin that we have returned. Come this way, please, Mr Gilchrist.'

She led me into a square and lofty hall, the walls of which were decorated with different trophies of the chase. The floor was of ash, slippery and dark with age, and although the evening was by no means cold, a fire burned on the hearth at one side of the room. The fire looked cheerful, and I stepped up to it not unwillingly.

'From the first of October to the first of May I never allow that fire to go out,' said the young hostess, coming forward and rubbing her hands before the cheerful blaze. 'This, as I have told you, Mr Gilchrist, is a solitary place, and we need all the home comforts we can get. I am vexed that my husband is not in to receive you—but, ah! I hear him.' She started and listened attentively.

A side door which I had not before noticed opened, and Kruse and his extraordinary dark companion both entered the room. They were accompanied by a couple of pointers, and were both dressed in thick jerseys and knickerbockers. Kruse offered me his hand in a calm, nonchalant manner, but Lewin who could evidently never check his impetuosity, came eagerly forward, grasped my hand as if in a vice, and said, with emphasis:

'We are much obliged to you, Mr Gilchrist—welcome to Castle Lewin. I am sorry the night is such a bad one, or, late as it is, we might have had a walk round the place before dinner.'

'No, no, Paul,' said Mrs Kruse, 'you must not think of taking Mr Gilchrist out again—he has had a long railway journey and a tiring drive, and would, I am sure, like to go to his room now to rest and dress for dinner.'

'I will show you the way,' said Kruse.

He took me up a low flight of stairs—we turned down a corridor, and he threw open the door of a pleasant, modern-looking bedroom. A fire blazed here also, the curtains were drawn at the windows, and the whole place looked cheery and hospitable. My host stepped forward, stirred up the fire to a more cheerful blaze, put on a log or two, and telling me that dinner would be announced by the sounding of a gong, left me to my own meditations.

I stood for a short time by the fire, and then proceeded to dress. By and by the gong sounded through the house, and I went down-stairs into the hall. The pointers were lying in front of the fire, and a great mastiff had now joined their company. The mastiff glanced at me out of two blood-shot eyes, and growled angrily as I approached. I am always fond of dogs, and pretending not to notice the creature's animosity, patted him on his head. He looked up at me in some astonishment; his growls ceased; he rose slowly on

his haunches, and not only received my caresses favourabl
but even went to the length of rubbing himself against n
legs. At this moment Mrs Kruse, in a pretty evening dres
tripped into the hall.

'Ah, there you are,' she said, 'and I see Demoniac has mad
friends with you. He scarcely ever does that with any one

At this instant Lewin and Kruse entered the hall.
gave my arm to Mrs Kruse, and we went into the dining
room. During dinner the gale became more tempestuous
and Kruse and his wife entertained me with tales o
shipwreck and disaster.

The cloth was removed, and an old mahogany table
nearly black with age and shining like a looking-glass
reflected decanters of wine and a plentiful dessert.

'Pass the wine round,' said Lewin. 'Pray, Mr Gilchrist,
help yourself. I can recommend that port. It has been in
bins at Castle Lewin since '47, and is mellow enough to
please any taste.'

So it was, being pale in colour and apparently mild and
harmless as water. I drank a couple of glasses, but when
the bottle was passed to me a third time, refused any more.

'I never exceed two glasses,' I said, 'and perhaps as we
have a good deal to do and to see . . .'

'I understand,' said Mrs Kruse, who was still seated at
the table. 'We will have coffee brought to us in my
husband's study; shall we go there now?' She rose as she
spoke, and we followed her out of the room. We crossed the
hall, where the fire still smouldered on the hearth, and
entered a large low-ceiled room at the opposite side. Here
lamps were lit and curtains drawn; the place looked snug
and cheerful.

'We may as well look over your document before we
repair to the laboratories, Mr Gilchrist,' said Kruse. 'I
gather from what you said in town that you do not care to
impart any of your knowledge to us until we have signed
the agreement.'

'I have brought it with me,' I answered. 'With your permission I will go and fetch it.'

I left the room, went up to my bedroom, took my lawyer's hastily prepared agreement from its place in my suit-case, and returned to the study. As I did so, the following words fell upon my ears—

'It will be the third cup, Carl—you will not forget?'

I could not hear Kruse's reply, but the words uttered by his wife struck on my ears for a fleeting moment with a sense of curiosity, then I forgot all about them. The full meaning of that apparently innocent sentence was to return to me later.

Lewin, who was standing on the hearth with his hands behind him, motioned me to a chair. Mrs Kruse sat down by the table—she leant her elbows on it, revealing the pretty contour of her rounded arms; her eyes were bright her cheeks slightly flushed—she certainly was a very pretty young woman; but now, as I gave her a quick, keen glance, I observed for the first time a certain hardness round the lines of her mouth, and also a steely gleam in the blue of her eyes which made me believe it just possible that she might have another side to her character. As I looked at her she returned my gaze fully and steadily—then raising her voice she spoke with some excitement.

'Carl,' she said, 'Mr Gilchrist is ready, and we have no time to lose. Remember that tonight, if all goes well, we perfect the great explosive. Now, then, to work.'

'Here is the agreement,' I said, taking the lawyer's document out of its blue envelope. 'Will you kindly read it? We can then affix our signatures, and the matter is arranged.'

Kruse was the first to read the document. I watched his eyes as they travelled with great speed over the writing. Then he drew up his chair to the table, and dipped his pen in ink preparatory to signing his signature.

'Hold a moment,' I said, 'we ought to call in a servant to witness this.'

A slightly startled look flitted across Mrs Kruse's face, but after an instant's hesitation she rose and rang the bell.

The footman appeared; he watched us as we put our names at the end of the paper, and then added his own signature underneath. When he had left the room Kruse spoke.

'Now that matter is settled,' he said, 'and we can set to work. You know, I think, Mr Gilchrist, exactly how far we have gone.' Here he produced his pocket-book and began to read aloud.

I listened attentively—Mrs Kruse and Lewin stood near— I noticed that Mrs Kruse breathed a little quicker than usual; her breath seemed now and then to come from her body with a sort of pant.

'At this point we are stuck,' said Kruse, pulling up short. 'We have tried every known method, but we cannot overcome this difficulty.'

'And for the success of the experiment,' I interrupted, 'it is almost an initial knowledge.'

'Quite so, quite so,' said Lewin.

'I can put you right,' I said; 'you are working with a wrong formula—you do not know, perhaps.' I then began to explain to them the action of a substance as yet never used in the combination in which I had worked it. I was interrupted in my speech by Kruse.

'Anna,' he said, 'get paper. Write down slowly and carefully every word that Mr Gilchrist says. Now, then, sir, we are ready to listen. Are you all right, Anna?'

'Quite,' she answered.

I began to explain away the main difficulty. Mrs Kruse wrote down my words one by one as they fell from my lips. Now and then she raised her eyes to question me, and her use of technical terms showed me that she was completely at home with the subject.

A Race with the Sun

'By Jove! Why did we not think of that for ourselves?' said Lewin, interlarding his remark with a great oath.

'We are extremely obliged to you, Mr Gilchrist,' said Kruse. 'This sweeps away every difficulty, the discovery is complete.'

'Complete? I can scarcely believe it,' said Mrs Kruse.

At this moment the servant entered with coffee; it was laid on the table and we each took a cup.

'You told me,' I said, when I had drained off the contents of the tiny cup which had been presented to me, 'that you have failed in this initial difficulty, and yet you have conquered in a matter which baffles me.' I then named the point beyond which I could not get.

'Yes, we certainly know all about that,' said Kruse.

'You will give me your information?'

'Of course, but the best way of doing so is by showing you the experiment itself.'

'That will do admirably,' I replied.

'If you are ready we will go now,' said Mrs Kruse.

She started up as she spoke, and led the way.

We left the study, and, going down some passages, found ourselves in the open air. We were now in a square yard, surrounded on all sides by buildings. Lewin walked first, carrying the lantern. Its light fell upon an object which caused me to start with surprise. This was nothing less than a balloon about twenty feet in diameter, which was tied down with ropes and securely fastened to an iron ring in the pavement. It swayed to and fro in the gusts of wind.

'Halloa!' I cried, in astonishment, 'what is this?'

'Our favourite chariot,' answered Mrs Kruse, with a laugh. 'Wait a moment, Paul, won't you? I want to show our balloon to Mr Gilchrist. Is it not a beauty?' she added, looking in my face.

'I do not see any car,' I replied.

'The car happens to be out of order. You do not know, perhaps, Mr Gilchrist, that I am an accomplished aeronaut.

I do not think I enjoy anything more than my sail in the air. It was only last Monday . . .'

'My dear Anna, if you get on that theme we shall not reach the laboratories tonight,' interrupted her husband. 'This way, please, Mr Gilchrist.'

He opened a door as he spoke, and I found myself in a large laboratory fitted up with the usual appliances.

Kruse and his companion, Lewin, began to show me round, and Mrs Kruse stood somewhere near the entrance.

The laboratory was full of a very disagreeable smell. Kruse remarked on this, and began to explain it away.

'We were making experiments until a late hour this afternoon,' he said, 'with some isocyanides, and as you are aware, the smell from such is almost overpowering, but we thought it would have cleared away by now.'

'I hope you don't mind it?' said Lewin.

'I know it well, of course,' I answered, 'but it has never affected me as it does now. The fact is, I feel quite dizzy.' As I spoke I reeled slightly and put my hand to my head.

'The smell is abominable,' said Kruse. 'Come to this side of the laboratory; you may be better if you get nearer the door.'

I followed my host.

'What is the matter with you, Mr Gilchrist?' said Mrs Kruse, the moment she looked at my face.

'It is those fumes, my dear,' said her husband; 'they are affecting Mr Gilchrist in a curious way—he says he feels quite dazed.'

'I do,' I answered. 'My head is giddy; it may be partly the long journey.'

'Then I tell you what,' said the wife, in an eager voice, 'you shall not be worried with any more experiments tonight. The best thing you can do is to go straight to bed, and then in the morning the laboratory will be fresh and wholesome. Carl and Paul Lewin will experiment for you in the morning to your heart's content.'

'Yes, really it is the best thing to do,' said Kruse.

I sank down on a bench.

'I believe you are right,' I said.

My sensations puzzled me not a little. When I entered the laboratory I was full of the keenest enthusiasm for the moment when Kruse and his companion should sweep away the last obstacle towards the perfecting of the grand explosive. Now it seemed to me that I did not care whether I ever learned their secret or not. The explosive itself and all that it meant might go to the bottom of the sea as far as I was concerned. I only longed to lay my throbbing and giddy head on my pillow.

'I will take your advice,' I said. 'It is quite evident that in my tired state these fumes must be having a direct and poisoning effect upon me.'

'Come with me,' said Kruse. 'You must not stay a moment longer in this place.'

I bade Mrs Kruse and Lewin good-night, and Kruse, conducting me through the yard where the balloon was fastened, took me to my bedroom. The fire burned here cheerfully—the bed was turned down, the snowy sheets and befrilled pillows seemed to invite me to repose. I longed for nothing more in all the world than to lay my head on my pillow.

'Good-night,' said Kruse. He held out his hand, looking fixedly at me as he spoke. The next moment he had left the room.

I sank into a chair when he was gone, and thought as well as I could of the events of the evening, but my head was in such a whirl that I found I could not think consecutively. I threw off my coat, and without troubling to undress, lay down and fell into a deep and dreamless slumber.

* * *

'Have you got the hydrogen and chlorine ready?'

These words, whispered rapidly, fell upon my ears with distinctness. They did not disturb me, for I thought they were part of a dream. I had a curious unwillingness to open my eyes or to arouse myself—an unaccountable lethargy was over me, but I felt neither frightened nor unhappy. I knew that I was on a visit to Lewin and Kruse in Cornwall, and I believed myself to be lying on the bed where I had fallen into such heavy slumber some hours ago. I felt that I had slept very deeply, but I was unwilling to awake yet, or stir in any way. It is true I heard people bustling about, and presently a vessel of some kind fell to the floor with a loud clatter. A woman's voice said, 'Hush, it will arouse him,' and then a man made a reply which I could not catch. My memory went on working calmly and steadily. I recalled how the evening had been passed—the signing of the document, the balloon in the yard, the horrible smell in the laboratory. Then I remembered as if I heard them over again Mrs Kruse's words when I returned to the study, '*It will be the third cup.*' What did she mean? Why should I be bothered with this small memory now? I never wanted to sleep as I did at this moment—I had never felt so unaccountably, so terribly drowsy.

'I hope that noise did not wake him,' said a voice which I knew was no echo of memory, but a real voice—I recognized it to be that of Mrs Kruse.

'He is right enough,' replied her husband. 'I gave you enough narceine to put into his coffee to finish off a stronger and a bigger man—don't worry. Yes, Lewin, 'I will help you in a moment to carry him into the yard.'

'The storm is getting less,' said Mrs Kruse. 'Be quick. Oh, surely he is dead!' she added.

'If not dead, all but,' replied her husband. I tell you I gave him a stiff dose—he never moved nor uttered a sigh when we took him from his bedroom.'

Lethargic as I undoubtedly was, these last words had

the effect of making me open my eyes. I did so, blinking with the stupor which was oppressing me. I stared vacantly around me. Where was I?—what had happened? My limbs felt as if weighted with lead, and I now experienced for the first time since I had heard the voices an unaccountable difficulty in stirring them. I tried to raise my hand, and then I was conscious of a hideous pang—the knowledge flashed across me that I was bound hand and foot. I was, then, the victim of foul play, but, good God! What? What awful discovery had I just made? My memory was becoming quite active, but my whole body felt numbed and dulled into a lethargy which almost amounted to paralysis. Making a great effort, I forced myself to turn my head. As I did so a woman's face peered down into mine. It was the face of my hostess, Mrs Kruse. She turned quickly away.

'He is not dead,' I heard her whisper, 'he is coming to.'

At that moment I knew where I was—I was lying on the floor of the laboratory. How had I got there?—what was about to happen? I found my voice.

'For God's sake, what is the matter?' I cried; 'where am I? Is that you, Mrs Kruse? What has happened?'

The moment I spoke Mrs Kruse stepped behind me, so that, bound as I was, I could no longer see her face or figure. The light in the laboratory was very dim, and just then the huge form of Lewin came between me and it. He bent over me, and, putting his hand under my shoulders, lifted me to a sitting posture. At the same moment Kruse took hold of my feet. In that fashion, without paying the slightest attention to my words, they carried me into the yard where the balloon was fastened. The contact with the open air immediately made me quite wide awake, and a fear took possession of me which threatened to rob me of my reason.

'What are you doing? Why am I bound in this fashion? Why don't you speak?' I cried.

They were dumb, as though I had not uttered a word. I struggled madly, writhing in my bonds.

'Mrs Kruse,' I cried out, 'I know you are there. As you are a woman, have mercy; tell me what this unaccountable thing means. Why am I tied hand and foot? If you really mean to kill me, for God's sake put me out of my misery at once.'

'Hold your tongue, or I'll dash your brains out,' said the ruffian Lewin. 'Anna, step back. Now, Carl, bring the ropes along.'

As the brute spoke he flung me with violence upon a plank, which ran across the iron hoop to which the meshes of the great balloon were attached. I struggled to free myself, but in my bound condition was practically powerless.

'What are you doing? Speak; tell me the worst,' I said. I was gasping with terror, and a cold sweat had burst out in every pore.

'If you want to know the worst, it is this: you are going to carry your secret to the stars,' said Lewin. 'Not another word, or I'll put an end to you on the spot.'

As he spoke he and his companion began to lash me firmly to the plank. My hands, which were already tied together round the wrists, were drawn up over my head and fastened securely by means of a rope to one end of the plank; my feet were secured in a similar manner to the other. Just at this instant a sudden bright flash of lightning lit up the yard, and I caught sight of a large dumb-bell-shaped glass flask, and also what appeared to be a tin canister. These Kruse held in his hand, and proceeded, with Lewin's assistance, to fasten round the underside of the plank, just under where I was lying. They were kept in their places by an iron chain. As soon as this operation was over Lewin began to slash away at the ropes which kept the balloon in the yard. I now found myself lying stretched out flat, unable to move a single inch, staring up at the great balloon which towered above me. It was just at that supreme moment of agony, amid the roaring of the gale, that Mrs

Kruse coming softly behind me, whispered something in my ear.

'I give you one chance,' she said. 'The loop which binds your hands to the plank is single.' She said nothing more, but stepped back.

The next instant, amid a frightful roar of thunder, the balloon was lifted from its moorings and shot up into the night. As it cleared the buildings the full force of the gale caught it, and I felt myself being swept up with terrible velocity into the heart of the storm. Blinding flashes of lightning played around me on every side, while the peals of thunder merged into one continuous deafening roar. Up and up I flew, with the wind screaming through the meshes of the net-work, and threatening each moment to tear the balloon to fluttering ribbons. Then, almost before I was aware of it, I found myself gazing up at a wonderful, star-flecked firmament, and was drifting in what seemed to be a breathless calm. I heard the thunder pealing away below me, and was conscious of bitter cold. The terrible sense of paralysis and inertia had now, to a great extent, left me, and my reason began to reassert itself. I was able to review the whole situation. I not only knew where I was, but I also knew what the end must be.

'Hydrogen and chlorine,' I muttered to myself. 'The dumb-bell-shaped glass vessel which is fastened under the plank contains, without doubt, these two gases, and the tin canister which rests beneath them is full of nitroglycerine.' Yes, I knew what this combination meant. *When the first glint of the sun's rays struck upon the glass vessel it would be instantly shattered. The nitro-glycerine would explode by the concussion, and the balloon and myself would be blown into impalpable dust beyond sight or sound of the earth.*

This satanic scheme for my destruction had been planned by the fiends in human shape who had lured me to Cornwall. Having got my secret from me they meant to destroy all trace of my existence. The deadly poison of narceine had been introduced into my coffee. I knew well the action of that pernicious alkaloid, and now perceived that the smell in the laboratory had nothing whatever to do with my unaccountable giddiness and terrible inertia. Narceine would, in short, produce all the symptoms from which I had suffered, and would induce so sound and deadly a sleep that I could be moved from my bed without awakening. Yes, the ruffians had made their plans carefully, and all had transpired according to their wishes. There was absolutely no escape for me. With insane fury I tore at my bonds. The ropes only cut into the flesh of my hands, that was all.

The storm had now passed quite out of hearing, and I found myself in absolute stillness and silence. I was sailing away to my death at the dawn of day. So awful were the emotions in my breast that I almost wished that death would hasten in order to end my sufferings. Why had not the hydrogen and chlorine exploded when I was passing through the storm? Why had the lightning not been merciful enough to hurry my death? Under ordinary circumstances they would certainly have combined if they had been subjected to so much actinic light. I could not account for my escape, until I suddenly remembered that in all probability the stop-cock between the two gases in the dumb-bell-shaped glass had only been turned just when the balloon was sent off, in which case the gases would not have had time to diffuse properly for explosion.

At the dawn of day the deadly work would be complete. The question now was this: how long had I to live, and was there any possible means of escape?

The action of the drug had now nearly worn off, and I was able to think with acuteness and intelligence. I recalled Mrs Kruse's strange parting words, 'The loop which binds your hands to the plank is single.' What did she mean? After all, it was little matter to me how I was bound, for I could not stir an inch. Nevertheless, her words kept returning to me, and suddenly as I pondered over them I began to see a meaning. The loop was single. This, of course, meant that the cord was only passed once round the rope straps which secured my wrists together. I nearly leapt as I lay upon my hard and cruel bed, for at this instant a vivid memory returned to me. Years ago I had exposed a spiritualist who had utilized a similar contrivance to deceive his audience. His wrists had been firmly tied together, and then a single loop was passed between them, and fastened to a beam above his head. He had been able to extricate himself by means of a clever trick. I knew how he had done it. Was it possible that my murderous hosts had tied my hands to the plank in a similar manner? If so, notwithstanding their sharpness, what an oversight was theirs!

In desperate excitement I began to work the cord between my wrists up and up between my palms until I could just reach it with my little finger, and by a supreme effort slipped it over my left hand. Great God, I was free! I could now move my hands, although they were still tightly tied together round the wrists. In frantic despair I began to tug and tear at the cords which bound them. Cutting hard with my teeth, I at last managed to liberate my hands, and then my next intention was to unfasten the horrible explosive from the plank. Here, however, I was met by what seemed to be an insuperable difficulty. The glass vessel and the tin canister had been secured round the plank by means of a chain, which was lashed in such a manner that by no possible means could I undo it. I was now free to move, but the means of destruction were still close to me. How long had I before the sun would rise? Even now the light in the heavens was getting stronger and stronger. What should I do? My hands were free and I could sit up. In another moment I had managed to untie the cords from my legs, and then, with many a slip and struggle, I contrived to clamber up the network till I came to the balloon itself, when I set to work to tear at the silk with my nails and teeth like a man possessed. After almost superhuman efforts, I managed to make a very small hole in the silk. This I enlarged first with my finger and then with my whole hand, tearing away the silk in doing so till I had make a huge rent in the side of the balloon. As soon as this happened, I knew that the balloon would slowly, but surely, begin to descend. The question now was this: how soon would the sun rise? Perhaps in an hour, but I thought sooner. The murderous explosive was so sccurcd to thc plank that there was not the smallest chance of my getting rid of it. My one and only chance of life was to reach the ground before the sun got up. If this did not happen, I should be blown to atoms.

The stars were already growing faint in the heavens, and, sitting on the plank, holding the meshes of the balloon on either side, I ventured to look below me. I saw, with a slight feeling of relief, that the wind must have changed, for instead of being blown seawards, as was doubtless the intention of my murderers, I had gone a considerable way inland. I could see objects, trees, villages, solitary houses dotted in kaleidoscope pattern beneath me—it seemed to me as I gazed that the world was coming up to meet me. Each moment the trees, the houses, assumed a more definite shape. Within a quarter of an hour I saw that I was only about six hundred feet from a large park into which I was descending.

A grey, pearly tint was now over everything—this, moment by moment, assumed a rose hue. I knew by past experience that in five minutes at the furthest the sun would rise, and striking its light across the glass vessel would hurl me into eternity. In an agony of mind, I once more directed all my attention to the terrible explosive. I knew that in this fearful race between me and the sun the sun must win unless I could do something—but what? That was the question which haunted me to the verge of madness. I was without my coat, having been lashed on to the plank in my shirt, or I might have tried to cover the dumb-bell-

shaped glass from the fatal light. The feasibility of breaking
the glass vessel, and so allowing the gases to escape, also
occurred to me for an instant, but I was afraid to try it—
first, because I had only my fists to break it with; and
second, if I did, the blow might explode the nitro-glycerine.
Suddenly I uttered a shout which was almost that of a crazy
person. What a fool I was not to have noticed it before—
there *was* a means of deliverance. By no possible method
could I unfasten the iron chain which secured the infernal
machine to the plank, but the plank itself might be un-
shipped. I observed that it was secured to the iron hoop by
thick and clumsy knots of rope. With all the speed I could
muster, for seconds were now precious, I gently worked the
chain along the plank till it and the infernal machine had
reached one end. I noticed with joy that here the chain was
loose, as the plank was thinner. Seating myself on the hoop
and clinging to the meshes with one hand, I tore and tugged
away at the knots which secured the plank with the other.
Merciful God! they were giving way! In another instant the
plank fell, hanging to the hoop at the opposite side, and as it
did so, the infernal machine slipped from the free end and
fell.

I was now within three hundred feet of the earth, and,
clinging for bare life to the meshes of the balloon, I looked
below. There was a sudden flash and a deafening roar. In
mid-air, as it fell, the machine exploded, for the sun had
just risen. In another moment my feet had brushed the
top of a huge elm tree, and I found myself close to the
ground. Seizing the opportunity of open space I sprang
from the balloon, falling heavily on the wet grass.

The instant I left it, the balloon, relieved from my
weight, shot up again into space, and was lost to view
behind the trees. I watched it disappear, and then consciousness forsook me.

I was picked up by a gamekeeper, who conveyed me to
his own cottage, where I was well and carefully nursed, for

the exposure and shock which I had undergone induced a somewhat severe illness. When the fever which had rendered me delirious abated, my memory came fully back, and I was able to give a faithful and circumstantial account of what had occurred to a neighbouring magistrate. Immediately on hearing my story, the superintendent of police in London was telegraphed to, and a detachment of his men went to Castle Lewin, but they found the place absolutely deserted. My would-be murderers had beyond doubt received news of my miraculous escape and had decamped.

I have only one thing more to say. On my return to London, amongst a pile of letters which awaited me, was one which I could not peruse without agitation. It ran as follows:

'You acted on my hint, and have escaped truly as if by a miracle. We are about to leave the country, and you will in all probability never hear anything of us again. But it gives me pleasure even in this crucial moment to let you know how easily you can be duped. Have you ever guessed how we got possession of that secret which was all yours and never ours? Do you recall the lady who, dressed as a nun, came to see you about six or seven months ago? You believed her story, did you not? May I give you one word of warning? In future, do not leave your alphabetically arranged note-books in a room to which strangers may possibly have access. Farewell.'

IX

The Contents of the Coffin

J. S. Fletcher

'Guilty!'

The foreman of the jury uttered the fatal word with the hesitation of a man who is loth to voice the decision which deprives a human being of his liberty. He and his fellow jurymen kept their eyes sedulously away from the man in the dock; every one of them at some time or another had partaken of his good fare, drunk his vintage wines, smoked his cabinet cigars, and now . . .

'You find the prisoner guilty; and that is the verdict of you all?'

'We find the prisoner guilty, and that is the verdict of us all,' repeated the foreman in dull tones. Something in his mien suggested that he was glad to have to say no more—he and his eleven companions in the cramped-in jury-box seemed to crave silence. They were wanting to get away, to breathe, to have done with an ugly passage in the life of their little town. What need of more talking? It had been impossible not to find their old friend and neighbour guilty. Of course he was guilty—guilty as Cain or Judas. Get the thing over.

The man in the dock seemed to share the opinion of the jury. His face was absolutely emotionless as he heard the fatal word drop limply from the foreman's lips, and he shook his head with something of a contemptuous smile when asked if he had anything to say as to why sentence should not be passed upon him. What was there to say?

'John Barr,' said the stern-faced embodiment of justice whom he faced. 'You have been convicted on the clearest evidence of the very serious crime of embezzlement. There were no less than nine counts in the indictment against you. It was only considered necessary to proceed with one—that relating to your embezzlement during the month of July, 1898, of a sum of three thousand seven hundred pounds, the moneys of your employers, the Mid-Yorkshire Banking Company—and upon that charge you have been found guilty. But it has been clearly established during the course of your trial that this sum forms almost an infinitesimal part of your depredations upon your employers' funds. It seems almost incredible to me, who know little of banking affairs, that it should have been possible for you to commit these depredations, but I note that the sums mentioned in the nine counts total up to the immense aggregate of one hundred and eighty-seven thousand pounds, and we have heard it stated by the prosecution that there are further sums to be accounted for, and that the probable total loss to the bank will exceed a quarter of a million sterling. Now there are several unfortunate features about the case, and not the least unfortunate lies in the fact that it is believed— and, from what I have gathered, justly believed—by the prosecution that a very considerable portion of the money which you have embezzled is at this moment, if not at your disposal, still within your cognizance. Appeals have been made to you from time to time, since you were first committed for trial, with respect to making restitution. All these appeals have been in vain. The last of these appeals was made to you here, in this court, this morning. You paid

no regard to it. Now, if it be a fact that any part of the
money of which you have robbed your employers is re-
coverable, let me beg of you to make proper restitution for
the sake of your own conscience and the honour of your
family, which, as I am informed, has long occupied a foremost position in this town. This has been a singularly
painful case, and it is a painful thing for me, in the dis-
charge of my duty, to feel obliged to pass upon you a
sentence of ten years' penal servitude.'

John Barr heard his sentence with as little show of
emotion as he had heard the verdict of the jury. He looked
round the court for a moment as if seeking some face. A
man sitting in a retired seat caught his eye—a man who
bore a distinct resemblance to himself, and who had listened
to the whole of the proceedings with downcast head. This
man was now regarding the convict with an intent look.
John Barr, for the fraction of a second, returned it; then,
with a quick glance round him—the glance of a man who
looks at familiar objects and faces for the last time—he
bowed to the seat of justice, turned, and was gone.

The people who had crowded the court since the doors
first opened that morning, streamed out into the Market
Place. There were several cases to come on yet, but the
great case of the day was over, and all Normancaster
wanted to get somewhere—home, inn-parlour, by-way,
anywhere—to talk over the result. Ten years' penal servitude!—well, it was only what anyone could expect. And a
quarter of a million of money—and had John Barr disposed of some of it in such a fashion that he could handle
it when he 'came out' of whatever penal settlement he
would be sent to? Men were gabbling like geese over these
questions, and particularly over the last, as they crossed
the cobble stones of the Market Square, making for their
favourite houses of resort.

Two men, leaving the court together, drew aside from
the throng and turned into a quiet street. One of them, a

big, burly, bearded man was obviously excited; the other, an odd-looking little individual, dressed in an antique frock-coat and trousers much too short to reach the tops of his shoes, who wore a rusty, old-fashioned hat far back on his head, and carried a Gamp-like umbrella over his shoulder. You would have thought him an oddly-attired, respectable old party, who, after certain years of toil as operative, artisan, or the like, had retired on a competency. In that you would have been right—but (as you might have gathered from his impassive face, his burning eyes, his rigid mouth) he was something more. Yet working in the dark as he did, mole-like, none of the people in the court that day had known him for Archer Dawe, the famous amateur detective, expert criminologist, a human ferret—none, at least, but the man at whose side he was now walking.

This man led Archer Dawe down a side street to the door of an office which formed part of the buildings of a big brewery. He unlocked the door; they entered; he locked the door behind them. Then, without a word, but pointing Archer Dawe to a seat, he went over to a cupboard, brought out whisky, soda, and glasses, and a box of cigars, and motioned the little man to help himself. They had both lighted cigars, both taken a hearty pull at their glasses before the big, bearded man spoke—vehemently.

'Dawe, it's a damned plant!'

Archer Dawe took another pull at his whisky-and-soda.

'What's your notion, Mr Holland?' he inquired.

Mr Holland stamped up and down his office for a few minutes. Then he fell to swinging his arms.

'It's a damned plant, Dawe!' he repeated. 'And that chap Stephen Barr is in it as well as John. John's going to take the gruelling—being the younger and stronger. He'll be a model prisoner—he'll get out in some seven and a half years. Lord! What's that? And then . . .'

He fell to stamping the floor, to waving his arms again.

'You mean?' said Archer Dawe. 'You mean . . .'

'I mean that they've got the money. It hasn't gone on the Stock Exchange. It's not gone on the Turf. It's not gone over the card table. They've got it. It's planted somewhere as safe as—as safe as I am standing here, Dawe! Did you see John give Stephen that look before he left the dock? Eh?'

'I did,' replied Archer Dawe.

'Now, I wonder what that meant? But—or, hang it,' exclaimed Mr Holland, 'don't let's theorize—I want you to keep an eye on Stephen Barr. It's lucky that nobody knew you here in Normancaster—they would think this morning that you were some old fogey interested in the Castle and so on, who'd just dropped into the Court for an hour or so—you know, eh?'

'The matter stands thus,' said Archer Dawe, slowly. 'John Barr, who for ten years has been manager of the Mid-Yorkshire Bank here in Normancaster, has been to-day convicted of the crime of embezzlement and sentenced to ten years' penal servitude. You, as a director of that bank, know that he has secured close upon a quarter of a million of your money; you, personally, believe that—eh?'

'I believe, as a private individual, that both of them have been in at this, that John's going to do his seven and a half years, and that in the meantime Stephen's going off to some other clime, there to prepare a comfortable place for his brother,' said Mr Holland. 'Why bless me, John Barr will only be three and forty when he comes out, even if he serves his whole ten years—which he won't. And Stephen isn't anything like fifty yet. I've known them both since they were boys.'

'Your plan of campaign, Mr Holland?' said Archer Dawe.

'Well, I have one, I'll confess, Dawe,' answered Mr Holland. 'I'm going to have it communicated to Stephen Barr by a secret channel this afternoon that application for a warrant for his arrest is to be made to the borough magistrates first thing to-morrow morning. I want to see if that won't stir him. Now, I happen to live exactly opposite his house, and I shall have a watch kept on his movements. I want you to stay here in my private office— there, you see, is a bedroom attached to it, with all conveniences, so that you'll be comfortable if you have to stay the night, and, of course, I'll see that you have everything in the shape of food and so on. If I telephone you that Stephen Barr makes a sudden move from his house, you'll be ready to follow him—you've plenty of disguises, I suppose?'

'Oh, yes,' answered Archer Dawe, with a glance at his old portmanteau. 'But, Mr Holland, do you think that Stephen Barr would set off from here like that? Wouldn't it look like—giving himself away?'

'No,' replied Mr Holland. 'And for this reason—Stephen Barr always goes up to town once a week—has done so for the last two years—why, nobody knows. He has no particular day; sometimes it's Monday, sometimes Thursday, sometimes Friday. My notion is that if he's startled by the rumour about the warrant he'll go to-night. If he does I want you to go with him, and to keep an eye on him.'

'Then in that case I shall hold myself in readiness an hour before the night train starts,' said Archer Dawe.

'And in the meantime,' said Mr Holland, 'I shall put you in charge of a confidential clerk of mine who will see that you are properly taken care of, and will be at your disposal. At half-past four tea shall be sent in, and at half-past six dinner—after that, Dawe, make your toilet, and be on the *qui vive* for the telephone. The clerk will be with you to the end—here, I'll have him in and introduce him.'

If anybody had been able to look through the carefully-closed blinds of Mr Holland's office at a quarter-past seven o'clock that evening they would have seen a dapper little gentleman who from his attire might have been a judge, a doctor, or a barrister, leisurely finishing a bottle of claret in company with a younger man who was obviously lost in admiration of his elderly friend's cleverness in the art of making up.

'Well, you're a perfect marvel in that line, Mr Dawe,' said the confidential clerk. 'I go in a good deal myself for amateur theatricals, but I couldn't make up as you do, sir. Now that you've got into these clothes and done your hair in a different fashion, you look another man. And it's your attention to small details, sir—that black stock with the old-fashioned gold pin, and the gold-rimmed spectacles instead of your ordinary ones—my word, those little touches do make a difference!'

'It's the details that do make a difference, young man,' said Archer Dawe. 'And no detail is too small or un-dignifi . . .'

A sharp tinkle of the telephone bell interrupted him. He nodded to the clerk.

'Take the message,' he said. 'If it's from Holland, tell me word for word what he says.'

In another minute the clerk turned to him. 'Mr Holland says: "Barr has just left his house, obviously for the station. Tell Dawe to follow him wherever he goes."'

'Answer, "All right",' said Archer Dawe.

He drank off his claret as the clerk hung up the receiver again, and began to button his smartly-cut morning coat. His glance wandered to an overcoat, a rug, a Gladstone bag, and a glossy hat which lay out in orderly fashion on a side-table.

'There's lots of time, Mr Dawe,' said the clerk, interpreting the glance. 'You see, Barr lives opposite to Mr Holland, a good three-quarters of a mile from here. He'll walk to the station and he'll have to pass down this street—the station's just at the bottom. We can watch him pass this window—there, you can see out.'

Archer Dawe nodded. With a tacit understanding he and

the clerk posted themselves at the window, arranging one of the slats of the Venetian blinds so that they could see into the street beneath. There was a yellowish autumn fog there, and everything was very cold and still. No one came or went, up or down, until at last a man, cloaked to the eyes, carrying a bag in one hand, a rug in the other, hurried into the light of the opposite gas-lamp, crossed it, and disappeared into the gloom again. 'That's Barr!' whispered the clerk.

Archer Dawe looked at his watch.

'Eight minutes yet,' he said. 'Plenty of time.'

The clerk helped the amateur detective on with his fashionable fur-lined overcoat, and handed him his fashionable broad-brimmed silk hat and gold-mounted umbrella.

'By George, you do look a real old swell!' he said, with an admiring chuckle. 'Wish I could get myself up like that for our theatricals—it's fine.'

'Good-bye,' said Archer Dawe.

He slipped quietly out into the fog, and made his way, rug over arm, bag in hand, to the station, where he took a first-class ticket for King's Cross. There was no one on the platform but Stephen Barr and two or three porters, moving ghostlike in the fog. The mail came steaming in and pulled up, seeming to fret at even a moment's delay; a door was opened, Stephen Barr stepped in. Archer Dawe followed; the train was off again. He was alone with his quarry.

During the four hours' run to London these two scarcely spoke, except to remark on the coldness of the night. But as they were at last running into King's Cross and were putting away their travelling caps and arranging their rugs, Archer Dawe remarked pleasantly:

'It's a great convenience to have an hotel attached to these London termini—one doesn't feel inclined to drive far after a four hours' journey at this time of night and this season of the year. It's something to be able to step straight from the train into the Great Northern Hotel.'

Stephen Barr nodded.

'Yes,' he said, 'and a very comfortable hotel it is, too. I always stay there when I come to town—it is very convenient, as you say.'

'And to those of us who happen to be passing through town,' said Archer Dawe, with a marked emphasis on the penultimate word, 'it is much more pleasant to break the journey here than to be driven across London at midnight to another station. Old men like me, sir, begin to appreciate their little comforts.'

The same porter carried Stephen Barr's bag and Archer Dawe's bag into the hotel; the clerk in the office gave Stephen Barr number 45, and Archer Dawe number 46. Stephen Barr and Archer Dawe took a little hot whisky and water together in the smoking-room before retiring, and enjoyed a little friendly conversation. Archer Dawe was perhaps a little garrulous about himself—he gave Stephen Barr to understand that he, Archer, was a famous consulting physician of Brighton, that he had been north to an important consultation, and that he had spent a few hours at Normancaster on his way back in order to look over the castle. He also mentioned incidentally that he might stay in town for a day or two, as he was anxious to see one or two experiments which were just then being carried on in some of the medical schools. Stephen Barr thought his travelling companion a very pleasant old gentleman.

In the privacy of number 46, Archer Dawe sized up Stephen Barr as a man who at that moment was brooding over some big scheme and would probably lie awake all night thinking about it. As for himself he meant to sleep, but he had first of all some work to do, and he set to work to do it as soon as the corridor was quiet.

Had any of the hotel officials seen what it was that Archer Dawe did they would have jumped to the conclusion that a burglar was in the house. For he produced from his bag a curiously ingenious instrument with which he swiftly and noiselessly cut out of the door of his room a solid plug of wood about one-third of an inch in diameter—cut it out cleanly, so that it could be fitted in and withdrawn at will. Withdrawn, the orifice which it left commanded a full view of the door of 45 opposite: fitted in again, nobody could have told that it had ever been cut out.

This done, Archer Dawe went to bed. But early in the morning he was up and at his peep-hole, waiting there patiently until Stephen Barr emerged and made his way towards the bathroom. This was a chance on which Archer Dawe had gambled. He seized it at once. He darted across the corridor, secured the key of 45, and in a moment had secured an excellent impression of it in wax.

The specialist from Brighton, more talkative and urbane than ever, begged permission to seat himself at Stephen Barr's table when he entered the coffee-room and found that gentleman breakfasting alone. They got on very well, but Archer Dawe decided that his travelling companion of the previous evening was still deep in thought, and had spent most of the night awake. He noticed also that Stephen Barr had a poor appetite.

Going into the smoking-room an hour later, Archer Dawe found Stephen Barr in conversation with a man of apparently thirty years of age—a man who seemed to have a strong family likeness to him. They were in the quietest corner of the room, and their conversation was being carried on in whispers. Presently they left the room, and Arthur Dawe saw them go upstairs together.

After a time Archer Dawe walked out of the hotel, went across to the station, and wrote out two telegrams. The first was addressed to Robert Holland, Esq., Normancaster, and ran as follows:

'*I have him here and under observation. He is in con-*

versation with man of apparently thirty, medium height, light complexion, sandy hair and moustache, blue eyes, wears eye-glasses, has strong resemblance to Stephen and John. Say if you know anything of this man.'

The other was addressed to a certain personage at Scotland Yard:

'*Send Mason here in character of clergyman, to lunch with me at half-past one. Tell him to ask for Dr Archer, and to meet me in smoking-room.'*

This done, Archer Dawe, carrying his wax impression with great care, took a hansom and set off to a certain establishment which he knew of, where, before noon, a quick workman turned him out a brand-new key. Getting back to the hotel a little before one he found a telegram awaiting him. He carried it into the smoking-room and opened the envelope.

'*The man you describe is undoubtedly their nephew, James. He was at one time a solicitor, but was struck off the rolls three years ago, after conviction for mis-appropriation. Watch them both and spare no expense. Holland.'*

Under the very eyes of Stephen Barr and his nephew, who were again conversing in a quiet corner, Archer Dawe tore this communication into minute shreds. He affected to take no notice of the Barrs, but he saw that they had a companion with them—a man, who, from his general appearance, he set down as a medical practitioner. Glancing at this person from time to time Archer Dawe formed the conclusion that he was much of a muchness with the younger Barr—there was something furtive, and shifty, if not absolutely sinister in his face. And Archer Dawe was a past-master in the art of reading character in faces.

Whatever the conference was about between these three

it broke up just before Archer Dawe was expecting Mason. The two Barrs rose, shook hands with the third man, and walked with him towards the door.

'Then I'll expect you and Dr Hislop at seven o'clock to-night, doctor?' said Stephen, in a loud voice. 'We'll dine and go to the theatre afterwards. And, by the bye, I wish you'd bring me another bottle of that medicine you gave me last time; I've had a touch of the old complaint again this morning.'

'I will,' replied the third man. 'But if you've felt any symptom of that sort, let me advise you to keep quiet this afternoon. You'd better lie down for a while after lunch.'

Stephen Barr nodded and smiled, and the stranger left, as Mason, in the correct attire of a prosperous-looking clergyman, entered the room. He and Archer Dawe greeted each other in a manner befitting their respective parts, and were soon in apparently genial and friendly conversation. The two Barrs had retired to their corner again; in the centre of the room three young gentlemen in very loud clothes were discussing in equally loud voices the merits of certain sporting guns which they had come up to town to purchase. Otherwise the room was empty.

Archer Dawe gave Mason a brief outline of the case as it had so far been revealed to him. His notion, he said, was that some plot was afoot by which Stephen Barr was to get clear away without exciting suspicion, and that that plot was to be worked there, in the hotel:

'And that's why I sent for you,' he concluded. 'I can't work the thing alone. I want you to find men who can keep a steady watch on every exit from this place and can be trusted to follow Stephen Barr wherever he goes, whether it's day or night. I've a strong notion that some coup is in brewing for to-night.'

'That's done easily enough,' answered Mason, 'if we can keep a watch on him for the next two hours I'll engage that he won't move a yard without being followed. Here,

I'll go round to the nearest station and telephone at once, and then come back to lunch with you.'

Two hours later the pseudo-clergyman and the pseudo-doctor having lunched together and afterwards taken their ease over coffee and cigars, the former again absented himself for a while, and came back smiling.

'That's all right, Mr Dawe,' he said. 'He can't move a foot out of this place without being shadowed—night or day. Make yourself easy. And now I must be off—let me know at the Yard if you want anything further, and let's hear how it goes on.'

Then the two separated, and Archer Dawe, knowing that his man was under the strictest surveillance, went out for a constitutional. Returning to the hotel just after six o'clock, he was met on turning out of the Euston Road by a plainly-dressed man who first smiled, then winked, and as he passed him, whispered his name.

'One of Mr Mason's men, sir,' he said, as Archer Dawe came to a standstill. 'The man has been out this afternoon. He and the younger man drove first to an office in Bedford Row, stayed there a quarter of an hour, and then drove to the Bank of Argentina. They were there half an hour; then came back here. They're safe inside, sir. We're keeping a strict watch—there's plenty of us on the job.'

Archer Dawe had a table all to himself that night at dinner. Mr Stephen Barr's party occupied one close by. There were five of them—Stephen himself, his nephew, the man Archer Dawe had seen with them that morning, another man whom he conjectured to be the Dr Hislop he had heard mentioned, and a lady of apparently thirty, whom he soon put down as the nephew's wife. There was a good deal of laughing and talking amongst the party, and Stephen Barr himself seemed to be its life and soul.

Dinner was nearly over, and Archer Dawe, straining his ears for all they were worth, and using his eyes when he dared, had neither seen nor heard anything that gave him

assistance. But there was suddenly a slight commotion at the next table. Looking round, he saw that Stephen Barr had fallen back in his chair, and was pressing one hand over the region of his heart—the other was crushing his eyes and forehead, whereon a frown as of deep pain had gathered. A groan was slowly forced from his lips.

The men at Stephen Barr's table sprang to their feet. One of them beckoned to a waiter. Ere the rest of the people in the room had grasped the situation, the three men and the waiter were carrying Stephen Barr away. The lady, obviously much distressed, followed in their wake.

Archer Dawe beckoned to the head-waiter, who was standing near.

'I'm afraid that gentleman's very ill,' he said.

'Yes, sir. I've seen him like that before, sir. It's his heart, sir. Well-known customer here, sir. Those two medical gentlemen have attended him here before, sir, often—Dr Hislop and Dr Brownson. Very weak heart, I should say, sir. Carry him off some day—sudden.'

Archer Dawe finished his dinner hurriedly and slipped upstairs to his own room, slipped into it unobserved by anyone. And once inside, he drew out the plug from the hole in the door, and settled himself for what might be a long and wearying vigil.

During the next hour Archer Dawe saw many strange things. A few minutes after he had posted himself with his eye to the peep-hole which his foresight had devised, the man whom he now knew as Dr Brownson came hurriedly out of 45, and sped away along the corridor. Archer Dawe heard the key turned upon him as he left the room. This was exactly at 8.20.

At 8.40 this man came just as hurriedly back. He was accompanied by a tall, middle-aged woman in the garb of a district nurse, and he carried a small black bag in his hand. He tapped twice at the door of 45, and he and the woman

were instantly admitted. Once more Archer Dawe heard the key turned in the lock.

At 8.48 the door was opened again. Three people came out. One of them was the man who, from what the waiter had said, was Dr Hislop; another was James Barr; the third was the lady who had made the fifth at Stephen Barr's dinner-table. She leaned on James Barr's arm and held a handkerchief to her eyes. And again the door was locked as soon as those leaving the room had crossed the threshold.

Archer Dawe slipped out of his room as soon as he thought these people would be clear of the corridor and the stairs. He reached the hall in time to see the two men assisting the lady into a four-wheeled cab. She still held the handkerchief to her eyes and seemed to be in great grief. When the cab had driven away the two men stepped back into the hotel and went to the manager's office. There they remained for some minutes. Coming out at length, they went upstairs again.

Archer Dawe strolled out of the door, making pretence of examining the weather. Turning in again he was met by the under-manager, who smiled in an apologetic manner.

'I believe, sir,' he said, in a low voice, 'you are the gentleman in 46?'

'I am,' replied Archer Dawe.

'Well, sir, of course it is necessary to keep these sad affairs very quiet in an hotel, as you are aware. The poor gentleman in 45, the room opposite yours, is dead.'

'Dead?'

'Yes, sir—he died twenty minutes ago. Heart failure. You are, I believe, a medical man, sir. Yes, then you will understand. He had his own two doctors with him at the time—nothing could be done. He has had these attacks here before. I was wondering if you would like to be transferred to another room, sir?'

'No, I don't know that I should—I am not squeamish about these things,' replied Archer Dawe.

'Well, sir, I thought it best to mention it to you. Certainly the—the body will not be in the house all night. As the doctors were well acquainted with the deceased gentleman's complaint they will be able to certify, so there will be no need for an inquest. A—a coffin is coming at half-past ten, sir, and they are going to remove the body to Normancaster, where the dead gentleman lived, by the night mail. These two gentlemen are going to make arrangements now, sir, I believe.'

Archer Dawe turned and saw James Barr and Dr Hislop descending the staircase. They passed him and the under-manager, went down the steps of the front entrance, and separated, Barr crossing over to the Station, and Hislop entering a hansom cab.

'No, you need not change my room, thank you,' said Archer Dawe to the under-manager, and left him. 'I do not mind at all.'

He dawdled about the smoking-room for a while, then went upstairs again. And once more he applied himself to the hole in the door. At 9.10 the nurse came out, followed by the man whom he knew as Dr Brownson. Brownson locked the door and put the key in his pocket. He and the nurse went along the corridor whispering. Archer Dawe cautiously opened his door and tip-toed after them until he saw them descend the stairs. Then he hurried back. Now was his chance! The two women were gone; the three men were gone. There could be nothing in 45 but—what?

In another instant he had whipped out the key which he had caused to be made that morning, had slipped it into the lock of the door behind which so much mystery seemed to be concealed, and had entered the room. His hand sought and found the electric light, and as it flashed out he took one swift glance around him.

The Contents of the Coffin

The room was empty. Empty! There was neither dead man nor living man in it. Everything was in order. Two large travelling trunks stood side by side against the wall; a large Gladstone bag, strapped, stood near them; a smaller one, which Arthur Dawe recognized as that which Stephen Barr had had with him the night before, stood, similarly strapped, on the stand at the foot of the bed. But on the bed itself there was no stark figure. The room was empty of dead man or living man.

Archer Dawe saw all these things in a moment. He turned out the light, re-locked the door, and went downstairs into the smoking-room, where he lighted a cigar and sipped a whisky-and-soda. On the other side of the room Dr Brownson was similarly employed. As Archer Dawe looked at him he thought of Holland's words of the previous afternoon. 'Dawe, it's a damned plant!'

But where could Stephen Barr be? How had he slipped out of the hotel unobserved? Well, anyway, unless he had very skilfully disguised himself, Mason's men would follow him. He must wait for news. At ten minutes past ten James Barr came back and joined Brownson; at twenty minutes past Archer Dawe, having somewhat ostentatiously betrayed symptoms of sleepiness and weariness, betook himself upstairs. And once more he glued his eye to the little peep-hole which his ingenious centre-bit had made the night before.

A few minutes later James Barr and Brownson came upstairs and entered 45. Five more minutes went by, and then the watcher heard the tread of several men's feet sounding on the corridor in the opposite direction. Then Hislop came into view—followed by four men carrying an oak coffin. Two other men came behind.

And now Archer Dawe noted a significant circumstance. When Hislop tapped at the door and James Barr opened it, these two and Brownson took the coffin from the men and carried it within the room. Then the door was locked. Five,

[236]

ten, fifteen, twenty, twenty-five minutes went by—the door was opened. The six men entered the room—came out again, carrying the coffin. They went away with it by the way they had come, Hislop following them. Then James Barr and Brownson came out of the room, locked the door, and went downstairs. When Archer Dawe, following them, reached the hall, they were crossing from the hotel to the station.

At that moment a hansom, the horse of which had obviously been urged to its full extent, dashed up to the entrance. Mason sprang out and ran up the steps. He saw Archer Dawe—seized him.

'Dawe!' he exclaimed. 'We got him—got him at Victoria! He was off for the Continent, and then for the Argentine. We got him to the Yard, and by George! he's given us the slip after all—for ever! He must have had something concealed in a hollow tooth—he's poisoned himself!'

'Dead!' exclaimed Archer Dawe.

'As a door-nail!' said Mason. 'But—we found two hundred thousand pounds' worth of securities on him. And . . .'

Archer Dawe dragged him out of the hotel and across to the station.

'Quick, man, quick!' he cried. 'The coffin—the coffin—and the other three men. We must have them. Get half-a-dozen police—quick!'

When they had dispatched James Barr, Dr Brownson and Dr Hislop, to the nearest police-station in charge of certain stalwart constables, Archer Dawe, Mason and some inquisitive and wondering railway officials broke open the coffin in which, according to the plate upon it, the remains of Stephen Barr were supposed to rest. There was a moment of suspense when the lid was removed . . .

Lead ingots, carefully and skilfully packed tight in cotton-wool.

X

The Mystery of Room 666

Jacques Futrelle

It was only a fleeting glimpse I caught of her as she sped along the brilliantly lighted hallway, past the half-open door of my room. A young woman she was, with the splendid grace of youth in her carriage, lithe as a leopard, supple of limb—a young woman, and yet such a face! Youth was no longer there—it had been obliterated by the merciless hand of sorrow; but beauty there was—the cold, colourless, deadly beauty of marble. Her lips were slightly parted, her great, dark eyes widely distended, and it seemed to me in that bare instant there was something of fear in them— horror even. Flying tendrils of her hair, escaping from the heavy veil, coupled with the pallor of her face, gave to her a weird, witch-like appearance.

For ten, perhaps fifteen, minutes I had been standing beside my open window overlooking the adjoining roofs, breathing in deeply the clean, cool, salt-tinged air swept in from the sea. I had been in my room no longer than that. I had not even paused to turn on the electric lights on entering, but had gone straight to the window, opened it, and had remained beside it, motionless there in the darkness. Of late I had not been well. It was some absurd nervous trouble, accompanied by giddiness, a pounding of blood in my ears, and queer, throbbing pains in my head, which at times drove me well-nigh frantic. The breeze at the window was grateful; it dissipated the oppressiveness of the room, and the tormenting pains were eased.

As I say, I had been standing there some ten or fifteen minutes, staring out over the gloomy, uneven roofs below me. Perhaps you know the fascination of a single scintillant point in the darkness? Perhaps you know how it compels your attention? Well, after a little time I had noticed such a point of light, a mere glint on the roof of the house twice removed. I thought at first it was a fragment of glass shining by reflected light from some window in the hotel where I lived. For no other reason than the sheer brightness of it, I continued to stare at the point of light; and finally it seemed to become a tangible object! A revolver! The thought startled me a little. Yes, a revolver! The longer I looked the more certain I grew. The light was flashed back to me by the short nickelled barrel of it, and it seemed somehow to grow clearer as I looked. I couldn't see, and yet—I knew.

Perhaps a minute passed, and then a trap-door in the roof opened suddenly, and the head and shoulders of a man appeared darkly. He carried a small electric flashlight, and turned it about inquiringly. Finally he stepped out on the gravel, and glanced about cautiously, after which he made a tour of the roof. He paused inevitably at that point where I had seen the scintillant point of light, and, stooping— picked up a revolver! I had known it was a revolver and yet a sort of shudder ran over me. By the light he carried he examined the weapon, and I, from my window fifty feet away, shrouded in the night, looked with a curiosity no degree less than his. It was a singular appearing firearm— short, sturdy, and rather bulky as to barrel; indeed, it seemed to have two barrels, one above the other, in general

shape not at all unlike an old-fashioned Derringer pistol . . .
After a time the man disappeared down the trap, and gloom
fell again on the roof. The scintillant point was gone!

All this was before I saw the woman in the hallway. I
don't know just how many minutes had elapsed before my
reverie was broken by the quick, distinct swish-swish of
skirts. That, too, startled me a little, I think, because it
seemed so near, almost in the room. I whirled about. My
door was half open—I had not been aware of it—and I took
a couple of steps in that direction. It was then that the
woman flashed by, along the lighted hallway. Brief as my
glimpse of her was, I noted every detail—the deadly pallor
of her face, the terror in her dark eyes, the splendid youth
of her body.

Certainly it was not more than half a minute that I stood
staring at the spot where she had been, and then, impelled
by nothing save curiosity, unless, indeed, it was a suggestion of stealth in her manner, a mocking noiselessness in
her tread, and the strangeness of her face, I went to the
door and peered out. It was a hallway without turns in the
direction she had gone, but she was not in sight. Obviously,
then, she had entered one of the rooms beyond mine. Which
one? I didn't know, and besides, it was no concern of mine.
It was only midnight; there was nothing startling about her
being there, and the fact that I had not heard a door open
or close was of no consequence in itself. Yet I wondered
which room she had entered. Perhaps it was simply that
my imagination had been whetted by the singular incident
I had witnessed on the roof.

I was just on the point of closing my door and turning on
the electric lights when there came to me the muffled crash
of a revolver shot! There was no mistaking the sound. It
came from somewhere down the hallway, in the direction
the woman had gone. For an instant I stood still, listening,
but only for an instant; then I flung my door wide and ran
out. I don't know just where I intended to go, or what I

intended to do. However, events in their natural course shaped my decision, for the door of Room 666 burst open almost in my face, and there was the woman coming out!

She paused at sight of me, and snatched her veil down, hiding her features.

'What's the matter?' I demanded excitedly. 'What happened?'

She didn't answer; instead she tried to dart past me. Instinctively I put out both hands to stop her and seized one of her wrists. It slipped through my fingers, as a serpent might have done; I was pushed violently backward, stumbled a little, and went reeling against the wall behind me. When I straightened up again I was just in time to see the woman vanishing down the stairs.

I made no effort to pursue her; I didn't even pause to investigate the cause of her flight. Instead I ran into my own room, three doors away, and telephoned to the office.

'Someone has been murdered in Room 666!' I explained hastily to the telephone girl. 'A woman fired the shot. I tried to stop her, but she escaped and ran down the stairs. She is still in the hotel. Don't let her get away.'

And then for a little time, I don't know just what happened. My best recollection is of a sudden, crushing return of the hideous pains in my head, due probably to the quick excitement, and a sickening weakness in my legs. I may have fallen; I don't know. Finally, I heard the rattle and clatter of the lift door as it opened, immediately followed by the rush of heavy feet in the hallway. I peered out. Here was the house detective, and with him Verbeck, the head night-clerk, a policeman in uniform, and a couple of frightened page boys.

'Did you catch the woman?' I queried breathlessly.

'No,' responded the house detective, Garron by name. 'Was it you that 'phoned the office?'

I nodded. Garron stopped still and regarded me curiously. He was tall, slight, with deep-set eyes, and the face of a ferret, done in chalk. I don't believe I've ever seen another man who shows in his countenance so little the colour of life.

Suddenly he turned away and went on to Room 666, with the rest of us at his heels. The door stood wide open, and we paused at the darkened threshold, waiting for him to turn on the light. It came at last, a flood of it . . . The thing I saw there wrung a scream from my lips. It was the figure of a man lying prone upon the floor, face down, with his right hand outstretched towards us, grasping a revolver. Beside him was a dark crimson stain, and from that, leading backward into the room, disappearing beyond the bed, was a little trail of blood. It was as if, wounded, he had dragged himself across the floor. Perhaps he had been trying to reach the door, or the telephone beside the door.

'Is he dead?' demanded the policeman.

Not dead! My heart leaped, and then seemed to stand still. I laid a hand upon Verbeck's shoulder to steady myself.

Garron dropped on his knees beside the prostrate man, and pressed his ear to the body over the heart.

'He's dead all right,' he said brutally.

With the assistance of the policeman he turned the body over. Fascinated, unable to avert my eyes, I looked into the upturned face, and, looking, screamed again. I believe I should have fallen had not Verbeck been there to support me.

'Do you know him?' Garron asked abruptly. 'You, I mean, Mr Meredith?'

Thus directly addressed, I suppose I faltered. The horror of the crimson stains, the little trail the dying man had left behind him as he crept across the floor, the agony on the dead face must have unnerved me. I remember my heart was pounding frightfully; my head seemed bursting.

'Yes, I know him,' I replied, the words coming with an effort. 'Frank Spencer, his name is. I have known him for years; he's an old friend of mine.'

'You didn't happen to know he was stopping in the hotel?' Garron went on.

His deep-set eyes were glowing into mine with a fire which suddenly aroused an unaccountable anger within me; I seemed to feel a note of accusation in the curt, abrupt questions.

'Why do you ask?' I demanded defiantly.

'If he had been an old friend, and you had known he was in the hotel where you lived, in all probability you would have known the number of his room, particularly as it is only three doors from your own,' Garron explained, patiently. 'You 'phoned downstairs that someone had been murdered in Room 666. You didn't mention Mr Spencer's name—only the number of his room; therefore I assume that you did not know he was in the hotel?'

'No, I didn't know he was in the hotel,' I replied, hesitating at the vague menace in Garron's manner. 'I didn't know he was here.'

Garron turned to the night clerk.

'How long has Spencer been here, Mr Verbeck?'

'Nearly a week,' was the reply.

'As a matter of fact,' Garron went on, 'there has been no one living in this section of the hotel—I mean on this floor—for the last three or four days, except Mr Meredith, here, and Mr Spencer?'

'No one at all.'

'And certainly no woman?'

Verbeck shook his head.

'But there was a woman,' I blazed angrily. 'I *saw* her. If you had taken the trouble to guard the entrance to the hotel instead of rushing up here, where you can do a dead man no good, you might possibly have caught her.'

'If the woman was in the hotel when you 'phoned to the office she has not escaped, believe me,' Garron assured me quietly. 'Every exit is guarded; she would not be allowed to pass.'

'If she *was* in the hotel?' I repeated. 'I *say* she was; I saw her!'

All this time Garron had been on his knees beside the dead man. Now he arose, said something aside to the policeman, who instantly turned and stared at me, from top to toe.

'We know you have been ill, Mr Meredith,' Garron was saying with quick courtesy, 'and this excitement has probably been too much for you. I would suggest that you go to your room, and if you have any stimulant there, take it. You are white as a sheet.'

Supported by Verbeck, I returned to my room. It was only a little while after that Garron rapped on the door and entered. Under the influence of a quieting potion I was quite myself again; the pains in my head had almost gone. He dropped into a chair.

'The woman?' I inquired. 'Did they catch her?'

He shook his head slowly.

'No woman left the hotel from the time you 'phoned to the office,' he replied. 'If she is in the hotel she will be caught, take my word for it. I should like to have a description of that woman as you remember her; and just whatever else you know of all this.'

I told him, frankly, everything I have set down here, even to the apparently unconnected detail of a man having picked up what seemed to be a revolver on the roof two houses away. I concluded by giving him a minute description of the woman. During all that time he said nothing—only stared at me, stared until I came to feel a sort of hypnotic influence in the deep-set eyes.

'You didn't turn on the electricity when you entered this room, and you did leave your door open?' he queried at the end.

'I didn't leave the door open,' I corrected. 'I remember distinctly having closed it behind me. It must have swung open.'

He arose, opened the door, then closed it casually. The bolt didn't catch; it swung back on its hinges. The incident, trivial as it was, brought to me a thrill of elation.

'Why didn't you turn on your light?' he resumed as he sat down.

'The room was hot and stuffy, I was feeling ill, and my first thought was to open the window.'

'I believe I stated the facts correctly when I said you had 'phoned downstairs that someone had been murdered in 666, did I not?' he asked.

'Yes.'

'You used the word "murdered"?'

'As I remember it I did.'

'Why?'

'I had heard the shot, I had seen the woman escape, and naturally my first thought was of murder,' I explained. 'I was excited when I went to the 'phone.'

'But you didn't know there had been *murder*!'

'No, I didn't *know* it.'

'You say you heard the shot. You didn't by any chance hear more than one shot?'

'Only one. Was more than one fired?'

'Two shots, at least. One of them entered Spencer's body in the back, just below the heart; the other was embedded in the woodwork of the door.' He paused a moment. 'The shot that was embedded in the woodwork of the door was fired from Spencer's revolver—the one he held in his hand when we found him.'

There was a pause.

'If the two shots had been fired simultaneously,' I suggested, 'there would have been the sound of only one.'

'If they had been fired simultaneously Spencer must have been standing with his back towards his assailant, and would have been shooting in the opposite direction,' Garron explained patiently. 'Therefore one of the shots must have been fired after the other.'

I offered no explanation of this fact, an obvious one, now that he had called attention to it.

'I heard only one shot,' I insisted.

Suddenly the mask of courtesy dropped from Garron, his tone hardened.

'You didn't enter Room 666 from the time you heard the shot fired until I came upstairs?' he asked.

'No,' I replied.

'You are positive?'

'Absolutely positive.'

'You didn't so much as lay a finger on Spencer's body while you were in the room with me?'

'No.' I shuddered.

'Don't you know,' he went on mercilessly, 'don't you know that there was no woman concerned in this affair at all?'

The question brought me to my feet, and I stood for an instant swaying giddily under the blinding anger which possessed me. I tried to speak; no words came.

'As a matter of fact, now, what motive led you to murder Spencer?' Garron demanded.

'How dare you ask me such a question?' My voice came at last. 'You make a direct accusation. Why?'

'Your hand, man—your hand!' Garron exclaimed violently. 'The back of it is covered with blood. I saw it when you met us at the door just after we came up here. There, by Spencer's body, I called the policeman's attention to it.'

I glanced down at my right hand, amazed, speechless. Blood, yes—a great splotch of it; it seemed to expand and grow until there was a perfect crimson sea of it! How came it there? How could it have been there all that time to have passed unnoticed? So this was why Garron had suspected me from the first, and I had not misinterpreted his brutal questions!

... For a long time I remembered nothing ... When semi-consciousness came I seemed to be looking down a long, narrow passageway, hedged with steel bars. At its end hung a rope ... A man was being bound and capped; he was shrieking ... When I opened my eyes a doctor was sitting beside my bed. A few minutes later I was formally placed under arrest, charged with the murder of Frank Spencer.

On the following day a lawyer came to see me in my cell. He was an old friend of my father. He found me at the tiny wash-basin scrubbing the back of my right hand. He asked many questions in no way touching upon the murder, the while he studied my face, my eyes, with an expression of growing surprise.

'I think perhaps you ought to know,' he said gravely, 'that the pistol with which you—with which Spencer was shot was picked up on the roof of the house two doors away.'

'Yes. I told Garron that I had seen a man find it.'

'It was thrown from a window of the hotel,' he went on. 'The servant in the house who occupied the room immediately beneath the spot where the pistol fell heard it strike, and thinking that someone was trying to force the trapdoor, dressed and went up to investigate. He found the weapon, which proved to be a *Maxim noiseless*!' I was silent. 'It looks something like an old Derringer, the part underneath, which looks like a second barrel, is really the muffler.'

'Yes, I know.'

'Garron got possession of it,' he continued slowly. 'It was turned over to the police, and they managed to find a man who says he sold it. *He will swear he sold it to you! You paid for it with a personal cheque!*'

If he had expected to startle me with this accusation, he was disappointed. There were two shots fired in Room 666, according to Garron. If one had been fired with a noiseless weapon, of course I *could* have heard only one! In a way it was a point for me.

'My boy,' the lawyer said solemnly, after a long time, and as he talked his stern eyes grew dim, 'I've known you ever since you were a little chap. Then you were sickly, nervous —a weakling. I've watched you grow into manhood with an awful fear upon me of what was coming. It has come. Your mother died in a sanatorium. Thank God that neither she nor your father is alive now to know.' He paused, and his eyes grew stern again; his lips were rigid. 'As the friend of your father I shall do the best I can for you. But there's only one thing to do—you must plead insanity!'

I came to my feet in a rage, my arms outstretched to throttle him. Across the back of my right hand was a great crimson splotch; I shuddered, and thrust it behind me.

'You mean that you *believe* I am guilty?' I almost screamed. 'And you've just called yourself a friend of my father!'

'The circumstantial chain is complete,' said the lawyer gently; 'perhaps with the exception of having established a motive.'

'Ah!' I exclaimed triumphantly. 'There *was* no motive; there could be none. That's where I shall beat them; and beat you, since you believe I murdered him.'

'Insane men need no motives,' was the answer. 'I will admit, to please you, that you *believe* you saw this woman you mentioned; I will even admit that you don't *remember* having shot Spencer. But you are not yourself, my boy. The disease that wrecked your mother's life—well!' he arose. 'I shall plead insanity when you are arraigned.'

'And I shall deny it!' I declared violently. 'I shall prove that I am not insane!'

'The minute you do you send yourself to the scaffold,' he said gravely, 'and all the skill of all the lawyers in all the world won't save you!'

. . . After a time he went away, and I lay stretched on my cot for hours, thinking, thinking . . . The blood splotch still glowed crimson on my right hand! . . . A long, narrow passageway, hedged with steel, and at its end a rope! . . . Finally, I slept.

When I awoke some great change had been wrought in me. I saw clearly the way to save myself, to rend the circumstantial net which bound me. They all believed me guilty, even my own lawyer—this friend of my father! I would prove them mistaken, and I would prove it by evidence.

Strangely enough, I began by sending for Garron. He came into my cell with only a word of greeting, and seated himself opposite me, with expectation burning in his deep-set eyes, his chalky face expressionless.

'It is not a confession,' I told him. 'I know you believe that I lied about having seen a woman pass my door, about having heard a single shot. I know that the blood-spot on my hand, coupled with the finding of a Maxim noiseless pistol, which is *supposed* to be mine, will be damning evidence in a court of law. I know all these things, and yet I am going to ask you to save me, because I know you to be clever, and I don't believe you would do any man an injustice.'

'Thank you,' he said quietly.

'In the beginning you must assume that my story of the woman is true,' I continued. 'You need not really believe it, but you must act is if you *did* believe it—act, in other words, as if you were trying to save me rather than convict me?'

'I understand.'

'Only one question,' I rushed on with the feverish exaltation of confidence and enthusiasm in my manner. 'Was any trace found of a woman by any of your men? Did you find any?'

'No,' he replied. 'If there was a woman she didn't leave the hotel that night; and there was not one woman in the hotel who answers the description you gave. Not even a servant,' he added. 'I may say, too, that no one connected with the hotel remembers that a woman entered the building that night.'

'I am not assuming that she was in the hotel. She left it, and I dare say she left it within fifteen minutes of the time I saw her.'

'How?' he queried curiously.

'There are always fire-escapes,' I suggested. 'It would be only a drop of a few feet from the bottom platform to the ground; and behind the hotel at least two of these fire-escapes open on an alley. Now, the woman ran downstairs from the sixth floor, where my room is; therefore, if she did get away by a fire-escape, it was either from the fifth floor, or one below that. All the fire-escapes open by windows into the halls.'

'I hadn't thought of that,' he admitted frankly.

'As a matter of fact, when you saw the blood on my hand you were so firmly convinced of my guilt, that no particular effort was made to locate the woman, except to guard the exits, was there?' I asked. 'Now—we are always assuming that there *was* a woman—if a woman opened a window and clambered out upon a fire-escape, she would probably leave some trace of it somewhere. And, of necessity, she would be compelled to leave the window unlocked behind her.'

'Of course!' A strange expression was creeping into Garron's eyes. I was unable to read it.

'Further, it is well to remember that a woman is hampered by skirts,' I continued. 'That being true, she may have taken hold of the window-frame to pull herself up and—Heavens! Man! Don't you see? There is a chance she left a blood-stain on the window-frame, if she did touch it!'

For a minute or more Garron merely stared at me.

'In all this,' he said measuredly at last, 'we must forget, of course, the blood-stain on *your* hand?'

'No, don't forget it!' I exclaimed sharply. 'Remember

it! But remember, too, that I tried to stop that woman; that I even took hold of her wrist. She wriggled away like a snake, and pushed me backward against the wall. If'—I leaned forward eagerly—'if there was blood on her hand, *that's where I got it on mine!*'

'I hadn't thought of that,' Garron said again.

'You hadn't thought of any of these things, because you assumed off-hand that I was the murderer,' I declared bitterly. 'Yet you haven't found a motive—you never will find a motive.'

Some subtle change was working in Garron's face. Had I convinced him of this new possibility? I wondered.

'I think you have a right to assume,' he remarked finally, 'that we didn't go as far in our investigation as we should. Believe me, now, I'll go to the end.'

'And search Spencer's room,' I urged. 'Search it closely. If that woman had dropped a handkerchief—a jewel—anything!'

He nodded. A fever of madness was upon me, but it was the madness of relief . . . He went away, and for hours, it seemed, I sat staring dully at the crimson splotch on the back of my right hand . . .

*   *   *

Garron came again about dusk. At sight of him I fairly leaped at the bars of my cell. The turnkey opened the door, and Garron entered, silent, inscrutable. Good news or bad? Which?

'Well?' I demanded fiercely.

'On the ledge of the window which opens to the fire-escape from the hall of the fourth floor,' he began, without preliminary, 'I found certain scratches and marks, which may have been made by somebody clambering out at that window. The window was unlocked.'

I tried to shout my joy! I couldn't. My vocal cords seemed paralysed; my body was tense.

'It so happens,' Garron went on evenly, 'that the fire-escape has been recently painted. The even surface of the paint was broken by unmistakable marks of foot-prints—the foot-prints of a woman.'

Again I tried to speak; there was only an inarticulate cry. Then suddenly came again those crushing pains in my head; the cell spun about me.

'The paving in the alley beneath the fire-escape is cement,' Garron continued, 'so it is impossible to say whether anyone dropped from the last landing to the ground.'

'But the foot-prints?' I gasped. 'They would show if the woman was going up or down?'

'They indicate that she was going down,' came the cautious reply. 'Also I found on one side of the window-frame, at about the point where a person would take hold of it . . .'

'A blood-stain!' I burst out. It was too good to be true! . . . 'Thank God!'

'It seemed to be a blood-stain, a small one,' Garron corrected in the same unemotional voice. 'I cut away the wood with the stain on it, and have turned it over to a skilled analyst for examination.'

'And if he says it *is* a blood-stain?'

'Your story begins to sound plausible,' Garron answered in the same monotonous voice. 'Meanwhile, at your suggestion, I made another search of Spencer's room.' He paused, and there came some perceptible change in the ferret-like face, a narrowing of the deep glowing eyes, a tightening of the pale lips. It was warning enough. 'I found this,' he added.

Casually he extended his open hand. In it lay a tie-pin—a solitary ruby surrounded by pearls . . . I didn't scream . . . Again that long, narrow passageway, and at its end a rope! . . . Here was a critical point; he had tried to trick me . . . If I had so much as lifted my hand to my tie! . . .

'One of the page-boys has identified this pin as yours,' Garron was saying.

'Mine?' I queried, and I was surprised at the cool steadiness of my voice. 'No. I have one something like it, a pearl surrounded by rubies. You'll find it somewhere in my belongings.' I took the pin in my hand. 'In just what part of the room did you find this?'

'All the way across the room from where we found Spencer,' was the reply. 'It had been dropped near a window—the window from which the pistol must have been thrown. It's the only one in that room overlooking the roof; it was open.'

'Seems to me it's Spencer's pin,' I remarked, heedless of his other statements. 'I think I've seen him wear it. Anyway, it's of no value as a clue to the woman.'

'But,' Garron suggested quickly, 'if that pin *is* yours, if it could be *proved* to be yours, it would be the last link needed. You wouldn't have a chance to clear yourself.'

'True,' I agreed, and I smiled a little. 'I bought my pearl and ruby pin from Spink's. Perhaps there's a record there. And now this Maxim noiseless pistol,' I went on. 'The police are prepared to prove, I understand, that the pistol with which Spencer was killed—the one that was found on the roof—is one that I bought and paid for with a personal cheque?'

'Yes,' he nodded.

'I did buy such a weapon a few months ago, on the eve of my departure for Germany. I paid for it with a personal cheque, and either lost it, or it was stolen, in Berlin. There are possibly not more than three or four hundred of these pistols in existence; they are all alike, and they are not numbered. If the woman came to this hotel to kill Spencer, and she knew such a thing as a noiseless pistol existed, isn't it quite possible that she, too, purchased one? In that case she could have walked in and shot him, and walked away with no one any the wiser. I heard one shot. Now we know that was the shot fired by Spencer after he himself had been shot in the back!'

After a long time Garron nodded his understanding.

'Therefore, there remain only three things for you to do,' I rushed on. 'First, look through my belongings, and see if you can find the tie-pin with the pearl and small rubies, and if you don't, go to Spink's and satisfy yourself I bought such a pin; second go to the gun shop where I bought the noiseless pistol—it's the sole agency in London—and see if one has ever been sold to a woman; third, find the woman who left the blood-stain on my hand, whose foot-prints lead *down* the fire-escape. You must find that woman! You've gone so far with me; you know there *is* a woman—she must be found!'

I extended both hands towards him in entreaty; on the back of the right still glowed that crimson splotch! I thrust it behind me, cursing.

I didn't see Garron again for more than two weeks, but the following day I received a short note from him. It was like this:

'*I found the pearl and ruby pin in your belongings. It has been identified by Spink's as one you bought there.*'

Three days later there came a telegram for me, dated at a small town sixty miles from London:

'*Analyst reports that stain on window-frame is human blood.   Garron.*'

That's all there was of it, but no man who has never stood in the shadow of death may know what it meant to me.

Then came a long silence, a week, ten days, and no word from Garron. Where was he? What was he doing in the small country town? My lawyer, this friend of my father, came to see me. I cursed him and he went away, shaking his head.

On the morning of the eleventh day Garron came, inscrutable of face, silent as ever. I beat upon the bars frantically at sight of him. The turnkey admitted him; he dropped down on my cot and sat without speaking, while the gaoler's footsteps died away in the distance. Then from a pocket he produced a small paper parcel. He opened it, and held up—a woman's glove! Some cry escaped me: I reached for it.

'Keep your hands off!' he commanded sharply. 'There are bloodstains on it. Your life depends upon them remaining undisturbed.'

'You found the woman?'

'I found her—yes,' he replied quietly. 'I traced her through a photograph I found in Spencer's trunk. It was a picture of a boy, a mere baby, made by a photographer in a little Sussex town. I went to that town; the photographer told me whose boy it was. The woman is that boy's mother; the boy is Spencer's son.'

'Spencer's son?' I repeated incredulously. 'To my knowledge Spencer was never married.'

'There's the tragedy of it,' Garron responded gravely. 'It's the same old story—a woman who trusted a man. The boy was born and, in a way, Spencer was fond of him. He made liberal allowances to the mother, and they lived quietly in the small town. She is known there as Mrs Rosa Warren, a widow.'

There was a little pause.

'But the glove?' I demanded suddenly. 'Where did you get that? What has the woman to say? Where is she now?'

'She is under arrest,' Garron resumed. 'She admits that she went to Spencer's room about midnight at his request, and showed me his note making the appointment for a last conference previous to his departure for a long trip abroad. He was to transfer a sum of money to her.'

'And she shot him?' I broke in fiercely.

'Her story of what happened in that room is beyond belief,' Garron continued. 'She tapped on the door, she says; there was no answer. She opened it and went in, closing it behind her. The room was dark. She heard some

sort of noise and spoke. After a moment came a pistol shot
—the shot you heard. She thought Spencer was trying to
kill her—remember, this is her story—and opened the door
to escape. She ran almost into your arms. You seized her;
she struggled free, and ran down two flights of stairs. She
knew there would be an alarm, and more to hide her own
shame than anything else, she went through a window to a
fire-escape, and thence to the ground. The drop from the
last platform is only about eight feet.'

The tortures of hell broke loose in my brain. I rose,
clasped both my hands to my head, and fell prone. Garron
lifted me to the cot. After a long time he went on:

'Of course, now we know the motive for the murder. She
loved this man. He had deceived her, and he was going
away. At the gun-shop a clerk remembered that a noiseless pistol had been sold to a woman, but it is doubtful if
she could be identified after so long a time. Of course, she
denies this. And the glove!'

Again he held it aloft; I turned on the cot and stared at
it fascinated.

'I found it in her house,' Garron went on calmly. 'There
had been no attempt to conceal it, or even clean it. I think
that's all. I believe the woman will confess.'

'And she would have let me go to the scaffold!' I com-
plained.

. . . A long, narrow passageway, hedged with steel. At
its end was a rope . . . A woman was being bound . . .
She was shrieking!

I was arraigned and dismissed without trial. The woman
had made further statements of a damaging nature, and
despite her pitiful protestations of innocence, she was held.
The chain of evidence against her was complete. I remember only the final words of the judge who set me free:

'. . . an insane man who, by the sheer cunning of his
madness, has broken down the circumstantial evidence
against himself and proven the probable guilt of a woman

now under arrest. The prisoner is discharged in the custody of his friends.'

Two days after that I went into the consulting room of a surgeon and held out my right hand.

'Please amputate that hand at the wrist,' I requested.

He stared at me as if I were mad.

'Amputate it?' he repeated. 'Why?'

'It's covered with blood, and it won't come off,' I told him.

*   *   *

Mr Howard Meredith, whose statement is set forth above, committed suicide four days after he was set free. In a short note, incoherent and barely decipherable, he said:

'It is not just that a woman should die for what she did not do. I killed Spencer. I shot him in the back and I thought I had killed him; then threw the pistol out of a window. He had said I was insane, so my act was justifiable. He shot at the woman who entered in the dark, thinking it was me. I bought the tie-pin in Germany. Garron is a fool; so is the judge who set me free.'

XI

The Man Who Cut Off My Hair

Richard Marsh

My name is Judith Lee. I am a teacher of the deaf and dumb.
I teach them by what is called the oral system—that is,
the lip-reading system. When people pronounce a word
correctly they all make exactly the same movements with
their lips, so that, without hearing a sound, you only have
to watch them very closely to know what they are saying.
Of course, this needs practice, and some people do it better
and quicker than others. I suppose I must have a special
sort of knack in that direction, because I do not remember a
time when, by merely watching people speaking at a distance, no matter at what distance if I could see them
clearly, I did not know what they were saying. In my case
the gift, or knack, or whatever it is, is hereditary. My
father was a teacher of the deaf and dumb—a very successful one. His father was, I believe, one of the originators of
the oral system. My mother, when she was first married, had
an impediment in her speech which practically made her
dumb; though she was stone deaf, she became so expert at
lip-reading that she could not only tell what others were
saying, but she could speak herself—audibly, although she
could not hear her own voice.

So, you see, I have lived in the atmosphere of lip-reading all my life. When people, as they often do, think my skill at it borders on the marvellous, I always explain to them that it is nothing of the kind, that mine is simply a case of 'practice makes perfect.' This knack of mine, in a way, is almost equivalent to another sense. It has led me into the most singular situations, and it has been the cause of many really extraordinary adventures. I will tell you of one which happened to me when I was quite a child, the details of which have never faded from my memory.

My father and mother were abroad, and I was staying, with some old and trusted servants, in a little cottage which we had in the country. I suppose I must have been between twelve and thirteen years of age. I was returning by train to the cottage from a short visit which I had been paying to some friends. In my compartment there were two persons beside myself—an elderly woman who sat in front of me, and a man who was at the other end of her seat. At a station not very far from my home the woman got out; a man got in and placed himself beside the one who was already there. I could see they were acquaintances—they began to talk to each other.

They had been talking together for some minutes in such low tones that you could not only not hear their words, you could scarcely tell that they were speaking. But that made no difference to me; though they spoke in the tiniest whisper I had only to look at their faces to know exactly what they were saying. As a matter of fact, happening to glance up from the magazine I was reading, I saw the man who had been there first say to the other something which gave me quite a start. What he said was this (I only saw the fag-end of the sentence):

'. . . Myrtle Cottage; it's got a great, old myrtle in the front garden.'

The other man said something, but as his face was turned from me I could not see what; the tone in which he spoke was so subdued that hearing was out of the question. The first man replied (whose face was to me):

'His name is Colegate. He's an old bachelor, who uses the place as a summer cottage. I know him well—all the dealers know him. He's got some of the finest old silver in England. There's a Charles II salt-cellar in the place which would fetch twenty pounds an ounce anywhere.'

The other man sat up erect and shook his head, looking straight in front of him, so that I could see what he said, though he spoke only in a whisper.

'Old silver is no better than new; you can only melt it.'

The other man seemed to grow quite warm.

'Only melt it! Don't be a fool; you don't know what you're talking about. I can get rid of old silver at good prices to collectors all over the world; they don't ask too many questions when they think they're getting a bargain. That stuff at Myrtle Cottage is worth to us well over a thousand; I shall be surprised if I don't get more for it.'

The other man must have glanced at me while I was watching his companion speak. He was a fair-haired man, with a pair of light blue eyes, and quite a nice complexion. He whispered to his friend:

'That infernal kid is watching us as if she were all eyes.'

The other said: 'Let her watch. Much good may it do her; she can't hear a word—goggle-eyed brat!'

What he meant by 'goggle-eyed' I didn't know, and it was true that I could not hear; but, as it happened, it was not necessary that I should. I think the other must have been suspicious, because he replied, if possible, in a smaller whisper than ever:

'I should like to twist her skinny neck and throw her out on to the line.'

He looked as if he could do it too; such an unpleasant look came into his eyes that it quite frightened me. After all, I was alone with them; I was quite small; it would have been perfectly easy for him to have done what he said he would like to. So I glanced back at my magazine, and left the rest of their conversation unwatched.

But I had heard, or rather seen, enough to set me thinking. I knew Myrtle Cottage quite well, and the big myrtle tree; it was not very far from our own cottage. And I knew Mr Colegate and his collection of old silver—particularly that Charles II salt-cellar of which he was so proud. What interest had it for these two men? Had Mr Colegate come to the cottage? He was not there when I left. Or had Mr and Mrs Baines, who kept house for him—had they come? I was so young and so simple that it never occurred to me that there could be anything sinister about these two whispering gentlemen.

They both of them got out at the station before ours. Ours was a little village station, with a platform on only one side of the line; the one at which they got out served for quite an important place—our local market town. I thought no more about them, but I did think of Mr Colegate and of Myrtle Cottage. Dickson, our housekeeper, said that she did not believe that anyone was at the cottage, but she owned that she was not sure. So after tea I went for a stroll, without saying a word to anyone—Dickson had such a troublesome habit of wanting to know exactly where you were going. My stroll took me to Myrtle Cottage.

It stood all by itself in a most secluded situation on the other side of Woodbarrow Common. You could scarcely see the house from the road—it was quite a little house. When I got into the garden and saw that the front-room window was open I jumped to the very natural conclusion that some one must be there. I went quickly to the window —I was on the most intimate terms with everyone about the place; I should never have dreamt of announcing my presence in any formal manner—and looked in. What I saw did surprise me.

In the room was the man of the train—the man who had

been in my compartment first. He had what seemed to me to be Mr Colegate's entire collection of old silver spread out on the table in front of him, and that very moment he was holding up that gem of the collection—the Charles II salt-cellar. I had moved very quietly, meaning to take Mr Colegate—if it was he—by surprise; but I doubt if I had made a noise that that man would have heard me, he was so wrapped up in that apple of Mr Colegate's eye.

I did not know what to make of it at all. I did not know what to think. What was that man doing there? What was I to do? Should I speak to him? I was just trying to make up my mind when some one from behind lifted me right off my feet and, putting a hand to my throat, squeezed it so tightly that it hurt me.

'If you make a sound I'll choke the life right out of you. Don't you make any mistake about it—I will!'

He said that out loudly enough, though it was not so very loud either—he spoke so close to my ear. I could scarcely breathe, but I could still see, and I could see that the man who held me so horribly by the throat was the second man of the train. The recognition seemed to be mutual.

'If it isn't that infernal brat! She seemed to be all eyes in the railway carriage, and, my word, she seems to have been all ears too.'

The first man had come to the window.

'What's up?' he asked. 'Who's that kid you've got hold of there?'

My captor twisted my face round for the other to look at.

'Can't you see for yourself? I felt, somehow, that she was listening.'

'She couldn't have heard, even if she was; no one could have heard what we were saying. Hand her in here.' I was passed through the window to the other, who kept as tight a grip on my throat as his friend had done.

'Who are you?' he asked. 'I'll give you a chance to

answer, but if you try to scream I'll twist your head right off you.'

He loosed his grip just enough to enable me to answer if I wished. But I did not wish. I kept perfectly still. His companion said:

'What's the use of wasting time? Slit her throat and get done with it.'

He took from the table a dreadful-looking knife, with a blade eighteen inches long, which I knew very well. Mr Colegate had it in his collection because of its beautifully chased, massive silver handle. It had belonged to one of the old Scottish chieftains; Mr Colegate would sometimes make me go all over goose-flesh by telling me of some of the awful things for which, in the old, lawless, blood-thirsty days in Scotland, it was supposed to have been used. I knew that he kept it in beautiful condition, with the edge as sharp as a razor. So you can fancy what my feelings were when that man drew the blade across my throat, so close to the skin that it all but grazed me.

'Before you cut her throat,' observed his companion, 'we'll tie her up. We'll make short work of her. This bit of rope will about do the dodge.'

He had what looked to me like a length of clothes-line in his hand. With it, between them, they tied me to a great oak chair, so tight that it seemed to cut right into me, and, lest I should scream with the pain, the man with the blue eyes tied something across my mouth in a way which made it impossible for me to utter a sound. Then he threatened me with that knife again, and just as I made sure he was going to cut my throat he caught hold of my hair, which, of course, was hanging down my back, and with that dreadful knife sawed the whole of it from my head.

If I could have got within reach of him at that moment I believe that I should have stuck that knife into him. Rage made me half beside myself. He had destroyed what was almost the dearest thing in the world to me—not

because of my own love of it, but on account of my mother's.
My mother had often quoted to me, 'The glory of a woman
is her hair,' and she would add that mine was very beautiful. There certainly was a great deal of it. She was so
proud of my hair that she had made me proud of it too—
for her sake. And to think that this man could have robbed
me of it in so hideous a way! I do believe that at the
moment I could have killed him.

I suppose he saw the fury which possessed me, because
he laughed and struck me across the face with my own
hair.

'I've half a mind to cram it down your throat,' he said.
'It didn't take me long to cut it off, but I'll cut your throat
even quicker—if you so much as try to move, my little
dear.'

The other man said to him:

'She can't move and she can't make a sound either. You
leave her alone. Come over here and attend to business.'

'I'll learn her,' replied the other man, and he lifted my
hair above my head and let it fall all over me.

They proceeded to wrap up each piece of Mr Colegate's
collection in tissue paper, and then to pack the whole into
two queer-shaped bags—pretty heavy they must have been.
It was only then that I realized what they were doing—
they were stealing Mr Colegate's collection; they were
going to take it away. The fury which possessed me as I
sat there, helpless, and watched them! The pain was bad
enough, but my rage was worse. When the man who had
cut off my hair moved to the window with one of the bags
held in both his hands—it was as much as he could carry—
he said to his companion, with a glance towards me:
'Hadn't I better cut her throat before I go?'

'You can come and do that presently,' replied the other,
'you'll find her waiting.' Then he dropped his voice and
I saw him say: 'Now you quite understand?' The other
nodded. 'What is it?'

The face of the man who had cut my hair was turned towards me. He put his lips very close to the other, speaking in the tiniest whisper, which he never dreamed could reach my ears: 'Cotterill, Cloak-room, Victoria Station Brighton Railway.'

The other whispered, 'That's right. You'd better make a note of it; we don't want any bungling.'

'No fear, I'm not likely to forget.' Then he repeated his previous words: 'Cotterill, Cloak-room, Victoria Station, Brighton Railway.'

He whispered this so very earnestly that I felt sure there was something about the words which was most important; by the time he had said them a second time they were printed on my brain quite as indelibly as they were on his. He got out of the window and his bag was passed to him; then he spoke a parting word to me.

'Sorry I can't take a lock of your hair with me; perhaps I'll come back for one presently.'

Then he went. If he had known the passion which was blazing in my heart! That allusion to my desecrated locks only made it burn still fiercer. His companion, left alone, paid no attention to me whatever. He continued to secure his bag, searched the room, as if for anything which might have been overlooked, then, bearing the bag with the other half of Mr Colegate's collection with him, he went through the door, ignoring my presence as if I had never existed. What he did afterwards I cannot say; I saw no more of him; I was left alone—all through the night.

What a night it was. I was not afraid; I can honestly say that I have seldom been afraid of anything—I suppose it is a matter of temperament—but I was most uncomfortable, very unhappy, and each moment the pain caused me by my bonds seemed to be growing greater. I do believe that the one thing which enabled me to keep my senses all through the night was the constant repetition of those mystic words: 'Cotterill, Cloak-room, Victoria Station,

The Man Who Cut Off My Hair

Brighton Railway.' In the midst of my trouble I was glad
that what some people call my curious gift had enabled
me to see what I was quite sure they had never meant
should reach my understanding. What the words meant I
had no notion; in themselves they seemed to be silly words.
But that they had some hidden, weighty meaning I was
so sure that I kept saying them over and over again lest
they should slip through my memory.

I do not know if I ever closed my eyes; I certainly never
slept. I saw the first gleams of light usher in the dawn of
another morning, and I knew the sun had risen. I wondered
what they were doing at home—between the repetitions
of that cryptic phrase. Was Dickson looking for me? I
rather wished I had let her know where I was going, then
she might have had some idea of where to look. As it was
she had none. I had some acquaintances three or four miles
off, with whom I would sometimes go to tea and, without
warning to anyone at home, stay the night. I am afraid
that, even as a child, my habits were erratic. Dickson might
think I was staying with them, and, if so, she would not
even trouble to look for me. In that case I might have to
stay where I was for days.

I do not know what time it was, but it seemed to me
that it had been light for weeks, and that the day must be
nearly gone, when I heard steps outside the open window.
I was very nearly in a state of stupor, but I had still sense
enough to wonder if it was that man who had cut my hair
come back again to cut my throat. As I watched the open
sash my heart began to beat more vigorously than it had
for a very long time. What, then, was my relief when there
presently appeared, on the other side of it, the face of Mr
Colegate, the owner of Myrtle Cottage. I tried to scream—
with joy, but that cloth across my mouth prevented my
uttering a sound.

I never shall forget the look which came on Mr Colegate's
face when he saw me. He rested his hands on the sill as if

he wondered how the window came to be open, then when he looked in and saw me, what a jump he gave.

'Judith!' he exclaimed. 'Judith Lee! Surely it is Judith Lee!'

He was a pretty old man, or he seemed so to me, but I doubt if a boy could have got through that window quicker than he did. He was by my side in less than no time; with a knife which he took from his pocket he was severing my bonds. The agony which came over me as they were loosed! It was worse than anything which had gone before. The moment my mouth was free I exclaimed—even then I was struck by the funny, hoarse voice in which I seemed to be speaking:

'Cotterill, Cloak-room, Victoria Station, Brighton Railway.'

So soon as I had got those mysterious words out of my poor, parched throat I fainted; the agony I was suffering, the strain which I had gone through, proved too much for me. I knew dimly that I was tumbling into Mr Colegate's arms, and then I knew no more.

When I came back to life I was in bed. Dickson was at my bedside, and Dr Scott, and Mr Colegate, and Pierce, the village policeman, and a man who I afterwards knew was a detective, who had been sent over post-haste from a neighbouring town. I wondered where I was, and then I saw I was in a room in Myrtle Cottage. I sat up in bed, put up my hands—then it all came back to me.

'He cut off my hair with MacGregor's knife!' MacGregor was the name of the Highland chieftain to whom, according to Mr Colegate, that dreadful knife had belonged.

When it did all come back to me and I realized what had happened, and felt how strange my head seemed without its accustomed covering, nothing would satisfy me but that they should bring me a looking-glass. When I saw what I looked like, the rage which had possessed me when the outrage first took place surged through me with greater force than ever. Before they could stop me, or even guess what I was going to do, I was out of bed and facing them. That cryptic utterance came back to me as if of its own initiative; it burst from my lips.

'"Cotterill, Cloak-room, Victoria Station, Brighton Railway!" Where are my clothes? That's where the man is who cut off my hair.'

They stared at me. I believe that for a moment they thought that what I had endured had turned my brain, and that I was mad. But I soon made it perfectly clear that I was nothing of the kind. I told them my story as fast as I could speak; I fancy I brought it home to their understanding. Then I told them of the words which I had seen spoken in such a solemn whisper, and how sure I was that they were pregnant with weighty meaning.

'"Cotterill, Cloak-room, Victoria Station, Brighton Railway"—that's where the man is who cut my hair off—that's where I'm going to catch him.'

The detective was pleased to admit that there might be something in my theory, and that it would be worth while to go up to Victoria Station to see what the words might mean. Nothing would satisfy me but that we should go at once. I was quite convinced that every moment was of importance, and that if we were not quick we should be too late. I won Mr Colegate over—of course, he was almost as anxious to get his collection back as I was to be quits with the miscreant who had shorn me of my locks. So we went up to town by the first train we could catch—Mr Colegate, the detective, and an excited and practically hairless child.

When we got to Victoria Station we marched straight up to the cloak-room, and the detective said to one of the persons on the other side of the counter:

'Is there a parcel here for the name of Cotterill?'

The person to whom he had spoken did not reply, but another man who was standing by his side.

'Cotterill? A parcel for the name of Cotterill has just

been taken out—a hand-bag, scarcely more than half a minute ago. You must have seen him walking off with it as you came up. He can hardly be out of sight now.' Leaning over the counter, he looked along the platform.

'There he is—some one is just going to speak to him.'

I saw the person to whom he referred—a shortish man in a light grey suit, carrying a brown leather hand-bag. I also saw the person who was going to speak to him; and thereupon I ceased to have eyes for the man with the bag. I broke into exclamation.

'There's the man who cut my hair!' I cried. I went rushing along the platform as hard as I could go. Whether the man heard me or not I cannot say; I dare say I had spoken loudly enough; but he gave one glance in my direction, and when he saw me I had no doubt that he remembered. He whispered to the man with the bag. I was near enough to see, though not to hear, what he said. In spite of the rapidity with which his lips were moving, I saw quite distinctly.

'Bantock, 13 Harwood Street, Oxford Street.' That was what he said, and no sooner had he said it than he turned and fled—from me; I knew he was flying from me, and it gave me huge satisfaction to know that the mere sight of me had made him run. I was conscious that Mr Colegate and the detective were coming at a pretty smart pace behind me.

The man with the bag, seeing his companion dart off without the slightest warning, glanced round to see what had caused his hasty flight. I suppose he saw me and the detective and Mr Colegate, and he drew his own conclusions. He dropped that hand-bag as if it had been red-hot, and off he ran. He ran to such purpose that we never caught him—neither him nor the man who had cut my hair. The station was full of people—a train had just come in. The crowd streaming out covered the platform with a swarm of moving figures. They acted as cover to those two eager gentlemen—they got clean off. But we got the bag; and, one of the station officials coming on the scene, we were shown to an apartment where, after explanations had been made, the bag and its contents were examined.

Of course, we had realized from the very first moment that Mr Colegate's collection could not possibly be in that bag, because it was not nearly large enough. When it was seen what was in it, something like a sensation was created. It was crammed with small articles of feminine clothing. In nearly every garment jewels were wrapped, which fell out of them as they were withdrawn from the bag. Such jewels! You should have seen the display they made when they were spread out upon the leather-covered table—and our faces as we stared at them.

'This does not look like my collection of old silver,' observed Mr Colegate.

'No,' remarked a big, broad-shouldered man, who I afterwards learned was a well-known London detective, who had been induced by our detective to join our party.

'This does not look like your collection of old silver, sir; it looks, if you'll excuse my saying so, like something very much more worth finding. Unless I am mistaken, these are the Duchess of Datchet's jewels, some of which she wore at the last Drawing Room, and which were taken from Her Grace's bedroom after her return. The police all over Europe have been looking for them for more than a month.'

'That bag has been with us nearly a month. The party who took it out paid four-and-sixpence for cloak-room charges—twopence a day for twenty-seven days.'

The person from the cloak-room had come with us to that apartment; it was he who said this. The London detective replied:

'Paid four-and-sixpence, did he? Well, it was worth it—to us. Now, if I could lay my hand on the party who put the bag in the cloak-room, I might have a word of a kind to say to him.'

I had been staring, wide-eyed, as piece by piece the contents of the bag had been disclosed; I had been listening, open-eared, to what the detective said; when he made that remark about laying his hands on the party who had deposited that bag in the cloak-room, there came into my mind the words which I had seen the man who had cut my hair whisper as he fled to the man with the bag. The cryptic sentence which I had seen him whisper as I sat tied to the chair had indeed proved to be full of meaning; the words which, even in the moment of flight, he had felt bound to utter might be just as full. I ventured on an observation, the first which I had made, speaking with a good deal of diffidence.

'I think I know where he might be found—I am not sure, but I think.'

All eyes were turned to me. The detective exclaimed:

'You think you know? As we haven't got so far as thinking, if you were to tell us, little lady, what you think, it might be as well, mightn't it?'

I considered—I wanted to get the words exactly right.

'Suppose you were to try'—I paused so as to make quite sure—'Bantock, 13 Harwood Street, Oxford Street.'

'And who is Bantock?' the detective asked. 'And what do you know about him anyhow?'

'I don't know anything at all about him, but I saw the man who cut my hair whisper to the other man just before he ran away, "Bantock, 13 Harwood Street, Oxford Street"—I saw him quite distinctly.'

'You saw him whisper? What does the girl mean by saying she saw him whisper? Why, young lady, you must have been quite fifty feet away. How, at that distance, and with all the noise of the traffic, could you hear a whisper?'

'I didn't say I heard him; I said I saw him. I don't need to hear to know what a person is saying. I just saw you whisper to the other man, "The young lady seems to be by way of being a curiosity."'

The London detective stared at our detective. He seemed to be bewildered.

'But I—I don't know how you heard that; I scarcely breathed the words.'

Mr Colegate explained. When they heard they all seemed to be bewildered, and they looked at me, as people do look at the present day, as if I were some strange and amazing thing. The London detective said: 'I never heard the like to that. It seems to me very much like what old-fashioned people called "black magic".'

Although he was a detective, he could not have been a very intelligent person after all, or he would not have talked such nonsense. Then he added, with an accent on the 'saw':

'What was it you said you saw him whisper?'

I bargained before I told him.

'I will tell you if you let me come with you.'

'Let you come with me?' He stared still more. 'What does the girl mean?'

'Her presence,' struck in Mr Colegate, 'may be useful for purposes of recognition. She won't be in the way; you can do no harm by letting her come.'

'If you don't promise to let me come I shan't tell you.'

The big man laughed. He seemed to find me amusing; I do not know why. If he had only understood my feeling on the subject of my hair, and how I yearned to be even with the man who had wrought me what seemed to me such an irreparable injury. I dare say it sounds as if I were very revengeful. I do not think it was a question of vengeance only; I wanted justice. The detective took out a fat notebook.

'Very well; it's a bargain. Tell me what you saw him whisper, and you shall come.' So I told him again, and he wrote it down. '"Bantock, 13 Harwood Street, Oxford Street." I know Harwood Street, though I don't know Mr Bantock. But he seems to be residing at what is generally understood to be an unlucky number. Let me get a message through to the Yard—we may want assistance. Then we'll pay a visit to Mr Bantock—if there is such a person. It sounds like a very tall story to me.'

I believe that even then he doubted if I had seen what I said I saw. When we did start I was feeling pretty nervous, because I realized that if we were going on a fool's errand, and there did turn out to be no Bantock, that London detective would doubt me more than ever. And, of course, I could not be sure that there was such a person, though it was some comfort to know that there was a Harwood Street. We went four in a cab—the two detectives, Mr Colegate and I. We had gone some distance before the cab stopped. The London detective said:

'This is Harwood Street; I told the driver to stop at the corner—we will walk the rest of the way. A cab might arouse suspicion; you never know.'

It was a street full of shops. No. 13 proved to be a sort of curiosity shop and jeweller's combined; quite a respectable-looking place, and sure enough over the top of the window was the name 'Bantock.'

'That looks as if, at any rate, there were a Bantock,' the big man said; it was quite a weight off my own mind when I saw the name.

Just as we reached the shop a cab drew up and five men got out, whom the London detective seemed to recognize with mingled feelings.

'That's queered the show,' he exclaimed. I did not know what he meant. 'They rouse suspicion, if they do nothing else—so in we go.'

And in we went—the detective first, and I close on his heels. There were two young men standing close together behind the counter. The instant we appeared I saw one whisper to the other:

'Give them the office—ring the alarm-bell—they're 'tecs!'

I did not quite know what he meant either, but I guessed enough to make me cry out:

'Don't let him move—he's going to ring the alarm-bell and give them the office.'

Those young men were so startled—they must have been quite sure that I could not have heard—that they both stood still and stared; before they had got over their surprise a detective—they were detectives who had come in the second cab—had each by the shoulder.

There was a door at the end of the shop, which the London detective opened.

'There's a staircase here; we'd better go up and see who's above. You chaps keep yourselves handy, you may be wanted—when I call you come.'

He mounted the stairs—as before, I was as close to him as I could very well get. On the top of the staircase was a landing, on to which two doors opened. We paused to listen: I could distinctly hear voices coming through one of them.

'I think this is ours,' the London detective said.

He opened the one through which the voices were coming. He marched in—I was still as close to him as I could get. In it were several men, I did not know how many, and I did not care; I had eyes for only one. I walked right past the detective up to the table round which some of them were sitting, some standing, and stretching out an accusatory arm I pointed at one.

'That's the man who cut off my hair!'

It was, and well he knew it. His conscience must have smitten him; I should not have thought that a grown man could be so frightened at the sight of a child. He caught hold, with both hands, of the side of the table; he glared at me as if I were some dreadful apparition—and no doubt to him I was. It was only with an effort that he seemed able to use his voice.

'Good night!' he exclaimed, 'it's that infernal kid!'

On the table, right in front of me, I saw something with which I was only too familiar. I snatched it up.

'And this is the knife,' I cried, 'with which he did it!'

It was; the historical blade, which had once belonged to the sanguinary and, I sincerely trust, more or less apocryphal MacGregor. I held it out towards the gaping man.

'You know that this is the knife with which you cut off my hair,' I said. 'You know it is.'

I dare say I looked a nice young termagant with my short hair, rage in my eyes, and that frightful weapon in my hand. Apparently I did not impress him quite as I had intended—at least, his demeanour did not suggest it.

'By the living Jingo!' he shouted, 'I wish I had cut her throat with it as well!'

It was fortunate for him that he did not. Probably, in the long run, he would have suffered for it more than he did—though he suffered pretty badly as it was. It was his cutting my hair that did it. Had he not done that I have little doubt that I should have been too conscious of the pains caused me by my bonds—the marks caused by the cord were on my skin for weeks after—to pay such close attention to their proceedings as I did under the spur of anger. Quite possibly that tell-tale whisper would have gone unnoticed. Absorbed by my own suffering, I should have paid very little heed to the cryptic sentence which really proved to be their undoing. It was the outrage to my locks which caused me to strain every faculty of observation I had. He had much better have left them alone.

That was the greatest capture the police had made for years. In one haul they captured practically every member of a gang of cosmopolitan thieves who were wanted by the police all over the world. The robbery of Mr Colegate's collection of old silver shrank into insignificance before the rest of their misdeeds. And not only were the thieves taken themselves, but the proceeds of no end of robberies.

The Man Who Cut Off My Hair

It seemed that they had met there for a sort of annual division of the common spoil. There was an immense quantity of valuable property before them on the table, and lots more about the house. Those jewels which were in the bag which had been deposited at the cloak-room at Victoria Station were to have been added to the common fund—to say nothing of Mr Colegate's collection of old silver.

The man who called himself Bantock, and who owned the premises at 13 Harwood Street, proved to be a well-known dealer in precious stones and jewellery and bric-a-brac and all sorts of valuables. He was immensely rich; it was shown that a great deal of his money had been made by buying and selling valuable stolen property of every sort and kind. Before the police had done with him it was made abundantly clear that, under various *aliases*, in half the countries of the world, he had been a wholesale dealer in stolen goods. He was sentenced to a long term of penal servitude. I am not quite sure, but I believe that he died in jail.

All the men who were in that room were sent to prison for different terms, including the man who cut my hair—to say nothing of his companion. So far as the proceedings at the court were concerned, I never appeared at all. Compared to some of the crimes of which they had been guilty, the robbery of Mr Colegate's silver was held to be a mere nothing. They were not charged with it at all, so my evidence was not required. But every time I looked at my scanty locks, which took years to grow to anything like a decent length—they had reached to my knees, but they never did that again—each time I stood before a looking-glass and saw what a curious spectacle I presented with my closely clipped poll, something of that old rage came back to me which had been during that first moment in my heart, and I felt—what I felt when I was tied to that chair in Myrtle Cottage. I endeavoured to console myself, in the spirit of the Old World rather than the New, that, owing to the gift which was mine, I had been able to cry something like quits with the man who, in a moment of mere wanton savagery, had deprived me of what ought to be the glory of a woman.

XII

The Affair of the German Dispatch-Box

Victor L. Whitechurch

A slight delicate-looking man with pale face and refined features, light red hair and dreamy blue eyes.

Such is a brief description of Thorpe Hazell, book collector and railway enthusiast, a gentleman of independent means, whose knowledge of book editions and bindings was only equalled by his grasp of railway details.

At least two railway companies habitually sought his expert advice in the bewildering task of altering their time-tables, while from time to time he was consulted in cases where his special railway knowledge proved of immense service, and his private note-book of such 'cases' would have provided much interesting copy to publishers.

He had one other peculiarity. He was a strong faddist on food and 'physical culture'. He carried vegetarianism to an extreme, and was continually practising various 'exercises' of the strangest description, much to the bewilderment of those who were not personally acquainted with his eccentricities.

Thorpe Hazell often said afterwards that the most

daring case which he ever undertook was that of the German Dispatch-Box. It was an affair of international importance at the time, and, for obvious reasons, remained shrouded in mystery. Now, however, when it may be relegated to the region of obsolete diplomatic crises, there is no reason why it should not, to a certain extent, be made public.

Hazell was only half through his breakfast one morning at his house in Netherton, when a telegram arrived for him with this message:

'*Am coming by next train. Wish to consult you on important question.* MOSTYN COTTERELL.'

'Cotterell, Cotterell,' said Hazell to himself. 'Oh, yes, I remember—he was on the same staircase with myself at St Philip's. A reading man in those days. I haven't seen him for years. Surely he's something in the Government now. Let me see.'

He got his Whitaker and consulted its pages. Presently he found what he wanted.

'Under-Secretary for Foreign Affairs—Mostyn Cotterell.'

As soon as he had finished his breakfast, including his pint of lemonade, he produced a 'Book of Exercises', and carefully went through the following directions:

'Stand in correct position, commence to inhale, and at the same time commence to tense the muscles of the arms, and raise them to an extended front horizontal position; leave the hands to drop limp from the wrists. While doing this change the weight of the body from the full foot on to the toes; in this position hold the breath and make rigid and extended the muscles of the arms, sides, neck, abdomen, and legs. Repeat this fifteen times.'

Half-an-hour or so later Mostyn Cotterell was ushered into his room. He was a tall, thin man, with a black moustache that made his naturally pale face look almost white. There was a haggard look about him, and certain dark lines under his eyes showed pretty plainly that he was suffering from want of sleep.

'It's a good many years since we met, Hazell,' he began, 'and you have gained quite a reputation since the old college days.'

'Ah, I see you have read my monograph on "Nerve Culture and Rational Food",' replied Hazell.

'Never heard of it,' said Cotterell. 'No, I mean your reputation as a railway expert, my dear fellow.'

'Oh, railways!' exclaimed Hazell in a disappointed tone of voice. 'They're just a hobby of mine, that's all. Is that why you've come?'

'Exactly. I called at your flat in town, but was told you were here. I want to consult you on a delicate matter, Hazell; one in which your knowledge of railways may prove of great value. Of course, it is understood that what I am going to say is quite private.'

'Certainly.'

'Well, let me put a case. Suppose a man was travelling, say, from London to the Continent by the ordinary boat train; and suppose that it was desirable to prevent that man from getting to his destination, would it—well—would it be possible to prevent him doing so?'

Hazell smiled.

'Your enigma is a difficult one to answer,' he said. 'It would all depend upon the means you cared to employ. I daresay it could be done, but you would probably have to resort to force.'

'That would hardly be politic. I want you to suggest some plan by which he could be got into a wrong train, or got out of the right one, so that, let us say, something he was carrying would be lost, or, at least, delayed in transit.'

'You are not very clear, Cotterell. First you speak of the *man* being frustrated, and then of something he is carrying.

What do you mean? Which is of the greater importance—the man or his property?'

'His property.'

'That puts a different aspect on it. I take it this is some intrigue of your profession. Why not place confidence in me, and tell me the whole thing? I never like to work on supposition. Once some fellows tried to draw me on a supposed case of wrecking a train. I could have told them half-a-dozen theories of my own invention, but I held my tongue, and lucky it was that I did so, for I found out afterwards they belonged to an American train robber gang. I don't accuse you of any nefarious purposes, but if you want my advice, tell me the exact circumstances. Only, I warn you beforehand, Cotterell, that I won't give you any tips that would either compromise me or be of danger to any railway company.'

'Very well,' replied the Under-Secretary, 'I will tell you the leading facts without betraying any State secrets, except to mention that there is a great stake involved. To cut matters short, a very important document has been stolen from our office. We pretty well know the culprit, only we have no proof. But we are certain of one thing and that is that this document is at present in the hands of the German Ambassador. You will understand that the ways of diplomacy are very subtle and that it is a case which makes action very difficult. If we were to demand the surrender of this paper we should be met, I have no doubt, with a bland denial that it is in the Ambassador's possession.

'Of course we have our secret agents, and they have told us that Colonel von Kriegen, one of the messengers of the German Embassy, has been ordered to start at mid-day with dispatches to Berlin. It is more than likely—in fact it is a dead certainty—that this particular document will be included in his dispatches. Now, if it once gets into the possession of the German Chancellery, there will be a bad international trouble which might even land us in a Continental war. If you can devise any means of obstructing or preventing the transit of this dispatch you would be rendering the country a real service.'

Hazell thought for a moment.

'Do you think this Colonel von Kriegen knows of the document he is carrying?' he asked presently.

'I shouldn't think so, its contents are of far too much importance to trust even to a regular messenger. No, he will probably be told to exercise the greatest care, and his journey will be watched and himself guarded by the German secret police.'

'How is he likely to carry the document?'

'In his dispatch-box, together with other papers.'

'And he will probably travel with secret police. My dear fellow, you have given me a hard nut to crack. Let me think a bit.'

He lit a cigarette and smoked hard for a few minutes. Presently he asked Cotterell if the dispatch-box had a handle to it.

'Yes—of course,' replied the Under-Secretary, 'a leather handle.'

'I wish I knew exactly what it was like.'

'I can easily tell you. All the dispatch-boxes of the German Embassy are of the same pattern. It is our business to know the smallest details. It would be about a foot long, eight inches broad, and about five inches deep, with a handle on the top—a dark green box.'

Hazell's face lit up with sudden interest.

'You haven't one exactly like it?' he asked.

'Yes, we have. At my office.'

'Will the key be with the Colonel?'

'Of course not. The Ambassador here will lock it, and it will not be opened till it is in the hands of the Chancellor in Berlin.'

Hazell jumped to his feet and began to stride up and down the room.

'Cotterell!' he exclaimed, 'there's just one plan that occurs to me. It's a very desperate one, and even if it succeeds it will land me in prison.'

'In England?' asked the other.

'Rather. I'm not going to play any tricks on the Continent, I can tell you. Now, suppose I'm able to carry out this plan and am imprisoned—say at Dovehaven—what would happen?'

He stopped abruptly in his walk and looked at Cotterell. A grin broke over the latter's face, and he said, quietly:

'Oh—you'd escape, Hazell.'

'Very good. I shall want help. *You'd* better not come. Have you got a knowing fellow whom you can trust? He must be a sharp chap, mind.'

'Yes, I have. One of our private men, named Bartlett.'

'Good. There are just two hours before the Continental train starts, and a quarter of an hour before you get a train back to town. You wire Bartlett from Netherton to meet you, and I'll write out instructions for you to give him. He'll have an hour in which to carry them out.'

He wrote rapidly for five minutes upon a sheet of paper, and then handed it over to the Under-Secretary.

'Mind you,' he said, 'the chances are terribly against us, and I can only promise to do my best. I shall follow you to town by another train that will give me just time to catch the boat express. What is this von Kriegen like?'

Cotterell described him.

'Good—now you must be off!'

Three-quarters of an hour later Hazell came out of his house, somewhat changed in appearance. He had put on the same dark wig which he wore in the affair of Crane's cigars, and was dressed in a black serge suit and straw hat. A clerical collar completed the deception of a clergyman in semi-mufti.

*　　*　　*

The Affair of the German Dispatch-Box

A stiffly-upright, military-looking man, with the ends of his fair moustache strongly waxed, dressed in a frock coat suit and tall hat, and carrying a dispatch-box, walked down the platform beside the boat train, the guard, who knew him well by sight—as he knew many who travelled on that line with their precious dispatches—giving him a salute as he passed.

Two men walked closely, but unobtrusively, behind the Colonel; two men whose eyes and ears were on the alert, and who scrutinized everyone carefully as they passed along. Of their presence the Special Messenger took not the slightest notice, though he was well aware of their companionship. He selected a first-class compartment, and got in. The two men followed him into the carriage, but without saying a word. One of them posted himself by the window, and kept a steady look out on to the platform.

The train was just about to start, and the guard had just put his whistle to his mouth, when a man came running down the platform, a small bag in one hand, a bundle of papers and an umbrella in the other. It was only a clergyman, and the man at the window gave a smile as he saw him.

With a rush, the clergyman made for the compartment, seizing the handle of the door and opening it. Frantically he threw his bag, umbrella, and papers into the carriage. The train had just begun to move.

The man near the window had retreated at the onslaught. He was just about to resent the intrusion with the words that the compartment was engaged, when a porter, running up behind the clergyman, pushed him in and slammed the door.

'I thought I'd lost it!' exlaimed the intruder, taking off his hat and wiping the perspiration from his forehead, for it was a very hot day, and he had been hurrying. 'It was a close shave! Oh, thank you, thank you!' he added, as one of the men rather ungraciously picked up his bag and papers from the floor, at the same time eyeing him closely.

But Hazell, in his disguise, was perfectly proof against

any suspicion. He sat down and opened the *Guardian* with
an easy air, just looking round at each of his three companions in such a naturally inquisitive manner as to
thoroughly disarm them from the outset. The Colonel had
lighted a cigar and said, half apologetically, as he took it
from his lips:

'I hope you don't mind smoking?'

'Oh, not at all. I do it myself occasionally,' returned the
clergyman with an amiable smile.

The train was now fairly under way, and Hazell was
beginning, as he read his paper, to take mental stock of his
surroundings and the positions in which the other three
were seated.

He, himself, was facing the engine on the left-hand side
of the compartment, close to the window. Immediately
opposite to him sat Colonel von Kriegen, watchful and
alert, although he seemed to smoke so complacently. Beside the Colonel, on the seat on his left, was the precious
dispatch-box; and the Colonel's hand, as it dangled negli-
gently over the arm-rest, touched it ever and anon. On the
next seat, guarding the dispatch-box on that side, sat one
of the secret police agents, while the other had placed
himself next to Hazell, and, consequently, opposite the box,
which was thus thoroughly guarded at all points.

It was this dispatch-box that Hazell was studying as
he apparently read his paper, noting its exact position and
distance from him. As he had told Mostyn Cotterell, the
chances of carrying out his plan were very much against
him, and he felt that this was more than ever the case now.
He had really hoped to secure a seat beside the box. But
this was out of the question.

After a bit he put down his paper, leant forward, and
looked out of the window, watching the country as they
sped through it. Once, just as they were passing through a
station, he stood up and leant his head out of the window
for a minute. The three men exchanged glances now that

his back was turned, but the Colonel only smiled and shook his head slightly.

Then Hazell sat down once more, yawned, gathered up his paper, and made another apparent attempt to read it. After a bit, he drew a cigarette case from his pocket, took out a cigarette, and placed it in his mouth. Then he leant forward, in a very natural attitude, and began feeling in his waistcoat pocket for a match.

The German Colonel watched him, carelessly flicking the ash from his cigar as he did so. Then, as it was apparent that the clergyman could find no matches, his politeness came to the front.

'You want a light, sir,' he said in very good English, 'can I offer you one?'

'Oh, thanks!' replied Hazell, shifting to the edge of his seat, and leaning still more forward, 'perhaps I may take one from your cigar?'

Every action that followed had been most carefully thought out beforehand. As he leant over towards the German he turned his back slightly on the man who sat beside him. He held the cigarette with the first and second fingers of his right hand and with the end of it in his mouth. He kept his eyes fixed on the Colonel's. Meanwhile his left hand went out through the open window, dropped over the sill, remained there for a moment, then came back, and crossed over the front of his body stealthily with the palm downwards.

It was all over in a second, before either of the three had time to grasp what was happening. He had his face close to the Colonel's, and had taken a puff at the cigarette, when suddenly his left hand swooped down on the handle of the dispatch-box, his right hand flew forward into the Colonel's face, instantly coming round with a quick sweep to his left hand, and, before the Colonel could recover or either of the others take action, he had tossed the dispatch-box out of the window.

They were on him at once. He sprang up, back to the window, and made a little struggle, but the Colonel and one of the others had him on the seat in no time. Meanwhile the third man had pulled the electric safety signal, and had dashed to the window. Thrusting his head out, he looked back along the level bit of line on which they were running.

'I can see it!' he cried triumphantly, as his eye caught a dark object beside the track. The whole affair had taken place so suddenly that the train began to pull up within fifteen or twenty seconds of the throwing out of the dispatch case. There was a shrill whistle, a grinding of brakes, and the train came to a standstill.

The guard was out of his van in an instant, running along beside the train.

'What is it?' he asked, as he came up to the carriage.

The police agent, who still kept his eyes fixed back on the track, beckoned him to come up. Heads were out of windows, and this matter was a private one. So the guard climbed on to the footboard.

'A dispatch-box has been thrown out of the carriage,' whispered the police agent, 'we have the man here. But we *must* get the case. It's only a little way back. We pulled the signal at once—in fact, I could see it lying beside the track before we stopped.'

'Very good, sir,' replied the guard quietly, commencing to wave an arm towards the rear of the train. The signal was seen on the engine, and the train began to reverse. Very soon a small, dark object could be seen alongside the rails. As they drew close, the guard held out his hand motionless, the train stopped, and he jumped off.

'Is this it?' he asked, as he handed in the dispatch-box.

'Yes!' exlaimed the Colonel, 'it's all right. Thank you, guard. Here's something for your trouble. We'll hand over the fellow to the police at Dovehaven. It was a clumsy trick.'

The Affair of the German Dispatch-Box

Colonel von Kriegen lit another cigar as the train went on, and looked at Hazell, who sat between the two police agents. There was a half smile on the Colonel's lips as he said:

'I'm afraid you did not quite succeed, sir! It was a sharp thing to do, but it didn't go quite far enough. You might have been sure that in broad daylight, and with the means of stopping the train, that it was impossible. Who put you on to this?'

'I accept the entire responsibility myself,' replied Hazell —'failure and all. I have only one favour to ask you. Will you allow me to eat my lunch?'

'Oh, certainly,' replied the Colonel grimly, 'especially as you won't have a chance of doing so when we arrive at Dovehaven. I should like you to travel all the way with us, but the exigencies of international law prevent that.'

Hazell bowed, and the next moment was placidly consuming Plasmon biscuits and drinking sterilized milk, expatiating at intervals on 'natural food'.

'Try a diet of macaroni and Dutch cheese,' were his last words to the Colonel. 'They both help to build up the grey brain material. Useful in your position!'

When the train arrived at Dovehaven, Hazell was given into the charge of the police there, and marched off to the station. Here the superintendent looked at him curiously. Hazell met his gaze, but nothing was said. It was strange, however, that he was not locked up in an ordinary cell, but in a small room.

It was also strange that the bar of the window was very loose, and that no one was about when he dropped out of it that night. The German police, when they heard about it, smiled. Diplomatic affairs are peculiar, and they knew that this particular 'criminal' would never be caught.

Meanwhile, the Colonel journeyed on to Berlin, with the full assurance in his mind that the papers in his dispatch-box were intact. He duly handed the latter over in person to the Chancellor, who, as the result of a cypher telegram, was eagerly expecting it.

Somehow, his key did not fit the lock of the dispatch-box. After trying it for a few moments, he exclaimed:

'Colonel, how is this? This is not one of our boxes, surely?'

The Colonel's face turned pale, and he hesitated to reply. Snatching up a knife, the Chancellor forced open the box, a cry of dismay issuing from his lips as he drew out the contents—the current number of *Punch*, in which he figured in a cartoon, and a copy of the *Standard* containing an article, carefully marked, on the foreign policy of the Government. Insult to injury, if you like.

German oaths never look well in print, and, anyhow, it is needless to record the ensuing conversation between the Chancellor and Colonel von Kriegen. At about the time it was taking place the German Ambassador in London received by post the original dispatch-box and its contents, minus the incriminating document, which now reposed safely in the custody of the Foreign Office, thanks to the ingenuity of Thorpe Hazell.

* * *

'How was it done?' said Hazell afterwards, when telling the story to a companion. 'Oh, it was a pure trick, and I hardly expected to be able to bring it off. Fortunately, Bartlett was a 'cute chap, and followed out all my instructions to the letter. Those instructions were very simple. I told him to wear an Inverness cloak, to provide himself with the duplicate dispatch-box, a few yards of very strong fishing twine, a fair-sized snap-hook, and a light walking-stick with a forked bit of wire stuck in the end of it. The only difficulty about his job was the presence of other travellers in his compartment, but, as it happened, there were only two maiden ladies, who thought him mad on fresh air.

'Of course, I told him how to use his various articles, and also that on no account was he to communicate with me either by word or look, but that he was to get into the compartment next to that in which the Colonel was travelling, and to be ready to command either window by reserving a seat with a bag on one side and seating himself on the other.

'The cloak served for a double purpose—to hide the dispatch-box and to conceal his movements from the occupants of his carriage when the time for action came. Fortunately, both his companions sat with their backs to the engine, so that he was easily able to command either window.

'I was to let him know which side of the train was the sphere of action by putting out my head as we ran through Eastwood. He would then look out of both windows and get to work accordingly.

'What he did was this. He had the snap-hook tied tightly to the end of the fishing line. By leaning out of the window and slinging this hook on the fork of his walking-stick he was able to reach it along the side of the carriage— holding his stick at the other end—and slip the hook over the handle outside my door, where it hung by its cord.

'He then dropped the stick and held the cord loosely in his right hand, the slack end ready to run out. This, you will observe, kept the hook hanging on my handle. With his left hand he drew the dispatch-box from under his cloak and held it outside the carriage, ready to drop it instantly.

'Of course he was standing all the time, with his head and shoulders out of the window.

'When I leant forward to light my cigarette at the Colonel's cigar, I slipped my left hand out of the window, easily found the hook hanging there, grasped it, and kept it open with one finger. Bartlett, who was watching, got ready. You can easily guess the rest. I swung my left hand suddenly over to the dispatch box, Bartlett allowing the line to run through his hand, snapped the hook over the handle before they could see what I was about, and pitched it out of the window as lightly as possible.

'The same instant Bartlett dropped the duplicate box from the train, grasped the line tightly as the real dispatch-box flew out, and hauled it in, hand over hand. He very soon had the dispatch-box safely stowed under his cloak, and, on reaching Dovehaven, took the next train back to town, to the no small satisfaction of his chief.

'Unluckily, I quite forgot to ask Cotterell to mention in the wire I knew he would be sending to the police at Dovehaven to have a dish of lentils ready for me in my brief imprisonment. It was very awkward. But they made me an exceedingly well-cooked tapioca pudding.'

XIII

The Tragedy at Brookbend Cottage

Ernest Bramah

'Max,' said Mr Carlyle, when Parkinson had closed the door behind him, 'this is Lieutenant Hollyer, whom you consented to see.'

'To hear,' corrected Carrados, smiling straight into the healthy and rather embarrassed face of the stranger before him. 'Mr Hollyer knows of my disability?'

'Mr Carlyle told me,' said the young man, 'but, as a matter of fact, I had heard of you before, Mr Carrados, from one of our men. It was in connection with the foundering of the *Ivan Saratov*.'

Carrados wagged his head in good-humoured resignation.

'And the owners were sworn to inviolable secrecy!' he exclaimed. 'Well, it is inevitable, I suppose. Not another scuttling case, Mr Hollyer?'

'No, mine is quite a private matter,' replied the lieutenant. 'My sister, Mrs Creake—but Mr Carlyle would tell you better than I can. He knows all about it.'

'No, no; Carlyle is a professional. Let me have it in the rough, Mr Hollyer. My ears are my eyes, you know.'

'Very well, sir. I can tell you what there is to tell, right enough, but I feel that when all's said and done it must sound very little to another, although it seems important to me.'

'We have occasionally found trifles of significance ourselves,' said Carrados encouragingly. 'Don't let that deter you.'

This was the essence of Lieutenant Hollyer's narrative:

'I have a sister, Millicent, who is married to a man called Creake. She is about twenty-eight now and he is at least fifteen years older. Neither my mother (who has since died) nor I cared very much about Creake. We had nothing particular against him, except, perhaps, the moderate disparity of age, but none of us appeared to have anything in common. He was a dark, taciturn man, and his moody silence froze up conversation. As a result, of course, we didn't see much of each other.'

'This, you must understand, was four or five years ago, Max,' interposed Mr Carlyle officiously.

Carrados maintained an uncompromising silence. Mr Carlyle blew his nose and contrived to impart a hurt significance into the operation. Then Lieutenant Hollyer continued:

'Millicent married Creake after a very short engagement. It was a frightfully subdued wedding—more like a funeral to me. The man professed to have no relations and apparently he had scarcely any friends or business acquaintances. He was an agent for something or other and had an office off Holborn. I suppose he made a living out of it then, although we knew practically nothing of his private affairs, but I gather that it has been going down since, and I suspect that for the past few years they have been getting along almost entirely on Millicent's little income. You would like the particulars of that?'

'Please,' assented Carrados.

'When our father died about seven years ago, he left three thousand pounds. It was invested in Canadian stock and brought in a little over a hundred a year. By his will my mother was to have the income of that for life and on her death it was to pass to Millicent, subject to the payment of a lump sum of five hundred pounds to me. But my father privately suggested to me that if I should have no particular use for the money at the time, he would propose my letting Millicent have the income of it until I did want it, as she would not be particularly well off. You see, Mr Carrados, a great deal more had been spent on my education and advancement than on her; I had my pay, and, of course, I could look out for myself better than a girl could.'

'Quite so,' agreed Carrados.

'Therefore I did nothing about that,' continued the lieutenant. 'Three years ago I was over again but I did not see much of them. They were living in lodgings. That was the only time since the marriage that I have seen them until last week. In the meanwhile our mother died and Millicent had been receiving her income. She wrote me several letters at the time. Otherwise we did not correspond much, but about a year ago she sent me their new address— Brookbend Cottage, Mulling Common—a house that they had taken. When I got two months' leave I invited myself there as a matter of course, fully expecting to stay most of my time with them, but I made an excuse to get away after a week. The place was dismal and unendurable, the whole life and atmosphere indescribably depressing.' He looked round with an instinct of caution, leaned forward earnestly, and dropped his voice. 'Mr Carrados, it is my absolute conviction that Creake is only waiting for a favourable opportunity to murder Millicent.'

'Go on,' said Carrados quietly. 'A week of the depressing surroundings of Brookbend Cottage would not alone convince you of that, Mr Hollyer.'

'I am not so sure,' declared Hollyer doubtfully. 'There was a feeling of suspicion and—before me—polite hatred that would have gone a good way towards it. All the same there *was* something more definite. Millicent told me this the day after I went there. There is no doubt that a few months ago Creake deliberately planned to poison her with some weed-killer. She told me the circumstances in a rather distressed moment, but afterwards she refused to speak of it again—even weakly denied it—and, as a matter of fact, it was with the greatest difficulty that I could get her at any time to talk about her husband or his affairs. The gist of it was that she had the strongest suspicion that Creake doctored a bottle of stout which he expected she would drink for her supper when she was alone. The weed-killer, properly labelled, but also in a beer bottle, was kept with other miscellaneous liquids in the same cupboard as the beer but on a high shelf. When he found that it had miscarried he poured away the mixture, washed out the bottle and put in the dregs from another. There is no doubt in my mind that if he had come back and found Millicent dead or dying he would have contrived it to appear that she had made a mistake in the dark and drunk some of the poison before she found out.'

'Yes,' assented Carrados. 'The open way; the safe way.'

'You must understand that they live in a very small style, Mr Carrados, and Millicent is almost entirely in the man's power. The only servant they have is a woman who comes in for a few hours every day. The house is lonely and secluded. Creake is sometimes away for days and nights at a time, and Millicent, either through pride or indifference, seems to have dropped off all her old friends and have made no others. He might poison her, bury the body in the garden, and be a thousand miles away before anyone began even to inquire about her. What am I to do, Mr Carrados?'

'He is less likely to try poison than some other means now,' pondered Carrados. 'That having failed, his wife will always be on her guard. He may know, or at least suspect, that others know. No. ... The common-sense precaution

would be for your sister to leave the man, Mr Hollyer. She
will not?'

'No,' admitted Hollyer, 'she will not. I at once urged
that.' The young man struggled with some hesitation for a
moment and then blurted out: 'The fact is, Mr Carrados,
I don't understand Millicent. She is not the girl she was.
She hates Creake and treats him with a silent contempt that
eats into their lives like acid, and yet she is so jealous of him
that she will let nothing short of death part them. It is a
horrible life they lead. I stood it for a week and I must say,
much as I dislike my brother-in-law, that he has something
to put up with. If only he got into a passion like a man and
killed her it wouldn't be altogether incomprehensible.'

'That does not concern us,' said Carrados. 'In a game of
this kind one has to take sides and we have taken ours. It
remains for us to see that our side wins. You mentioned
jealousy, Mr Hollyer. Have you any idea whether Mrs
Creake has real ground for it?'

'I should have told you that,' replied Lieutenant Hollyer.
'I happened to strike up with a newspaper man whose office
is in the same block as Creake's. When I mentioned the
name he grinned. "Creake," he said, "oh, he's the man with
the romantic typist, isn't he?" "Well he's my brother-in-
law," I replied. "What about the typist?" Then the chap
shut up like a knife. "No, no," he said, "I didn't know he was
married. I don't want to get mixed up in anything of that
sort. I only said that he had a typist. Well, what of that?
So have we; so has everyone." There was nothing more to
be got out of him, but the remark and the grin meant—
well, about as usual, Mr Carrados.'

Carrados turned to his friend.

'I suppose you know all about the typist by now,
Louis?'

'We have had her under efficient observation, Max,'
replied Mr Carlyle, with severe dignity.

'Is she unmarried?'

'Yes; so far as ordinary repute goes, she is.'

'That is all that is essential for a moment. Mr Hollyer opens up three excellent reasons why this man might wish to dispose of his wife. If we accept the suggestion of poisoning—though we have only a jealous woman's suspicion for it—we add to the wish the determination. Well, we will go forward on that. Have you got a photograph of Mr Creake?'

The lieutenant took out his pocket book.

'Mr Carlyle asked me for one. Here is the best I could get.'

Carrados rang the bell.

'This, Parkinson,' he said, when the man appeared, 'is a photograph of a Mr . . . What first name by the way?'

'Austin,' put in Hollyer, who was following everything with a boyish mixture of excitement and subdued importance.

'. . . of a Mr Austin Creake. I may require you to recognize him.'

Parkinson glanced at the print and returned it to his master's hand.

'May I inquire if it is a recent photograph of the gentleman, sir?' he asked.

'About six years ago,' said the lieutenant, taking in this new actor in the drama with frank curiosity. 'But he is very little changed.'

'Thank you, sir. I will endeavour to remember Mr Creake, sir.'

Lieutenant Hollyer stood up as Parkinson left the room. The interview seemed to be at an end.

'Oh, there's one other matter,' he remarked. 'I am afraid that I did rather an unfortunate thing while I was at Brookbend. It seemed to me that as all Millicent's money would probably pass into Creake's hands sooner or later I might as well have my five hundred pounds, if only to help her with afterwards. So I broached the subject and said that I should like to have it now as I had an opportunity for investing.'

'And you think?'

'It may possibly influence Creake to act sooner than he otherwise might have done. He may have got possession of the principal even and find it very awkward to replace it.'

'So much the better. If your sister is going to be murdered it may as well be done next week as next year as far as I am concerned. Excuse my brutality, Mr Hollyer, but this is simply a case to me and I regard it strategically. Now Mr Carlyle's organization can look after Mrs Creake for a few weeks, but it cannot look after her for ever. By increasing the immediate risk we diminish the permanent risk.'

'I see,' agreed Hollyer. 'I'm awfully uneasy but I'm entirely in your hands.'

'Then we will give Mr Creake every inducement and every opportunity to get to work. Where are you staying now?'

'Just now with some friends at St Albans.'

'That is too far.' The inscrutable eyes retained their tranquil depth but a new quality of quickening interest in the voice made Mr Carlyle forget the weight and burden of his ruffled dignity. 'Give me a few minutes, please. The cigarettes are behind you, Mr Hollyer.' The blind man walked to the window and seemed to look over the cypress-shaded lawn. The lieutenant lit a cigarette and Mr Carlyle picked up *Punch*. Then Carrados turned round again.

'You are prepared to put your own arrangements aside?' he demanded of his visitor.

'Certainly.'

'Very well. I want you to go down now—straight from here—to Brookbend Cottage. Tell your sister that your leave is unexpectedly cut short and that you sail tomorrow.'

'The *Martian*?'

'No, no; the *Martian* doesn't sail. Look up the movements on your way there and pick out a boat that does. Say you are transferred. Add that you expect to be away only two or three months and that you really want the five hundred pounds by the time of your return. Don't stay in the house long, please.'

'I understand, sir.'

'St Albans is too far. Make your excuse and get away from there to-day. Put up somewhere in town, where you will be in reach of the telephone. Let Mr Carlyle and myself know where you are. Keep out of Creake's way. I don't want actually to tie you down to the house, but we may require your services. We will let you know at the first sign of anything doing and if there is nothing to be done we must release you.'

'I don't mind that. Is there nothing more that I can do now?'

'Nothing. In going to Mr Carlyle you have done the best thing possible; you have put your sister into the care of the shrewdest man in London.' Whereat the object of this quite unexpected eulogy found himself becoming covered with modest confusion.

'Well, Max?' remarked Mr Carlyle tentatively when they were alone.

'Well, Louis?'

'Of course it wasn't worth while rubbing it in before young Hollyer, but, as a matter of fact, every single man carries the life of any other man—only one, mind you—in his hands, do what you will.'

'Provided he doesn't bungle,' acquiesced Carrados.

'Quite so.'

'And also that he is absolutely reckless of the consequences.'

'Of course.'

'Two rather large provisos. Creake is obviously susceptible to both. Have you seen him?'

'No. As I told you, I put a man on to report his habits in town. Then, two days ago, as the case seemed to promise some interest—for he certainly is deeply involved with the typist, Max, and the thing might take a sensational turn at any time—I went down to Mulling Common myself. Although the house is lonely it is on the electric tram route. You know the sort of market garden rurality that about a dozen miles out of London offers—alternate bricks and cabbages. It was easy enough to get to know about Creake locally. He mixes with no one there, goes into town at irregular times but generally every day, and is reputed to be devilish hard to get money out of. Finally I made the acquaintance of an old fellow who used to do a day's gardening at Brookbend occasionally. He has a cottage and a garden of his own with a greenhouse, and the business cost me the price of a pound of tomatoes.'

'Was it—a profitable investment?'

'As tomatoes, yes; as information, no. The old fellow had the fatal disadvantage from our point of view of labouring under a grievance. A few weeks ago Creake told him that he would not require him again as he was going to do his own gardening in future.'

'That is something, Louis.'

'If only Creake was going to poison his wife with hyoscyamine and bury her, instead of blowing her up with a dynamite cartridge and claiming that it came in among the coal.'

'True, true. Still . . .'

'However, the chatty old soul had a simple explanation for everything that Creake did. Creake was mad. He had even seen him flying a kite in his garden where it was bound to get wrecked among the trees. A lad of ten would have known better, he declared. And certainly the kite did get wrecked, for I saw it hanging over the road myself. But that a sane man should spend his time "playing with a toy" was beyond him.'

'A good many men have been flying kites of various kinds lately,' said Carrados. 'Is he interested in aviation?'

'I dare say. He appears to have some knowledge of scientific subjects. Now what do you want me to do, Max?'

'Will you do it?'

'Implicitly—subject to the usual reservations.

'Keep your man on Creake in town and let me have his reports after you have seen them. Lunch with me here now. 'Phone up to your office that you are detained on unpleasant business and then give the deserving Parkinson an afternoon off by looking after me while we take a motor run round Mulling Common. If we have time we might go on to Brighton, feed at the "Ship", and come back in the cool.'

'Amiable and thrice lucky mortal,' sighed Mr Carlyle, his glance wandering round the room.

But, as it happened, Brighton did not figure in that day's itinerary. It had been Carrados's intention merely to pass Brookbend Cottage on this occasion, relying on his highly developed faculties, aided by Mr Carlyle's description, to inform him of the surroundings. A hundred yards before they reached the house he had given an order to his chauffeur to drop into the lowest speed and they were leisurely drawing past when a discovery by Mr Carlyle modified their plans.

'By Jupiter!' that gentleman suddenly exclaimed; 'there's a board up, Max. The place is to be let.'

Carrados picked up the tube again. A couple of sentences passed and the car stopped by the roadside, a score of paces past the limit of the garden. Mr Carlyle took out his notebook and wrote down the address of a firm of house agents.

'You might raise the bonnet and have a look at the engines, Harris,' said Carrados. 'We want to be occupied here for a few minutes.'

'This is sudden; Hollyer knew nothing of their leaving,' remarked Mr Carlyle.

'Probably not for three months yet. All the same, Louis, we will go on to the agents and get a card to view whether we use it to-day or not.'

A thick hedge, in its summer dress effectively screening the house beyond from public view, lay between the garden and the road. Above the hedge showed an occasional shrub; at the corner nearest to the car a chestnut flourished. The wooden gate, once white, which they had passed, was grimed and rickety. The road itself was still the unpretentious country lane that the advent of the electric car had found it. When Carrados had taken in these details there seemed little else to notice. He was on the point of giving Harris the order to go on when his ear caught a trivial sound.

'Someone is coming out of the house, Louis,' he warned his friend. 'It may be Hollyer, but he ought to have gone by this time.'

'I don't hear anyone,' replied the other, but as he spoke a door banged noisily and Mr Carlyle slipped into another seat and ensconced himself behind a copy of *The Globe*.

'Creake himself,' he whispered across the car, as a man appeared at the gate. 'Hollyer was right; he is hardly changed. Waiting for a car, I suppose.'

But a car very soon swung past them from the direction in which Mr Creake was looking and it did not interest him. For a minute or two longer he continued to look expectantly along the road. Then he walked slowly up the drive back to the house.

'We will give him five or ten minutes,' decided Carrados. 'Harris is behaving very naturally.'

Before even the shorter period had run out they were repaid. A telegraph-boy cycled leisurely along the road, and, leaving his machine at the gate, went up to the cottage. Evidently there was no reply, for in less than a minute he was trundling past them back again. Round the bend an approaching tram clanged its bell noisily, and, quickened by the warning sound, Mr Creake again appeared, this time with a small portmanteau in his hand. With a backward glance he hurried on towards the next stopping-place, and, boarding the car as it slackened down, he was carried out of their knowledge.

'Very convenient of Mr Creake,' remarked Carrados, with quiet satisfaction. 'We will now get the order and go over the house in his absence. It might be useful to have a look at the wire as well.'

'It might, Max,' acquiesced Mr Carlyle, a little dryly. 'But if it is, as it probably is, in Creake's pocket, how do you propose to get it?'

'By going to the post office, Louis,'

'Quite so. Have you ever tried to see a copy of a telegram addressed to someone else?'

'I don't think I have ever had occasion yet,' admitted Carrados. 'Have you?'

'In one or two cases I have perhaps been an accessory to the act. It is generally a matter either of extreme delicacy or considerable expenditure.'

'Then for Hollyer's sake we will hope for the former here.' And Mr Carlyle smiled darkly and hinted that he was content to wait for a friendly revenge.

A little later, having left the car at the beginning of the straggling High Street, the two men called at the village post office. They had already visited the house agent and obtained an order to view Brookbend Cottage, declining with some difficulty the clerk's persistent offer to accompany them. The reason was soon forthcoming. 'As a matter of fact,' explained the young man, 'the present tenant is under *our* notice to leave.'

'Unsatisfactory, eh?' said Carrados encouragingly.

'He's a corker,' admitted the clerk, responding to the friendly tone. 'Fifteen months and not a doit of rent have we had. That's why I should have liked . . .'

'We will make every allowance,' replied Carrados.

The post office occupied one side of a stationer's shop. It was not without some inward trepidation that Mr Carlyle found himself committed to the adventure. Carrados, on the other hand, was the personification of bland unconcern.

'You have just sent a telegram to Brookbend Cottage,' he said to the young lady behind the brasswork lattice. 'We think it may have come inaccurately and should like a repeat.' He took out his purse. 'What is the fee?'

The request evidently was not a common one. 'Oh,' said the girl uncertainly, 'wait a minute, please.' She turned to a pile of telegram duplicates behind the desk and ran a doubtful finger along the upper sheets. 'I think this is all right. You want it repeated?'

'Please.' Just a tinge of questioning surprise gave point to the courteous tone.

'It will be fourpence. If there is an error the amount will be refunded.'

Carrados put down his coin and received his change.

'Will it take long?' he inquired carelessly, as he pulled on his glove.

'You will most likely get it within a quarter of an hour,' she replied.

'Now you've done it,' commented Mr Carlyle, as they walked back to their car. 'How do you propose to get that telegram, Max?'

'Ask for it,' was the laconic explanation.

And, stripping the artifice of any elaboration, he simply asked for it and got it. The car, posted at a convenient bend in the road, gave him a warning note as the telegraph-boy approached. Then Carrados took up a convincing attitude with his hand on the gate while Mr Carlyle lent himself to the semblance of a departing friend. That was the inevitable impression when the boy rode up.

'Creake, Brookbend Cottage?' inquired Carrados, holding out his hand, and without a second thought the boy gave him the envelope and rode away on the assurance that there would be no reply.

'Some day, my friend,' remarked Mr Carlyle, looking

nervously towards the unseen house, 'your ingenuity will get you into a tight corner.'

'Then my ingenuity must get me out again,' was the retort. 'Let us have our "view" now. The telegram can wait.'

An untidy workwoman took their order and left them standing at the door. Presently a lady whom they both knew to be Mrs Creake appeared.

'You wish to see over the house?' she said, in a voice that was utterly devoid of any interest. Then, without waiting for a reply, she turned to the nearest door and threw it open.

'This is the drawing-room,' she said, standing aside.

They walked into a sparsely furnished, damp-smelling room and made a pretence of looking round, while Mrs Creake remained silent and aloof.

'The dining-room,' she continued, crossing the narrow hall and opening another door.

Mr Carlyle ventured a genial commonplace in the hope of inducing conversation. The result was not encouraging. Doubtless they would have gone through the house under the same frigid guidance had not Carrados been at fault in a way that Mr Carlyle had never known him fail before. In crossing the hall he stumbled over a mat and almost fell.

'Pardon my clumsiness,' he said to the lady. 'I am, unfortunately, quite blind. But,' he added, with a smile, to turn off the mishap, 'even a blind man must have a house.'

The man who had eyes was surprised to see a flood of colour rush into Mrs Creake's face.

'Blind!' she exclaimed, 'oh, I beg your pardon. Why did you not tell me? You might have fallen.'

'I generally manage fairly well,' he replied. 'But, of course, in a strange house . . .'

She put her hand on his arm very lightly.

'You must let me guide you, just a little,' she said.

The house, without being large, was full of passages and

inconvenient turnings. Carrados asked an occasional question and found Mrs Creake quite amiable without effusion. Mr Carlyle followed them from room to room in the hope, though scarcely the expectation, of learning something that might be useful.

'This is the last one. It is the largest bedroom,' said their guide. Only two of the upper rooms were fully furnished and Mr Carlyle at once saw, as Carrados knew without seeing, that this was the one which the Creakes occupied.

'A very pleasant outlook,' declared Mr Carlyle.

'Oh, I suppose so,' admitted the lady vaguely. The room, in fact, looked over the leafy garden and the road beyond. It had a French window opening on to a small balcony, and to this, under the strange influence that always attracted him to light, Carrados walked.

'I expect that there is a certain amount of repair needed?' he said, after standing there a moment.

'I am afraid there would be,' she confessed.

'I ask because there is a sheet of metal on the floor here,' he continued. 'Now that, in an old house, spells dry rot to the wary observer.'

'My husband said that the rain, which comes in a little under the window, was rotting the boards there,' she replied. 'He put that down recently. I had not noticed anything myself.'

It was the first time she had mentioned her husband; Mr Carlyle pricked up his ears.

'Ah, that is a less serious matter,' said Carrados. 'May I step out on to the balcony?'

'Oh yes, if you like to.' Then, as he appeared to be fumbling at the catch, 'Let me open it for you.'

But the window was already open, and Carrados, facing the various points of the compass, took in the bearings.

'A sunny, sheltered corner,' he remarked. 'An ideal spot for a deck-chair and a book.'

She shrugged her shoulders half contemptuously.

'I dare say,' she replied, 'but I never use it.'

'Sometimes, surely,' he persisted mildly. 'It would be my favourite retreat. But then . . .'

'I was going to say that I had never even been out on it, but that would not be quite true. It has two uses for me, both equally romantic; I occasionally shake a duster from it, and when my husband returns late without his latchkey he wakes me up and I come out here and drop him mine.'

Further revelation of Mr Creake's nocturnal habits was cut off, greatly to Mr Carlyle's annoyance, by a cough of unmistakable significance from the foot of the stairs. They had heard a trade cart drive up to the gate, a knock at the door, and the heavy-footed woman tramp along the hall.

'Excuse me a minute, please,' said Mrs Creake.

'Louis,' said Carrados, in a sharp whisper, the moment they were alone, 'stand against the door.'

With extreme plausibility Mr Carlyle began to admire a picture so situated that while he was there it was impossible to open the door more than a few inches. From that position he observed his confederate go through the curious procedure of kneeling down on the bedroom floor and for a full minute pressing his ear to the sheet of metal that had already engaged his attention. Then he rose to his feet, nodded, dusted his trousers, and Mr Carlyle moved to a less equivocal position.

'What a beautiful rose-tree grows up your balcony,' remarked Carrados, stepping into the room as Mrs Creake returned. 'I suppose you are very fond of gardening?'

'I detest it,' she replied.

'But this *Glorie*, so carefully trained . . .?'

'Is it?' she replied. 'I think my husband was nailing it up recently.' By some strange fatality Carrados's most aimless remarks seemed to involve the absent Mr Creake. 'Do you care to see the garden?'

The garden proved to be extensive and neglected. Behind the house was chiefly orchard. In front, some semblance of order had been kept up; here it was lawn and shrubbery, and the drive they had walked along. Two things interested Carrados: the soil at the foot of the balcony, which he declared on examination to be particularly suitable for roses, and the fine chestnut-tree in the corner by the road.

As they walked back to the car Mr Carlyle lamented that they had learned so little of Creake's movements.

'Perhaps the telegram will tell us something,' suggested Carrados. 'Read it, Louis.'

Mr Carlyle cut open the envelope, glanced at the enclosure, and in spite of his disappointment could not restrain a chuckle.

'My poor Max,' he explained, 'you have put yourself to an amount of ingenious trouble for nothing. Creake is evidently taking a few days' holiday and prudently availed himself of the Meteorological Office forecast before going. Listen: "*Immediate prospect for London warm and settled. Further outlook cooler but fine.*" Well, well; I did get a pound of tomatoes for *my* fourpence.'

'You certainly scored there, Louis,' admitted Carrados, with humorous appreciation. 'I wonder,' he added speculatively, 'whether it is Creake's peculiar taste usually to spend his week-end holiday in London.'

'Eh?' exclaimed Mr Carlyle, looking at the words again, 'by gad, that's rum, Max. They go to Weston-super-Mare. Why on earth should he want to know about London?'

'I can make a guess, but before we are satisfied I must come here again. Take another look at that kite, Louis. Are there a few yards of string hanging loose from it?'

'Yes, there are.'

'Rather thick string—unusually thick for the purpose?'

'Yes; but how do you know?'

As they drove home again Carrados explained, and Mr Carlyle sat aghast, saying incredulously: 'Good God, Max, is it possible?'

An hour later he was satisfied that it was possible. In reply to his inquiry someone in his office telephoned him the information that 'they' had left Paddington by the four-thirty for Weston.

It was more than a week after his introduction to Carrados that Lieutenant Hollyer had a summons to present himself at The Turrets again. He found Mr Carlyle already there and the two friends awaiting his arrival.

'I stayed in all day after hearing from you this morning, Mr Carrados,' he said, shaking hands. 'When I got your second message I was all ready to walk straight out of the house. That's how I did it in the time. I hope everything is all right?'

'Excellent,' replied Carrados. 'You'd better have something before we start. We probably have a long and perhaps an exciting night before us.'

'And certainly a wet one,' assented the lieutenant. 'It was thundering over Mulling way as I came along.'

'That is why you are here,' said his host. 'We are waiting for a certain message before we start, and in the meantime you may as well understand what we expect to happen. As you saw, there is a thunderstorm coming on. The Meteorological Office morning forecast predicted it for the whole of London if the conditions remained. That was why I kept you in readiness. Within an hour it is now inevitable that we shall experience a deluge. Here and there damage will be done to trees and buildings; here and there a person will probably be struck and killed.'

'Yes.'

'It is Mr Creake's intention that his wife should be among the victims.'

'I don't exactly follow,' said Hollyer, looking from one man to the other. 'I quite admit that Creake would be immensely relieved if such a thing did happen, but the chance is surely an absurdly remote one.'

'Yet unless we intervene it is precisely what a coroner's

jury will decide has happened. Do you know whether your brother-in-law has any practical knowledge of electricity, Mr Hollyer?'

'I cannot say. He was so reserved, and we really knew little of him . . .'

'Yet in 1896 an Austin Creake contributed an article on "Alternating Currents" to the American *Scientific World*. That would argue a fairly intimate acquaintanceship.'

'But do you mean that he is going to direct a flash of lightning?'

'Only into the minds of the doctor who conducts the post-mortem, and the coroner. This storm, the opportunity of which he had been awaiting for weeks, is merely the cloak to his act. The weapon which he has planned to use—scarcely less powerful than lightning but much more tractable—is the high voltage current of electricity that flows along the tram wire at his gate.'

'Oh!' exclaimed Lieutenant Hollyer, as the sudden revelation struck him.

'Some time between eleven o'clock to-night—about the hour when your sister goes to bed—and one-thirty in the morning—the time up to which he can rely on the current—Creake will throw a stone up to the balcony window. Most of his preparation has long been made; it only remains for him to connect up a short length to the window handle and a longer one at the other end to tap the live wire. That done, he will wake his wife in the way I have said. The moment she moves the catch of the window—and he has carefully filed its parts to ensure perfect contact—she will be electrocuted as effectually as if she sat in the executioner's chair in Sing Sing prison.'

'But what are we doing here!' exclaimed Hollyer, starting to his feet, pale and horrified. 'It is past ten now and anything may happen.'

'Quite natural, Mr Hollyer,' said Carrados reassuringly, 'but you need have no anxiety. Creake is being watched, the house is being watched, and your sister is as safe as if she slept to-night in Windsor Castle. Be assured that whatever happens he will not be allowed to complete his scheme; but it is desirable to let him implicate himself to the fullest limit. Your brother-in-law, Mr Hollyer, is a man with a peculiar capacity for taking pains.'

'He is a damned cold-blooded scoundrel!' exclaimed the young officer fiercely. 'When I think of Millicent five years ago . . .'

'Well, for that matter, an enlightened nation has decided that electrocution is the most humane way of removing its superfluous citizens,' suggested Carrados mildly. 'He is certainly an ingenious-minded gentleman. It is his misfortune that in Mr Carlyle he was fated to be opposed by an even subtler brain . . .'

'No, no! Really, Max!' protested the embarrassed gentleman.

'Mr Hollyer will be able to judge for himself when I tell him that it was Mr Carlyle who first drew attention to the significance of the abandoned kite,' insisted Carrados firmly. 'Then, of course, its object became plain to me—as indeed to anyone. For ten minutes, perhaps, a wire must be carried from the overhead line to the chestnut-tree. Creake has everything in his favour, but it is just within possibility that the driver of an inopportune train might notice the appendage. What of that? Why, for more than a week he has seen a derelict kite with its yards of trailing string hanging in the tree. A very calculating mind, Mr Hollyer. It would be interesting to know what line of action Mr Creake has mapped out for himself afterwards. I expect he has half-a-dozen artistic little touches up his sleeve. Possibly he would merely singe his wife's hair, burn her feet with a red-hot poker, shiver the glass of the French window, and be content with that to let well alone. You see, lightning is so varied in its effects that whatever he did or did not do would be right. He is in the impregnable position of the body showing all the symptoms of death by lightning shock and nothing else but lightning to account for it—a dilated eye, heart contracted in systole, bloodless lungs shrunk to a third the normal weight, and all the rest of it. When he has removed a few outward traces of his work Creake might quite safely "discover" his dead wife and rush off for the nearest doctor. Or he may have decided to arrange a convincing alibi, and creep away, leaving the discovery to another. We shall never know; he will make no confession.'

'I wish it was well over,' admitted Hollyer. 'I'm not particularly jumpy, but this gives me a touch of the creeps.'

'Three more hours at the worst, Lieutenant,' said Carrados cheerfully. 'Ah-ah, something is coming through now.'

He went to the telephone and received a message from one quarter; then made another connection and talked for a few minutes with someone else.

'Everything working smoothly,' he remarked between times over his shoulder. 'Your sister has gone to bed, Mr Hollyer.'

Then he turned to the house telephone and distributed his orders.

'So we,' he concluded, 'must get up.'

By the time they were ready a large closed motor car was waiting. The lieutenant thought he recognized Parkinson in the well-swathed form beside the driver, but there was no temptation to linger for a second on the steps. Already the stinging rain had lashed the drive into the semblance of a frothy estuary; all round the lightning jagged its course through the incessant tremulous glow of more distant lightning, while the thunder only ceased its muttering to turn at close quarters and crackle viciously.

'One of the few things I regret missing,' remarked Carrados tranquilly, 'but I hear a good deal of colour in it.'

The car slushed its way down to the gate, lurched a

little heavily across the dip into the road, and, steadying as it came upon the straight, began to hum contentedly along the deserted highway.

'We are not going direct?' suddenly inquired Hollyer, after they had travelled perhaps half-a-dozen miles. The night was bewildering enough but he had the sailor's gift for location.

'No; through Hunscott Green and then by a field-path to the orchard at the back,' replied Carrados. 'Keep a sharp look out for the man with the lantern about here, Harris,' he called through the tube.

'Something flashing just ahead, sir,' came the reply, and the car slowed down and stopped.

Carrados dropped the near window as a man in glistening waterproof stepped from the shelter of a lich-gate and approached.

'Inspector Beedel, sir,' said the stranger, looking into the car.

'Quite right, Inspector,' said Carrados. 'Get in.'

'I have a man with me, sir.'

'We can find room for him as well.'

'We are very wet.'

'So shall we all be soon.'

The lieutenant changed his seat and the two burly forms took places side by side. In less than five minutes the car stopped again, this time in a grassy country lane.

'Now we have to face it,' announced Carrados. 'The inspector will show us the way.'

The car slid round and disappeared into the night, while Beedel led the party to a stile in the hedge. A couple of fields brought them to the Brookbend boundary. There a figure stood out of the black foliage, exchanged a few words with their guide and piloted them along the shadows of the orchard to the back door of the house.

'You will find a broken pane near the catch of the scullery window,' said the blind man.

'Right, sir,' replied the inspector. 'I have it. Now who goes through?'

'Mr Hollyer will open the door for us. I'm afraid you must take off your boots and all wet things, Lieutenant. We cannot risk a single spot inside.'

They waited until the back door opened, then each one divested himself in a similar manner and passed into the kitchen, where the remains of a fire still burned. The man from the orchard gathered together the discarded garments and disappeared again.

Carrados turned to the lieutenant.

'A rather delicate job for you now, Mr Hollyer. I want you to go up to your sister, wake her, and get her into another room with as little fuss as possible. Tell her as much as you think fit and let her understand that her very life depends on absolute stillness when she is alone. Don't be unduly hurried, but not a glimmer of a light, please.'

Then minutes passed by the measure of the battered old alarum on the dresser shelf before the young man returned.

'I've had rather a time of it,' he reported, with a nervous laugh, 'but I think it will be all right now. She is in the spare room.'

'Then we will take our places. You and Parkinson come with me to the bedroom. Inspector, you have your own arrangements. Mr Carlyle will be with you.'

They dispersed silently about the house, Hollyer glanced apprehensively at the door of the spare room as they passed it, but within all was as quiet as the grave. Their room lay at the other end of the passage.

'You may as well take your place in the bed now, Hollyer,' directed Carrados when they were inside and the door closed. 'Keep well down among the clothes. Creake has to get up on the balcony, you know, and he will probably peep through the window, but he dare come no farther. Then when he begins to throw up stones slip on this dressing-gown of your sister's. I'll tell you what to do after.'

The next sixty minutes drew out into the longest hour that the lieutenant had ever known. Occasionally he heard a whisper pass between the two men who stood behind the window curtains, but he could see nothing. Then Carrados threw a guarded remark in his direction.

'He is in the garden now.'

Something scraped slightly against the outer wall. But the night was full of wilder sounds, and in the house the furniture and the boards creaked and sprung between the yawling of the wind among the chimneys, the rattle of the thunder and the pelting of the rain. It was a time to quicken the steadiest pulse, and when the crucial moment came, when a pebble suddenly rang against the pane with a sound that the tense waiting magnified into a shivering crash, Hollyer leaped from the bed on the instant.

'Easy, easy,' warned Carrados feelingly. 'We will wait for another knock.' He passed something across. 'Here is a rubber glove. I have cut the wire but you had better put it on. Stand just for a moment at the window, move the catch so that it can blow open a little, and drop immediately. Now.'

Another stone had rattled against the glass. For Hollyer to go through his part was the work merely of seconds, and with a few touches Carrados spread the dressing-gown to more effective disguise about the extended form. But an unforeseen and in the circumstances rather horrible interval followed, for Creake, in accordance with some detail of his never-revealed plan, continued to shower missile after missile against the panes until even the unimpressionable Parkinson shivered.

'The last act,' whispered Carrados, a moment after the throwing had ceased. 'He has gone round to the back. Keep as you are. We take cover now.' He pressed behind the arras of an extemporized wardrobe, and the spirit of empti ness and desolation seemed once more to reign over the lonely house.

From half-a-dozen places of concealment ears were straining to catch the first guiding sound. He moved very stealthily, burdened, perhaps, by some strange scruple in the presence of the tragedy that he had not feared to contrive, paused for a moment at the bedroom door, then opened it very quietly, and in the fickle light read the consummation of his hopes.

'At last!' they heard the sharp whisper drawn from his relief. 'At last!'

He took another step and two shadows seemed to fall upon him from behind, one on either side. With primitive instinct a cry of terror and surprise escaped him as he made a desperate movement to wrench himself free, and for a short second he almost succeeded in dragging one hand into a pocket. Then his wrists slowly came together and the handcuffs closed.

'I am Inspector Beedel,' said the man on his right side. 'You are charged with the attempted murder of your wife, Millicent Creake.'

'You are mad,' retorted the miserable creature, falling into a desperate calmness. 'She has been struck by lightning.'

'No, you blackguard, she hasn't,' wrathfully exclaimed his brother-in-law, jumping up. 'Would you like to see her?'

'I also have to warn you,' continued the inspector impassively, 'that anything you say may be used as evidence against you.'

A startled cry from the farthest end of the passage arrested their attention.

'Mr Carrados,' called Hollyer, 'oh, come at once.'

At the open door of the other bedroom stood the lieutenant, his eyes still turned towards something in the room beyond, a little empty bottle in his hand.

'Dead!' he exclaimed tragically, with a sob, 'with this

beside her. Dead just when she would have been free of the brute.'

The blind man passed into the room, sniffed the air, and laid a gentle hand on the pulseless heart.

'Yes,' he replied. 'That, Hollyer, does not always appeal to the woman, strange to say.'

Sources

I. Catherine Louisa Pirkis: *The Experiences of Loveday Brooke, Lady Detective.* (Hutchinson, 1894)

II. Arthur Morrison: *Martin Hewitt, Investigator.* (Ward, Lock & Bowden, 1894) First published in the *Strand Magazine*, March to September 1894.

III. Dick Donovan: *Riddles Read.* (Chatto & Windus, 1896)

IV. Arthur Morrison: *The Dorrington Deed-Box.* (Ward, Lock n.d. [1897])

V. M. McD. Bodkin Q.C.: *Paul Beck, The Rule of Thumb Detective.* (C. Arthur Pearson, 1898)

VI. Fergus Hume: *Hagar of the Pawn-Shop.* (Skeffington & Son, 1898)

VII. M. McD. Bodkin Q.C.: *Dora Myrl, The Lady Detective.* (Chatto & Windus, 1900)

VIII. L. T. Meade and Clifford Halifax, M.D.: *A Race with the Sun.* (Ward, Lock, 1901) Title story first published in the *Strand Magazine*, January 1897.

IX. J. S. Fletcher: *The Adventures of Archer Dawe (Sleuth-Hound).* (Digby, Long, 1909)

X. Jacques Futrelle: (*The Story-Teller.* August, 1910) Not previously published in book form.

XI. Richard Marsh: *Judith Lee, Some Pages from Her Life.* (Methuen, 1912)

XII. Victor L. Whitechurch: *Thrilling Stories of the Railway.* (C. Arthur Pearson, 1912)

XIII. Ernest Bramah: *Max Carrados.* (Methuen, 1914)